AN IMPERFECT FUTURE

AN IMPERFECT FUTURE

UNIT-13

DAVID PENNY

RIVERTREE PRINT

ALSO BY DAVID PENNY

THE THOMAS BERRINGTON HISTORICAL MYSTERIES

The Red Hill

Breaker of Bones

The Sin Eater

The Incubus

The Inquisitor

The Fortunate Dead

The Promise of Pain

The Message of Blood

A Tear for the Dead

A Death of Innocence (prequel)

UNIT-13: A Paranormal Spy Thriller

An Imperfect Future

The Luck of the Devil - coming 2022

CHAPTER ONE

Squeezed into the cramped, freezing bomb-aiming space at the front of an Avro Lancaster heavy bomber, Calum Auger was trying to ignore the fear that threatened to swamp him. Two years doing the job and each night it became harder. The fear debilitated him, but he tried to ignore it, as he always did, because he had a job to do. He needed to enter that special zone which allowed him to see as far into the future as he could. About a minute, if he pushed himself. Not so much, he sometimes thought, but it was enough for tonight. Enough for all the other nights he had flown.

None of the other six crew knew exactly what his odd ability was, but they liked to fly with Calum because of it. Most of the time, ten or fifteen seconds was all he needed on the way out and back, and ten seconds was easy. Ten seconds was always there. A double vision of the world he had grown accustomed to over the last nine years, ever since the strangeness had first emerged inside him.

Staring ahead and down, it was as though he saw two

images laid one over the other. The now, the present, was the stronger, but if he concentrated in a certain way he still didn't understand, he could conjure up another reality. One that had not yet happened.

Calum pushed hard, extending the envelope as far as he could. A headache started up almost immediately, pulsing bright on the edge of his vision. He saw flak rising from below to burst harmlessly. Soon, it would rise higher. Calum saw nothing in the next sixty seconds to alarm him, so he switched his attention to the job at hand. He saw five-hundred-pound bombs he had not yet released tumble to bloom into flame far below. The first one missed as the blaze of its explosion hit a hundred yards to the right of a factory.

"Guy, a nudge to port... gently... hold it... a little more... that'll do nicely."

Above him, Guy Jordan obeyed his command and a new future opened up ahead, playing like a jerky black and white film. One of the old Keystone Cops comedies they showed between features. Calum saw his second bomb fall a little short and adjusted for it.

"Hold steady, Guy...." He whispered, knowing Guy could hear whether or not he shouted. He didn't know if the others heard, but Guy always did. Sometimes he wondered if words were even necessary.

Calum wrapped his thumb around the release trigger and waited. Anti-aircraft shells exploded close by, but he ignored them because he knew none had hit the plane in the future.

All those futures coalesced into one reality and he pressed down. The big Lancaster lurched as the first bombs dropped away like the spill of eggs from a gravid salmon. Guy brought the nose down, fighting the urge of the plane to rise. Calum counted to himself until he reached the point where he would have released the rest of the ordnance, then waited another second before allowing them to drop away.

This time when the plane lifted Guy let it have its head and turned away hard, above the other wing of bombers coming in behind. Calum twisted, looking back and down to where explosions lit the factories that were their target for tonight. He heard chatter in his headphones. Phil Hastings giving Guy a fresh course. Bob Sutherland updating everyone on the damage the other bombers had inflicted.

Calum closed his eyes and tried to ignore the headache but knew it was going to stay. He had pushed too hard. It would still be there when he went to bed, probably still there when he woke to prepare for the next mission. The pace was relentless, even now everyone knew the war was close to won. That knowledge made climbing into the aircraft each time all the harder.

Calum sometimes wondered if he was inflicting damage on himself, but what else could he do? Without this quirk he possessed they would all be dead by now. Every single one of the crew knew it, but they kept the thought to themselves. Calum was their secret weapon. Sometimes he wondered if anyone outside their close-knit unit knew what he could do. He prayed nobody did. The crew needed him.

When he opened his eyes again, it was because he had seen something coming. Half a dozen ME-110 night fighters. They shouldn't be here, not tonight, but here they were.

Calum toggled his radio. "Guy, six bogeys coming in fast at three-o'clock."

He rose from his prone position and worked himself upright until he could grip the firing mechanism of the twin .303 Browning machine guns available to him. The perspex nose-cone offered an unobstructed view and he could see the group of fighters descending towards their position. Calum waited, searching the future, knowing he might have only one moment. Possibilities came and went. The chaos of crossing futures made it difficult to concentrate, but as he pushed further, two moments became clear.

"Hold the old girl steady for a minute, Guy," Calum said. "Vick, they're going to break right of us."

"Got them."

Calum opened fire. The relatively small calibre ammunition, no match for the larger shells used by the oncoming fighters, was still enough for someone like Calum. He saw his rounds hit the lead fighter and smash through the perspex canopy. The airplane broke up in mid-air, but Calum had already dismissed it to fire on a second, which he took further back. He had allowed his concentration to slip, but his rounds were enough to shear the tail from the fighter and it spiralled towards the ground.

He felt the big plane lurch as it turned and dived. Without its cargo of heavy bombs, the Lancaster was agile and Guy used all his skill to counter the incoming attack. Calum heard the deep rattle of gunfire as Vick

Richardson loosed tracer rounds into the dark night air from his position perched at the top of the airframe.

"Cal, get upstairs now." Guy's voice carried a hint of panic. "I need you up here with me. Soon as you can, old chap, if not sooner."

Calum wriggled back from the claustrophobic nose bubble, too tight to allow him to wear a parachute. He picked it up from where he had left it, before scrambling through the belly of the Lancaster to where Guy, Phil Hastings, Pete Marshal and Ken Francis did their work.

As Calum climbed through the awkward space between the wing spars he saw glowing tracer rounds light up the sky as the surviving ME-110s dived on them and the remaining four bombers of their wing.

"Where the hell did they come from?" asked Pete Marshal, the wireless operator. "I thought all the fighters had been called up to Normandy."

"Never mind where they came from," said Guy, "they're here now. Phil, give your seat to Cal."

Phil Hastings, the navigator, grumbled but rose to push past Calum. No love lost there.

"Do your thing, Cal," said Guy. It was the closest he had ever come to acknowledging Calum's secret, the one that kept them all alive. Until tonight, at least.

Calum searched the chaotic, splintered futures. He didn't like what he saw. Didn't like it at all. He probed harder, trying to find a window of possibility that would not result in their plane plunging in flames to the ground below.

He couldn't.

Which meant he had to find the least bad option. He chose, discarded, chose again.

"We're going to take a hit, skip," he said. "Hard to port now. Hard as you can."

He saw the tracer come close. Saw it stitch through the starboard wing, and then a sudden blossom of fire as it punctured a fuel line on the outer engine. Guy fought the controls as Ken Francis, their flight engineer, cut off valves somewhere far away from them. Calum watched the broken skeins of unrequited futures tumble away from him. In one, the enemy fire sheared the starboard wing clean off. In another, the rounds cannoned through the cockpit, killing them all. Except those futures hadn't happened. Not in this reality. Not yet.

Guy feathered the prop of the outer engine and leaned across Calum to watch as the flames guttered and died to leave a trail of dark smoke.

"Dive!" Calum shouted, panic entering his own voice. They all knew the danger they flew into every night but had grown blasé. Calum had always brought them home safe, time after time. Tonight he didn't know if he could.

Two fighters took the starboard wing off one of the other Lancasters and it broke apart in mid-air. Calum watched for parachutes, but none appeared. He heard Bob Sutherland give a shout and claim he'd taken one fighter out. It still left three, and with one less bomber, they regrouped and picked their targets more carefully. Calum's Lancaster and one other were injured, so the fighters doubled their attack. They dived fast, then came up under the belly of the lone undamaged plane.

"Keith's going to go down," Calum said. "Take us as

low as you can, Guy, before they try the same trick on us. Don't let the buggers get underneath us."

Guy lowered the nose of the big bomber and dived hard. The airframe shook, but Calum was used to its creaks and rattles now. When he first flew, he kept expecting the plane to disintegrate around him. Now he trusted those who built it.

"Dutch coast a mile ahead." Phil Hastings crouched with his hands on the back of the seat Calum had taken from him.

"Go to a hundred feet once it's safe," Calum said. Then, as a vision came to him, "Up, Guy, now!"

The skipper reacted instantly, as he always did. Tracer rounds arced across the space they would have flown through seconds before.

"Hard to port!" As the big plane lumbered around, Calum heard the rattle of their own guns firing. A shout told them Vick Richardson had taken full advantage of Calum's strange prescience. He leaned to look through the canopy but saw nothing. He toggled his radio and said, "Did you get him, Vick?"

"Blew him to buggery," came the reply.

Which would explain why there was nothing to see. Calum pushed himself into the future again, searching out more attacks, but the remaining German fighters seemed cautious about following them out over the North Sea.

"How's that engine looking, Cal?" asked Guy as he fought the controls to keep them airborne.

Calum looked out again, grasping a stanchion for balance, careful not to touch anything else.

"It's trailing smoke, but I can't see any fire."

"Let's be thankful for small mercies. Ken, what's the fuel situation?"

"Give me a second, skip." Behind them, the flight engineer consulted dials and turned switches. "It's going to be close," he said.

"How close?" When Ken Francis made no reply, Guy raised his voice. "How fucking close, Ken?"

"I'd say too close, skip. We'll almost get home, but not near enough."

"What can you do?"

They flew on while Ken worked. Below them, the dark sea slid by. Calum leaned over to look to either side but saw only one other bomber off to their right and five hundred feet higher. It, too, trailed a dark line of smoke which showed as dawn chased them from behind.

"Take it down to two engines, skip," said Ken.

"Haven't done that since training," said Guy. "But that was then, and this is now. What can you give me if we do?"

"Enough to make home, I think."

"You think?"

"Yes, I think. If we keep three going we won't make the coast. We'll have to ditch in the drink. Oh, and one more thing, I think the hydraulics for the landing gear is shot."

"Any more good news to impart?" asked Guy.

"Not right now, skip, but I'll see what I can find."

Guy reached out and cut fuel to the outer port engine. The roar of the big Rolls Royce Merlin faded. Calum watched Guy fight with the controls until he restored some semblance of balance. He took the big plane even lower until it felt as if they were skipping across the surface of the waves like a flat pebble. If Guy kept them as close to the water as possible the ground-effect might help eke our their stock of fuel. Perhaps they'd make it after all.

A half-hour from the coast, a bank of dark clouds thickened to obscure the horizon. Ten minutes later, rain streamed back from the screen, forcing Guy to take them higher as visibility reduced. They crossed the Suffolk coastline as the rain grew heavier, and Guy took the big Lancaster up to three-hundred feet. It fought him all the way. The bomber was designed to limp home on two engines, one if it had to, but it didn't have to like it.

"Fuel's good for another five minutes," said Ken Francis.

"Four should see us home. What's the state of the undercarriage?"

"Do you want the truth or an approximation of it?"

"Truth might be best under the circumstances," said Guy.

"Then the port wheel will come down... I think. The starboard I'm not so sure about. And even if it deploys, I can't see it taking the strain of landing. Not even one of yours, Guy."

"Belly flop?" asked Guy.

"It'll give us the best chance, and we've trained for it."

Guy glanced across at Calum. "Find something to wedge yourself up against, Cal." Then he toggled his headset and spoke to the rest of the crew. "We're going to come in hard, chaps. Do what you can and I'll do what I can."

Calum slid from the flight engineer's jump seat and

wedged himself in the front corner. He saw Ken Francis do the same further back. Guy feathered the flaps, his face a grimace of concentration. Calum trusted him to bring them down safely. Everyone regarded him as the best pilot in the flight. Perhaps the best pilot in Suffolk.

Calum withdrew into himself. He didn't want to know what was about to happen, because there was nothing he could do to influence it. They would belly-flop and skid along the grass on one side of the runway. They would make it or not. He was aware of everything that could go wrong but preferred not to see his own death coming if that's what it was going to be.

Guy feathered the engines right back and a moment later Calum's body jerked hard as the belly of the Lancaster hit the ground. There was an almighty crash, followed by a splintering sound as the propellers shattered. Guy fought the controls with his feet, only the rear ailerons offering him the slightest chance of influencing their direction.

It wasn't enough.

Calum felt the fuselage drift sideways. The starboard wing dipped. It dug into the ground and pivoted the rest of the airframe into the sky. The Lancaster cartwheeled, came down hard, and continued to slide. But their speed was less now and gradually the world settled into, if not order, at least some semblance of it.

"Report," said Guy, his voice still calm as the plane came to a final, shuddering halt.

Calum listened as the men reported in. All except Vick Richardson, their upper gunner. Calum tried to get up and failed on the first attempt. By the time he gained his feet, Pete Marshall had already gone back to check on Vick. He returned, shaking his head.

Guy punched open the emergency hatch above his head but made no move to climb out himself. He unsnapped his harness and stood crouched over as he helped the others to clamber out. He held his hand out to Calum, who took it and pulled himself up. It was a drop to the grass and Calum rolled when he landed. As he came to his feet he saw a fire tender racing towards them, together with two jeeps. He knew questions were going to be asked. A sense of exhaustion flooded through him.

Guy punched him on the arm before walking to the remains of the Lancaster. He kissed the tips of his fingers, then touched the creased metal of the plane that had brought them home. "Thanks, old girl. You did good tonight."

CHAPTER TWO

The fire tender skidded to a halt and the crew jumped out, but it looked as if nothing was going to burst into flames. There wasn't enough fuel left for flames to feed on. Even if one did start, the rain was heavy enough to put it out. Two jeeps pulled up and Phil Hastings, Pete Marshall, and Ken Frances ran across to climb aboard one. Guy walked across to the fire tender and told them to check the upper gun position. Vick Richardson's body would need bringing out.

"I think I might have broken the old girl for good this time," said Guy.

Calum looked at the tthroughwisted airframe, amazed all but one of them had survived.

"I've seen them do amazing things with worse, skip. They'll salvage what they can." He glanced at Guy. "It wasn't your fault. If it had been anyone else at the controls, we'd all be goners."

"Still doesn't feel like any kind of victory though, does it?"

Calum walked to the second jeep but stopped when he heard another vehicle approach. An expensive Rover Light Six with green bodywork pulled up beside the other vehicles and the driver got out. His uniform was army rather than RAF.

"Very impressive landing," the man said, a note of disdain in his voice. "Are either of you gents Flight Sergeant Auger?"

"This is your man." Guy nodded at Calum. "Who's asking?"

"Major Simpson. Can I ask you to come with me, Auger?"

"What's this about?" Guy asked. "We have to debrief, Calum more than anyone."

"It's nothing to worry about. All above board and cleared with your superiors. Flight Sergeant Auger can debrief later." The Major stopped, waiting. "If you would like to come with me?" There was no hint Calum had any choice in the matter.

He nodded at Guy. "I'll catch up with you later, skip."

"The Bell at six if I don't see you before," said Guy as he went to the second jeep. "I've got my fingers crossed we won't be flying tonight. We can all tie one on and raise a glass for Vick."

"More than one." Calum turned and followed the uniformed man to the Rover and got into the passenger seat. "What's this all about?"

"As I said, nothing to worry about." Simpson started the engine and drove at speed towards a group of wooden huts set apart from Calum's usual quarters.

"You're not RAF, are you?"

"Army. Well, sort of Army."

"Sort of?"

"Kind of hush-hush, I suppose. I might be able to tell you more later, but for now, let's just say I'm a friend."

The smile on the man's face seemed genuine enough, but an uneasy feeling crawled through Calum's belly. This didn't feel right. They pulled up in front of one of the huts. The sound of the rain was loud on its roof, louder still when they entered.

Calum stopped in the corridor's shelter.

"I need to know what you want with me."

The Major looked at him, his eyes harder now. "You are a Flight Sergeant, Mr Auger, and I am a Major. Even if we serve different services that still means I don't have to explain why I want you, only that you are to come with me when I ask." His voice was firm, and it was clear he was used to being obeyed.

Calum stared back. He could be stubborn, too. For a moment they were locked in a minor battle of wills, but it was always going to be one Calum couldn't win. He had already seen that. He shrugged, as though it didn't matter to him one way or another, and started walking again, making the Major catch him up. Small, petty victories, he thought.

The door at the end of the corridor was open, but the Major closed it behind them once they entered. A small table had been set up, borrowed from the NAAFI by the look of it. A pot of tea and three cups were set at one end. An older man, not in uniform, sat on the far side.

"Mr Auger, it's a pleasure to meet you at last. I have

heard so much about you and your, ah, special abilities. Please, take a seat. Major, would you be mother?"

Major Simpson poured weak tea for each of them before sitting at the end of the temporary table as if his job was now complete. The man on the other side sat with hands folded in his lap, an expression of utmost patience on his face. He was dressed in civilian clothes, well-cut, expensive looking. A dark tweed jacket and matching trousers. A striped tie that would no doubt mean something to another of his class, but not Calum.

He stayed on his feet as he tried to decide whether to leave or not. The tension of their landing still thrummed through him. He made an attempt to ignore the pounding behind his eyes as he stared at the grey block wall, trying to evaluate his options. It took him less than half a minute before he knew he had none. If he tried to leave, his foresight showed him Major Simpson rising and moving fast to stop him before he could reach the door. If he objected, whatever conversation ensued lay too far in the future to discern. He saw nothing useful in the time-frame he could see into. Which meant he might as well sit and listen to whatever they had to say. Besides, he was curious how they seemed to know about him.

He sat and reached for his tea, added two sugars, and stirred. He sipped, too hot, but he needed to behave normally, and waited. The man behind the desk was tall, well over six feet, and unnaturally thin. He continued to stare at Calum as if he could wait all night.

Calum broke first. "What's this all about?" He thought he saw a tiny smile pass across the man's lips, but if it did it came and went too fleetingly to be sure. Using normal sight now, his headache was fading, but he knew it would return as a ravening monster if he wasn't careful. The raid had been long and the stress of their return would take days to leach from him. He was still trying to process Vick's death. All he wanted to do was swallow three fingers of good Scotch and sleep. If he could.

"It's about you, of course, Calum," said the still nameless man behind the desk.

Not Flight Sergeant. Not Mr Auger. Calum.

"You have the advantage of me, Mr… or do you have a rank?"

The man lifted a shoulder. Almost a shrug. "You have no need to know my name at the moment. Later, perhaps, depending on the outcome of our conversation, but I think for now I prefer to remain anonymous. It will be better for both of us."

"In that case…" Calum rose. He saw the Major tense in preparation. There was no reaction from the other man.

"I think we both know what the consequences will be if you try to leave."

Calum did, but how could the other man be so sure? Admittedly, the Major was taller and heavier than Calum, but he also looked a little soft around the edges. And Calum still had his service pistol tucked inside his flight jacket. It might be interesting to see what happened. Except his head hurt like hell, he was tired, and his bones ached. All he wanted to do was fall into bed and sleep six straight hours. And when he woke, he'd get drunk with the others as they toasted Vick. Perhaps he'd even try his luck with one of the pretty WAAFS that were usually around.

"In that case, perhaps you can explain why I'm sitting here instead of being debriefed with the rest of my crew." Calum crossed his arms. "The Major here saw us crash-land. We lost a man. Questions are going to be asked."

"We can do this several ways, Calum." The man was relaxed, his voice cultured. He was one of those upper-crust individuals who seemed to find themselves appointed into positions just a little above their ability. He gave every appearance of conviviality, but his voice carried a note of authority. An authority that came only after years of being instantly obeyed.

"I'd like to do this the quickest way possible if that's all right with you?" Calum said.

The man smiled, allowing it to show this time. "In that case, I am here to offer you a job. Another posting, if you like."

Calum shook his head. "I'd rather see this one out, thanks. I like my crew, and they need me."

"I am aware they do. I am also aware of exactly why they need you, and why you feel you owe them some loyalty. But your... talents, shall we say... would be better used in a different service to your country."

"Talents?" Calum asked.

"I thought you had already indicated you wished to do this the quickest way. Do I really need to go through all the rigmarole of telling you everything I know about you?"

Calum stared across the table and waited. He could also wait.

A minute passed. Two...

"Would anyone like more tea?" Major Simpson broke the lengthening silence.

The man shot him a sharp glance and the Major sat back in his chair.

Calum was tempted to say yes, please, and perhaps some biscuits, but the look from the other side of the table made him decide it would be the wrong response.

"What do you know about me?" he asked. "And how?" He looked into the eyes across the table. Light grey, as hard as steel but colder.

"We have certain sources of information available to us."

"But no one knows. No one."

"Perhaps you underestimate your colleagues. I believe most of the men on this base consider it a good day when they fly with Calum Auger."

"I always think whatever I might possess is rather a minor talent."

"There you go, underestimating yourself. How many times have you saved the lives of your crew, including what you will have done tonight? You might have lost one man, but the rest of you walked away. I suspect you can no longer recall how many times you have saved them, can you?"

"In those circumstances, I agree my ability might have its uses. But I don't see how it might be employed in other ways. A fluke, that's all it is. Of little benefit other than to myself and those close to me."

Finally, the other man moved, leaning forward and steepling his fingers, his elbows on the tabletop.

"I would like to propose a hypothetical situation to you."

"Propose away." Calum tried to make himself sit back, to match the relaxation he saw across the table, but knew he made a poor job of it.

The man turned aside for a moment and said, "I think we will have more tea after all, Major. Would you like to organise that? And perhaps some biscuits?"

The Major rose as though it was perfectly natural he should be the tea-boy.

"You can call me Teddy," the man said, once the Major had left the room.

Calum looked at him. "Is that your actual name?"

The man laughed. "I thought it might make you more comfortable if I had a name. Do you mind the small subterfuge, Calum?"

"Of course not, Teddy. You were going to tell me something, I believe." Calum knew that the man was dangerous but the whole situation was suddenly comical. The stress of the day, the strangeness of the situation, bubbled through him. It wanted to erupt in a guffaw which he fought to hold inside.

"You intimated you are unsure how your, ah, ability could prove useful. Well, imagine that we employed you to accompany the Prime Minister everywhere he went. Or the King. Or a General. I am sure we can both think of dozens of suitable subjects. Imagine how your gift could be used in those circumstances. Suppose some traitor tries to make an attempt on Winston's life. Half a minute's warning should be enough, don't you think?"

Calum said nothing. He wondered how close that half-minute was to a guess. Or did the man know a lot more about Calum than he had thought? And if so, how did he know?

Teddy waited. There was a clatter outside and the door opened, bringing the Major back with more tea and a plate of biscuits. Rather good biscuits.

"Is that the job you are offering me?" Calum asked. "As a babysitter for the Prime Minister?"

Teddy shook his head and held his hand out over the biscuits, choosing as though by divination. "Not necessarily. It is merely a hypothetical situation. To help you see how your gift has practical application outside of how you use it now." He dropped his hand and chose a shortbread. "I am certain that if we were to throw ideas around for a while, we could come up with many more applications."

"I'm not interested," Calum said.

The look of amusement that had been on the man's face drained away.

"Don't forget, Flight Sergeant, that you are a member of His Majesty's Armed Forces, and that this country is at war. All I have to do is give the word and they will transfer you out of here so fast your feet won't touch the ground"

"And then?" Calum asked, trying to keep his voice even.

"And then I can do whatever I want with you until you agree to help your country. We are at war, in case it has escaped your attention. My powers are more or less without limit."

"You are assuming the trauma of such an act would

not cause any minor talent I might possess to suddenly dry up," Calum said. "If I have any talent at all, that is."

Teddy dipped the corner of the biscuit into his tea, wafting it backwards and forwards before leaning over to bite the soft end away with small teeth that seemed out of place in a man so tall.

"I know some people who can be extremely persuasive."

"I'm sure you do, but it's not secrets you're trying to drag out of me, is it? It's something of a more delicate nature."

"And if I call on your patriotism? The sense of duty to your country?"

"What about my sense of duty to my crew? My friends? I can relate to them more easily than I do some vague concept like country."

The man sighed and sat back. "I thought you would have been more amenable to my proposal than this."

Calum allowed himself a smile. "I'm not unsympathetic, but I can't abandon my crew. Not now. Not when..."

The man waited for Calum to finish. When it was obvious he wasn't going to, he finished for him. "Not when the war is almost over? Is that what you were about to say? Is that what you believe, Calum?"

Calum looked across the table at him, then nodded. "Doesn't everybody? This feels like the end, Teddy, you know it does. We all know it. It's just a case of how long, and how to stay alive until that day arrives. That's what I meant. How would I feel after spending two years in that bloody bomber if I just walked away on another mission and abandoned my friends? What if on the next raid they don't come back? We lost one man tonight. I don't want to lose any more. We both know the war is almost done, but that doesn't mean it's not as deadly as it always has been."

"You make a persuasive argument, and I would be a fool if I tried to argue against your analysis of the situation. However, let me posit another hypothetical case. The war lasts another six months, even a year. What plans do you have then, Calum? I believe you had intended to study at Oxford."

Calum gave a brief nod.

"As I am sure you know, our country's more discreet organisations get many of their new recruits from that centre of study. That and the other one. And if they identify an individual they are particularly interested in, then it is not unknown for them to employ him in an unofficial capacity while he continues his studies. Would you not be interested in a more lavish lifestyle while you complete, or rather start, your studies?"

"And the price?" Calum asked.

"As our American cousins say, there is no such thing as a free lunch. I expect the demands on you would not be too onerous. We will allow you a freedom not accorded most of our recruits."

"And if I say no?"

The man stared at Calum, the benign expression still on his face, if not in his eyes.

"You are free to leave whenever you want, Mr Auger." He glanced at Major Simpson and gave an almost imperceptible nod.

Calum didn't believe him, but decided to test what would happen. He rose and turned away. He got as far as the door before the man spoke again.

"The Major and I intend to stay here a while longer, should you change your mind."

Calum opened the door and walked from the room. His feet sounded loud on the uncarpeted floor. Outside, the rain was still falling hard as he ran across to the debriefing hut only to find it closed up. He huddled beneath the locked door, trying to work out how long he had been in the interview room. Only thirty minutes, he was sure. Debrief usually took at least twice that long. Tonight it should have been longer still. So where the hell was his crew, and all the other crews who had returned?

He tried the mess hall first. Everyone was always starving by the time they returned, and an early breakfast would go down well with Calum, too. When he walked in, the heat and noise almost drove him back out. The air was thick with the mouth-watering smell of bacon, fried potatoes and sausage – though what the sausage consisted of might not be quite so mouth-watering. Calum saw Guy and the others seated at a table on the far side, their heads together, and he made his way past the other crews and pulled out a chair.

Nobody said anything, but all faces turned to look at him.

"What happened?" he asked. "Why was there no debrief?"

Phil Hastings rapped the bare table-top with a knuckle. "You're what happened, you bastard."

"There's no need for that kind of language," said Guy. "This isn't Cal's fault. These things happen."

"What things?" Calum's stomach grumbled, and he reached over and took a remnant of fried bread from Guy's plate. It was all that was left.

"They've broken the team up," said Guy. "We're all assigned to new crews. Some of us to new bases."

"Why?"

"Because of you," said Phil, bringing another sharp look from Guy. "They told us you were moving on, and without you, there's no reason to keep the rest of us together. Which is bollocks of the first order."

Calum looked at Guy. "Is this true, skip?"

Guy nodded.

"Even if they take me out of the crew, surely it's simpler just to bring in a new man."

"I expect they want you for something more important than us."

"That's enough, Phil," snapped Guy. He rose to his feet and touched Calum on the shoulder. "Come on, let's take a walk."

Calum laughed, his tension needing some release. "It's pissing down outside."

Guy smiled and looked around the mess hall. "Another table, then. Just you and me. And get yourself some breakfast, you look all done in."

Guy found an empty table while Calum went to the canteen counter and picked up as much as the serving woman would allow, which was quite a lot. The women liked Calum, he knew. They thought he was both handsome and cheeky, and Calum made no effort to disabuse them of the notion if it let him pile his plate a little higher. Not that it did any good. Whatever he ate never seemed to make any difference to his weight.

He carried the plate in one hand and a mug of tea in the other – proper tea this time, dark and strong, unlike the stuff the Major had poured – towards the quiet corner where Guy was waiting for him.

CHAPTER THREE

"What is it you don't want to say to me in front of the others, skip?" Calum took a bite from the bacon sandwich he had constructed. He patted crumbs from his flying suit, only then aware he should have changed into either uniform or civvies.

Instead of answering his question, Guy had one of his own. "Who was that man who took you away?"

"Not exactly sure I can tell you." Calum washed the remnant of bread down with more tea. "Hush-hush, I was told."

"I thought it might be something like that. When we reached the briefing hut, they stopped us from going inside and took us away to another one. The Wingco came and told us the team was being broken up." Guy stared at Calum, a hardness in his eyes.

"Because of the crash, or because of me?"

"They didn't say, but it makes sense it's you. It might be the crash, of course, but I've never heard of a crew being broken up because of a bad landing." Guy took a breath and held it a moment before letting it go. "Look, Cal, all of us know about you."

Calum couldn't meet Guy's eyes. "Who ratted me out?"

Guy shrugged. "Not me, and I doubt it was Bob or any of the others. They like you. If pushed, I'd probably say Phil."

"As would I. He's never taken to me." Calum stared at Guy. "Do you talk about me between yourselves?"

"Never. I mean that, Cal, nobody ever said anything to me. Oh, Phil drops the odd hint now and again, but he never comes right out and makes an accusation."

"An accusation of what? You know without me everybody on the crew would be dead. Do you mean that kind of accusation?" Calum put his half-eaten sandwich down, no longer hungry. "Tell me what the Wingco had to say."

"Quid pro quo?" said Guy. "I'll show you mine if you show me yours?" A smile lifted one side of his mouth.

Calum didn't care about quid pro quo. All he cared about was the man sitting across from him, and the crew he had recently returned from flying over Nazi Germany with.

"They want me to work for them."

"Doing what?"

"Doing what I've been doing for you."

"And the crew," said Guy.

"Yes. For you and the crew."

"We've never talked about it, have we?"

"Do you want to talk about it now?"

Guy looked into his eyes for a long moment, then pulled out a pack of Players. He tamped the end of one, put it between his lips and struck a match. He offered the pack to Calum, who took one and waited for the match. He inhaled the smoke deep.

"I'd prefer we don't talk about it," said Guy, smoke drifting out as he spoke. "I don't think I want to know. There are times you spook me, Cal. It makes me uncomfortable."

"Is that how everyone feels?"

"I told you, we never talk about you. So, are you going to do it?"

"Work for them?" Calum drew on the cigarette, giving himself a moment to decide if he was going to or not. "It depends. Quid pro quo works in other ways, too. How long do you think the war's going to last?"

A frown narrowed Guy's eyebrows. "What's that got to do with the price of fish?"

Calum laughed. "God, I'd kill for a piece of fresh fish. What I mean is, if these people I'm not allowed to talk about promise me something, such as making sure the crew are offered safe postings for the duration, I might be more amenable to going with them. At least until I find out what they want."

"I don't want a safe posting," said Guy. "Yes, we're winning the war now, but only because people like me and you, and everyone else climb into those rattling death-traps several times a week and fly over the enemy with a belly full of thousand-pounders."

"You know what's going to happen if I turn them down, don't you? The crew gets broken up anyway. You may not even get a flying job. I can give up what I have here and step into the unknown, but for that to happen you have to give up being a hero."

"I'm no hero."

"You say that, but it's how the others see you. It's how I see you. If you refuse, then I have to refuse them. You might want to keep flying, but I know the others don't. Without me, you have no guarantee you'll come back the next time or the time after that. You know what the odds are, Guy."

"Do it for the others then, but leave me out of it. I'll find a new posting. Pilots are in short supply. Good pilots even more so." Guy stubbed his cigarette out in the tin ashtray where Calum's burned, ignored. Guy looked beyond Calum and gave a nod at someone. "The boys are ready, I have to go. Do what feels right to you, Cal. I'm behind you whatever decision you make."

Guy rose to his feet and offered his hand. Calum stared at it, the implications of shaking it ripe with finality. He stood and took the proffered hand, then turned and walked past his waiting crew without meeting their eyes.

The rain had lessened as Calum ran across to the hut where he had left Teddy and Major Simpson. As he approached the door, he saw a woman in a smart two-piece suit emerge from the hut. She stopped beneath the small shelter and fumbled in her shoulder bag. She glanced up as Calum slowed, for a moment a look of almost panic on her face. He watched as she attempted to control herself, wondering when he had got so scary.

"Have they gone?" Calum asked.

"Has who gone?"

"The Major and Teddy."

"Who?"

"Major Simpson and the other man."

"Ah… I see. No, they're both still inside." She found what she was looking for and drew out a pack of cigarettes. Pall Mall, marking her either as someone with taste or someone wanting to appear to have taste. "I assume you are Calum Auger."

"Who's asking?"

"I am." She shook out a cigarette and lit it, her lipstick marking the filter.

"When you tell me your name, I'll think about telling you mine."

"I know perfectly well who you are. They're inside waiting for you, but they're starting to think you're not coming back. Have you reached a decision, Calum?"

Whoever the woman was, she clearly had some connection with the two inside. Was she their senior or junior, or something else? She looked too young to be in command of either of the men in the hut. Too pretty, though what that had to do with any seniority was another matter altogether. Calum brushed past her and went into the corridor. Major Simpson stood at the far end. He was facing away but turned when he heard the door. The faintest of smiles touched his lips, and he walked back into the room.

"I need something," Calum said, as he drew out the

hard metal chair and sat. The man who wanted to be called Teddy remained as still as he had before, his expression showing nothing.

"Do you want more tea?" He glanced past Calum. "If you would you be so kind, Simpson?" When they were alone, the man set his palms on the table in front of him. "What kind of deal are you looking for?"

"I want you to stand my crew down. Furloughed for the duration. Offered safe postings if they want them. Guy says he wants to keep flying, so I'd like you to arrange that as well. A posting to a good squadron. I'm sure you could assign him to the Pathfinders if you wanted. Guy's more than good enough."

"I suspect you may have an inflated idea of my influence, Mr Auger, but I will see what I can do. And in return?"

"I'll do as you ask. At least until I find out whether it's something I can do."

Teddy leaned forward and held out his hand. He waited.

Calum experienced a sense of déjà vu, something he was more than familiar with. He pushed himself to see what the implications would be if he shook the hand, what they were if he refused. For as far as he could see ahead, the choice made no difference at all. Which meant the decision was down to him. And because Calum had been raised to be polite, he reached out and shook the offered hand. The handshake was firm, a test of some kind perhaps, but if so it was one Calum passed with ease. He was used to the brotherhood of such moments among men, even if the one sitting across from him was not the same manner of man as Calum himself.

Teddy only released Calum's hand when the door opened again.

"Sorry, Simpson, we seem to have concluded. Unless Dr Grierson would like to make a start with Calum now? Set the tea down and go ask her if you would."

When they were alone again Calum said, "I assume you are his senior?"

"In some ways, but not in others. I have no rank, as you can see."

"Is Dr Grierson the woman I met outside?"

"Elizabeth Grierson, yes. Pretty young thing." The man's eyes met Calum's. "If you like that sort of thing."

On the desktop, the pot of tea curled steam into the air. A clock on the wall counted off the seconds. The sweep of its arms blurred under Calum's gaze. They became a hundred different hands, each telling a slightly different time.

When the door opened again Major Simpson said, "She says she'd rather talk to him when we get there, or perhaps tonight over dinner if we don't make it that far."

The tall man offered a nod and rose to his feet. An operation that seemed to go on for a long time. "I may see you later, Calum. If you would be so kind as to go with the Major and Dr Grierson now. And good luck."

Outside, the woman wasn't in sight, but the sleek Rover Light Six idled on the nearest patch of tarmac. Beyond it, a single Lancaster powered up and started searching for enough speed to get airborne. No doubt it was a test flight for some repair the ground crew had undertaken. One of them might even be at the controls, taking advantage of the chance to pretend to be something they were not. Beyond it, Calum caught sight of the wreckage of their plane. One wing had come loose and more men swarmed over it, cutting it apart. It amazed him all but one of them had walked away from the landing.

Major Simpson came past Calum and walked to the car. He opened the passenger door wide enough for Calum to climb into the back and sit beside Dr Grierson, then walked around the long nose and got in behind the wheel.

"Where are we going?" Calum asked.

"You'll find out when we get there." Major Simpson accelerated hard along the tarmac.

"What about my kit?" Calum asked. "Everything I own is in my hut."

"Not any longer. It's in the boot of the car. There was plenty of room. Now talk with Elizabeth if you want some amusement, I'm going to be busy. This car is a bit of a beast."

They followed the perimeter road until the main gate appeared ahead. It opened without them having to slow, the tyres protesting as Major Simpson bullied the long car onto the road that would lead them to the A14. They headed west, so Calum knew they were not going to the coast or south to London. He considered whether he cared where they were going and decided he didn't. Making the decision felt as if it cut him loose and he drifted, no destination in mind.

Ahead of him, the Major drove fast, as if impatient to reach whatever destination lay ahead.

"Can we talk?"

Calum turned to look at Dr Grierson. She was older than him, but not by much. Not the age he expected of a Doctor, whatever kind she was. He suspected it had little to do with the body and more to do with the mind. He had already noted she was pretty, but now he took a moment to study her more closely. Only a little shorter than him as she sat, perhaps not much shorter when she stood from the way she had to tuck her slim legs sideways. Blonde hair cut to the shoulder. Hazel-brown eyes and perfect, pale skin. She wore just a touch of lipstick, enough to enhance, too little to be brash. Her teeth, when she smiled, were very white, with one slightly overlapping another at one side, which only added to their perfection. Calum wondered what she saw in return and wished he had changed out of his flight suit. But he knew some women found it attractive – a little devil-may-care. More for what it meant than how it looked, though he was aware women liked him. Enough of them to make his nights off into an interesting game. Calum was not one for self-study, but he knew how he looked. He looked exactly like his twin brother would have had he still lived.

"We can talk if you want," he said when Dr Grierson blinked.

"I thought it might help pass the time. We have at least four hours ahead of us, I'm afraid."

Four hours west, Calum thought, trying to work out where that would take them. As far as Wales? Possibly, the way Major Simpson drove. He knew that side of England well because he had been raised in Shrewsbury, and for a moment he thought they might take him there, to his home, though why they would do so he didn't know. Unless it was to see his parents, who continued to live in their large house on the old Roman road.

"What do you want to talk about?" Calum asked.

"You."

He tried to offer a smile but knew from her expression he didn't get it quite right.

"Can we do this later? I've just landed from a six-hour flight, which ended rather badly, and I'm exhausted."

She gave a smile that offered Calum something, but exactly what was lost on him. She leaned forward and placed her hand on Major Simpson's shoulder. "Pull over if you can, John. I'll come in the front with you so Calum can stretch out and sleep."

The Major didn't wait for a lay-by but braked hard to pull up in the middle of the narrow road. Dr Grierson leaned forward and pulled the door handle, slipped out and then slipped back in. By the time the car was up to speed again Calum was asleep, his dreams jostled by the movement of the car and the hum of the engine. Dreams of flying. Dreams of falling. Uneasy dreams of a pretty, blonde-haired woman.

CHAPTER FOUR

Calum came awake with a jolt. The car had stopped with such force it had thrown him into the narrow space between the seats. He freed himself as both doors opened, then climbed out and looked around. They were in the countryside, with extensive views to the west into what he recognised as Wales. He made out the long bulk of Black Hill, with its sharp scarp dropping to Hay-on-Wye. The distinctive double-peak of Pen y Fan rose in the distance beyond. The car had stopped on a gravel driveway in front of a rather unimpressive but large house built of harsh red brick. The only redeeming feature was an attempt at a porch over the entrance. Behind the house, a wooded hill rose, though not to any great height. An explosion of sound made him turn to see a small training plane speed across a grass runway and lurch into the air.

"Where are we?" he asked, but received no response. Calum washed a hand across his face, trying to dispel his tiredness and failing. He glanced at his watch, surprised to see it showed a little after 1400 hours. He must have slept a good four hours.

Major Simpson went to the rear of the car, opened the boot and lifted out a cardboard suitcase. He set it on the ground.

"Your things," he said, then got back behind the wheel and drove off.

"Is he always like that?" Calum asked Dr Grierson, who stood beside him watching the car disappear. A trail of dust settled back to earth to show where it had passed.

"Sometimes he smiles, but rarely. I hadn't seen him for a while until yesterday."

"You drove across the country to meet me?"

Dr Grierson offered Calum her pretty smile. He was starting to like it, but wouldn't get his hopes up. Despite her relative youth, there was something knowing about her. She seemed more mature than her years. And from the way she was treated, she must have some seniority.

"The Service informed me you were someone it would be worth my time talking to," she said.

"Did you have to bring me all the way here to have that conversation? Couldn't we have done it on the base?"

"I was following orders. We all follow orders these days."

"Whose orders?"

"I thought it was me asking the questions. Come on, I'll show you to your room, and you might want to shave and take a bath before we start." She looked him up and down. "Perhaps civvies would be more comfortable, too. I'll get Dottie to wash your flight suit if you leave it out."

"Dottie?"

"Our housekeeper," said Dr Grierson. "Dorothy Powell, but everyone calls her Dottie. Local girl. Husband's in the navy. She does all the cooking and cleaning, but we might need to get some more help in when the others arrive."

Calum was about to ask her who she meant by the others, but as they approached the wide door it opened, and the tall man who had spoken with Calum on the base stepped out. Calum stared at him, confused.

"You must have driven like the very devil to get here before us."

The man offered a smile. "Why drive when you can fly? I cadged a lift with a mail crate headed this way. Well, not exactly this way, but I can be persuasive when needs must." He looked towards Dr Grierson. "As you already know, my dear. I assume you haven't started yet?"

"I thought Calum might like to see where he'll be sleeping and clean up first."

"Capital idea. I'll see if I can rustle up some late lunch, and then you can start. I need to be somewhere else later today, but I'm content to stay for a while if it helps."

"I'm not sure it will. You can get away early if you like, Sir Edward. I'm sure I can sort out lunch for Calum and myself, even if it is a little late."

"If you're sure, my dear?" He glanced to where a second training plane taxied to the end of the runway. "I expect I can find a hotel in Hereford. And I'll be back in the morning for the briefing."

The man appeared unconcerned he had flown across England for little reward. Watching the interplay, Calum was again puzzled at the young woman's authority, as if she was the senior partner in whatever relationship existed between the pair.

"Stay if you want, but I'd rather the talk is between Calum and myself. You're more than welcome to hang around the house if you think it worthwhile. I can probably find you a room for the night here, but I suspect a hotel will be more comfortable. Carden House is big, but a little spartan."

Carlton offered his hand to Calum, taking it in both of his as if they had become best of friends, then went into the house, presumably to sort out his accommodation.

When he had gone Calum said, "Sir Edward? He told me his name was Teddy, and I assumed it was an outright lie. Only a slight one, it seems."

"He likes to play games." Dr Grierson caught the corner of her bottom lip between her teeth, a strangely coquettish gesture. "Have I let slip an official secret, do you think?"

"He didn't seem to mind."

"No, he wouldn't. Edward keeps a lot to himself." A shadow of a smile.

Calum noticed she had dropped the Sir from the name. He waited, half-expecting her to reveal the man's full name. Instead, Dr Grierson led him inside. Sir Edward was talking on a telephone in the wide hallway. He raised a hand as Dr Grierson led Calum up a staircase and along a corridor on the first floor. She opened the door to a small room. There was a single bed pushed against one wall, a narrow table set before a tall window that offered a view west to the same hills Calum had noted on arrival. The vista was made even more impressive by the addition of height. There was a chair, a bedside table, and a small chest of drawers. In one corner was a sink with a single cold tap. Dr Grierson allowed Calum to drop his suitcase on the bed, then showed him where the large bathroom was at the end of the hall. She told him to come downstairs when he was ready.

Calum ran a bath, relieved to discover there was hot water. He neglected to shave the fine stubble from his cheeks because he had left his razor in his suitcase. At least he hoped it was there. When he was ready, he wrapped a towel around his waist, opened the door and peered into the hallway to check it was clear before running back to his room. He dressed in a shirt and slacks, not bothering with a tie, and left his flight suit in a pile on the floor for the housekeeper to take care of. He had seen no staff yet, heard nobody else in the house. Calum sat on the bed and gazed through the window at rolling parkland that gave way to fields where sheep and cattle grazed. He felt his eyes grow heavy again and stood abruptly, pushing the fatigue away. There were tablets in his flight suit that would help, but he preferred not to use them. He wanted answers, not pills.

He was still staring through the window, unaware how long he had been doing so when there came a soft knock on the door. Or rather, he heard the echo of a knock so that by the time he opened the door, Dr Grierson was raising her fist. She made no show of surprise.

"If you're ready, Calum, I'd like to make a start before the others arrive. There's good strong tea and ham sandwiches downstairs. I left the mustard out of yours because, well, I wasn't sure if you liked it or not, but there's some on the table if you do. Help yourself."

Calum wondered again who she meant by the others. The apparent nervousness evidenced by her chatter also puzzled him. If she was nervous, it was the first sign of it so far.

"Mustard is fine." He waited for her to lead the way.

They descended the wide, curved staircase and crossed a parquet floor, her heels clicking, Calum's soles making a squeak with each step he took. He gazed around. As always, when he saw a house like this, he wondered how it must have been for a single family to live in all this space and grandeur. Now, the war had requisitioned many of these old houses for its own purposes. Despite the opulence of the staircase, the wide hallway, the high ceilings, there was something utilitarian about the place. As if whoever had commissioned it knew all the right elements but had failed to implement them properly.

Dr Grierson led the way into a small room devoid of decoration. An oak desk sat squarely in the middle. Behind it, a bookcase took up half of one wall. A single tall window offered a view over grounds that were growing wild. A plate of thick sandwiches made with home-baked bread sat in the centre of the table. Set to one side lay a writing pad and pen. Calum took the seat opposite, a comfortable captain's chair that wrapped around him.

Dr Grierson slipped out of her jacket and hung it over the back of her own chair before sitting. She had also changed and now wore a white blouse open at the neck. Calum took a moment to appreciate the curve of her breasts while she busied herself arranging the items on the desk. She opened the empty writing pad and uncapped the fountain pen.

"Help yourself to a sandwich, Calum."

He reached out and took one, peeled the bread back to see if it was the one with mustard or not. It lacked any condiment, so he smeared a good portion on one slice and set it on the small plate in front of him while the doctor poured tea for them both. When he looked up she was staring at him with a strange intensity. Calum expected her to look away, embarrassed, but she only continued to look at him.

"Sorry, I should have shaved," he said. "I left my razor in the room." He was aware of his own nerves. Also of a potent attraction to her.

Her eyes tracked his face. "No, the rugged look suits you. You're a handsome man, Cal, though I don't suppose I'm the first woman to tell you that, am I?" She tilted her head to one side. "Is it all right to call you Cal? Or should we continue to be more formal?"

Calum bit into his sandwich and nodded. "Cal is fine," he said once he had swallowed. "Why am I here?" He wiped his mouth with the palm of his hand.

Dr Grierson's eyes remained locked on his. Her sandwich lay ignored on the plate.

"I can tiptoe around what you are, what you can do, or you can accept that you are going to tell me everything eventually and save us both some time."

Calum smiled. "Is that a threat, Dr Grierson?"

"I hope it doesn't need to be. And please, call me Elizabeth."

"Elizabeth?"

"It is my name, and as I'm calling you Cal, it seems only fair."

"Elizabeth," Calum said again, this time not making it a question. "So – exactly what do you want to know about me?"

She leaned forward a little. "How long have you known you can see into the future?"

CHAPTER FIVE

When Calum laughed, a frown caused Elizabeth Grierson's eyes to narrow. Light hazel with a touch of green. Beautiful eyes. High cheekbones and a full mouth. It was a lovely face. Calum knew it was wrong to judge her that way, but it was difficult not to. There was something about her that made it hard to do anything else.

"You might as well ask me how long I have been self-aware. What is your first ever memory, Elizabeth?"

A brief smile. "I believe I'm supposed to be asking the questions."

Calum thought of his conversation with Guy. "Quid pro quo," he said.

She sighed, as if she meant to humour him, for a while at least.

"I suppose I was three or four. We were at the beach, and there were enormous waves." She laughed. "Well, they seemed enormous waves to me. I don't suppose they would do so now. And then Daddy lifted me onto his shoulders because there was a school of porpoise swimming just beyond the surf. They looked close enough to touch. I remember I reached out my hand, making Mummy laugh." Elizabeth's eyes had taken on a distance, which remained only a moment before they sharpened. "Your turn now, Cal."

"I suppose I had my first sense of myself as a person when I was about the same age as you were. Three or four." He knew he used her answer to evade the real question she had asked. "You don't know your age when you're that young, do you? Only when other people tell you on birthdays and afterwards. Only when you learn how to count the candles. And yes, everyone has a first memory. I like yours, by the way. Where was the beach?" He knew it was his turn to answer but was curious.

Her lips thinned. "The Welsh coast, I expect. My family lived near Shrewsbury, so it was the closest seaside. Barmouth was where we went in later years, so most likely it was there. We always took the train because that was part of the holiday."

"I like the rail bridge at Barmouth," Calum said.

"Yes, so do I." She tapped the end of her pen on the open page in front of her. "You're from Shrewsbury originally, aren't you?"

"I am. Which makes us neighbours, I suppose. My first memory wasn't as idyllic as yours. I got bitten by a dog. He was a new puppy, and we called him Max. He was a lab. We had him until he was fifteen years old, a good age for a lab. He died in his sleep in front of the living room fire. But this memory was from when he came home for the first time." He met Elizabeth's eyes. "Did you ever have a dog?"

"My family are cat people."

Calum nodded. "Most folks are one or the other. We always had dogs. I miss a dog even now, but you can't have one on base, not unless you're the Wingco." Calum closed his eyes, searching for another memory. One he didn't want to reveal because it carried too much sorrow. "But you don't want to know about my dog, do you?"

"I want to know everything about you, Cal." And then, as if she had revealed too much of herself, "It's my job to know everything. I have all the details, of course. I know you are twenty-three-years-old, but give the appearance of being older. War can do that to you, can't it? I know you joined up in thirty-nine at the age of eighteen. Then two years training before you were assigned to Lancasters as a bomb-aimer. And I know you possess a special kind of talent, which brought you to my attention. Tell me when you first became aware you were different."

Calum raised his eyes to meet hers, thinking that Dr Elizabeth Grierson was amazingly beautiful. He pushed ahead, and in a future that had not yet happened, he reached out and put his hand against her face. A tender touch. She jerked away sharply, and Calum allowed the unrequited future to spill away into non-existence.

"I suppose the first time was when I was thirteen, at a friend's house. They had a new dog too, and I wanted to see it."

"Because you like dogs." She gave a smile. Everything returned to stability in this world.

"Exactly. It was outside in the garden. Summertime. I remember playing with the puppy, a brown and white terrier. A scrapper. He was down on his front legs with his backside in the air. I was touching his paws, and he was biting at my fingers. Then he bit me for real, and I jerked my hand away, except he didn't bite me because my hand had already gone." Calum raised his eyes to find Elizabeth staring at him. A faint flush brought colour to her pale throat. "I turned it into a game. I teased the puppy, and each time he bit my finger, it was no longer there. I had seen... no, I had *felt* it bite me and moved before he could do it."

"You felt him bite you even though he didn't?" Another note in the journal, longer this time. "So you experienced pain even though there was none?"

Her insight impressed Calum. "Yes, I felt it. But as soon as I moved my fingers, as soon as the moment when he was going to bite me disappeared, there was no memory of the pain. It faded almost immediately."

"But it was there in the beginning? It prompted you to move, so it must have been."

"I expect so. But the moving wiped it from existence. It didn't happen, so there was no pain. All I kept was a faint memory of something, which quickly faded."

Elizabeth stared down at her notes for a long time. Calum waited. He tried to imagine what this must be like for her. He had lived with the strangeness for half his life. It was part of him. It felt over-intimate to be sharing the ability he possessed, how he felt about it, with this woman.

"Summer of…" She gazed into space for a moment "…thirty-four?"

"Yes, I suppose it was. When we didn't know what lay ahead."

"Oh, I expect some of us did. So this happened the year your brother George died?"

It was clear she knew everything about him, and Calum experienced a sense of unease. "Yes," was all he said.

"Before or after he drowned?"

Calum stared across the desk as he tried to work out whether or not to answer. And if he did answer, whether to tell her the truth. The question showed she had already made some connection, and Calum wished his explanation hadn't been a lie.

"After," he said. "A week after. It was another reason I went to the house because I was looking for a distraction from my thoughts."

She noted far more than his words in her journal before looking up. "When did you learn you could control your ability?" she asked, as if he could dismiss the enormity of his twin brother's death so easily.

"I didn't. I still can't. I have no idea what it is, how I do it, how it came about. Whether there are others like me." Calum met her eyes. "Are there others like me?"

She gave a shake of her head, blonde curls brushing her face. "Tell me what it feels like when you turn your ability on."

Calum laughed, seeing her eyes widen at his response.

"I don't turn it on or turn it off. It simply is. Nothing

more and nothing less. How does it feel? As if everything happens to me twice. Once in the future, then again in the present. My now is an echo of the future, and most of the time the echo and the reality are the same thing. Only when there is danger can I make them separate, can I push harder, further ahead. To protect myself, I suppose. To protect Guy and the crew when we're up there. So I suppose I must be able to control it to some extent, but if I can, I have no idea how I do it."

She wrote six lines, the nib of her pen scratching on the paper.

"But you must have honed your ability over the years."

"Perhaps. But it's like growing up, isn't it? You get better at life."

Elizabeth gave a small laugh. "Some people. I'm still waiting."

The confession, small as it was, endeared her to him even more. Calum wondered what it would be like to fall in love with Elizabeth Grierson before dismissing the thought. She was his boss. She was also way out of his league.

"Do you see it all the time?" she asked. "Both the future and the present?"

Calum stared through the window as he tried to come up with an answer. It wasn't as easy as yes or no.

"It's always there, this shimmer on the horizon, but I've learned to ignore it. I can't turn it off, but I can forget it's there. I expect it must be like someone with a vision problem. Don't scientists say what our eyes see is upside down, but our brain interprets it as the right way up?"

"There were experiments," said Elizabeth. "They put a series of lenses on people that turned everything upside down. Within a few days, their brains adjusted, and they saw everything the right way up again. Is that how it is for you, Calum?"

"I don't know. You're the doctor. Perhaps you can find out and let me know when you do."

"Are the future and the present equally real to you? Can you control this… this talent of yours? How far into the future can you push yourself?" There was a tension beneath her words, and Calum suspected they were getting close to the crux of the matter. Close to what she had been sent to find out.

Even so, they were good questions. Ones Calum would like to know the answers to himself. But they were also ones he needed a little more time to think about what those answers might be.

"Would it be all right if I went for a walk? I need to consider how to answer you. I don't mean to evade your questions, but I don't know the answers myself. Not yet."

"Take all the time you need. Go outside, but not too far away."

Calum rose, feeling a stiffness from sitting too long, both here and in the car. A headache was starting up behind his eyes. Walking to the door was strange as he analysed everything he did. He saw himself reach for the doorknob and turn it. He felt the cold metal against his palm, then felt it again ten seconds later when his hand, his actual hand, met it, turned it. By then, his future self was already outside, and he followed. The world shimmered in and out of focus, and he wondered which vision was the real one.

Calum took out a cigarette and lit it as he went through the door. He inhaled smoke deep into his lungs. Twice. Then and now. He smoked fast, the repetitive nature soothing him because then and now became one, only slightly out of step because he drew on the cigarette every ten seconds until it burned his fingers. He dropped it on the grass and stubbed it out beneath the sole of his shoe. In the distance, a small training plane banked before straightening out to come in to land. Calum recalled the training school, only part of the grass runway visible, the buildings out of sight from where he stood at the side of the house.

How do I do this? Can I control it, or does it control me?

"Yes, I can control it." Calum sat across from Elizabeth again. She had also smoked a cigarette, the smell of it in the air, the evidence a stubbed out filter in the plate on the desktop. She had finished her sandwich while Calum was outside.

"Explain it to me." Her face had grown flushed again. Calum wondered if she found him attractive or only wanted him to think she did. He knew he was overthinking things, the same way he always did. Elizabeth wasn't much older than him, but her confidence and knowledge were that of someone ten or twenty years her senior.

"Ask me the question again, I've forgotten what it was."

She consulted her notes. The question should have been the last thing she had written, but it took her a while to find it. Perhaps she had recorded her own thoughts while Calum was outside.

"Are the future and the present the same to you?"

"Not quite. It's like watching two movies on two screens side by side. Except they're not side by side. They're one behind the other, and the movies are running at different speeds. The same movie, but one happens before the other. Does that make any sense?"

Elizabeth nodded and wrote in her journal.

"I can look at one, but the other never really goes away. I can concentrate on the one, and the other becomes a shadow, but it's always there. When we are in the air, I see mostly what's going to happen to the bird in the future. It's how I can tell Guy to avoid the flak, how I can tell Bob and Vince there's an ME-110 coming in from above, and if they don't kill it, it's going to kill us." A sense of loss rose through him. Vince was dead, and Calum had abandoned the crew who had become his family. He only hoped the promise made to him would be kept and they would be safe.

"How far ahead can you see?" Elizabeth returned to the other question she had asked.

Calum heard a rap on the door and turned his head, only as he did so, realising the event had not yet happened. He watched a woman enter and speak. Then the rap sounded and Elizabeth also heard it and called out for whoever was there to come in.

"The others are here," said a woman Calum hadn't seen before. She was in her early thirties, buxom and pretty with freckled cheeks. She wore a print dress with a striped pinafore over it, her pale hair covered with a scarf.

He assumed she was the housekeeper. "I've put them in the dining room for now." She glanced at Calum, not attempting to hide her curiosity. "I took your flight suit to wash. Hope you don't mind, my dear."

Elizabeth rose to her feet and dismissed the woman with a nod. "Thank you, Dottie. Come and meet your compatriots, Cal. You might find this interesting."

CHAPTER SIX

Two people stood in the long dining room with their backs to the door. They turned as Calum and Elizabeth entered. One was a broad-shouldered, sandy-haired man in his mid-thirties, the second a slim woman at least ten years younger, with dark hair cut long. Elizabeth went to the woman first and shook her hand before turning to the man.

"Welcome to Carden House, both of you. It's a pleasure to have you accept my invitation."

"They gave me the impression we had little choice in the matter," said the man. His accent was coloured with the sound of the south-west. Bristol, Calum thought.

"Everyone here volunteered," said Elizabeth. "You are all free to leave at any time you wish. That should have been made clear to you. I apologise if such was not the case."

"Are you in charge?" The woman's voice carried a hint of sharpness.

Calum stood to one side, studying her. She wore a blue dress that fell to the knee, narrow at the waist, flaring over her hips. She was pretty, with a narrow nose and generous mouth that showed a tightness that hinted at unease Calum could understand. The entire situation was new to them all. She tilted her head to one side as she waited for Elizabeth to provide an answer.

"For the moment, I suppose I am." She waved a hand. "What am I thinking? Let me introduce you all." She looked around. "We are waiting for one other to join us, but perhaps he has been delayed." She glanced at Calum, who stood watching the interplay.

Some spark of mischief brought a smile to his lips, and before Elizabeth could offer the introductions, he stepped forward with his hand out.

"Hola, Maria, mucho gusto."

Her slim hand was warm within his, and she flashed a smile that made her beautiful. "Hables español?"

Calum laughed. "Sorry, no. I've just used up my entire stock of words. I'm Calum Auger, by the way, before Elizabeth tells you my name." He glanced across to see her standing to one side with a frown on her face.

Maria's smile remained. "No problem, I believe my English is fairly good." She gave a sweet laugh. Her English was perfect. Her accent sounded as if she had been brought up in the Home Counties. The western side of Surrey, Calum thought.

He released her hand and turned to the man. "I'm sorry, but I've used up my store of party tricks. You are?"

"Harry Parker. Good to meet you, Cal. Do you have

any idea why we're all here? Nobody's told us anything. Practically snatched off the streets, we were. Ain't that right, Maria?"

She made no response, deliberately not acknowledging Harry's question. Despite the moment of tension, Calum decided he liked them both. Maria might be sweet when she got over her unease. Harry appeared solid and dependable, a man you wanted at your side if there was going to be trouble – also with a hint he might be the one to start it.

Calum turned to Elizabeth. "Yes, I'd rather like an answer to Harry's question as well." He tilted his head to one side.

"As soon as the last man arrives, I will explain everything, but I'd rather not have to go over it more than once. There's a lot you may need to take in. Hopefully, Richard will arrive before dinner, and I can tell you everything then."

A cough sounded from a corner of the room, and everyone turned. A man rose from an armchair. As Calum watched him, he wanted to turn away. Wanted to ignore the figure, though he couldn't say why. The man was around forty years of age, handsome, with a strong face and muscular body. He wore a tailored pin-stripe suit in dark charcoal. A white shirt and plain tie. Highly polished black shoes completed the outfit. His dark hair was full and recently cut, the faint sheen of some oil setting it off perfectly. There was nothing at all wrong with him, except he seemed to keep fading into the background.

Elizabeth Grierson came past Calum and shook the

man's hand. "Welcome to Carden House, Mr Williams. I believe you have all been introduced to each other now." For a moment, she looked at a loss for what to do next, then gave a small laugh. "It might be an idea if you attempted to ensure people know when you are present, Richard."

"Of course." The man took a pack of cigarettes from an inside pocket and held it up. "All right if I smoke?"

"Of course, go ahead."

He shook an unfiltered cigarette out, replaced the pack and brought out a gold lighter and tapped the tobacco down on the side of it. By the time he had lit the cigarette and returned the lighter, everyone had lost interest in him. Apart from Calum, who was trying not to do so. The man looked around, gave a shrug and returned to his seat. As he sat, Calum felt an urge to turn away and did so almost without thinking. He found Elizabeth's eyes on him, perhaps searching for his reaction.

"It would be a good idea if you all got to know each other a little better. I have things I need to do in any case. We can carry on with your evaluation tomorrow, Cal, if that's all right with you?"

He offered a nod of agreement, and she gave a wave of her hand before striding from the room.

"She's a looker, isn't she?" said Harry. "How long have you been here, Cal?"

"I arrived less than two hours ago. And I'm exhausted. I spent last night flying over Germany."

Maria touched his wrist. "You do look a little tired. Don't think you have to stay if you'd rather rest. We can get to know each other over dinner. We were told it was at seven, and there was no need for formality."

"What is it you do?" Harry asked. "Are you a pilot? You look like you could be."

"I drop bombs from a Lanc. No – I used to drop bombs. Now… now I don't know what I'm supposed to do."

"The same as the rest of us then, mate. But that's not what I meant. What is it you can do? Maria and Dicky told me what they could–"

"Richard, please," said a voice from the corner. "Call me Dicky one more time and I may have to ask you to come outside, Harold."

"Don't mean nothing by it, old chap," said Harry. "It's just my way."

"Then learn to control your way."

Maria gave the impression she had heard this conversation before and was becoming tired of it.

"I would be interested to hear what you can do as well," she said. "We talked about it on the train from London, though Harry claims he has no particular talent."

"So you know about each other?" Calum asked.

"Me and Maria do," said Harry, then laughed. "What Dicky – sorry, Richard – over there does is pretty obvious. We were past Oxford before either of us even realised we had a third bod in our compartment." He gave a smile. "First class, too. Never ridden that way before. I fix things, and Maria is a genius with words."

Calum frowned. "Fix things?"

"Engines. Electrics. Anything broken or about to

break. I have a friendship with machinery." Harry shrugged. "Always have had, guess I always will. I thought nothing of it until I was approached a few weeks back. I assumed everyone could do what I did, but it seems not. So, Cal, what about you? What can you fix?"

"The future."

Calum watched their faces, not sure what he was searching for, but both of them seemed to accept what he said, even though he knew it wasn't an answer.

"I can see into the future," he added.

Harry gave a long whistle. "So when's this bloody war going to end, Cal? Who's going to win the election when it does? Winnie, I expect. Be worth getting a bet on if you give me the gen."

"Sorry to disappoint, but I can only see a minute into the future."

"Damn, not much use for the gee-gees then. Is it any use at all?"

"I told you what I did. I was a bomb-aimer in a Lancaster. A minute's a long time when your ordnance only takes thirty seconds to reach the ground. It gave me enough time to adjust for maximum damage. Then there's the flak and the fighters."

"Well, bugger me," said Harry. He glanced at Maria. "Pardon my French, but it makes me and you look ordinary, don't it?"

Maria offered him a tight smile before turning to Calum.

"Harry's right – what we do is a bit clever, even the spook over there doesn't do anything spooky, but you…"

She broke off to look around the room. "Are you still here, Richard?"

"Yes, still here, my dear. Carry on, I'm taking everything in."

Calum looked around until he found Richard Williams sitting upright in the easy chair, one leg crossed over the other. The creases in his suit trousers were perfect. As soon as Calum looked away, he forgot he was there.

"There's more to it than you say," Calum said. "You tell me you can fix anything, Harry, right?"

Harry gave a nod.

"And you, Maria, how many languages do you speak?"

She waved a hand in the air. "I don't keep count. Dozens, most likely."

"Do you retain them all?"

"That depends how much I use them. English, clearly. Spanish, which is my native tongue. I was born in Malaga. French, German and Russian, all useful at the moment. Some more obscure ones would take me a day or two to recover."

"And how long does it take you to learn a new one?"

"If I'm in the country a week at most. If I have to use books, perhaps two or three times as long."

"And that's not spooky?"

She offered a smile. "Not spooky like seeing into the future, no."

"I still want to know why us, why here," said Harry.

"We all want to know that," Calum said.

"Except you have a head start on us, old man. You've already had a session with the pretty young filly. Did she give you the third degree, or did she give you something else?" Harry waggled his eyebrows in a poor imitation of Groucho Marx, complete with an invisible cigar.

"Questions, that was all." Calum took a breath, let it go. "If you don't mind, I'm going to get a bit of shut-eye. My crate landed at six this morning, and I managed only a couple of rather uncomfortable hours in the back of a car. I'm going to get my head down until dinner."

"Want me to give you a knock if you're still asleep when the gong sounds?" asked Harry. "Which room are you in?"

"Second floor…" Calum turned, orienting himself. "West-facing, so pretty much above where we are now."

"Same as the rest of us, then. How many doors from the bathroom are you?"

Calum tried to remember but couldn't. "A few."

"I'll have to knock on all the doors, then. I'm three down from the bathroom. Maria here's next to me and Dicky there's… well, I don't exactly know where he is because you never see him coming or going, do you?"

"End of the hallway," said the voice from the armchair. Richard sounded as if he had given up on Harry doing as asked.

Calum glanced at Maria and offered a nod. She had been quiet during Harry's interrogation, and he wondered what she was thinking. Her eyes were on him, and he saw a cool appraisal that made him uncomfortable. Harry was a chancer. Richard was nothing at all. Maria looked like she might be trouble.

He wondered if she had a boyfriend back in Surrey, or more likely she lived in London now. Or perhaps she worked at one of those hush-hush operations set up throughout the country. Just as this one had been set up here. No doubt he would find out over the next hours and days and… how long, he wondered? Months? Years? A lifetime? Were they brought together to help the war effort and be disbanded when it ended, or was there more to Elizabeth Grierson's plans?

CHAPTER SEVEN

Calum came awake slowly to find a hand on his shoulder. He smelled perfume, became aware of slim fingers on him. He rolled onto his back and stared up at Maria Carmen. His head was fuzzy, and he knew he could have done with a few more hours of sleep. He saw Maria's hand reach out again and rolled off the bed before she could touch him.

"You need to brush your hair before coming down. A shave might be a good idea, too." She offered a smile, a promise of something that confirmed his earlier thought she might be trouble. But was it the kind of trouble he might welcome?

Calum ran a hand across his cheek. "How long until dinner?"

"The gong hasn't sounded yet." Maria turned away. "Have you heard it, Richard?"

Calum hadn't noticed the man. Now he saw him standing at the window. Richard shook his head without turning.

"Where's Harry?"

Maria laughed. "He's outside tinkering with the Major's car. He says it's a fine motor, but he heard something he could make better. I heard nothing, but Harry says he's never wrong about these things."

"Major Simpson's back?" Calum smoothed his hair with his fingers and looked around for his shoes, glad he had done nothing more than slip them off and lie fully clothed on the bed.

"It was the Major who brought us from the station. I don't know what he's been doing since. Talking with that woman, I expect."

The way Maria said 'that woman' made Calum wonder if there was a touch of jealousy. He sat on the bed to tie his shoes, glanced at his watch and frowned. The hands showed 2:17.

"What time is it?" He wound the watch, a little annoyed he had forgotten to do so. It was a pilot's watch, one of the thousands the government had commissioned from Swiss manufacturers. Longines had crafted Calum's, but he knew there had been a dozen other makers involved.

"Five before seven," said Maria. "The doctor said dinner at seven sharp, so you'd better have a quick splash and come downstairs. We'll go ahead if that's all right with you?"

"Please."

Calum took extra care to ensure Richard Williams left the room. Once alone, he used the small sink in the corner to wash his face and wet his hair before combing it. He lathered his cheeks and shaved quickly, then rinsed.

He hunted for his tie but couldn't find it. He left his shirt collar open and pulled on his jacket. By the time he reached the top of the stairs, the gong in the hallway was sounding. Calum saw Major Simpson doing the honours.

"I thought you had returned to London," Calum said as he approached.

"Sorry, old chap, I'm Elizabeth's liaison, so you're stuck with me for the time being."

"Liaison for who?"

"Ah, now that's a question I can't answer."

Calum shrugged as if it was no matter. That was the trouble with fighting a war. Everyone wanted their secrets kept close. Sometimes even when they had no secrets.

The housekeeper Dottie appeared in a checked apron, a tray of drinks grasped in both hands. Calum and Major Simpson allowed her to enter first before following into the dining room. The others were already present, standing at the head of the long table. Elizabeth had changed into a light red dress that accentuated her slimness. Her freshly washed hair was caught in a tortoise-shell clip on one side.

Dottie held the tray out to each of them in turn – some pale liquid in small glasses. When Calum took his and sniffed, he believed it to be some kind of sherry, though he couldn't be altogether sure. He kept hold of the glass out of politeness, intending to set it down as soon as he could. The others were chatting without purpose, probing each other's stories of the war, where they were from, had they siblings, were their parents still alive? All except Richard Williams, who stood off to one side, ignored.

Calum thought he was learning to see the man more easily. He wondered if that was him or Richard allowing himself to be seen. Was it even something the man could control, like Calum's own ability?

A drift of scent made him to turn to find Elizabeth beside him. Her skin was freshly scrubbed and shone with health. She had applied red lipstick, and a little rouge to her cheeks.

"Are there any more like us due?" Calum asked, with a nod towards the others.

"Not tonight."

He met her eyes. "But you're looking, aren't you?"

"I am aware of a few others at the moment I would like to recruit, yes. One man in particular by the name of William Harrison, but he's a bit of an awkward customer."

"Another one like us?"

"Like you? There's nobody else like you, Calum. Nobody else like Maria or Harry or Richard."

"How can you be so sure? We're not freaks. All we have is the ability to do something that's of little use unless we're in specific circumstances. Is that why you brought us here?"

"You'll find out why you're here soon enough."

Calum kept his gaze on her. "Tonight?"

"I have been authorised to tell you everything I know." She offered a brief smile. "Which doesn't mean everything, of course. But whatever I can, I will reveal."

"What if we don't like what we hear?"

"I hope you will wait and see what I have to say before pre-judging anything."

Before Calum could reply, the housekeeper returned

with a trolley holding food. She had already laid plates on the crisp tablecloth and opened bottles of wine. Glasses waited, ready to accept whatever the bottles contained. Better than the sherry, Calum hoped, putting his untouched glass on a side table. He waited as Elizabeth moved away to usher everyone to their seats as if the places were pre-assigned. Then only Calum remained. He strolled to the last vacant chair.

In the centre of the table sat a side of beef, slices already carved. The smell of it conjured up memories for them all, who had not seen such a mythical joint since the start of the war. Calum took a small bite of the meat and closed his eyes in momentary bliss.

"Local Hereford," said Major Simpson, who sat at the end of the table to Calum's left. "The farm has a small herd, and we stock our kitchen pretty well."

Elizabeth sat at the opposite end of the table, with the remaining four arrayed two to a side. For several minutes nobody spoke, too intent on enjoying the food. Each of them knew it wouldn't last, and eventually it was Major Simpson who broke the spell by picking up his glass and tapping it with his knife.

"Ladies and gentlemen, I know you are all wondering exactly why you are here, so I have asked Dr Grierson to explain everything to you. I would ask that you hear her out before raising questions. It will save us all time. And in this endeavour, like many others in the war, time may be in short supply." He looked along the length of the table. "Elizabeth?"

"Please continue eating as we talk," she said. "And I would prefer it if you would all follow Major Simson's example and call me Elizabeth, not Dr Grierson. We are not all members of the military here, are we, Major?" When he met the question with a brief shake of the head, she said, "In that case, perhaps you can call Major Simpson by his first name as well. Is that all right with you, John?"

His expression showed it might not be, but he said, "Looks like the cat's out of the bag now, so go ahead."

"Good. Now, help yourselves to wine and more of this delicious food while I try to explain why you are all here." She looked around at them, ensuring each met her sharp gaze before continuing.

"Very well. I think it is no secret," she gave a brief smile, "that each of you has a talent that cannot be explained using normal, rational science. Agreed?"

"Apart from me," said Harry Parker. "I fix things, there's nothing spooky about that."

"Perhaps you do. We shall see." Elizabeth turned to Maria. "You, my dear, can learn a new language inside a week, is that right?"

Maria smiled and leaned closer to show her willingness to hear something about why they were here. Anything at all.

Elizabeth switched her attention across the table. "And Calum here can see a little way into the future. You could explain Maria's ability through rational science and impressive intelligence. I don't believe Calum's can. Agreed?" Her eyes scanned them.

Harry offered a nod of acknowledgement. The others seemed to prefer to wait until they heard more.

Calum glanced at his watch and discovered its lack of

winding hadn't been the problem. He shook his wrist, raised the chronometer to his ear. Nothing.

"Are you all right?" asked Elizabeth.

"I think my watch is broken. It was working fine this morning. Not working now." He slipped the band over his wrist and placed the watch on the table. "Had it since I joined up. Don't suppose I'll get another one now I'm not flying. Not to worry, carry on. Not your problem."

"But it is yours," said Elizabeth. "Harry, would you look at it for Cal?"

"Sure thing, old girl." He reached across the table but didn't yet touch the watch. He glanced at Calum. "All right with you, mate?"

Calum offered a nod, and Harry took the watch, turning it through his fingers. "Nice watch."

"Please, carry on," Calum said.

"Very well. Where was I? Oh yes, Calum's special ability. Do any of you believe what he can do is not something special?"

"How do we know he can do anything?" Richard Williams spoke, drawing attention to himself, an attention that faded almost as soon as he stopped speaking. The Major's request to save questions for later was already forgotten.

"Can you explain why nobody can see you, Richard?"

"I'm just an ordinary sort of bloke, I suppose. There's nothing much to remember about me."

"Except it's more than that, isn't it? Like when you walked into that bank in Pall Mall and helped yourself to a hundred pounds."

Richard said nothing as he faded again. It was as if the

surrounding air folded in on itself, taking him with it. Even staring directly at him, Calum found it difficult to keep him in sight.

"Did you really do that, Dicky?" Harry asked. He had stopped fiddling with Calum's watch without opening the back. Now he placed it between his palms and held it there. "By God, but that's a handy talent to have." Harry opened his palms and glanced at the watch before holding it out to Calum. "There you go, my old mucker, good as new."

Calum took the watch and looked at it. The second hand swept smoothly, and he heard a soft ticking when he held it to his ear. The time was also right, except he hadn't seen Harry touch the crown to set it. He looked up at Harry, who was watching where Richard was with a frown. When Calum looked along the table at Elizabeth, she gave a small nod and a smile, as if in confirmation of something. Exactly what was lost on him.

Elizabeth's eyes remained on his, making Calum uncomfortable. He looked away, deliberately concentrating on where he knew Richard sat, waited until he could make him out. Richard returned the stare, curiosity on his face.

"I don't wish to pre-empt what you will be shown and told tomorrow, but I do want you all to understand each of you has a unique talent. You are all different to most people."

"I can think of a way Calum can prove himself," Richard said.

"Tell us." Elizabeth steepled her hands and rested her chin on them. It was a coquettish gesture, and Calum wondered who she intended it for. Not Richard, he was sure. Harry? Equally unlikely. Almost certainly Major Simpson.

"Do we have a pack of cards?" asked Richard.

"Do we, John? There must be some in a place like this." Elizabeth gave a brief smile. "It strikes me as a house that has a games room."

"It does," said Major Simpson. "But I think we should leave all such nonsense until you have completed your explanation as to why we are all here. And after we have finished this excellent meal."

"I think it's pretty clear why we're here," said Harry.

Amusement showed on Elizabeth's face. "And why is that?"

"We're spooks," he said. "All of you, apart from me, has some weird ability or other. Someone, somewhere, thinks they can use us. Thinks we can make a difference, even if the war is almost over."

Elizabeth looked around at them all before her gaze returned to Harry.

"Something like that," she said. "Now, as John says, we don't want our food going cold, do we? Is that acceptable to you all? Calum can prove himself to everyone when we have finished." She didn't wait for any of them to offer agreement.

A moment after Calum started to eat again, he realised she hadn't told them anything at all. He wondered if the omission had been deliberate.

CHAPTER EIGHT

"Why am I the only one who has to prove himself?" Calum asked as he shook a cigarette from a pack of Players and tapped the tobacco down before lighting it. Dottie had cleared the table, and now brandy sat in mismatched glasses.

"Because your talent is easier to demonstrate," said Elizabeth. "Besides, you have already witnessed an example of what Harry can do. Everyone saw how he fixed your watch."

"I did nothing," said Harry. "Cal must've forgotten to wind it, that's all."

Elizabeth offered a smile. "If you say so." She glanced around the table at the others. "I think it's fairly obvious what talent Richard has. Quite handy when a man is short of a hundred pounds, I'm sure we all agree." Another fleeting smile crossed her lips. "As for Maria, her talent might be a little more difficult to demonstrate. Unless we drive into Wales and see how long it takes before she speaks the language fluently."

"I already can," said Maria. "I spent a fortnight there with a boyfriend the year before the war."

Harry laughed. "Good grief, girl, what were you, fifteen years old? A bit young to start on the boyfriends, don't you think?"

"I was seventeen," said Maria. "And he wasn't my first boyfriend."

"Had a lot of them, have you?" asked Harry.

"Wouldn't you like to know, old man?"

"Now, now, children," said Elizabeth. "If I can bring us all back to the present. We should adjourn to the games room so Calum can show us his ability." She rose to her feet. Tall, slim and elegant. "Lead the way, John. You appear to know where it is."

Calum remained in his seat as the others rose. He smoked his cigarette, trying to decide whether to cooperate. He felt as if Elizabeth had cornered him into doing something he didn't want to.

When he looked up, she stood beside his chair. She reached out a hand and rested it on his shoulder. Calum took a last pull on his cigarette before stubbing it out in the ashtray.

"I need to get everyone on side, Cal," she said. "They're not convinced about the reason I have brought them here. Not yet. And despite what Harry says, I saw the look on your face when he handed your watch back to you. That's Harry's gift. All of you have something, but not all of you have accepted what it is yet. I need everyone on side if this is going to work."

"If what is going to work?" asked Calum. He remained where he was, Elizabeth's hand still on his shoulder. He liked the way it felt. "It might help if someone explained what the hell is going on here. Why have you pulled us all together? Or are there more to come?"

"Nobody else, not at the moment, but that could change at any time."

"You mentioned a man to me earlier. What can he do? I assume it's another… something." He wasn't sure what to call their abilities. What was it Elizabeth referred to it as – talent?

"He can read conversations locked in walls."

It surprised Calum she answered. He hadn't expected her to.

As he rose to his feet, Elizabeth's hand slipped from his shoulder.

"What's that supposed to mean?" he asked.

"It's difficult to explain. Let me think about it for a while, and I'll let you know once I can. I'm not trying to be secretive. One thing we are going to have to do among ourselves is to forget all about secrets."

"Does that include you and the Major?"

"All of us," said Elizabeth. "Now come on, before they get restless and start talking about us."

"Too late for that, I expect."

When they entered the games room, Harry was playing darts with Richard, while Maria stood talking to John Simpson, who held a fresh pack of cards in his hand. Elizabeth clapped once to draw their attention.

"All right, I know some of you have reservations, but Calum has agreed to demonstrate his talent for you. Perhaps when he has done so, it will allow you to consider what each of you can contribute to our small group. We don't have a great deal of time to prove our worth, so the sooner we can pull together, the better for us and the country." Elizabeth put her hand on Calum's wrist and drew him to an armchair. "Sit here. John, take this seat. The rest of us can perch wherever we can; I don't suppose this will take long."

"Any chance of getting another drink?" asked Harry.

"When we finish, perhaps."

John Simpson sat on a straight-backed chair opposite Calum, a low coffee table set between them. Simpson opened the card pack and shuffled using only one hand, a grin on his face.

Elizabeth perched on the arm of Calum's chair. "I want you to read what card John is about to place on the table, Cal. Can you do that?"

"I expect so." He looked around and met the eyes of the others, even Richard, who, for once, appeared to be fully present. Maria's eyes showed a brightness, and a flush coloured her cheeks.

"Ten of clubs," Calum said a few moments before Major Simpson placed the first card face up on the table.

Maria clapped her hands together, bouncing on her toes.

"You must've seen the card before he turned it over," said Harry. He looked around and pointed. "In that mirror over there, I expect."

"Take it down if you would, Harry," said Elizabeth.

Calum waited while Harry set the mirror on the floor and turned it to face the wall.

"Ace of spades... deuce of hearts... five of diamonds..."

"Lucky bugger," said Harry. His voice was less sure than it had been.

"John, I want you to take your time," said Elizabeth. "Count to ten before turning each card over." She squeezed Calum's arm. "Push yourself, Cal. Push yourself further."

Simpson's lips moved as he counted silently.

"Eight of spades," Calum said, casting himself into the future, concentrating on the double image that was then and now. As he did so, the present faded into the background, as it always did.

By the time Simpson had turned half the pack over, a headache had started behind Calum's right eye.

"Stop," said Elizabeth before Simpson finished the pack. "Pick the cards up, John. Reshuffle them, but this time I want you to turn the cards over as fast as you can, one on top of the other. But only start when I tell you."

John Simpson nodded and gathered the cards together, shuffled them one-handed again.

Elizabeth's fingers circled Calum's wrist. "Can you do this?"

"I'll try."

"You've gone a little pale."

"I can do it." Calum was aware of the shortness of his answer. "Sorry, yes, let's show them."

"I'm going to count to twenty, and then John will start to put the cards down. Begin when you're ready, Cal."

He closed his eyes and took a breath. When he let it go, he pushed himself hard. He heard Elizabeth counting, and when she reached twelve, he spoke.

"Six of spades, ten of diamonds, jack of clubs, ace of

spades, three of hearts, queen of hearts..." The words spilled out as fast as he could say them, the cards slapping down twenty seconds in the future. By the time the others saw the first card turned over, Calum had already reeled off half the pack.

"Holy shit..." Harry's voice was barely a whisper.

"Stop," said Elizabeth, her voice sharp.

But Calum was near the end of the pack by then and finished reading them off until finished. When he looked at John Simpson, he saw the man still held a dozen or more cards. Calum raised a hand and rubbed his nose, discovered blood on his fingers when he took them away.

"Turn the rest over if you would, John," said Elizabeth.

Simpson did as asked, revealing the cards more slowly. Half a minute passed before he turned the last one over, and Calum frowned, unsure exactly what had just happened.

"Are you all right, Cal?" Elizabeth's fingers touched the back of his neck. The throbbing in his head caused the light in the room to pulse in and out of focus.

"Need to sleep," he said.

Elizabeth stood, smoothed her dress and patted her hair. She looked around at the array of faces, each reflecting their confusion.

"We'll talk more about this in the morning," she said. "Go to your rooms and think about what Calum has just shown us. I also want you to each consider your talents and how they might best serve the war effort."

Harry turned and left without a word, his shoulders bunched. Maria came towards Calum as he rose to his feet, dizzy for a moment until John Simpson grabbed his arm.

"Careful, old man. Can you make it to your room all right?"

"I think so," Calum said.

Elizabeth handed him a handkerchief, and he used it to dab at his nose. When he looked around, only the three of them remained. The pack of cards lay scattered across the coffee table, some on the floor.

Elizabeth slipped her arm through his. "Come on, I'll see you upstairs. Just in case you have a relapse. I want to talk to you in private anyway."

Calum allowed her to lead him up the curving staircase and along the hallway. Ahead, a door opened, and Maria trotted towards them before darting into the bathroom.

"I think she likes you," said Elizabeth, squeezing Calum's arm.

"I doubt it." His headache was spreading, and he knew sleep was going to be hard to find despite the hours he had spent awake.

"Why not? You're a good-looking man, and you have a presence about you women like. Take it from a woman who knows about such things."

Calum laughed, then stopped when his head hurt more.

"What's this secret you want to tell me? Assuming it's not that Maria might like me, that is."

"That's no secret." Elizabeth opened the door to his room and guided him inside.

Calum crossed to the bed and sat down hard. When he

looked up, Elizabeth was closing the door. She walked to the sink, ran the cold tap and wetted the flannel that hung on a hook on one side and came across to him. She wiped his face and neck, then handed the flannel to him and sat on the end of the bed.

"I thank you for what you did tonight, Cal," said Elizabeth. "It will help when Sir Edward returns tomorrow. He's bringing something with him to show you all what other talents there are throughout the world. Your demonstration will make what everyone is going to see be accepted in a better light."

"Is Sir Edward your boss?" Calum asked. He hadn't been impressed by the man, but he had too little experience of titled gentry. Perhaps they all gave the same air of nonchalance – as if nothing mattered. Not even the war.

"That's a good question."

"Another one you can't, or won't, answer?"

"We can talk about it tomorrow after I've had a little time to work out exactly what Sir Edward is to me and this unit." She rose to her feet and handed the damp flannel to Calum. "Now, get some sleep. You'll all find out more tomorrow, and then the real work starts."

CHAPTER NINE

Harry was already in the dining room when Calum entered.

"Do you think we're going to find anything out today or not? I tell you, I'm wondering what the hell we've let ourselves in for here. It's all a bit fanciful for a simple bloke like me."

"Let's see what the toff says when he gets here." Calum stood at the sideboard where Dottie had provided them once again with a marvellous array of food. "Did you meet Sir Edward Carlton, Harry?"

"Never even seen the cove, nor heard of him. What's he like?"

"Posh," Calum said, as if that's all that was needed. "You'll have met his like before, no doubt."

Calum chose sausage and eggs and took his plate to the table. "Thanks for fixing my watch, by the way." He offered Harry a knowing smile.

"Winding it you mean, don't you?"

"More than likely that's what I meant."

"That trick you did was bloody clever, mind. How did you manage it? Was the Major in on the secret? It's well past time for us to be told the reason we're all here if you ask me."

"I didn't intend to ask you, Harry, but thanks for your opinion all the same," Elizabeth said as she entered the room. Calum suspected she had been standing outside the door, eavesdropping on them. "Maybe Sir Edward will tell us the reason when he gets here. I'm sure you'll all find out why you have been invited here soon." She carried a small sheaf of papers in her hand, which she set on the table before going to see what was to eat. "Sir Edward is due to arrive around ten, so we'd better all get some breakfast before it's time for lunch."

Harry glanced at her. "It's you and Cal who are the stay-in-beds. Maria and Richard were down earlier. I'd be finished as well if I hadn't been admiring the Major's Rover. I'm sure I can double the horsepower with a bit of tinkering."

"I'm not sure I'd welcome John driving an improved car. He seems to go more than fast enough in it already." Elizabeth stood at the sideboard, deciding what to add to her plate.

"It's me we're talking about," said Harry, "so it'll be safe enough. When Dottie brought the food in, she told us about a dance in town this Saturday. What about you, Lizzie, are you going to come?"

"How do you know I'm going to let any of you go?"

"Because it'll be good for morale," said Harry.

"Let's see what Sir Edward wants with us first. We might not even be here come Saturday." Elizabeth pushed one of the sheets of paper she had brought towards Harry, another at Calum. "You need to read these and sign them before Sir Edward arrives."

Harry turned the page around and scanned it. "I've signed this before." He slid the sheet back to Elizabeth, but she simply returned it.

"Not this version. Read it, Harry, then sign it or not. But if you refuse, you'll need to leave here today, and you cannot tell a soul about anything you might have learned."

"That wouldn't be difficult, would it? None of us has any idea why we're here. Isn't that right, Cal?"

Calum said nothing. He scanned the document, took Elizabeth's fountain pen from the middle of the table and signed his sheet. Harry might claim to know nothing, but Calum wasn't sure he didn't know more than he wanted to.

Sir Edward Carlton was whisked straight into Elizabeth's office while his driver, an army Corporal, carried in a white screen, a film projector, and finally a metal box into the games room and set them on the floor. Then the man left without saying a word. It was apparent he was not allowed to see what the rest of them were going to be shown.

"Have you ever worked one of these things?" Calum asked Harry.

"Never even see one. They always keep them in that little room above the rest of us when I visit the flicks." Harry examined the seemingly complex projector and grinned. "It's a machine though, so I expect I can work it out. Unless that toff is going to set it up."

"Toffs don't do any actual work, do they," said Maria. She and Richard were already in the games room when Calum and Harry entered.

Harry opened the metal box and took out a circular film can. He showed it to Calum. "Look, they're even labelled with numbers. Should I put them on in random order? Do you think he'd even notice?"

"Best not, just in case. I get the impression he'd not take well to being messed around with."

Calum watched as Harry took a moment to study the projector, then he threaded the film as if he had done it a hundred times before. Calum left him to it and set the screen up. It wobbled on its tripod, and he adjusted it until satisfied it wasn't going to collapse. Then he went and drew the heavy curtains across both windows. He had just finished when Elizabeth led Sir Edward Carlton into the room. His expression was sour, but Calum couldn't recall when it had been anything else. He wondered if Elizabeth had been briefing him on the scepticism of the day before. She had told Calum the man knew the purpose of their group, but did he involve himself in the day-to-day management? Sir Edward didn't give the impression he would be bothered with them. Which suited Calum just fine. He expected it suited Elizabeth just fine, too.

She crossed the room and stood in front of the screen. "Sir Edward has agreed to provide background information on why our group has been brought together." She made sure to look at each of them. "Do you know how to work that thing, Harry? If we're all ready, then let's start."

Elizabeth went to the light switch and turned it off, leaving only a standard lamp to provide some illumination. The projector started to clatter. There was no other sound, no roaring lion, just a flickering black-and-white image of a sparely furnished room with two men in white coats. They looked like scientists of some sort. After a moment, a third figure entered, a woman wearing a shapeless dress, her hair hanging lank almost to her waist. Dark shadows sat beneath her eyes, but the eyes themselves were bright. Perhaps too bright.

The woman sat at a table and placed her hands on the smooth surface. At the far end sat a single object. A small vase, devoid of any decoration. A brief conversation took place, but still no sound. Then the woman stared hard at the vase.

"Well, she's not Mae West, is she?" said Harry, who had taken a seat next to the projector.

"Shh," hissed Elizabeth.

When Calum looked back at the screen, the vase on the table wobbled. There was nobody near it. The image showed nothing that might have caused it, and the woman had not moved her hands. Then the vase shifted again, sliding a few inches to one side. As Calum wondered what the trick was, the vase rose into the air by a quarter inch. It drifted to the left, the right, then climbed further. Suddenly it moved fast, flying to one side to smash into the plain wall.

Calum looked back at the woman on the film, who remained passive as if nothing had happened. The tail of the film clattered through the projector and flapped loosely. Harry turned it off, and Elizabeth brought up the lights.

"What did we just see?" asked Maria. "Was that real or some kind of trick?"

"Got to be a trick," said Harry, who was loading the second film.

"If you would be good enough to explain what we have seen, Sir Edward?" said Elizabeth.

Sir Edward Carlton went to stand in front of the white screen.

"The segment I have shown you – and there is more to follow shortly – was smuggled out of the Soviet Union six months ago at the expense of the lives of two of our agents." He glanced at Maria. "And what you saw was no trick."

"I saw King Kong at the Odeon last week," said Harry. "Are you telling me that wasn't a trick either?"

"I am sure all of us here know that what we see on a screen can be manipulated to fool our senses. What you saw here is real." Carlton looked at each of them. "Dr Grierson has not yet told you the real purpose of you being brought together because I asked her not to. I wanted to do that myself and in person."

"About time somebody told us," said Harry.

"Let me assure you that my purpose in coming here is to answer all your questions and explain why you are here."

"So that was real?" Calum asked. "The woman actually smashed the vase?"

"As far as we can discern, yes, she did."

"When? Where?"

"The when is less clear, but we estimate no more than a year ago, and no less than nine months. The where is sixty miles south of Moscow. And the ability she demonstrated is called telekinesis."

"Tele-what?" asked Harry.

"The woman can move objects through the power of her mind alone."

Harry made a dismissive sound, shook a cigarette out of his pack and lit up. For a moment, he disappeared in a cloud of smoke. When it cleared, his usual expression of scepticism had faded, replaced by something closer to worry.

"I understand one of you performed a demonstration of something similar only last night," said Carlton. His gaze settled on Calum. "I'm sorry I missed out on that. It must have been fascinating." Something hungry in his attention made Calum uneasy, and for a moment he wondered whether the man might not prefer members of his own sex.

"Nobody smashed anything," said Elizabeth, "but yes, Cal showed his talent to the others."

"Spooky," said Harry, "that's what he is."

Carlton moved his attention to Harry. "And I hear you repaired Calum's watch without the need of opening it. You did so simply by holding it between your palms." He turned to Richard. "You can perform feats nobody can explain, and you, my dear," to Maria, "have an ability with language most would regard as verging on the supernatural."

Maria gave a tiny shrug but said nothing.

Carlton met each of their eyes again. "If nobody has anything constructive to add, I propose we continue. You need to see several other abilities, and then I must get back to London to report. Dr Grierson is authorised to tell you everything she knows and what your purpose here is. She will discuss all of this with you once I have left."

"Tail wagging the dog if you ask me," said Harry. "Why can't you tell us yourself?"

"Because Dr Grierson is the expert." Carlton moved away from the screen, and Harry started the projector, which now contained a fresh film roll. Calum glanced at the table beside the projector where five other metal cases sat, waiting to reveal their contents.

CHAPTER TEN

It was early afternoon before Dottie entered the games room with a plate stacked high with sandwiches. Carlton and his corporal were about to depart back to London with their equipment and secrets. Elizabeth had escorted them out to their car but not yet returned. Calum wondered if some explanation would be forthcoming about what they were shown, or only more of the same obfuscation he was getting used to from her.

Harry watched Dottie, dressed as always in a plain dress and patterned apron. He leaned across to Calum and whispered, "She's a bit of all right, ain't she? Do you think she's married?"

"Elizabeth told me she is," Calum said. "Husband's in the Navy. Why, do you fancy your chances?"

But Harry's mind had moved on. "It was all bollocks, wasn't it?" He bit into a ham and cheese sandwich.

"Was it?" said Maria.

Calum was pleased she had responded because he was reluctant to express his own thoughts yet. He knew the images would have surprised them all. Even so, their own talents could not match what they had been shown.

"Of course it was," said Harry. "People can't make things move through the air like that. As for the rest, that was even worse. I said it in front of that tall streak of piss, and I'll repeat it now. These filmmakers are clever buggers. They can make you believe anything."

"Except we all know those of us gathered here are different, don't we?" Richard Williams rose from the chair he had been sitting in unnoticed and walked across to examine the sandwiches. He chose one and took a delicate bite. "We saw what Calum could do last night. That was no movie director's trick. You have all seen, or rather not seen, my own ability."

"A magician could do what Cal did." Harry continued to hold his scepticism close, a protective blanket from the truth.

Calum rose as the door opened, and Elizabeth entered. "Oh good, food," she said. "I'm absolutely starving. Shall I see if I can get some beers rustled up? We're likely to be here for a while yet, I'm afraid." She glanced at Harry. "Would you be a dear and go find Dottie. Ask her if she can fetch us some. She'll still be in the kitchen, I expect."

Harry took the remains of his sandwich with him, a grin on his face.

Once the door closed, Calum said, "Why did you want to get rid of him?"

"Because he'll only start arguing. I need to know what the three of you think before we get into any of his fireworks."

"He'll still want to spark a row as soon as he gets back," said Maria.

"If the rest of us are united, it will fizzle out soon enough. Harry's scared. He doesn't want to believe what his own eyes have shown him."

Maria gave a shake of her head. "I accept what we saw, at least a little, hard as it is to believe. But what those people did isn't us, is it? They are at a completely different level of what… skill?"

"I believe they have been training for significantly longer than any of you. Who is to know what we can achieve given time and sufficient effort?"

"Not anything like that," said Maria, and Richard nodded in agreement.

"You said we, not us," Calum said. "Are you including yourself as one of us, then? What's your secret ability, Elizabeth?"

"Keeping us in line, isn't it?" said Harry, who returned with a crate of beer bottles in time to hear Calum's question.

Elizabeth laughed. "Oh, if only it was that easy. My contribution is to make each of you the best you can be, but you have to accept you can get better. Now, help yourselves to a beer and find a seat while I attempt to tell you everything I can."

"Which doesn't mean everything, I suppose," said Harry. He helped himself to two of the bottles and grabbed another sandwich before taking a seat.

Elizabeth walked to the window and drew back the curtains. When she turned back, sunlight illuminated her from behind and formed a halo around her head. Calum wondered if she had practised the move until satisfied with the effect.

"As you were told, the films you were shown were obtained at substantial cost to our country. You were also told the people in them were Russian, or as near as we can tell. What wasn't revealed is that Russia is not the only country developing individuals with such talents."

There's that word again, Calum thought.

"The Nazis," said Harry. "Is that what you're telling us?"

"They may be even more developed than the Russians."

"And what's that supposed to mean? Are they going to lob vases at us across the Channel? I don't think that's going to scare anybody much, do you?"

Elizabeth gave a thin smile. "It's all a matter of opportunity. Imagine a situation where this country wants to obtain secret documents from somewhere inside Germany itself. Can you not see how it might be done, even with the nascent abilities you already have?"

She waited. When Calum saw nobody was about to respond, he took it on himself.

"The four of us?" he said. "I don't know how we get there, a parachute drop perhaps, or a sub to the coast and then cross-country. I know how close some German cities are. I used to fly over them most nights. Richard can sneak his way into just about anywhere without being seen. I assume you're already fluent in German, Maria?"

She offered a nod and said something he didn't understand.

"Harry can sort out transport for us and keep it running sweetly."

"And you?" asked Elizabeth. Her eyes appraised him with an unfamiliar coolness. This was all business now. Both hers and theirs.

"I push myself as far as I can and warn us about what we might walk into. A minute ought to do it, and I can manage that far ahead for long enough."

Elizabeth turned her head slowly to take in each of them. "Do any of you disagree?" She raised a hand. "Yes, Harry, I assume you do, but think for a minute about what you can do and drop your scepticism."

"Whatever you say, old girl. What Cal says makes sense, but I can't see the Nazis letting us waltz in and steal their secrets, can you?"

Elizabeth's lips thinned again, and Calum knew she disliked the phrase Harry used for her.

"Calum is right, but so are you, Harry. What he proposes might succeed, or it might not."

"If not, it gets us all killed," said Richard.

"There is that possibility. Calum has been flying over Germany for the past two years and knows that fact well. As for the rest of you, we are at war, and sometimes people must make sacrifices."

"I'd rather someone else makes them," said Harry.

"As I'm sure every one of us would prefer. But you are all members of either the armed forces or government agencies, so your country has an expectation you will do your duty."

Calum saw what Elizabeth had done. Appealing to Harry's sense of duty was one of the few things that might bring him onside. He was less sure about Richard and Maria, but he also knew they were not so resistant to the idea of what was happening. As for himself, whatever was being asked couldn't be any more dangerous than how he had already spent half the war. The memory of sitting in the exposed bubble at the front of the Lancaster came to him. The cold, the wind and engines' roar, the thump of flak and tracer rounds as German fighters dived on them. Despite being less than a week in the past, it seemed as if it had happened to someone else. Calum felt a tension he had been unaware of leaving him. He walked to the crate of beer and took a bottle, caught the opener Harry tossed him in his left hand and eased the cap off. He took a long draught. The beer was cold and hit the spot perfectly. When he looked down at Maria, she was staring at him with a strange intensity.

"Tell me something, Cal," she said.

"If I can."

"When you caught the bottle opener, did you see yourself doing it first and then again when you actually did it?"

Calum laughed. "The truth? The first time I missed and it fell to the floor. I adjusted, same as I always do, and caught it the second time." He expected Maria to return his smile, but she only continued to stare at him before turning to Elizabeth.

"We need to have one of us in charge. Obviously, you are our boss, right? Or is our boss Edward Carlton?"

"As far as you are all concerned, you report to me. I report to Sir Edward."

"If we are to be a group with a solid foundation, it needs a structure," said Maria. "That means one of us should be a liaison between the rest of us and you. It will make things more efficient."

"There's only four of us," said Harry. "We don't need any ranks, do we?"

"Only four at the moment," said Maria. Once again, she looked at Elizabeth. "Am I correct in assuming there may be more coming or others being searched for?"

"You are right, of course," said Elizabeth. "We already have our eyes on one man, but he turned us down, which is a great shame. We have people scouring the country for rumours of anyone with strange gifts. I don't know how many of you there may be in the end. Perhaps there will be only those of you here right now, but you have a good point, Maria. It will help me if someone can be a conduit between the rest of you and me. It might make these discussions more efficient, for a start." She arched an eyebrow. "Are you putting yourself forward?"

"Of course not. Everyone knows who it should be."

"Sorry, old girl," said Harry, "but I refuse your generous offer."

Maria smiled without humour. "You know who I mean. We all do. There's only one person it can be. Isn't there, Cal?"

He knew Maria was right but opened his mouth to make some kind of objection when Elizabeth spoke across him.

"Of course it has to be Cal. It can hardly be Richard, can it? I'd never be able to find him. And I can see you don't want it for yourself, Maria, so it has to be him."

He noticed she omitted Harry. Neither did Harry object, for once.

"If you agree, Cal?"

"Do I have any choice in the matter?"

"Only if you want to see our unit fail."

"What unit? Do we even have a name, or is that top-secret as well?"

"In government circles, when we discussed the setting up this group, we referred to it as Unit-13."

Harry gave a loud laugh. "Damn, but that's original. Whatever happened to units one to twelve?"

"I believe most of those numbers are already used to designate other areas of the Service," said Elizabeth. "It was the next free number, that is all. I had little to do with it. I would ask if any of you object to the designation, but there's not much point. It has already been decided by people better than me."

"There's nobody better than you," said Harry. "And when you say the Service," he managed to say it with the same emphasis as Elizabeth, sounding the capitalisation, "do you mean the Secret Service?"

"We are a part – a very distant part – of MI5. Hence the necessity of you signing the additional forms I gave you at breakfast."

Calum looked at Harry, aware he had a bit of a crush on Elizabeth. The same as all the men. Possibly even Maria, too.

Something occurred to him he had meant to ask before. He wasn't sure if now was the right time, but the right time might never come. Elizabeth had a way of deflecting answers when asked.

"That man," said Calum. "Sir Edward Carlton."

"What about him?" Elizabeth's expression closed down.

"He was there on the base with John Simpson. He was here when I arrived. And he came here again today. It's pretty clear he's part of this group as well, but just how much does he know?"

"Sir Edward Carlton is involved. He is my boss, and no doubt he has another boss he must report to, and so and so on all the way to the top. As for what he knows, that should be eminently clear from the films he showed us. However, how much he truly understands is another matter entirely."

"You said it goes all the way to the top," said Harry. "Does that mean Churchill know about us?"

"Do you expect me to answer that?"

"You just have," Calum said.

"I don't like him," said Maria. "He has a purple aura."

Calum looked at her. "Winston Churchill?"

"Of course not. His aura is pale red. That Carlton man."

"What the devil is an aura?" asked Harry.

"Maria, like the rest of you I suspect, has more than a single talent. Each ability you possess is linked to who you are. What those abilities are is what I intend to tease out from each of you and then hone into the best they can be."

Nobody spoke for a while. When someone did, it was Harry, of course.

"When do you plan on doing that, old girl?"

"Tomorrow. Training for all of you starts tomorrow morning."

It was an hour before Calum found himself alone with

Elizabeth. The others had gone to the kitchen to find out more about the dance Harry had told them about.

"You mentioned you are looking for others with talent," he said. "How long have we got?" Calum asked.

"For what?"

"To prove ourselves. Sir Edward barely looked at those films, and when he spoke, it felt like he was reading from a prepared script. He's not interested in what we're doing, only in his position as our overseer. I'd wager he gets paid more than all of us put together."

"He could be working for nothing. It's not as if he needs the money, he's rolling in it. God knows why, because as far as I can tell, he doesn't do anything at all. But you're right, we're on a deadline. How long it is, I don't know, but safer to assume it's not long. This means you all have to work extra hard. Even you, Cal. Though you can go to the dance with the others tomorrow if you want."

"Are you coming?"

"I doubt it."

"I'm not much for dances. I'd rather stay here with you."

Elizabeth stared into his eyes, and he knew what she was going to say before she opened her mouth.

"All right, I get it. Strictly business. But you can't blame a chap for trying, can you?"

CHAPTER ELEVEN

Calum and Maria sat next to each other on a metal bench set at the house's western side. They watched as Elizabeth carried what appeared to be a heavy wooden box from the garage to a table where Harry waited. Five weeks had passed since Calum had first demonstrated his talent for the others, and a great deal had changed. In the outside world, the Allied Forces were pushing the Nazis back from captured territory. Here in Carden House, Elizabeth spent time every day with each of them, exploring their talent, trying to extend what they could do. Most times, it was individually, sometimes, as now, in plain view. This is how Calum knew that each of them, other than himself, possessed more than a single talent. He wondered whether that was because of how he appeared to have acquired it. As far as he could tell, each of the others had always possessed their own from birth.

"What is it this time, do you think?" asked Maria.

"It'll be mechanical if it's a test for Harry." Something occurred to Calum he had meant to ask Maria weeks before but always seemed to forget. Now, in the warmth of mid-afternoon, his belly filled with excellent food, it came back to him. "Tell me, what colour is Harry's aura?"

"So you believe me now, do you?"

"I believe everything these days. Hard not to, isn't it?"

Maria smiled. "Harry's is green, of course."

"Why of course?"

"Green tells me he's good with his hands. He's grounded, comfortable with himself."

Calum gave a shake of his head. "And Elizabeth?"

"Hers changes," said Maria.

"Why does it do that? Does Harry's?"

"Everybody's changes, but most people have a constant aura around them. Harry's is green, but it takes on some orange when he's around Dottie. Do you think he's persuaded her to lift her skirts yet?"

Calum laughed. "You're asking the wrong person. Have you asked Harry to his face?"

"Of course not."

"Harry's an open book. If you ask, he'll tell you. It's not for want of trying, I expect. Didn't Dottie go to that dance with the rest of you?"

"For all his talk, Harry was a complete gentleman. Mind you, there were several hundred women workers from the munitions plant, so Harry was like a kid in a sweetshop."

"But he still has this thing for Dottie, doesn't he?"

"Have you lifted her skirts, Cal?" asked Maria.

"Dottie's? Of course not. She's pretty enough, but... well, you know."

"Not Dottie. Elizabeth. Her aura changes when she's

around you, just like yours does when you're around her. Not all the time, only when you're both relaxed. It's one reason I suggested you be our liaison. You two have a connection."

Calum wanted to change the subject. If what Maria said was true, why did Elizabeth always treat him with such coolness? Perhaps it was nothing more than being professional, because it seemed to have increased after the others elected him as their spokesperson.

"So what colour is mine?" he asked.

Maria reached out and took his hand. He was used to her tactile nature by now, aware it meant nothing. At least as long as he made no response to her.

"Take a guess, Cal. Let me see how close you get."

"Grey," he said, without thinking, wondering if not thinking might conjure up the correct answer. Not that he had any idea what grey might mean.

Maria gave a bright laugh. "Close, but no cigar. Yours is one of the very rarest, Cal." Her face lost its amusement. "It's another reason I knew you were the right person to speak for us."

"So what is this rare beast?"

Elizabeth set the wooden box on the table. Harry upended it to a clatter of metal. Some parts fell off the side, and he knelt to pick them up. Elizabeth stepped back ten paces and crossed her arms as she watched him.

"Your aura is white most of the time, but it changes when you're around her." Maria still held his hand. "She wants me to give a talk on auras, so we all know about them."

"Even if we can't see them? What's the point of that?"

"You know what the point is, Cal. She wants us to know as much about each other as we can." She gave his hand a slight squeeze as if to communicate something about knowing each other differently. "Elizabeth spends time with each of us alone, more time with us like this, observing each other. She's trying to extend our talents, but she also wants us to unite as a team. Which I think is happening, don't you?"

"I feel comfortable with everyone now. Even Harry. He's more accepting, isn't he."

"That's because he's accepted his own talent. Richard and I had a chat with him a couple of weeks ago, and I think Harry was afraid of what he could do. He's a sensible sort of bloke, as you know, and sensible blokes don't hold with the ethereal."

"Do you think he does now? Do you hold with it?"

Maria laughed. "I always have. I know the way I learn a language isn't something ordinary. It comes from… I don't know where it comes from. Somewhere ancient. Something almost primaeval, as if all languages in the world have evolved from a common root. I know that root, so I know all languages. Even the ones I can't yet speak. And to answer your question, yes, Harry accepts what he does has some magical element to it."

Calum had never heard them use that term before. Magical. He wasn't sure he accepted that himself. Except science couldn't explain what he could do or what the others could do. Not yet, perhaps never. But did that only leave magic?

When he looked up, Harry was putting the pieces of metal together, his hands moving fast and sure as he assembled whatever had been broken down and handed to him. There were tools beside the table, but he didn't need them. He tightened nuts and bolts with his fingers. Calum knew they would be tight enough to hold together whatever the device was. They always were when Harry finished.

Maria leaned against Calum's shoulder. "I can try to teach you how to see auras if you want. I think we should all try to teach each other more about what we can do. I can always come to your room and get you in the right frame of mind if you like."

Calum laughed and extricated his hand from within hers. "I thought you and Richard were an item."

"We are. But it's not exclusive."

"To you, or him?"

"To both of us."

"That sounds too complicated for a simple man like me," Calum said.

"I told you, you have a white aura. That means you're no simple man. Far from it. Look, I think Harry's finished."

It was a motor. A small one, perhaps for a water pump.

Elizabeth approached the table as Harry wrapped a length of cord around a flywheel at the side. He touched a few parts, then tugged. The motor burst into life before settling into a steady rhythm.

"How long did he take?" Cal asked.

"Ten minutes."

"Faster than last time."

"How far can you see ahead now, Cal?" asked Maria.

"Four minutes, but that feels like some kind of limit.

Elizabeth's tried to push me further, but no luck so far. What has she been doing with you? It's got to be hard testing you on languages."

"There are books. She even gave me one on a supposedly lost language. Scratches on clay tablets."

"Is that where you heard about this proto-language?"

"We spoke about it, but these scratches come well after that. If there ever was one. It was Elizabeth's suggestion, so I suspect it has some basis in truth."

"How are you getting on with the scratches?"

"I'm still working on them, but it's coming together. Whatever we do is like a muscle. Use it, and it gets stronger. We've just witnessed that."

Harry turned the small engine off, and he and Elizabeth walked back towards them. Harry offered a cheeky salute to Calum, blew a kiss at Maria, then walked around to the rear of the house where the kitchen door lay. Perhaps he was hungry.

Elizabeth tried to sit between Calum and Maria, wriggling her backside until they made room. There was just enough space for the three of them, but it was cosy. Calum was acutely aware of the softness of her against his arm.

"Who wants to go next?" she asked.

"You did me this morning," Calum said.

"Indeed I did, but that doesn't mean you're excused duties. What about you, Maria?"

"You did me as well."

Elizabeth sighed. "I expect I'll have to find Richard, then."

Maria laughed. "I'll come with you. I can always see

him, and it will be good practice for me as well." She rose to her feet and moved away.

There was space now, but Elizabeth stayed pressed against Calum.

"You again tomorrow then, Cal, all right?"

"If you say so. You're the boss."

"Indeed, I am supposed to be, am I not?"

She rose, and Calum's arm felt suddenly cold. He watched the two women walk around to the front of the house, both young and beautiful, but there was only one he wanted to be with.

Calum and Elizabeth once more sat side by side, this time at the big dining table, but there was no food laid, and no other team members were present. A scatter of papers covered half the surface, roughly grouped into four piles. Each of the groups had a small card with their names printed on them. Harry. Maria. Richard. Calum.

"Where do you want to start?" asked Elizabeth. She was dressed in slacks and a cream blouse, her hair tied up with a clip at the back. She looked stunning.

"You're the boss. Which do you want to start on?"

"Am I really the boss?"

"Don't pretend. You know you are."

"Sir Edward is threatening to come down next week. I suspect he might beg to differ over who is in charge."

"Sir Edward is an idiot. You know it. I know it. Everybody knows it apart from him."

"He has influence," said Elizabeth.

"Is this a distraction from you deciding?" Calum asked. "If so, then all right, I'll do it for you." He reached out and drew one of the stacks of papers close. He did it without looking who it belonged to, trusting in some instinct he didn't even know whether he possessed or not. It turned out perhaps he did because at least they weren't his, but Maria's.

"You know, Cal," said Elizabeth, "I think she might be the most interesting of all of us."

"I might agree with you after a conversation we had earlier today. Tell me why she's so interesting to you."

"It's the combination of talents she shows. She was chosen because of her language skills, but I'm thinking they're not what we all thought they were."

"Do you mean the aura thing? It's impressive, I admit, but hardly of much use."

"That depends. As you so eloquently put it, the aura thing is only a by-product of what else she can do. Which is to demonstrate a rudimentary talent for telepathy. I don't think she was even aware of it herself until this last month, but I've been working her hard, and she acknowledges it now." Elizabeth moved a little closer, her chair squeaking on the parquet floor. She reached out and took a few of the sheets. "Look here. I took her over to the base, and she could read several people over there. She even exposed a store worker who was stealing fuel and rations."

"Does he know it was you or how you did it?"

"Of course not. As far as anyone knows, we were there asking questions on behalf of the war office. It's the kind of bumph that gets done all the time. Nobody raised an eyebrow."

"Did you find anything else of interest?" Calum reached for some pages and scanned them. Most were in Elizabeth's tiny but ornate handwriting. He saw nothing that might embarrass anyone. "I take it you got her to try it out on all of us."

"Not with any malign intent, Cal, but yes, of course I did."

"And I suppose you won't tell me any more than that?"

"You suppose right." Elizabeth tapped a fingernail on the stack of papers. "I need to dig deeper. I think Maria is going to be the star among us." She reached out and touched the back of Cal's hand, which remained on the tabletop. "No hard feelings, I hope."

"None. I know I'm a bit of a one-trick pony. I'm different to the others, aren't I?"

"You are. I'm still trying to work out why."

"Are you going to call in experts to help you out with Maria, or any of us?"

"Not yet. I still have a few things I can try first. The fewer people involved in what we do, the better. Not everyone would understand."

"But you must have some outside resources?"

"Not as many as you might think. There is an academic at Oxford who has been a great help, but he's not young, and I don't want to saddle him with extra work until I'm more sure of what I want from him."

Elizabeth tidied the papers relating to Maria and set them aside. She reached out for Richard's. "Now, these are interesting, too. I had an inkling of what he was doing, but Maria confirmed it for me."

"Another secret you can't reveal, I expect," Calum said.

"Not at all. Though again, Richard wasn't aware of it. But now he is, we can work on that talent as well. When he disappears, it's both something he does to himself and something he does to others. Maria explained it better to me than that. She says he can suck the very essence from people. He makes them lazy, unobservant. Clearly, he can't make himself invisible, but as good as. Maria calls him a psychic vampire, except he extracts a person's will rather than their blood."

"Thank God for that, at least. Now you mention it, I recall occasions when I've become tired around him. More so than you working us hard accounts for, anyway. You know he and Maria are an item, I take it?"

"Are you jealous?"

"Of course not."

"Perhaps. But yes, I am aware they are in some manner of relationship. She has spoken with me about that as well but… well, let's just say it's too intimate to discuss with you."

Calum felt a pang of disappointment that she felt she couldn't tell him everything, followed by relief that she wouldn't. Womens' matters, he suspected. Emotions, or worse.

"Another one you need to work on, then?" he asked.

"Of course, along with the rest of you. No sitting back around here, Cal. I need you all up on your toes. Especially at the moment."

Calum glanced at her. "Why at the moment?"

"Do you remember me telling you I had people looking out for those with abilities that couldn't be explained rationally?"

"Like you had someone looking out for me and the others?"

"Exactly. I told you about the other man I want to recruit, but he's still playing hard to get. I had word this morning about someone else I need to look at. I had planned to give everyone a few days leave, but I think we can work around that. I'd like you to come with me to see this woman."

"Where is she?"

"Derbyshire, close to the start of the Pennines."

"That's bloody miles away. How are you going to swing that? Get John Simpson to take us?"

"I'd prefer he doesn't know anything about it yet."

Calum looked at her. "Don't you trust him?"

"Of course I do. We go back a long way. But sometimes I wonder if he's not reporting to someone else." Elizabeth gave a shake of her head. "I'm probably getting paranoid. Too many secrets, Cal. So, will you help me?"

"If I can. When do we leave?"

"Not from here. I'd rather the other's don't know about this woman either until we've talked to her. I was going to arrange for a few days leave for everybody if they wanted it. We can use it as an excuse. I'll even let you spend a night at home with your parents if you'd like that. Shrewsbury, isn't it?"

Calum nodded. "It is. And yes, I'd like that. It must be a year since I've seen them."

"And my family home is nearby, so we both have an excuse to take the train north. Then, if this woman doesn't work out, we have no need to tell anyone about her."

Calum was uncomfortable at being drawn into Elizabeth's web of deceit. Still, he would welcome seeing his mother and father again.

"Is this woman dangerous?"

Elizabeth frowned. "Why would she be dangerous?"

"A couple of people in those films Carlton showed us looked like they might be dangerous."

"Which is why I need someone at my side I can rely on." Elizabeth patted his hand and smiled. "A big strong man."

"Or failing that, me," Calum said, and she laughed.

CHAPTER TWELVE

"So where do your folks live?" Calum asked. The train sat in the small station for Marshbrook. Only one passenger had boarded, but something was stopping them up from departing.

"Pontesbury," said Elizabeth.

She sat across from Calum, with her feet up on his seat. His own legs went the other way. Like her, he had slipped his shoes off to avoid marking the material. He had spent most of the journey admiring Elizabeth's legs. It would have been impolite not to because he was sure that was her intention. Her dress rose higher than if she stood, and he found the slim strength revealed to him attractive. That he might attract her, in turn, had occurred to him, he admitted, but more in hope than expectation.

"That's a few miles out of town," Calum said. "I'll see if Dad will let me borrow the car to give you a lift. Unless someone is coming to pick you up? We'll need some kind of transport to get to Derbyshire tomorrow, won't we?"

"We will, but nobody's coming, so thanks for the

offer." Elizabeth stretched, arching her back before settling again. The movement raised the hem of her dress for a moment before it returned to its starting point.

Calum laughed. "Depends what Dad says."

"He's a doctor, isn't he?"

"General practice. He works out of an annex on the side of the house, so hardly ever needs the car. Only when he needs to make a house call." Calum glanced through the window. He saw the guard talking with another uniformed man. It was clear there was no urgency about the train moving off. The guard had come to their carriage earlier to punch their tickets but not been since.

"Does your mother work?" asked Elizabeth.

"Housewife."

"And your sister?"

Calum looked into Elizabeth's eyes. "You do know a lot about me, don't you?"

"It's part of my job."

"Then perhaps you can tell me what Jeannie does because she won't tell me."

Elizabeth offered a smile. "Perhaps I could if I had ever asked, but I haven't. Would you like me to see if I can find out?"

Calum shrugged. "I don't suppose I'll be able to tell anyone what I'm doing either, will I?"

"Afraid not."

Calum met Elizabeth's eyes again. "Just how much do you know about me?"

"Pretty much everything."

"You told me that first day at Carden House that you knew about George. Do you know how he died?"

Elizabeth gave a nod. "Can you talk about it?"

Calum stared into her eyes. He had known this conversation would have to come but wasn't sure whether he was ready for it yet. He knew he might never be, so he took a breath and said, "I expect so. What do you want to know?"

"He drowned, didn't he? You were both thirteen."

"George was older than me by a little over four minutes. We were twins."

"Identical?"

"Pretty much to look at, though George was always the more outgoing. People liked George."

"I'm sure they liked you, too, Cal."

Calum gave a shrug. "I'd rather not relive all the details if you don't mind."

"He was caught in a tree branch, wasn't he?" It was as if Elizabeth hadn't heard him.

Calum thought about not answering, then changed his mind. They would need to have this conversation at some time. Better to get it over with now. Here, where it was only the two of them.

"The branch had always been there as long as we swam in that spot. It was the closest part of the river to our house and there was a good shingle beach. All the kids we knew swam there, but George was the only one taken by the tree. He was a better swimmer than me but the tree still got him."

Elizabeth set her feet on the floor and leaned forward. "You make it sound like the tree did it deliberately."

"Sometimes it feels that way." Calum met her gaze. "Do

you remember you asked me when I first became aware of my talent?"

She nodded, waiting for him to go on.

"I didn't tell you the whole truth. It was after George died. It was like his death flicked a switch in me. It took me a while to work out what was happening. At first, I thought it was my grief, but then…" Calum broke off because what lay in his mind was too strange, even after discovering what everyone else could do. He became aware of his talent in a way he hadn't for a long time, the future and present intertwined. Shards of possibility in a future that was not yet locked, that could be changed.

When Calum looked into Elizabeth's eyes he saw only compassion.

He searched the crossing futures. In one, he leaned forward and kissed her, and she allowed the touch before pulling away and saying it was inappropriate. In another, the kiss went on longer, reciprocated. But he couldn't discern which was the real future, which might become the present. Sometimes his talent let him down.

Elizabeth reached out and took his hands in both of hers. It was one of the moments he had seen, but he didn't respond, didn't follow the twisting threads of possibility. He was too afraid of rejection. Or ridicule. Elizabeth was too beautiful. Too perfect. She could never want a man like him. George might have been a different matter. Calum wondered what his twin brother would be like now. No doubt he'd be a Spitfire pilot with dozens of kills. One of the golden boys.

The touch of Elizabeth's hands sent a tingle along his arms and he knew he was about to tell her what he had never spoken of before. Not to anyone. Not his parents, not his sister. Definitely none of his friends. Not even Guy, and Calum felt he could tell Guy almost anything.

"I was messing around in the water with a girl. Her name was Sally Harrington, and she lived near to us, went to the same school. I was thirteen. It's what you do, isn't it?" He didn't wait for any response from Elizabeth. None was required. She would know what thirteen-year-old boys were like.

"When I looked around, I couldn't see George. I asked the others if they'd seen him, and one told me he'd been diving off the trunk of the old oak. We all did it. The water was deep there, but there was a strong current that could push you back towards it. It was a rite of passage among us to learn how to fight that current. I swam over and climbed on the trunk but couldn't see him. Then, and I have no idea why I did it, I looked down and saw something pale under the surface. I didn't hesitate. I dived down, let the current push me until I could reach George. He was still alive, but only just. His eyes were open, and he reached out a hand. I grabbed it and tugged, but he was stuck fast. I went deeper and found where his foot was trapped between two branches. They'd been there all these years waiting for someone to land just right." Calum raised his eyes to meet Elizabeth's again. "And yes, that's how I felt, how I still feel. That old oak was waiting to kill someone. A human sacrifice. It was sentient."

"What did you do?"

"I tried to free his foot, but it wouldn't come, so I had to go back to the surface to breathe. I didn't..." Calum broke off, his voice catching, and he knew there were tears in his eyes. He wished he had never started to tell her, but he had gone too far not to finish the story. This was why she had asked. This next moment, when George's life ended and Calum's changed forever. The reason he was sitting here with this beautiful women.

Calum took a deep breath, just as he had on that long-distant day, and started to finish the telling. His words came fast so he could finish and be done with the confession.

"I didn't want him to die alone, so I went back down and stayed there until something changed in his eyes. My own lungs were burning by then, but I couldn't leave him. I held his hand and waited. And then… well, you know what happened next, don't you?"

Elizabeth nodded for him to go on.

"I thought I was going crazy. My world splintered into a thousand motes, all spinning around each other. And…" No. It was too hard to say the rest.

Outside, the guard must have finished his conversation because he blew his whistle. The train jerked, stopped, jerked again, then headed on north.

"Finish it," said Elizabeth. "You need to tell me all of it."

The train picked up speed, the carriage swaying from side to side. Calum knew Elizabeth was right. If he stopped now he might never be able to tell her again. It felt important that she knew.

"I heard his voice," Calum said. "He spoke to me as clearly as if we were sitting on the sofa at home. He told me to live for both of us. Then he told me he would never leave me. He was inside me. I felt him inside me. Whatever life force we all possess exists outside our physical selves, and George's had passed from his discarded body into mine."

"Are you always aware of him?"

"No, hardly at all. Those first few months I was, but it faded. It's amazing what you can get used to. But sometimes, in times of stress, I hear him. Not the George who died, but George as he would be now, his voice that of a grown man." Calum smiled, gave a soft laugh. "His voice is different to mine, and it's George to a tee. Exactly how he would be if he had lived."

"It might be worth trying to bring him to the surface more if you're willing."

"I'm not sure I am. Is that why I can see into the future, because of George?"

"I believe so. What you told me confirms my theory that you are different to the others. Your talent came to you later than theirs. A gift from your brother to you. And you're right – each of us has a soul that can live on, and George's soul now lives inside you. Both of you together, for eternity."

"Or until I die."

"That won't end it. You know it won't. If George passed into you, then you can pass somewhere else. Heaven, the Christian Church calls it, but every religion has a different version of the story. We continue beyond death."

Calum sat up, his hands slipping from within Elizabeth's, the electricity of her touch leaving him instantly. "I'm not sure I want to believe that. Going on day after day into eternity?" He shook his head.

"Oh, I think it's not such a bad idea, provided you can hold onto your curiosity."

"Perhaps that's what Hell is. A place for those who lack curiosity. And Heaven for those who have it." Calum laughed, aware he was recovering his sense of self that had slipped from him during the telling of the tale. "Or maybe it's the other way around. I always did think Heaven sounded rather dull."

"Let's hope it's not something you'll discover for a long time yet," said Elizabeth.

CHAPTER THIRTEEN

Calum's mother smothered his face in kisses and almost squeezed the life from him. Then she held him at arms' length and surveyed him from top to toe.

"Why didn't you tell us you were coming home, Cal?"

"I didn't know myself until late last night."

"We have a telephone, you know."

"Sorry, but I'm here now. I thought it would be a nice surprise." He saw his mother glance at Elizabeth and give a frown. No doubt she was wondering who the beautiful woman was and drawing the wrong conclusion, as usual. Calum let her conjure her fantasies a while longer before dashing them.

"Who is your friend? Is she staying for lunch?" The expression on his mother's face showed a touch of panic at the thought of two extra mouths to feed.

Elizabeth stepped forward, her hand out. "I'm Elizabeth Grierson, Mrs Auger. It's a pleasure to meet you. I can't stay, I'm afraid, not if Cal can borrow your husband's car. He kindly offered me a lift."

Calum's mother shook the offered hand before glancing in his direction. "Your father's in the surgery, but I think he's finished with his patients. Introduce your friend, and I'm sure you can borrow the car. I can't remember the last time he took it out of the garage. Oh, and Jeannie's on her way home as well, so you can catch up with her later. In fact, you can pick her up from the station." She looked at Elizabeth, back to Cal. "Unless you have other plans?"

"No, no plans." As they went outside and walked around to the annex, he said, "I think Mum might have us married off already. I'm a big disappointment to her."

"All mothers are the same, aren't they?"

Calum laughed. "Is yours?"

"She died some time ago, but yes, she was."

"I'm sorry."

"What for? It was a very long time ago now."

Ahead of them, Calum's father, a tall, well-built man, stepped through a door in the side of a low building set to one side of the main house.

"Hello, Dad," Calum said.

Calum's father smiled, stepped forward and offered his son a hug. When he turned to take in his companion a look of puzzlement crossed his face.

"Elizabeth?" he said.

Cal frowned. "Do you know each other?"

His father stared at Elizabeth for a while longer, then shook his head. "No, we can't do. But you look so much like someone I used to know. A long time ago now, in the war. The other one, that is." Robert Auger gave a laugh. "Though the woman I knew could be your twin."

He shook his head. "Mind, she would be my age by now."

"Perhaps you knew my mother. She was an Elizabeth, too. We look very much alike, I've been told." Elizabeth stepped forward and shook the hand of Calum's father. She kept his hand in hers for a long time as she looked up at him. "Though if it was her, she never told me about a handsome devil like you. She was stationed in France during the war."

Calum saw a flush colour his father's face and suppressed a smile.

"So was I," said Robert Auger. "It's where I met Mairi…" His voice trailed off, something left unsaid.

"Elizabeth lives in Pontesbury," Calum said. "Can I pinch your car to give her a lift home?"

"You can borrow it. Did your mother tell you Jeannie's coming home later? You can pick her up from the station if you're back in time. She'll be on the three-fifteen from London."

"What's she doing now?" Calum asked as they started the short walk back to the main house.

"You can try asking her if you like, but she won't tell me. Hush-hush, she claims." Robert Auger shook his head. "It seems to me everything is hush-hush these days. How long are you staying, Cal?"

"Only the one night."

"Still flying?"

"Not at the moment. New job."

"What's that then?"

Calum offered his father a wink. "Sorry, Dad. Hush-hush."

They entered the big kitchen, where Mairi Auger was laying the table. She glanced up. "Are you sure you won't stay, Elizabeth?"

"I have to get home, I'm afraid. Perhaps another time."

"That would be lovely." His mother gave a meaningful glance in Calum's direction. "Try not to be too long, Cal, I've made shepherd's pie. Your favourite. I'm sure we can make it stretch to the three of us."

———

Several hours after dropping Elizabeth off at the end of a long driveway that hid her house from view, Calum stood on the station at Shrewsbury and watched the London train pull in. A cohort of soldiers and airmen poured out, followed by a few civilians. It was mid-afternoon, and the commuters, the few there were, wouldn't arrive until closer to six. Calum caught sight of the slim figure of his sister, Jeannie. She carried a small cardboard suitcase and wore a dark blue overcoat as if it was a shield. She had cut her pale red hair short since last he'd seen her, but was as pretty as ever. Perhaps more so. Calum was always protective of his younger sister. Though he suspected the war had finally offered her an opportunity to make use of her prodigious talents. Opportunities civilian life couldn't provide. Her skills came at a cost, but perhaps less of one now she could offer them in service to her country.

Jeannie walked half-way across the station yard before she caught sight of Calum. She came forward, then stopped, awkward as ever. Where Calum's mother was all hugs and kisses, Jeannie was more circumspect. He was sure she loved him, as he did her, but it wasn't in her nature to show that love in any physical sense. When he closed the gap and gave her a brief hug, he felt her tense and released her.

"I wasn't expecting to see you," she said.

"And I wasn't expecting to see you, either." He picked up her suitcase, which weighed barely anything. "Come on, Dad lent me the car so you can travel the rest of the way home in luxury."

Jeannie smiled. "Hardly luxury if it's still that old Austin. Can we stop off on the way?"

There was no need for her to state where. Calum wanted to visit the cemetery too, and it would be good to have Jeannie's company. It might soften the guilt he always felt. It occurred to him the coincidence of them both getting leave at the same time was rather convenient. He wondered if Elizabeth had anything to do with it.

Neither of them said anything as they travelled through town and pulled up in a side-street close to the Abbey. The silence between them wasn't unusual. Calum would have been more surprised if Jeannie had chattered away like most of the girls he knew.

"How long are you home for?" he asked as they walked along a gravel path lined on either side by old headstones, half of which had faded into obscurity. The stone they wanted required no feat of memory to recall the location of, and Calum barely noticed the turns they took.

"Three days," said Jeannie. It was close to a speech for her.

"Dad says you're doing something hush-hush these days."

"Can't tell you."

Calum thought he almost caught the hint of a smile on his sister's face.

They both slowed until they stood side by side in front of a small headstone inscribed with a terse message.

In Memory of George Auger
1922-35
Taken too soon

"I can never come home until I've stood here," said Jeannie. Her hand came out in search of Calum's and grasped it, her fingers cold.

"Me neither." He gave her hand a squeeze.

"You don't still blame yourself, do you?"

If anyone else had said the words Calum would have taken them to heart, but he knew it was only Jeannie. She always said what she thought, never considering her words might hurt others. It was part of who she was. Part of her genius and failing, all wrapped together.

"I'll never stop blaming myself, Jeannie. You know I won't. But it doesn't hurt as much as it did."

"I loved him so much."

"Me too."

Jeannie gave a sharp laugh, cutting it off. "The pair of you used to fight all the time."

"Isn't that what love is?"

"You're asking the wrong girl, Cal."

"Still nobody special, then?"

"What do you think? What about you? All those eager WAAFs still chasing after you fly-boys? It must make your head spin, never mind another part of your anatomy."

"I think I might have flown my last mission, sis, so no more WAAFs for me. More's the pity. Some of them were even quite pretty."

Jeannie went to the headstone and placed her hand on top of it. She said nothing. Shed no tear. It was her way, Calum knew. He also knew she felt George's loss as deeply as he did but would always hold it inside. George and Jeannie had been closer than he was to her. He wished he could tell her how his own pain felt, but knew Jeannie wasn't the right person for such a confession. He wondered if Elizabeth might be.

He glanced at the sky. "Come on, sis, we can't put it off any longer."

Jeannie turned back to him, her face expressionless.

"So what are you doing if you're no longer flying, Cal?"

He smiled. "Can't tell you."

"I hope it's important." Her lips thinned. "Fuck this war, Cal. Fuck it all to hell!"

"My, this new job has changed you, hasn't it?"

"The war's changed me, Cal. It's changed us all, you know it has." She looked directly into his eyes, an act unusual enough to make Calum uncomfortable. "At least now I don't have to worry about you getting shot out of the sky, do I?"

"That would never happen."

Jeannie made a snuffling sound that might have been an attempt at a laugh. "That's what everybody says. Doesn't make it happen though, does it?" She reached out and retook Calum's hand. "Come on, let's go and pretend we don't have to leave again soon."

***

"That friend of yours is downstairs, Cal."

When he opened his eyes, Calum saw his mother standing at the foot of his bed. A sense of unreality sparked through him. He hadn't slept in his bedroom at home for years, and he had forgotten how small it was.

"It's the middle of the night. Tell her to go away. Our train back isn't until eleven."

"It's five in the morning, so it's not the middle of the night, and she says she needs you to go with her."

"All right. Go and tell her I'll be down as soon as I'm dressed. Unless she wants to come up here?" Calum smiled when he saw his mother's expression, but she turned away without a word, as ever willing to do her duty for her family.

Elizabeth was talking with his mother as Calum descended the stairs, and he took a moment to study her, a sense of unworthiness settling through him. Then he thought of how George would behave, the adult George, the confident George, and stepped into the room.

Elizabeth turned to him with a smile. "Come on, sleepy-head, we've got work to do." She looked Calum up and down. "You might want to go and change, put something warmer on. Our transport is basic, to say the least."

When Calum followed her outside he saw what she meant. A Matchless G3 motorcycle sat precariously on its stand. It was painted dull army green, with two canvas panniers strapped behind the small rear seat. Both contained something bulky.

"I'll go find something else," Calum said. "Do I need to pack anything for overnight, or is this a day trip?" A moment of excitement passed through him at the thought of a night away with Elizabeth.

"Don't know yet, but a change of socks and underwear should be enough. We've got extra fuel in the panniers, so there's not much spare room. Can you ride a motorcycle, Cal?"

"Used to have one of my own. Don't suppose I'll have forgotten how. "There was no need to ask Elizabeth if she could. The Matchless gave all the answer needed.

Calum searched in his wardrobe until he found the black leather jacket he had bought at sixteen when he rode his first motorcycle, relieved to find it still fit. When he emerged, he carried a small rucksack into which he had packed enough for a couple of nights. Elizabeth sat astride the motorcycle, perched on the small rear seat. She looked utterly enchanting. So much so Calum had to force back his feelings about her. He stuffed his belongings into one of the panniers then stood for a moment.

"When you said you'd get us transport, I assumed it would be something a little bigger, with doors and everything. Do you want me to drive?"

Elizabeth looked him up and down. "Well, you're dressed for it. Leather suits you, by the way. And I'm afraid this is all I could get my hands on at short notice, but it will get us there. You did say you used to own a motorcycle, didn't you? I could do it, but to be honest this machine is a bit of a beast. More suited to a strong man."

"Or even me. We could do with Harry here."

"Harry wouldn't be any good for what we're about to do. I called through to Carden House and explained we might be away a few days more."

"I bet that's going to set tongues wagging."

"Let them wag. We know better."

"So where is this place, exactly? You said Derbyshire, didn't you?"

"Up on the moors. I've got the address here. I know roughly where it is, but we'll stop somewhere for a bite of lunch and ask the locals if they know who we're looking for. It's going to take us three or four hours, I expect." She patted the seat in front of her. "Come on, Cal, the sun's up and the day is wasting."

Calum stepped over the seat and settled into it. He checked the single dial, which showed speed but nothing else. He kicked the stand up and rocked the Matchless from side to side, relieved to hear the tank was full. Then he stood on the kickstarter and put all his weight on it. The big single-cylinder kicked back hard, and he cursed. The second time it burst into life and they set off along the old Roman Road, heading east. The air was cool, but a cloudless sky promised warmth later on. As they picked up the A5 and Calum gave the engine its head, Elizabeth's arms snaked around his waist, and she leaned against his back. He said nothing, not wanting to do anything that might make her loosen her hold. He was only grateful she couldn't see the grin plastered across his face.

CHAPTER FOURTEEN

They had been on the road for two hours when Elizabeth tapped Calum on the shoulder and pointed to the side of the road. He drew to a halt and turned off the engine. It wasn't their first stop. They had refuelled from the petrol cans twice, and Calum wondered if there was enough remaining to take them to their destination. Which, it turned out, Elizabeth had already thought of. She climbed off the rear pillion and walked up and down to ease the stiffness in her legs. Even dressed in thick trousers, a heavy sweater and a waxed jacket, she was the most beguiling creature Calum had ever seen.

"We need to get something to eat soon," she said. "There's an RAF depot ten miles ahead at Harpur Hill. It's not far out of our way, and we can fill the petrol cans up and get some food if we're lucky."

Calum climbed off the motorcycle and stretched his legs as well. "Do you want to take us there?"

"I'd rather not," said Elizabeth. "I thought you were

doing a pretty good job. Especially when that lorry pulled out without looking. I'd have ridden straight into it."

Calum grinned. "I do have the advantage of foresight, remember. You'll have to direct me, then."

"I'll tap you on one shoulder or the other when you need to take a turn."

Twenty minutes later they reached the depot. It was tucked away on a hillside Calum would never have found on his own. A high fence enclosed the site, but as soon as Elizabeth showed the guards her credentials they waved them through. They left the motorcycle at a maintenance shed with the promise their petrol cans would be filled, as well as the tank. Shortly after, they sat in an almost deserted canteen drinking tea and eating bacon sandwiches.

"What does this Alice Clare do that's dragging us halfway up the country?"

"She communes with spirits."

"I assume you mean ghosts, not the kind Harry drinks every chance he can."

"Not ghosts, Cal. Spirits."

"Is there a difference?"

"In this case, yes. I heard about Alice because the locals consider her to be a bit of a witch. Strange goings-on around her place is what came back to me."

"How many people have you got out there searching?" Calum asked. "And do they know what they're actually looking for? Might that not be a bit tricky if they learn too much?"

"I only use a couple, and both are trustworthy. The ones who found Alice are a married couple. He's in supplies, so has an excuse to track backwards and forwards across the country. His wife comes across as a little mouse of a woman, but she's sharp as a tack. They both are."

"Are they the people who found me?"

Elizabeth smiled. "Not saying, Cal."

"I expect they are if you say they're the only people you use. Makes sense, doesn't it?"

"Does it?"

"Do you actually have any kind of address for this Alice Clare?"

For once, Elizabeth didn't have an answer on the tip of her tongue. She searched in a pocket and pulled out a slip of paper. When she passed it to Calum he recognised her tiny, neat handwriting.

"Edale." Calum glanced up to meet Elizabeth's eyes. "Why do you want her?"

"I don't know if I do yet, but I investigate every report in this country personally."

"Like you did me."

"Yes, like I did you. Maria, Richard and Harry as well. I spoke with them two weeks before I did you. It took a little longer to get them released to me."

"I thought you could get anything you wanted."

"Most times I can, like I did with you. Sometimes there are hoops to jump through. Getting Richard released from prison was one of those hoops."

Calum stared at her. "Prison?"

"That's where they put you when you steal a hundred pounds."

"I thought he got away with it."

"So did Richard. Enough of the history lesson, I'd like to find this woman before the end of the day, so we should get back on the road. We're over halfway now, and we've enough fuel to get there. I'll worry about getting us home later."

"Perhaps we should find someplace to spend the night," Calum said, trying to keep his voice light.

Elizabeth smiled as she reached out to pat his cheek. "Oh, the innocent dreams of youth."

<hr>

There was a single pub in the village of Edale but it had closed for the afternoon, which was no barrier to Elizabeth. She instructed Calum to knock until a man opened the door.

"We open at six," he said.

"Which I am glad to hear," said Elizabeth. "I hear that some inns in isolated locations play fast and loose with opening hours. But we are not here to enjoy your no doubt excellent ale. I'm looking for a woman by the name of Alice Clare. Do you know her?"

"Everyone around her knows Spooky Alice. Have you come to lock her up?"

"I merely wish to have a conversation with her. Does she live in the village?"

"Up on the moor," said the man. "On the road out to Kinder Scout. Though road's too fine a word for it. What is it you want with her?"

Calum suspected people looked out for each other in these parts.

"Which way is this road?" asked Elizabeth, choosing not to answer his question.

He said nothing, and Elizabeth turned away.

"It's been a long day," Calum said before following her. When he glanced back, the man continued to stare at them. "I hope this Alice doesn't have a telephone, or he's going to warn her we're on our way."

Elizabeth pointed a finger upwards, confusing Calum.

"Take a look around you, Cal. Show me the telegraph poles and wires. I haven't seen any for the last ten miles. There are no phones all the way out here. Perhaps the village isn't even aware there's a war going on."

"They'll have the radio."

"Possibly, but we're a long way from such niceties here. Do you think that's why Alice Clare lives here? We go this way." Elizabeth pointed to the road that led around the side of the pub.

"How do you know that's the way?"

"Because it goes north. Actually, a little west of north, which is where Kindle Scout lies."

"Is there anything you don't know? How do you manage it?"

"I've had a lot of practice. Come on, I want to find her before dark."

"It's hours until then," Calum said.

"Better safe than sorry."

The first house they came to was set back from the road, which had been accurately described by the innkeeper. It was little more than an unpaved track through open fields where sheep grazed. The door was answered by a grizzled man who could have been any age between thirty and ninety. When Elizabeth asked if he knew where Alice Clare lived, he shut the door in her face and threw the bolt across.

They set off again. The next house was abandoned, the roof slowly dissolving into the interior. The third house was perched on a rocky outcropping with a fast-flowing stream almost enclosing it. The water split when it met rock and parted around the house, only drawing together again a hundred paces downstream. A stone slab offered the only access to the house without getting wet feet.

"This has got to be it, hasn't it?" said Calum. "I don't fancy taking the bike any further on this track. It was hard enough getting this far."

"This is the place," said Elizabeth. Her expression had changed, taking on an intense seriousness. Calum wondered if this is how she had looked before she encountered him.

As they crossed the stone bridge, the front door opened and a woman stepped out. She was younger than Calum had expected, and far prettier. He had conjured a vision of some old hag with white hair and a beaked nose. This woman was none of those things. Except something wasn't right. He sensed it without being able to pin down what it was.

"What is you after?" Her voice was soft, the accent so clipped it was difficult to understand.

"Are you Alice Clare?"

"Who be asking?"

"My name is Dr Elizabeth Grierson. If you are Alice, I would welcome a word with you."

"Why for?"

"My friend here is someone who shares a talent with you. Of a different nature, but a talent all the same."

"Talent? What can he do?" Alice Clare's first question was cancelled out by her second, which showed she knew precisely what Elizabeth was talking about.

"He can see the future."

Calum wasn't sure honesty was the right approach, but Elizabeth was in charge, so he stayed back. He saw something move in one of the windows.

"There's someone else," he said, his voice low so only Elizabeth could hear.

"Do you have a husband?" asked Elizabeth.

"Only me lives out here. Only me. No other people."

Calum caught another movement, this time in one of the upper windows. A pale shape that stood back from the glass so it could not be clearly seen.

"Who's in there with you?" Calum raised his voice so the woman could hear him. He reached out and tugged at Elizabeth's sleeve to make her take a step away from the house. He didn't see anything in the future, but he didn't need to. A sense of danger lay thick across this place.

Alice Clare took three steps forward to match those Calum and Elizabeth took backwards.

"Nobody here you'd wantin' to meet, boy."

Elizabeth jerked her arm out of Calum's grip and went towards the woman.

"I am authorised by the Crown to investigate all reports of paranormal incidents in the land. Your name crossed my desk. That is why I am here. And that is why you will answer my questions."

Alice Clare stared at Elizabeth without expression, and

then, as if a switch had been thrown, she smiled. It was as if the sun emerged from behind a cloud. Calum felt his fear disappear in an instant. He wanted to approach her. Wanted to kiss her soft lips. He fought against the urge, knowing it wasn't real. It was something Alice was doing to him.

"Why didn't you say that before, my dear?" Her voice had changed, all the sharpness lost from it. "Come on in, I'll make tea for all of us. There might even be a bit of cake left." She turned and walked into the house.

"No," Calum said.

Elizabeth gave him an impatient glance. "She can do things, Cal, don't you feel it? She's powerful."

"She's dangerous. That's what I feel."

"More dangerous than you and me? I think not. She's a slip of a girl."

"No, she's not. There's something badly wrong here."

"Then stay outside, but I'm going in."

Calum watched her walk towards the house. When she reached the door he followed, knowing he couldn't let Elizabeth face whatever lay inside its walls alone. As he entered directly into the kitchen, he felt a chill. A fire burned in an open hearth but threw out no heat. A pot of tea curled steam from its spout, but there had been no time for Alice Clare to make it. Half a rich cake sat on a plate, three other smaller ones set on the table. Three chairs were drawn up.

Alice picked up a wicked looking carving knife and held it out.

"Cake?"

"Yes, please," said Elizabeth.

Alice ignored Calum. Whatever was going on was happening between the two women. And then he heard a noise from above. A dragging sound, as if a sack of stones was being pulled across the floor. Elizabeth seemed not to hear anything.

"What is it you want with me?" asked Alice.

"I told you, I am looking for people with unusual abilities. A talent that cannot be explained by rational science."

"Then you come to the right place, ain't you?"

"I hope so."

"'Cept I don't want to work for no Crown, nor nob'dy else. I stay here where I belong. We all stay here where we belong."

"All?" said Elizabeth.

Alice laughed. "Yes, all'us." She waved the carving knife. The cake remained uncut.

A sudden sound came from the stairs, as if the sack of stones had been tossed down it. And then a shape appeared in the doorway. A tall shape without form. It roiled, dark and smoky, then resolved into a man in an anachronistic dress coat.

"Who be these folks, Alice?" His voice was made of the same stones that had been in the sack. "Be they friend or foe?"

"Foe, I thinks."

"Then best they be gone."

"Yes, best they be gone."

Elizabeth started towards the man, but Calum put himself between them. He turned to face her, scared at what he saw on her face. She was smiling, but there was little rationality in her eyes. Calum felt the power of Alice Clare. It whispered to him, but he fought it. Elizabeth appeared to have lost the battle, and her wits were gone.

Calum put his hands on her chest and pushed her backwards.

She fought him. Her hand came out and slapped his face hard. Calum ignored it, allowing the future slap to land on his cheek. Then he hit her back.

Elizabeth's head rocked with the force of the blow, but something changed in her eyes, and her smile disappeared.

"Out, Cal. Now!"

Calum needed no encouragement. He dragged Elizabeth across the kitchen, then stopped when he saw a future Alice Clare strike out with the knife. He hesitated, pushed Elizabeth aside, then gripped Alice's wrist as it descended. He twisted hard, making her drop the weapon. And then the man who wasn't a man started forwards.

Calum pulled Elizabeth outside and ran. They skidded on the wet grass, then they were across the bridge. Only then did he turn back.

The house stood unchanged, but in front of it now stood thirteen figures, Alice Clare at their centre. The eye of the storm. Calum looked at the figures, then looked away. He knew his sanity would be shattered if he stared at them too long. They stood unmoving. He had expected them to follow, but they remained where they were.

"I tol' you, we don't need nob'dy else here," Alice called out. "Now bugger off the pair of you 'fore I sets my friends on you."

Calum heard the engine of the Matchless fire. When

he turned, Elizabeth was riding away down the track. He ran after her, all the while Alice Clare's laughter following him.

He caught up with Elizabeth three hundred yards along the track, but only because she had stopped. She crouched over the fuel tank, her head down. When Calum gripped her shoulders, she jerked and cried out before realising it was him. She pulled him into an embrace, holding him tight. Calum could feel her shaking inside his arms.

He looked beyond her to the isolated house. Nobody stood outside. The door was closed. A curl of smoke rose from the chimney. The sun shone as if this was just another ordinary day.

"What the hell was that?"

"Not now, Cal. Take me away from here. Ride as fast as you can. Use your talent. I know you can do it. Ride as if the demons of Hell are on our tail, because that's what I think lives in that house." Elizabeth wiped a hand across her face to remove the tears that tracked her cheeks. "Take me home, Cal."

CHAPTER FIFTEEN

It was close to 2300 hours before Calum brought the Matchless to a stop outside Carden House. He killed the engine and lights, but anyone watching or listening would only have noticed the lack of the single cylinder firing. Their progress had been slow once dark came, the last hours difficult. Only Calum's talent had brought them home safely.

He looked up at the house, all the windows dark.

"Think anyone heard us arrive?" he asked.

Elizabeth eased herself off the small rear pillion seat as if she had become glued to it. Neither had wanted to stop on their way south, but were forced to get more fuel south of Stoke. They had covered the last few miles on little more than fumes.

"Harry will have," said Elizabeth. "He can hear an engine from half a mile away and tell you exactly what's wrong with it."

Calum patted the tank of the motorcycle. "She did

well. Brought us home, anyway. Do you have to send her back?"

"I don't suppose so. The man I took it from barely noticed me riding off. Why, do you want it, Cal?"

"Might be handy having our own transport, so we don't have to rely on John Simpson all the time."

"It's yours, then. Once Harry's taken a look at it." Elizabeth stretched, twisting from side to side. "How tired are you, Cal?"

"Pretty tired. You?"

"The same. But I don't want to sleep yet. Not after what we saw."

"Do you want to talk about it?" Neither had said anything, not even when they stopped. But Calum still held an image in his mind from when they passed through Edale. The pub was open, a few people standing outside. One of them was a tall man in a black frock coat. He had watched them with dark eyes as they rode through the village and out the other side. Calum hadn't looked back to see when the man had stopped watching them.

"I don't," said Elizabeth, "but I think we should. I need to make a decision, and best I make it tonight. Come on."

Instead of entering through the front door, she led him around the back to the kitchen. When she flicked the light switch, the single bulb almost blinded Calum. Elizabeth went to her knees in front of a cupboard and searched inside for something. Calum leaned against the scarred oak table and admired the view. He made sure she didn't catch him as she straightened up, a bottle of whisky in her hand.

"Find us a couple of glasses, Cal."

He got two mismatched tumblers and followed her out. He expected them to go to her office or the dining room, but Elizabeth climbed the stairs. Calum watched her for a moment, then followed.

Her room was larger than his, the bed wider, and a half-open door showed it had its own bathroom. There were two easy chairs and a narrow desk set in front of a bay window. Elizabeth drew the cork from the bottle and poured two generous measures before handing one to Calum. He took it and sank into one of the chairs as Elizabeth took the other. The whisky burned on its way down, lifting his mood.

"So," he asked, "did you expect any of that?"

Elizabeth stared into the swirling, peat-tinted nectar of her whisky. "Do you think I'd have taken you there if I thought anything like that was going to happen?"

"You told me she communed with spirits. Was that what they were? Spirits?"

Elizabeth drained her glass, shook her head. She rose and refilled it, poured more for Calum. Instead of sitting, she stood in front of him so he had to look up at her. It wasn't a difficult thing to do, and the view was fabulous.

"Not spirits. Something older, darker than spirits. Did you get a look at all of them, Cal?"

"As far as I could. They kept changing shape."

"I need to make a decision."

"About Alice Clare?"

Elizabeth nodded. Calum hadn't seen her drink, but her glass was empty again. So was his. He held it out, and she slopped amber liquid into his and her own. They were both getting a little tipsy, but he knew they both needed it.

"You can't send troops out there. Not to that."

"I know. Which is why I don't know what to do."

"I read books as a kid, fantasy stuff, Verne and Wells and others. Do you think her house was surrounded by running water on purpose?"

"There is often a kernel of truth in folklore, so yes. Except I thought running water kept demons out, not trapped inside. I know you saw the tall man outside the pub. The water didn't keep him in. It wouldn't keep Alice in either."

"It was hard to miss him, but I'm sure she wasn't with him. There was no way a normal man could have reached the village before us."

"I don't know enough. I need to talk to that professor I told you about as soon as I can."

"I thought you were the expert," Calum said.

"In talent, not witchcraft."

"Is that what it was?"

"I don't know!" Elizabeth's answer was almost a wail of anguish, and Calum stood. He hesitated a moment, then put his arms around her. It was as if a switch had been thrown and she clung against him. Some of her whisky spilled down his chest, the rich smell encompassing them both. It felt like some kind of protective shield.

"I don't want to be on my own tonight, Cal." Elizabeth's breath was warm against his neck.

"I'll stretch out in the chair. It's more comfortable than it looks."

Elizabeth gave a laugh. "It would have to be. But I didn't mean that. I want you to lie beside me." She looked up and met his eyes. "I want you inside me. I need human touch, Cal. I need you."

He kissed her. First in the future, and then again in the present. It was worth the repetition.

When Calum woke and opened his eyes, it was to discover Elizabeth propped on one elbow, staring at him with an almost unsettling hunger. Grey light filled the room, and he glanced at the small alarm clock on the bedside table. It read a little after five.

"What?" he asked.

"I'm working out whether I want to jump on you this very moment or keep the tension going a little longer."

"Do I have any say in the matter?"

"Of course you do. You did last night, didn't you?"

"That was all a bit frantic, to be honest."

"And this will be more relaxed, I promise. Besides, you're a man. There's little point in me asking if you want to or not."

"There is that."

"You know you can't tell the others about this. About us. Ever."

"I suspected it might come with a catch."

"And..." Elizabeth's voice trailed off. She ran a finger across Calum's chest, exploring him as if she had never touched a man before.

"I have no expectations," Calum said.

"We need to talk about yesterday, but not right now. Later today. You and me."

"You said you had other resources as well. How many are there who help you?" Calum reached out and touched Elizabeth in the same way she was touching him. Of course, her chest held much more interest than his own.

"Fewer than you might think, but yes, I have other resources. I told you about the academic in Oxford who studies the arcane. You already know Unit-13 is part of the Secret Service, but they're not much use at this kind of thing. I think it makes the few among their ranks who do know about us uneasy. So I prefer dealing with those who have spent their whole lives studying the esoteric. People who acquire knowledge for its own sake, with no expectation it will ever be used or appreciated. They like talking to me."

"I bet they do." Calum pushed the bedclothes to the bottom of the bed. It didn't seem they would be needed anymore. Not for what he had in mind.

Calum woke the next time with a start as he heard the door to Elizabeth's room open. He sat up as Dottie entered, carrying a tray holding a teapot, a small jug of milk, and a single delicate china teacup on a saucer. She stopped halfway across the room.

"Oh."

Calum thought she did well not to drop the tray.

Elizabeth sat up, pulling the sheet up to cover herself. "Is it that time already?"

"Six-thirty, yes." Dottie glanced down at the tray, then

crossed the room to set it on the desk. "I'll fetch another cup, shall I?"

"Please. And…" Elizabeth held a finger to her lips. "Not a word to anyone."

"Of course not."

When she was gone, Elizabeth slipped from the bed and poured herself tea, completely relaxed at her nakedness in front of Calum. Far less relaxed than he was in studying her.

"Dottie won't say anything," said Elizabeth as she walked back to the bed. She handed her cup to Calum. "Here, we can share until she brings another."

Which was only a few minutes. Dottie seemed to have recovered her usual equanimity when she returned with another cup, this time without a saucer. She set it on the desk before turning to face them.

"There was a phone call for you while you were away, Elizabeth."

"In what regard?"

Calum felt the urge to laugh at the normality of the conversation while they both lay naked, covered only by a thin bedsheet.

"They never told me. You know they never do. Said he'd call back on Monday. I told him I didn't know when you'd be back."

"Was it Sir Edward?" asked Elizabeth. She sipped at her tea.

"No, thank goodness. I'd have recognised his hoity-toity tones in a second."

"I take it she doesn't like him," Calum said once they were alone again. This time he crossed naked to the desk and filled the fresh cup. He held the teapot out to see if Elizabeth wanted more, and she nodded. It all seemed very domesticated, but he knew not to get used to it.

"There's not an awful lot to like, is there?"

"I've only met him twice, but I have to agree with you even on such short acquaintance. Do you have any idea who might have called?"

"No, but I expect we'll find out soon enough once I make a few calls of my own." She sipped her tea, set it down. "I expect we ought to get up and find out what's been going on while we've been away."

"I expect we should." Calum set his own cup down.

"In a minute, perhaps," said Elizabeth. "Be a sweetheart, Cal, and go lock the door, then come back to bed. I should have done it last night. It would have saved Dottie's blushes. I expect my mind must have been elsewhere."

Calum went to the door and turned the key. He wondered why Elizabeth was allowed one when the rest of them were not. One of the perks of being the boss, he supposed.

"I don't think Dottie was embarrassed, more amused once she got over the shock of seeing us together. Do you think Harry's managed to have his wicked way with her yet?"

"I don't care whether he has or not, as long as it doesn't cause any problems. They're both grown adults." She stretched like a cat. "Now, talking about having wicked ways with each other…" She glanced at the clock. "Though we might have to be quick if the others aren't to get suspicious."

CHAPTER SIXTEEN

Harry was on his own in the dining room when Calum entered.

"You're back then, are you? Did you have an exciting time gallivanting around the country? Nice motorbike, by the way. I took a quick look at it when I came down. Do you think Lizzie might let me strip it down and improve it? I need something to do, I tell you. I've had just about enough of this malarky, my old mucker. We need to organise a prison break or something."

Calum had slipped along the upstairs hallway to his own room for a quick wash and change of clothes before coming down. Elizabeth had gone to her office to see if she could find out more about the phone call.

"If you recall, we walked down to the pub in the village at the start of the week," Calum said. "And aren't you going to the dance in town tomorrow? Do you mean that kind of prison break?"

"The dance is tonight, Cal," said Harry. "Have you forgotten today is Saturday?"

"Is it? I suppose I must have. Got things on my mind, I expect."

"What things?"

Calum smiled and tapped the side of his nose. He regarded the offerings laid out on the sideboard and decided on the scrambled eggs with mushrooms. They had eaten barely a thing the day before and he was starving. Though perhaps Elizabeth's enthusiasm might have something to do with that, he thought.

"Come on, spill the beans. What were you and Lizzie up to that kept you away? A little hanky-panky in the shires, was it?"

"Government business."

Harry seemed, for once, to take the hint. "So are you coming to the dance tonight, Cal? Maria and Richard are up for it if you want to tag along. Might even find yourself a little distraction or two."

"Is Dottie going?"

"I think so." Harry tried to sound casual.

"And the Major? We might need him to drive us there and back."

"There's a bus goes from outside the village hall, the last one gets back around midnight."

Elizabeth entered the room. Calum suspected she had been standing outside the door eavesdropping on them. She carried a small sheaf of papers in her hand, which she set on the table before going to see what was to eat. "I was planning on catching up on all your training tomorrow. I don't want you staying out all night and then sleeping half the morning away."

Harry glanced at her. "It's you and Cal who are the

stay-in-beds. Maria and Richard were down early. I'd be finished as well if I hadn't been admiring that Matchless. Can I take it apart?"

"Can you put it back together again if you do?" Elizabeth stood at the sideboard, deciding what to add to her plate.

"It's me we're talking about," said Harry. "And if I can't, I'll get another one for us. It might be a good idea to do that anyway. There's plenty of space in the garage, even with that long car of the Major's. What about you, Lizzie? Are you coming to the dance tonight?"

"How do you know I'm going to let any of you go?" She came to the table with bacon and eggs and deliberately sat as far from Calum as she could.

"Because it'll be good for morale," said Harry.

"I suppose it would. And it means I can catch up on my work and have an early night."

***

The bus dropped them off in High Town at 1900 hours. Golden light filled the narrow square as they walked to St Peter's Square and the Shire Hall. The yard was packed with more people than could possibly attend the dance, but nobody seemed to mind. Dottie walked arm-in-arm with Harry, Maria arm-in-arm with Richard, who was attempting to be on his best behaviour, barely fading at all. Calum walked alone. He had called in on Elizabeth in her office in an attempt to persuade her to accompany them, but she had a stack of papers spread across her desk and a distracted frown on her beautiful face. She had ignored him all day, and he had gone to find her with some vague idea she might ask him to stay behind. But all she had said was for him to enjoy himself.

A swing band played a decent rendition of a Glenn Miller song which drifted out from doors thrown wide. The others showed their tickets and went inside. Calum stayed in the triangular square and smoked a cigarette. He gazed back the way they had come, past the black and white Old House, hoping he might see that Elizabeth had changed her mind and followed them. Instead, he saw someone else he recognised: John Simpson. He was talking with another man Calum didn't recognise, though the two of them seemed familiar enough. When the conversation ended, John Simpson turned and strolled in Calum's direction. He didn't notice him at all, his eyes on the Shire Hall, and Calum called his name as he passed.

John Simpson turned and offered a smile.

"What are you doing here?" Calum asked.

"Elizabeth had a spare ticket. She asked me to come along and offer you all a lift home. Should be room for everyone in the Rover at a pinch if the girls don't mind sitting on knees."

Calum laughed. "I expect Harry might like them both on his. Do you dance?"

"I move my feet around and hope my partner can avoid them most of the time," said John Simpson with a laugh. "Are you going in?"

"I expect I best had. Thanks for coming, by the way. Once Harry gets a few beers inside him he'll forget all about the last bus."

"That's what Elizabeth thought." John Simpson patted

Calum's shoulder and walked into the hall. Inside, the music was louder but still mostly American based. Calum didn't mind. He could dance, though not well, and had more or less decided to stand to one side and observe.

He glanced back along the square, but whoever John Simpson had been talking to had gone. Instead, he saw another familiar figure, and the sight sent a sudden chill through him. A tall man dressed in a dark frock coat. Calum stared at the man, sure it must be someone else, not Alice Clare's companion. But if it was, he looked exactly the same. Except this man's face wore a pleasant expression totally unlike the scowl it had worn in Derbyshire. If it was the same man. As he continued to stare at him, Calum began to convince himself it couldn't be. There were many tall men around, and Hereford wasn't known for throwing out old frock coats that might offer some comfort when the air grew chill.

And then the man turned his head, and his eyes met Calum's, and he knew exactly who he was. As the man did in return. For a moment, something linked the two of them. Then the figure turned away and dissolved into the crowd, exactly as Richard could make himself disappear.

Calum scanned the faces, but the throng was thick and he couldn't tell if any of Alice Clare's other companions were amongst them. It was unlikely. Most had been too other-worldly to pass in civilised company.

He lit another cigarette and smoked it down while he continued to stand where he was. People moved past him like water around a rock in the nearby River Wye. How long he might have stayed there Calum had no idea, but he jumped, startled when a hand slid through his arm.

Elizabeth stood looking up at him, a smile on her face.

"I thought you had to work."

"Changed my mind, Cal. What were you staring at so intently? You looked like you'd seen a ghost."

"Maybe I did. I thought I saw that tall man from Alice Clare's house, but I must have been wrong. Are you coming inside? Can you dance?"

"I dance like an angel, and you might very well have seen him. One of the reasons I stayed behind was because I received a report from my watcher. Alice Clare was seen leaving her house on foot, together with a tall man. My man tried to follow them but caught his foot on a rock and twisted his ankle. By the time he managed to reach the village, they had gone. He asked around, but nobody had seen them. Or so they claimed."

"I suppose if they had transport, it could be them. What do you think?"

"It's possible. Which is another reason I came. Though I am looking forward to dancing with you."

"Wait until you've tried it. What are you going to do if it is her? It can't be a coincidence. She's followed us, hasn't she?"

Elisabeth tugged Calum towards the open door. The sound of the band grew as they entered the vast ballroom.

"If she has – and I agree it's the most likely explanation – it may be a good sign. Perhaps she has changed her mind and wants to help the war effort."

"Or come to cause trouble."

"Why would she do that? She was safe in that house with her companions. I think she might be curious. Keep your eyes peeled and look out for her or the tall man. I did a little research and have come to the conclusion he's her great-grandfather."

"How old must he be?"

"He died when he was forty-eight."

"So it can't be him."

"Can't it? Come on, Cal, dance with me, and later we can find a quiet spot somewhere and do some kissing. If you want to, that is?"

Calum shook his head. He wondered why Elizabeth wanted to distract him, but inside the ballroom, surrounded by a raucous crowd, he was willing to go along with her. And there was the promise of kissing.

CHAPTER SEVENTEEN

Calum danced with Elizabeth. They even kissed a little when they were sure none of the others were looking. Then Maria demanded Calum dance with her as well, and there might have been a little kissing involved there, too. By that time, Calum was too drunk to recall or even care. Drunk on the company more than the beer and cider, but drunk all the same. He danced with Dottie, who pressed her fulsome body against his in a way that hinted Harry might not be the only one of them she was interested in. And then he found Elizabeth again.

"Did I see you kissing Dottie?" she asked, her face showing a mock sternness.

"Only a little. I think she's kissing everyone."

"Just so long as you didn't enjoy yourself. Or when you kissed Maria. She's the one I'm more worried about, to be honest."

"Are you worried about me, then?"

"Do you need to ask after last night?"

"I thought I might. Don't people say relationships sparked by trauma rarely last?"

Elizabeth laughed. "Speaks the man who flew Lancs almost every night for two years. How many relationships did you have as a result of that trauma, Cal?"

Calum shrugged, and Elizabeth laughed again and clung against him. "It's all right, I'm not jealous. Do you want me to tell you about my conquests?"

"I think I'd rather you didn't."

Elizabeth's face lost all trace of humour. Calum turned to see what had caused the change, knowing even before he did so the reason.

Alice Clare stood ten feet away from them. A small space had opened around her despite the crush inside the dance hall. Her hair hung long to her waist, falling in shimmering waves. She wore a light print dress that clung enough to reveal a good figure beneath. She was radiantly beautiful, and Calum felt drawn to her even with what he knew about the woman.

"Ask her to dance," said Elizabeth.

"What?"

"You heard me. I want to know what she's is here for. Does she wants to join our group, or has she come for some other reason?" Elizabeth gave him a push. "Go on, I won't be jealous, even if you do have to kiss her."

Calum shivered at the thought but stepped towards the girl. No, she was a grown woman, though her age was difficult to calculate. Older than twenty. Younger than mid-thirties. Except every moment he looked at her he changed his mind. He glanced around, searching for her companion, but couldn't see him.

"Why are you here?" he asked when he was two feet from her. He smelled a faint perfume that reminded him of pine trees and heather.

"Aren't you goin' t'ask me to dance, first? It's been a long time since I danced with a handsome man."

"I'll go and see if I can find one, shall I?"

Alice smiled, transforming herself from beautiful to radiant, and all at once Calum wanted nothing more than to hold her body against his own.

He held out his hand and she took it, coming inside his arms as their feet began to move. Calum knew he was no great dancer, he could not turn off his critical mind and simply move. Elizabeth and the others had been too kind to mention it, but he knew it was true. Alice was different. It felt as if she was made for dancing, and her skill transferred to him as they twisted and spun. Some American soldiers were doing the jitterbug with women from the armament factory in front of the bandstand. As Alice drew him in that direction Calum lost all his inhibitions. Alice moved lithely under his touch. When he swung her through the air, her legs flew above her head and her body wrapped around his.

Space opened around them, then grew wider still. Others stopped dancing and formed a circle, clapping their hands, and the two of them set the world aflame with their movements. The band played louder, faster, extending the music until it filled Calum's entire being and any sense of himself was lost. His talent shimmered with a hundred possibilities, present and future melding into one so he knew exactly what Alice wanted him to do and made his moves at the exact moment.

And then the music stopped. Around them, the crowd applauded.

Alice stood inside Calum's arms, her softness pressed against him, her face turned up to his, and he knew what she wanted.

The band started up again and their moment in the sun passed into history.

Calum looked beyond her, searching for the others, for Elizabeth, but he couldn't see them. Instead, he saw the tall man standing against the wall, watching. His presence broke the mood.

"I'm still waiting for you to tell me why you're here," Calum said.

"Come outside with me. I need some fresh air, and I'll tell you then."

She took his hand, her touch eroding his will to resist. When Calum searched again the tall man had gone. Instead, he saw Elizabeth with the others beside her. She offered a nod, giving permission for him to discover what Alice Clare had come for; even if it meant the loss of himself.

Outside, Calum lit a cigarette then held the pack out to Alice. She shook her head. The daylight had fled while they were inside, but the crowd was just as dense.

"Let's find somewhere quieter, Calum."

"How do you know my name?"

"You told me, I'm sure you did." She laughed, the sound sweet. "Though I might've been upside down showin' my knickers at the time."

As they entered a narrow alleyway, still with people around them, Calum glanced back. He was relieved to see

Elizabeth at the head of the others, keeping watch. Keeping him safe. Except Calum wasn't sure he wanted to be kept safe.

It was as if Alice knew the city. She turned, turned again until they found themselves on a steep grassed bank above the silver ripples of the Wye. Alice sat on the slope and patted the ground beside her.

"When you came, I panicked. After you was gone, I thought about what your friend Elizabeth said. We talked about it 'tween us."

"You and the tall man?"

"And the others."

"What are they?"

"What they are don't matter. I make the decisions. I need to know what Elizabeth wants. Why she wants me."

"She'll have to tell you that herself," Calum said.

"But you know, don't you? I sense something inside you. I sense something inside all of you except the Major and Dottie."

"How do you know all our names?"

"Because I have a talent, just like you do." Her face was turned up to his. "I like you, Calum. You know I do. And I think you like me too, don't you?"

He was going to tell her no, he loved someone else, wondering if what he and Elizabeth shared was love or not. Before he could do so, he found himself kissing Alice without knowing which of them had made a move. She pressed against him, her fingers searching out his arousal. He rolled on top of her on the grass, the world, his life, slipping away in the heat of the moment.

"Leave her alone!"

The tall man stood above them.

"I wants him, pa-pa," said Alice. "I deserve him."

"No." The man came close. He leaned down without bending his knees and put his hands on either side of Calum's head. He lifted him to his feet. Then off his feet.

Calum kicked, but to no effect.

He saw Alice move away. And then he saw Elizabeth and the others approach, except he knew they could do nothing. One shake of the man's hands and Calum's neck would snap like a twig.

"Put him down." It was Maria who spoke, but it wasn't her usual soft voice. Her words were darker, stronger, and filled with power.

"Make me, girl." The man pressed his hands harder against Calum's face.

"I tell thee, demon, put my friend down and to do it now!" Maria's words filled the air like thunder. They wrapped around Calum and the man. He felt his will erode beneath a raw wind. He also felt the man's grip loosen.

And then Maria spoke four words in a language Calum had never heard. A language that might not have been spoken for millennia. All at once, he was free, rolling down the slope. When he got to his knees all he saw were his friends, and he came back to himself in a rush. The world shimmered, returning to normal. Past and future intertwined once more.

Calum rose and walked to Maria. He hugged her.

"What the bloody hell was that, girl?" said Harry.

"I want to know the answer to that as well," said Elizabeth.

"What was what?" said Maria.

"Those words you spoke. What language was it?"

Maria frowned. "No language. Well, only English. I told them to go away and leave Cal alone."

Elizabeth stared at her, but it was clear Maria was unaware of what she had done. Instead, she turned to Calum.

"Are you all right?"

"I think so. Where did they go?"

"Ran off," said John Simpson. "Want me to go after them?

"Under no circumstances." Elizabeth's voice was sharp. She turned back to Calum, put her arm through his and led him away. "What does Alice Clare want?"

"I think she's curious about us. Our visit sparked something, and I think she wants to find out where it might lead."

"Her talent is prodigious, but I'm not sure we can cope with something that powerful. That primeval. She's different to the rest of you." Elizabeth stopped and looked around. "Now, where did John park the car?"

"Don't ask me, I came on the bus." When Calum looked back, none of the others were in sight. He and Elizabeth had followed the riverbank. A stone bridge lay ahead, a set of steps leading up to the road, a house standing with its foundations almost in the water. "What are you going to do when she comes back?"

"Don't you mean if she comes back?"

"When," Calum said.

"What would you have done with her if her spirit mentor hadn't stopped you?"

"I don't know. Alice had me under her spell by then." He looked at Elizabeth. "I'm sorry – it wasn't something I wanted."

"No need to apologise. She has enormous power, but I'm not sure she's altogether in command of it. It was lucky she chose you and not someone like Harry, who's an easy touch. Did you know Maria could do what she did?"

Calum shook his head as they climbed the steps. "I'm not even sure Maria knew she could do it, or even knows what she did. What was it, anyway?"

"Do you recall me telling you about my theory that her talent might be linked to some kind of proto-language that is the root of all others? I think she used that. She spoke words of power. I've read a little about it but never experienced it. If that's what she did, then she tapped into some language older even than humanity. It has enormous power. It stopped that man from killing you, so it must have. The car is this way, I think." Elizabeth started along the road.

"I had everything under control," Calum said.

"Yes, it looked as though you did. Lucky we all came along, wasn't it?"

"Where do you think she's gone?"

"Back home, most likely. Or she may be waiting for us at the house."

"And if she is?"

"We need to get her away from her mentor."

"Is that what he is? I thought he was, I don't know, a ghost or something."

"He's an elemental. What Alice has is nothing like the

rest of you. I don't know whether I can work with her or not."

"But you'd like to try, wouldn't you?"

"I'd like to find out what she can do, but only when it's Alice on her own."

"Do you have any idea how you might separate them?"

Elizabeth laughed. "None at all. Ah, there's the car. Quick." She dragged Calum into the doorway of a large house, pushed him against the stone wall and kissed him long and hard. When she came up for air, she said, "I needed to do that before we reached the others."

"Do you think they've guessed?"

"Guessed what?"

Calum watched her walk away, then followed at a distance. He saw the others catch sight of Elizabeth and wave. Harry had his arm around Dottie, and she leaned back against him. She looked as if she was enjoying the attention. It had been some night, Calum thought and wondered whether the strangeness would continue or not.

CHAPTER EIGHTEEN

Calum stood outside Carden House in the chill of midnight and watched as John Simpson drove the Rover into the garage. The dim headlamps briefly illuminated the Matchless, but the engine had been removed by Harry and lay in neatly arranged piles on the workbench. Calum scanned the grounds, looking for Alice Clare or her companion. He saw nothing but knew half an army could be hidden in the darkness. He recalled the feeling as the man's hands grasped his head and knew he had come close to dying tonight. His mood was lifted when he heard Dottie give a sultry laugh. He turned to see her dragging Harry around the side of the house to where she had a small suite of rooms off the kitchen. John Simpson offered a nod as he passed, and then Calum stood alone. He wrapped his arms around himself and wondered whether what he had got himself into might be even more dangerous than sitting in a Lancaster over Nazi Germany.

"I'd like a word if you're not going to bed right now."

Calum turned to see Elizabeth standing in the

doorway. She looked stunning, but he had no expectations, despite the kiss. Not after what he had done with Alice. It felt like a betrayal, even as he knew he'd had no choice in the matter. Alice had controlled him completely. She had wanted him to make love to her. The question was, why?

"I don't think I can sleep yet."

"There's whisky in my office, and the games room is empty. We won't be disturbed. Maria and Richard have gone upstairs together, and you know where Harry is."

"I hope he doesn't start getting any ideas," Calum said.

"I think he already has, but Dottie knows what she's getting into. The minute her Bert comes home, Harry will be out on his ear. At least Harry doesn't strike me as the kind of man to be heartbroken."

"Plenty more women in Hereford," Calum said. "There were a lot more women than men at the dance."

"They're from the big munitions works. Pretty much everyone there is female. Come inside, Cal. I promise not to attack you."

"Well, if that's the case..."

Elizabeth grinned as she turned away.

When Elizabeth returned, clutching a bottle of single malt and two tumblers, Calum was stretched out in the same easy chair from which he had demonstrated his talent to the others all those weeks before.

Elizabeth took the couch, then patted the seat beside her to indicate what she wanted. Calum rose and went across. She poured the whisky and handed a glass to him.

"Here's to the future, Cal." She clinked his glass. "Perhaps you can tell me what that future holds."

He drained his glass and held it out for her to refill.

"I know what I'd like it to be, but it's not up to me, is it?"

Elizabeth didn't take the hint by professing her undying love, which came as no surprise.

"I wasn't going to go into Hereford tonight but I'm glad I did. We're a unit, Cal, aren't we? We fought together tonight, all of us."

He smiled. "Unit-13."

"Yes, Unit-13. And I think we have our first mission. Our first real test. I made a call earlier and found out who rang while we were away and what they want from us. That's what I was working on when you came into my office. That and Alice. Do you really think she's done a runner?"

Calum shrugged. The late hour was starting to affect him, that and the lack of sleep the night before and a good single malt, not to mention the presence of a beautiful woman at his side. His aberration with Alice Clare was fading, as if it had been nothing more than a dream. He knew it was a protective mechanism but welcomed it all the same.

"What mission?"

"Something's gone missing, and they want us to find it."

Calum laughed. "Can't they get their hands on somebody better suited than us? What is this missing thing?"

"I don't know, but I get the impression it's so top secret we're not actually allowed to know what we're meant to be looking for."

"Won't that make the job a touch difficult?"

"I think they've tried everyone else and failed."

"So they thought of us? It feels to me like being the last boy picked for the football team."

"We can do it, whatever it is," said Elizabeth.

"Where did this info come from? Carlton?"

"Via him, yes. I think he might even have suggested us."

"Maybe he wants proof we can do what you claim," Calum said.

"Possibly. I got some other information as well. Do you remember me telling you I was looking for someone else?"

"Other than Alice?"

"Of course other than Alice. She just cropped up."

"From where? Was that Carlton, too? Do you think he knew how dangerous she was and that's why we were sent? I don't trust the man. He doesn't care about us, only himself. Typical toff."

"He's our boss, Cal. I do what he tells me. Anyway, I also had word that someone has the location of this Bill Harrison I want to talk to. I'm hoping he's less dangerous than Alice. I wish I knew where the hell she's gone to."

"Hell itself, I hope."

Elizabeth filled his glass again and this time he sipped instead of draining it. The amber liquid made his lips tingle, eroding the fear that had clung to him. He reached out with his free hand and took Elizabeth's, pleased when she didn't pull away. He thought he could get used to being close to her this way. Long evenings in front of a log fire. Kids, maybe. He smiled, knowing he was getting ahead of himself.

"So, when do we ride out to save the country from whatever it is we know nothing about?"

"First thing Tuesday. They wanted us tomorrow, but I told them it had to be Tuesday because I want to talk with Bill Harrison first. I'm keen that we prove ourselves. Nervous, too. This is why I intend to work you all hard tomorrow, so we're ready for whatever is needed."

"It might be too soon."

"I don't think so. You saw what Maria did tonight. And I know you can push yourself further than you could when you came here. Same with Richard. And haven't you noticed the difference Harry made to John's car? It feels twice as fast as it did, and it was pretty fast before. John once told me he'd taken it all the way up to seventy. Now, I think he could reach a hundred."

"I hope I'm not with him when he tries. I'm glad we're not rushing off in the morning. I don't think any of us are going to be in any fit state."

"Which means it's probably time for bed."

Calum put his empty glass down but made no move to stand.

"Your bed, or am I consigned to my lonely cell?"

Elizabeth stared straight ahead, not meeting his eyes. "I do like you, Cal. I like you an awful lot, you know I do. But I'm your senior officer. What we did could get us both drummed out of the Service."

"So I have to wait until the war ends, do I?" Calum hated the way his voice sounded.

"We might all be dead next week," Elizabeth said, which was no answer at all. She rose and left the room.

Calum stared at the bottle of single malt. He reached out and poured himself another good measure and took it upstairs. He thought of Harry and Dottie in her room. Thought of Maria and Richard. He suspected he knew what they were all up to. He felt bereft, without knowing why he should. Calum wondered how much of what he and Elizabeth had shared was due to their mutual fear, their need for comfort, as any concept such as love.

He stood at the window, staring out at the night, searching once again for Alice Clare and not finding her. Perhaps he would never see her again, which suited him just fine.

He woke some time later to the sound of the telephone in the hall ringing. He lay on his back, wondering if he ought to go downstairs and answer it. Then it stopped.

Calum turned over and went back to sleep.

"How many of us are going on this jaunt?" Calum asked as he pushed the door of Elizabeth's office shut behind him. She had asked to see him alone, leaving the others to discuss the news she had given them over a late Sunday breakfast. Calum set his mug of tea on the desk before taking a seat. Elizabeth picked the mug up and placed a beer mat beneath it.

"This is going to be no jaunt, it's deadly serious, so you tell me, Cal." Elizabeth had brought her own breakfast with her, a single slice of buttered toast spread with local jam. Her tea was in a fine china cup set on a saucer.

"Tell it to me again, but this time include the things you left out when you told the others"

"What makes you think I left anything out?"

"Because what you told us doesn't make enough sense to have us scramble this way. You said some information had gone missing. That's work the Service can do perfectly well on its own. They don't need our skills. I don't believe they would even welcome our skills." He watched Elizabeth's face, her passivity, her closed expression. "I take it they don't know what Unit-13 does, do they?"

"They know about us because we're part of the Service. But only a few at the top know exactly what we do."

"Alice Clare knew about us, and she's a civilian. I assume whoever you use to watch out for people like us know what we do, not to mention that buffoon Carlton. Does he also know about this assignment? It seems to me for an organisation that's meant to be secret there are too many people in the know."

"I had a phone call early this morning from my watcher in Derbyshire. Alice has returned to her house, so we can forget about her for now." Elizabeth spoke as if she hadn't heard him.

"Are you sure about that?"

"I'm assuming she's run back home, so she's no longer our concern."

"Let sleeping snakes lie?"

"Something like that, yes. This new assignment hasn't come from Carlton, who appears to have gone quiet since he came down here. Which, as far as I'm concerned, is a good thing."

"Where did the request come from? It seems strange if he's meant to be our supervisor that he wouldn't know."

"He'd have been in touch if he did, and not a dicky bird. This came from someone higher up. Seems he heard about the missing intelligence and wants it found as soon as. I thought they meant documents had been stolen, but they were careful only to use the term information, so I'm not sure if we're talking about theft or something else. Whatever it is, the government are none too pleased the Service hasn't been able to find out who took it."

"Why turn to us?"

"Because they are desperate. I've not been told what this information is, but it has to be pretty important if they're asking us, the organisation of last resort."

"It does show a little desperation, I agree." Calum meant it as a joke, but Elizabeth seemed to take him seriously.

"We can do this, Cal. There's nobody like you or the others. You know there isn't."

"Not here, perhaps, but we saw what Alice can do, as well as those people in Russia. You've dropped hints about the Germans and Americans, too."

"Except only one of those is our enemy."

"At the moment." Cal wondered which of the others he meant. "How high up is this contact of yours?"

"You know who I mean. In fact, you're going to meet the man in a day or two. He asked to be introduced to some of us, and I thought you might be the most presentable. Winnie has an open mind, unlike some of the others who think they're running this war."

"So it is him," Calum said. "Do you call him that to his face – Winnie?"

"I'm still waiting to hear what you think. How many should go?" Elizabeth gave his question the lack of attention it deserved. She took a delicate bite from the corner of her toast and washed it down with a sip of tea.

"Everyone," Calum said. "We don't know what we'll come up against or what talents we might need. You said the Service tried to uncover what happened. Do they also know we are being brought in?"

"They know somebody is, but not that it's us. I'll have to think of some lie to tell them if they ask what and who we are."

"It's going to make our job even harder."

"I trust you," said Elizabeth. "And agreed, all four of you must go, and of course I will be there. How long is it going to take, do you think?"

"You don't expect me to know the answer to that, do you? I don't even know what we're looking for. All you mentioned was unknown information." Calum shook his head in frustration. "I have to assume it's important if the powers that be are desperate enough to call on us. Do you have any idea what it concerns?"

Elizabeth looked at Calum for a long time, and he knew she was deciding whether or not to tell him the truth. When she finally responded, he had no clearer idea which she was telling him.

"I know little more than I told you. I'm hoping when we see Winnie he might tell us more. As much as he is willing to. Wheels within wheels, Cal, you know what it's like."

"Secrets," Calum said.

"Important secrets."

"Three months ago, I would assume we might be talking about the invasion plans. Now, I have no idea. We all know the way the war is going these days. It's going to take time, maybe even a couple of years, but there's only one end in sight now."

"What if the information that's been stolen could change that?"

"A weapon? I've heard rumours of a bomb that's a city-killer, but I don't believe it. Rockets? Jet engines? They're already here. The Nazis are ahead of us on most of that already and it's not making much of a difference."

Elizabeth leaned forward, almost upsetting her teacup, which she moved to one side. "Perhaps we may never know what this information is, Cal. If that's the case, then fine. We don't have to know what it is to expose who has it, only that we have to. Boxes inside boxes. You know how it is."

"I'm getting sick and tired of how it is."

"Which is pointless. None of us can do anything to change the situation. But we can do our duty. How we do it is the question. Do you have any ideas at all?"

"You know more than me. You call each of us in here at least once a day, sometimes more, and tease out everything inside our heads. You know more about our abilities than we do ourselves. So tell me, how are we going to do it?"

Elizabeth gave a brief smile. "Once we know what it is they want us to do?"

"There is that, of course."

"Richard will be key. He can gain access to places the rest of us can't. And then there's Maria. Has she spoken to you at all?"

"She's said a few things: auras, weird stuff like that. And the telepathy, and then that thing she did last night. Was she not supposed to say anything?"

"It's up to her what she tells you, but I believe it

important we all know as much about each other as possible. Tell me how your own talent has changed since you came here, Cal."

"You know that better than me." He held a hand up as Elizabeth objected, knowing he was being stubborn on purpose. "All right, here's how I see it. I can see the future more clearly than I could, thanks to the things you've taught me. Mostly because you persuaded me it was possible. There will be a limit, but I haven't reached it yet, and I don't know where it might be."

"I agree, though I have an idea on that. I'm sure you'll discover it yourself soon enough."

"You're not going to tell me?"

Elizabeth shook her head. "But I am going to tell you about the others. First, Richard. He already had excellent control over his ability when he came here, but he has improved, like the rest of you. I believe he can infiltrate himself into places nobody else can. He also has some other talent we're still exploring."

"I noticed last night that he was more present than I've ever seen him."

"There's no point being a ghost if people can tell you are one. Richard is learning to be as present as any normal person. It helps prevent suspicion. He is also learning how to disappear even more deeply than he already can, as well as exploring the means that allow him to do so. There are a few other things, too."

"Do you mean the life-force thing?"

"Has told you about it?"

"Maria did."

Elizabeth gave a strained smile. "Why doesn't that surprise me?"

"Maria's got no secrets, either about her own talents or anyone else's. She's an open book."

"I believe she may still carry a flame for you."

"Which is unreciprocated." Calum stared into Elizabeth's eyes until he was sure she got the message. "Do you have any idea how Richard can do what he does?"

"None, even though it's my job to know. However, I believe I have managed to enhance all of your talents. Can you explain how you do what you can?"

Calum laughed. "No. What about Harry?"

"Harry, as you know, can be difficult. When he came here, he was the most resistant to the idea that what he possesses is anything more than the ordinary skill possessed by any mechanic."

"And now?"

"These last few weeks, he's come around. As you already know, there are no keys to any of the rooms here."

Calum frowned, thinking the comment odd. "Other than yours, of course." He was pleased when his words brought a blush to her cheeks.

"Yes, well, with good reason perhaps. I wanted to talk to Harry the other day and went to his room. He called me in, but I found the door locked. Which is impossible. I heard him approach and he opened the door. I looked for a key, but there wasn't one, so I confronted him. He made some excuse that the door sticks, but I didn't accept that. In the end, he showed me. He put his hand over the lock mechanism for only a second. When he took it away, he told me to try opening the door, and I couldn't. When I touched the lock, it was warm."

"My watch was warm when he passed it back to me that first night," Calum said.

"I saw your reaction. It seems Harry generates some heat by what he does. I asked him what else he could do, and he showed me a few things. He can make solid metal bend like plasticine. He can disable a gun simply by holding it. The other day, I discovered he can achieve some of these things without even touching the object. So Harry will be useful. You will all be useful, but not in ways we might know about yet. That's why I believe in you all."

"And Maria?" Calum asked.

Elizabeth took another bite of her toast but pulled a face when she sipped her tea. It had gone cold.

"You are all magicians, but Maria might be the most amazing of you. When she came here, all she believed was that she had an uncanny ability for learning languages. I tested her, brought in a Polish flyer from the base, another from Kenya, and watched how she learned to speak their languages. Maria listened, of course, but listening isn't enough. Between us, we teased the truth out. Maria learns so fast because she can read the thoughts inside people's heads. Now she accepts that talent we can work on it to strengthen it." She looked at Calum for a long time. "You know, I'm wondering what the rest of you can do we don't yet know about."

CHAPTER TWENTY

Over dinner, Elizabeth filled them in on the arrangements she had spent several hours organising. Harry, Richard and Maria would take the train from Hereford to the small village of Bletchley. She placed three rail passes on the table.

Harry reached out and took one, examined it. "These are for Tuesday. And they're third-class."

"Afraid that's all I could get my hands on at late notice."

"Are you keeping the first-class ones for Cal and yourself, like you did when you took your little jaunt to Shrewsbury?"

"I'm taking Cal to meet someone else first thing in the morning. Our transport will be even less comfortable than yours, though admittedly a little swifter."

"Why can't John drive us to wherever this place is?"

"Because I have another job for him. If he finishes that, he can come and meet us."

Which is why, at a little after eight the following

morning Calum, Elizabeth and Harry took the car the short distance to the training base and stood looking at a Miles Magister being pulled from a hangar and left to stand on the grass. The small truck that had drawn the plane out drove off, leaving them alone.

"How the devil did you wangle this?" Harry was there to take the car back so the others could reach Hereford station the following morning.

"I have my ways."

"Who did you have to sleep with?" Harry walked closer, bending his knees to check the undercarriage and the single twin-bladed propellor.

Someone had painted the fuselage a strange yellow and brown camouflage colour, and the open cockpit gave the aircraft's age away. Most of the newer models had an enclosed one.

Calum glanced at Elizabeth and saw she had come prepared, dressed in a heavy jacket and wool trousers, her hair caught in a scarf. It would have been helpful if she'd told him this is how they would be travelling. He wondered if he could borrow a flight suit from somebody. If not, he was likely to reach whatever destination she had in mind frozen to the controls.

"It's an antique," said Harry. "I hope it runs all right. You want to start it up so I can check her over, Cal?"

"If I can remember how." He looked around until he found a wooden ladder on two wheels and brought it over.

"According to your records, you trained in one exactly the same as this," said Elizabeth.

"That was in 1939."

"You know what they say. Just like riding a bike."

"Not quite. How far do we need to go, and at what altitude? I could have done with a little warning."

"Look in the boot of the car. I brought the flight suit you arrived in. Remember that?"

"Start her up first," said Harry. He made sure the chocks were firm against the tyres to prevent the plane from moving, then watched as Calum manoeuvred himself into the front cockpit.

He surveyed the simple instrument cluster, its familiarity some small comfort. He touched the controls, tapped the fuel gauge until satisfied it read full, then turned on the fuel pump before lifting himself up so he could see Harry.

"Is there a cartridge loaded?"

Harry went to a panel on the side and opened it. "Looks that way. Is it electrical or mechanical?"

"Judging by the age of this thing, it'll be mechanical. You want to fire her up? Make sure you stand to the side in case it blows back."

"Not on me she won't."

Harry reached in, his hand cupping the mechanism, then pressed a trigger. A loud bang sounded and the explosive charge ejected into the cylinders to turn the engine. Calum pushed the throttle forward, rechecking the fuel gauge as he did so. The needle swung wildly, but that was nothing new. Every one he had ever seen did the same.

The engine caught and settled into a steady rhythm. Calum listened, trying to judge the sound. It seemed a little rough, but that might only be the cold start. He stood again and climbed down, leaving the engine to idle. Harry remained at the side of the plane, his hand still inside the open flap. Calum watched, knowing better than to ask what he was doing. Anyone else would lose fingers, or worse, but he knew nothing mechanical would ever injure Harry. As he watched, he heard the engine settle and grow smoother. That was also Harry's doing.

Calum went to the car and opened the boot. There was one small overnight bag, a flight suit, and two leather helmets. He slipped off his shoes and pulled the suit on, zipping it up the front, then tied his shoes again and carried both the bag and two helmets to Elizabeth. He handed one to her and set the bag on the ground.

"You're going to have to hold this on your knee the whole time," he said. "I'll hand it to you once you're settled. These birds don't come equipped for luggage."

"Which is why I packed only enough for one night. I'm afraid you must make do with what you've got, Cal."

"A little notice would have come in handy. Where are we headed, anyway?"

"East."

Cal laughed. "How far east?" Though he believed he knew.

"Northolt." Elizabeth tucked her hair inside the leather helmet and seated it snugly. "I take it you can fly that far?"

"Have you ever flown in something as small as this before?" Calum asked. "It's going to be bumpy if you're not used to it."

"I've flown in crates a lot older than this one, so I think I can cope." Elizabeth climbed the ladder and stepped into the rear cockpit. Usually, the trainer sat in the back seat while the student took the front to make it feel like they were in command. No doubt that same arrangement suited Elizabeth.

Calum nodded to Harry, who removed his hand from inside the open compartment and clipped the cover back on.

"She'll run sweet long enough for what you need," he said.

Calum shook his hand, warm from being against the engine. He picked up the overnight bag, climbed the ladder and handed it to Elizabeth. He looked at her a moment. At the coarse jacket and trousers, at the helmet, and thought she looked more beautiful than he had ever seen her. Calum wondered what she thought about him as he slipped into the confines of the front cockpit. Something had changed between them since what had happened with Alice Clare, and he knew he would have to get over his sense of rejection.

Harry pulled the ladder away and jerked the chocks from under the wheels.

Calum opened the throttle and checked the controls again. He looked sideways at the ailerons as he moved the stick and pedals, back at the tail. Satisfied, he fed more fuel to the cylinders and the small plane began to move.

He knew morning training flights would typically be preparing for take-off and landing. This morning, the other planes remained in their hangars, and he could see nobody. He shook his head at the number of favours Elizabeth must have called in for such a thing to happen.

The windsock showed a breeze from the south-west, so he taxied to the eastern end of the runway. Then, before he could overthink what he was about to do and how long since he had last piloted a small plane, he pushed the throttle all the way forward.

The grass runway was pitted and uneven, and the small plane bounced along, twitching. Calum used his feet on the pedals to keep a tall tree directly ahead, and when he judged their speed high enough, he drew back on the stick. The wheels left the grass, and immediately the bouncing stopped. He let the plane rise to a hundred feet, then pulled back harder. The open cockpit buffeted him, the wind growing fierce, but the small perspex panel kept most of it away.

He banked left, bringing them around a hundred and eighty degrees. The house that formed their base appeared to the left. Calum waggled the wings just in case anyone was watching.

He glanced across at the instruments as the plane rose, almost flying itself. He discovered there was no radio, an annoyance but unsurprising. What gave him slightly more pause was the lack of any means of communication at all. There should be a socket to insert a wire from his helmet so the trainer and trainee could communicate. He found the socket but no means of connecting to it. Calum cursed himself for not checking before they took off.

Ahead, he found the bulk of the Malvern Hills and steered a course slightly south of them. He was hoping to pick up the A40 and follow it all the way to London.

When the altimeter showed six thousand feet he levelled off and eased the fuel to the engine. The howl of wind lessened a little. The engine noise became a roar rather than a cacophony. He twisted around in his seat to check on Elizabeth. She was looking over the side at the tiny houses, trees and roads below. Calum tapped on her screen to attract her attention and made a gesture with his thumb to ask if she was all right. Elizabeth put a thumb up in return and grinned, her face flushed with the pleasure of flight. As Calum turned back and checked the dials, he smiled. He had grown used to climbing into the belly of a Lancaster as it fought to grab enough air to rise into the sky. This plane was a different creature altogether. He banked for no reason other than he could, testing out the controls. He knew the Miles Magister was used to train Spitfire and Hurricane pilots, designed to offer an experience almost on a par with those fighters. Those who went on from training to fly the faster planes said the transition was virtually seamless. He wondered what Elizabeth's reaction would be if he attempted a barrel roll. Best not, he thought, or she might lose her overnight bag.

He banked right, picking out the silver ribbon of the Severn estuary to the south, the smoke-stain of Gloucester ahead. He brought them down five hundred feet as they crossed the city, the docks busy with men loading squat freighters to take goods upstream along the river for transfer to the canal network. Cheltenham passed on his left, the rising Cotswolds beyond, and then he picked out the winding A40 heading east.

An hour later, Calum performed a low pass over the airfield at Northolt, this one far busier than the one they had left from. He saw Hurricanes and Spitfires spread across the grass, watched as six rose into the air in formation and headed south. They showed him the correct direction to land in, so he flew another few minutes east, then banked hard to the left and let the plane drift towards the ground. Fifteen feet up, he throttled back the engine and drew the stick toward himself, waiting for the wings to lose lift. They banged down harder than he wanted, but at least they were down.

Calum taxied around the edge of the runway, looking for somewhere to park the plane. He saw a black car pulled up in front of a small hangar, a man waving his arms in their direction.

Calum eased himself out, only as he did so aware of how stiff his body had become. He offered a hand to Elizabeth, who took it and drew herself up as though she had been sitting in a comfortable armchair. They waited as the man who had waved brought a ladder, then Calum took the bag from Elizabeth and allowed her to climb to the ground first.

She was already seated in the back of the car when he got there, her small bag in the middle as he slipped inside. The driver said nothing. He started the engine and circled the runway before pulling onto the same road Calum had followed. This time it would take them most of the way to Westminster.

Elizabeth glanced at the man in front, then leaned across and touched the back of Calum's hand. He leaned closer so she could whisper in his ear.

"That was so exciting," she said, her breath warm. "Thank you, Cal." She kissed his cheek. "I have to admit I was a little worried, but your record showed you were one of their better pilots. How did you end up in Lancasters?"

"Good question. If I ever find an answer to that, you'll be the first to know."

Elizabeth's hand remained on his, a sense of closeness enveloping them which Calum attempted to dismiss. He had been here before, only to suffer disappointment. He drew his hand back to his lap and turned to stare through the window at the grey, battered landscape of the country's capital city. He wondered how long after the war ended it would take to rebuild, and what that rebuilding would look like.

CHAPTER TWENTY-ONE

Calum expected the driver to take them to the House of Commons. He only realised his naivety when the car turned into Horse Guards Parade while the bulk of the Commons still lay ahead, then right into King Charles Street. The driver pulled up at a nondescript door where a single private stood on guard. Calum climbed out first and offered his hand to Elizabeth, but she ignored it.

Elizabeth approached the private and spoke a few words. He turned and rapped on the door. When it opened, she walked through. After a moment, Calum followed, picking up the overnight bag she had left on the pavement.

They entered a corridor strung at intervals with bare lightbulbs. Nobody was assigned to them, but Elizabeth appeared to know exactly where she was going. She turned several times before coming to a staircase that led down. Without a word, she descended. Unpainted concrete walls lay on four sides as the stairs turned at right angles, always descending. Another guarded door barred their way at the bottom, but this too opened at a few brief words. Beyond, the atmosphere transformed. Men and women moved purposefully, most in uniform, some in civilian clothes. A few glanced in their direction as they passed, but none challenged them. Calum assumed once someone had made it this far, they were meant to be here.

They passed a large room with maps stuck to a board, an enormous table taking up most of the floor space. The ceilings were low, a palpable sense of being underground making Calum wonder what it must be like to live your working life down here.

The corridors grew less busy as they progressed. Elizabeth turned into a doorless room where a secretary sat behind a desk. A tall black typewriter sat in front of her, clattering away at speed. She looked up with a smile of recognition, rose and came around the desk to kiss Elizabeth on both cheeks.

"So nice to see you again," she said. "He's expecting you, but whether he's dressed yet is another matter. Ask if he wants breakfast. I'll organise some tea for you both; you've had a long trip, I expect."

Calum moved closer to Elizabeth as they entered a narrow corridor. "How well known are you down here?"

"Oh, pretty well. In this area, at least. Most of these people have been working down here for the duration. It takes skill and knowledge which are too valuable to waste."

A further door admitted them to a second secretary who tapped on a door behind her and disappeared through it. She was gone only a moment before returning.

"In you go, Elizabeth, he's expecting you. I should warn you he's still in bed, and you might need a gas mask because he's got a cigar going."

A sense of unreality clung to Calum as he followed Elizabeth into a compact room. There was a desk, an easy chair, and a narrow bed on which lay the Prime Minister of Great Britain, Winston Churchill. He had a cigar set between his lips and was reading a stack of papers, dropping each to the floor as he finished. He glanced up and took the cigar from his mouth.

"Elizabeth, my dear, how wonderful to see you again. Come and give an old man a kiss."

Elizabeth obliged. When she stepped away, Churchill looked past her at Calum.

"Is he one of them?" he asked.

"He is. Calum Auger. Used to be a bomb-aimer, but now he works for me."

"Lucky bugger is all I can say. How did you like flying… what was it, Lancs, Mosquitos?"

"Lancasters, sir."

Churchill smiled. "Polite, too, unlike half the bastards down here. What can he do?"

Calum's sense of strangeness increased. Elizabeth was not only known down here, but she was also on first-name terms with the Prime Minister. The man who had saved the country from humiliation and defeat. A man who seemed to know exactly why she had brought together their small group.

"Cal can see into the future, Winnie."

"Can he, be damned? Bloody useful talent, I expect." His gaze met Calum's. "Came in handy up there, I expect."

"Yes, sir."

"How good is he?" Churchill returned his attention to Elizabeth. Calum didn't blame him. She was far easier on the eye, even in the clothes she wore.

"I think he's going to be useful," she said. "As are the others. The last time I was here I mentioned another man I was looking for. Do you recall?"

"You know me, old girl, I forget nothing."

"Other than breakfast," said Elizabeth. "Pam mentioned you hadn't eaten yet."

Churchill waved the papers he was holding. "Too much bloody work, my dear, more and more bumph all the time. I'll grab a sandwich or something for lunch and eat tonight. Need to get to the House by noon, so we'd better get on with business. I tracked down this William Harrison – not personally, of course; I had someone do it for me. One of the perks of being PM, what? I've got a note of where he works if I can find it..." He looked around, then threw the bedclothes back and stood up. He wore only pyjamas, and the buttons on the trousers were undone so that a thatch of coarse hair showed. Churchill appeared oblivious. Calum saw Elizabeth avert her eyes.

"In the desk somewhere... where did I put it? Only got the info a couple of days ago, hence my message to you." He opened a drawer. Closed it. Opened another. "Ah, here we go." He handed a slip of paper to Elizabeth. "You'll find him there if I'm not mistaken. Have the rest of your crew gone ahead?"

Elizabeth read the note, then nodded. "They'll be there in the morning, Winnie. We'll track this man down and join them, more likely tomorrow than today."

"Don't spend too long buggering about if you don't find him, my dear, there's still a war to win. I need to know who's spilling our bloody secrets." He glanced at Calum. "You trust him, I take it?"

"Implicitly, as I do the entire team."

"Good. Good." Churchill came across to Calum and held his hand out. "It's a pleasure to meet you, Flight Sergeant Auger. Elizabeth will brief you on what's gone missing, but I want you to know its recovery is of the highest importance." He glanced at Elizabeth. "Take care of him, my dear. We've lost too many good young men already."

She smiled. "I'll do my very best. There is another matter I hoped to raise with you."

"Is there? Can't it wait?"

"I expect it can, but you need to know Sir Edward is turning into a bit of a problem, and now he appears to have gone AWOL. I'd like to get someone else assigned to oversee our operation."

Churchill laughed. "He always has been a problem. I thought assigning him to your group might keep him out of everyone else's hair, but it seems I was wrong. Is it urgent?"

"Not as urgent as our mission."

"Then save it for another day. Perhaps you and Calum would like to come for dinner one evening, once you've sorted out this matter. You can tell me again why you were so keen to set up this Unit-13. I've put a lot of trust in you, my dear. Don't let me down, and find out where that information has gone. There is no need for me to state how important it might be to the war effort. So get to it. Get to it."

Churchill turned away, got back into bed and picked up the discarded papers. They had been dismissed. Elizabeth stopped in the outer office and asked to use the telephone. Calum stood beside the door, waiting, trying to come to terms with where he was, and failing.

"Say again?" said Elizabeth, then, "Do you have a home address for him?" Another pause. "What?" Elizabeth held the telephone out. "Be a dear, Pam, and tell this jobsworth where I'm calling from, then get him to give you Bill Harrison's home address."

She turned to Calum while the secretary pulled rank on whoever was on the other end. "He's not been at work for two days. Apparently, it's usually difficult to get him to stay away."

"Has he done a runner, do you think?"

"Strange if he has because I got a message he wanted to talk to me."

"Cold feet, perhaps?"

"Possibly. Damn it." She turned as the secretary held up a slip of paper.

On the street, the car that had brought them was gone.

"Where does this man live?" Calum asked.

Elizabeth glanced at the scrap of paper still clutched in her hand. "Shooters Hill. Someplace called Mayday Gardens." She gave a shake of her head. "Sounds like a call for help if I ever heard one."

"Any idea where it is?"

"South of the river if it's Shooters Hill." She glanced around as if searching for something, but it seemed she was only thinking. "A 161 or 132 bus should get us there if we cross the river. Come on, the day's passing. Looks like we might have to stay in town tonight after all. It's a good hour or more to this place, even after we find a bus going the right way."

Calum fell into step beside her. "I didn't think to bring any money."

Elizabeth smiled. "Not to worry, I did."

They crossed Westminster bridge and had to run to catch a number 161 just as it was pulling away. They climbed to the top deck and fell into their seats, laughing. The tension and strangeness of the day had leached half the strength from Calum. He stared through the window at rows of terraced houses that stood like rotten teeth. Here and there, a molar had come loose where a bomb or doodlebug had done its worst. He felt his moment of good humour fade.

"What do we do if he's not there?"

"Go back to the Royal Arsenal where he works and see if they have any idea where he might have gone," said Elizabeth. "But with luck, we'll find him sitting at home nursing a summer cold. We can always live in hope, can't we?" Elizabeth reached out and took Calum's hand. She rested it in her lap, cradled inside hers like they were a newly married couple.

If only, he thought, then wondered if that was really what he wanted. He was beginning to wonder if Elizabeth wasn't turning out to be too complicated for him.

It was a long walk from where the bus dropped them, and they strode out as if hurrying home for their lunch. The streets were quiet, only an occasional housewife off to the shops with a basket to break the monotony.

Mayday Gardens turned out to be a 1930s block of almost identical semis arranged on a curved road, their gardens backing on to those of others behind. Number 65 stood to the right of its neighbour, pebble-dashed and neat. A driveway led to a wooden garage. Beyond lay a back garden given almost entirely over to the growing of vegetables. Half a dozen sleek hens picked their way among rows of beans and peas.

Elizabeth gave Calum a nod, indicating he should do the talking.

"Does he know about us?" Calum asked.

"Not as such, but he definitely has talent, and he's not stupid. He'll have worked out why I wanted him when we talked before. I'm hoping he's ready to change his mind and join us now."

Calum opened the metal gate and walked along the short pathway to knock on the front door.

"If he asked to see you, why has he disappeared? Did you tell him you were coming down, and that's why he's scarpered?"

"I made sure he had no idea we were coming. If he's missing, it's for some reason of his own, nothing to do with me. We can ask him why if we ever find him."

"What is it he can do? His talent? Did you say it was something about hearing conversation in bricks, or was that someone else?" He was learning the language of their strangeness.

"No, you remember right. It's no odder than the rest of you, and it would be bloody useful about now."

Calum knocked again, but there was no movement

inside the house. He was starting to fear they had come on a wild goose chase.

"Put Bill Harrison in a room where secrets have been spoken and he can hear what the words are," said Elizabeth. "The more recent the conversation, the more he can hear."

Calum knocked a third time, harder, but with little hope. He thought about what Elizabeth had said and knew she was right. They were all strange in their own individual ways.

"What secrets?" he asked.

"If we knew that, we wouldn't need him, but something has gone missing from somewhere it shouldn't have." Elizabeth shook her head. "The people telling me all this are too vague. It doesn't make any sense. But whatever it is is so top secret I haven't even been told what the information concerns. Not even a squeak of a hint, and that's unusual."

Calum knew Elizabeth was far closer to the wheels of power than she had let on so far. On first-name terms with Churchill. Privy to top-secret information – even if not all of it. For a woman still to turn thirty, that was some track record.

"This is a waste of time. He's not home, is he?"

"We'll have to go back and see if his works knows where he might have got to. I was stupid thinking he'd be here. We'll do that as soon as we've taken a quick peek around back."

Calum looked around at the quiet street. "Are we going to break in?"

Elizabeth gave a smile. "Well, it is a matter of national security. I think they might expect it of us."

"And if someone calls the police?"

"I think I can handle the police."

Yes, Calum thought, you probably can.

CHAPTER TWENTY-TWO

There was a recently built lean-to at the rear of the house that enclosed the kitchen door. The door to the lean-to was unlocked. The door to the kitchen was not. Calum gave it a thump with his shoulder but, though the glass rattled, it remained shut.

"I could break the glass," he said, "but then he'd know we've been here. Does it matter?"

"Probably not," said Elizabeth, "but give me a minute. Take a look down the garden and in the garage, see if there's a car in there. If not, he might have done a runner."

The garage had a padlock on it, but it wasn't locked, and the doors swung open with only a minor complaint from unoiled hinges. The interior was empty. It smelled strongly of the pitch used to waterproof the wooden walls, and petrol. A recent oil stain on the concrete floor told Calum it had recently contained a vehicle. Finding fuel might be a problem if Bill Harrison intended a long journey, but he could have been saving his ration for a while. Calum scanned the floor, finding cleaner places where cans might have sat. Four of them, which explained the smell of petrol.

The bench at the far end held the usual collection of tools, and Calum rummaged through them until he found what he was looking for. A length of stiff wire he could twist into shape. He doubted the lock on the kitchen door would prove too much of a challenge. However, when he returned, the door stood open. There was no sign of Elizabeth, but a key sat in the lock, and a flowerpot was tipped over, the only one in a neat row of six not to stand upright.

"Elizabeth!" Calum called as he entered.

"Through here, in the front room."

There was a step up from the kitchen into a narrow hallway, with the living room on the right. There were two easy chairs set on either side of an empty fire-grate, but no couch. A radio sat alongside a bookcase, next to it a dark wood dining table with the drop-leaves let down to make more space. A single place mat sat on the table, together with a half-drunk cup of tea. It was cold when Calum lifted the cup to check.

Elizabeth was examining a cork-board that covered one wall. It held photographs and clippings from newspapers, as well as schematics. One small square in the top right-hand corner was empty, and Calum wondered if that had contained similar items which had been taken down.

When he approached, Elizabeth glanced at him, her face showing nothing.

Calum examined the images, but they made no sense to him. They seemed to be random. Newspaper stories concerning bombed houses. Pictures of firefighters which must have come from the blitz. A doodlebug schematic with the parts exploded out to reveal the inner workings was the most unusual thing. Most of the flying bombs had been turned into a thousand shards when they came down. Other blueprints meant nothing at all to him.

"Have you any idea what any of this means?" Calum asked.

"None, but it clearly means something to him. Assuming he's not totally crazy, that is." She reached out and touched some of the images with her fingertip. As she did so, Calum noticed she wore a wedding ring on her left hand. He tried to recall if he had ever seen one there before but could not. Was Elizabeth still married? A widow?

"Here, here and here," she said, touching the images. "I have no idea what these plans are for, but I suspect Bill Harrison shouldn't have them."

"Where did he get them from?" Calum asked.

"He works at the Royal Arsenal. It's a research centre now, and Bill is one of their brightest stars. I hear he's always been fascinated by weaponry. I suspect most of these plans are for some kind of weapon. Top secret, no doubt."

"There's no car in the garage, but one was there not so long ago. He might have driven to work, but that's unlikely with the petrol ration, and they did say he wasn't there. It looks to me like he's done a runner. I noticed a telephone in the hallway. Maybe you should call his work and find out if they have any idea where he might have gone. Or try Churchill again."

"Winnie's got more important things on his mind than my insignificant problems," said Elizabeth. "But it's a plan, I suppose."

"It is?"

Calum was pleased when she smiled and patted his cheek. "Have a look upstairs, see if he's taken any clothes, or if there's any clue where he might have gone."

"Why do you want him so much?" Calum asked. "Because he can hear secrets buried in walls? If so, does that make him one of us?"

"It does. He'd be damned useful right now if we're supposed to find out who took this information. I'll make that call while you check upstairs"

Two bedrooms led off from the top of the stairs, as well as a small bathroom. The front bedroom was the larger, with a curved bay window looking over the deserted road. The bed was made up but looked as if it hadn't been slept in for a while. There was a door set in one corner, but when Calum opened it he found only a long, narrow water tank tucked beneath the sloping eaves.

Calum heard the click-click of metal-heeled shoes as he emerged from the cobweb-strung eaves. When he looked through the window he saw a dark-suited man walking along the far pavement. He assumed it was someone returning early from work until the man stopped opposite the house and turned to stare at it. Calum drew back so he was hidden in the shade beside the window. He watched the man for several minutes, neither of them moving. He wondered if it was Bill Harrison, checking to see if it was safe to return home. Calum was on the point of running down the stairs to accost him when a car pulled up and the man climbed into the passenger seat. Calum shook his head. Nothing more than some worker waiting to be picked up by a friend or colleague.

The back room was where Bill Harrison slept. A step down mirrored the one from the kitchen below. Calum wondered why the man used the smaller bedroom because it wasn't as if there was much in the way of traffic noise. He hadn't seen a single vehicle since they arrived.

He could faintly hear Elizabeth downstairs on the telephone but ignored her.

Calum opened a walnut wardrobe and ran his hand across the contents. There were gaps, but he didn't know if it meant Bill Harrison owned few clothes or had taken some with him. He looked around for a suitcase but couldn't see one. Which again might or might not indicate something. He hoped Elizabeth was having more success, grateful he wasn't a detective because he would make a terrible one.

"Anything?" asked Elizabeth when Calum descended the stairs.

"There might be some clothes missing from his wardrobe, and there might be a suitcase missing as well, but their lack could equally well mean nothing at all. Why would he run?" Calum laughed. "I thought I'd found him just now. A man was watching the house from across the street. I thought it might be him, come back to see if the coast was clear. I was about to go out and confront him when he got in a car and it drove off."

"What did he look like?"

"Short, dark-haired, dark suit."

"It wasn't Bill Harrison, then," said Elizabeth. "I wish I knew what those pictures were all about." She looked around, standing close to Calum in the narrow hallway. "His works said they might be able to show us what they've got on him. They've sent someone to check, but it could take a while."

"Do you know where the place is?"

"This side of the river, fortunately."

"I expect you also know which bus will get us there."

Elizabeth gave a smile "As a matter of fact, I do. Don't forget my overnight bag, it's still in the lean-to."

Calum took a last look around the kitchen but saw nothing of interest, other than five eggs sitting in a bowl on the windowsill. He thought about taking them before realising he had no way to use them. They'd probably break in his pocket and stink to high heaven for a week afterwards.

The bus dropped them off opposite the Royal Arsenal works. As they stood side by side across the road from it, Elizabeth explained it no longer acted as a factory for creating munitions but more as a research centre to develop new explosives.

"Then that must be what all those pictures and cuttings are about," Calum said. "Work and hobby combined. Does he never take a break?"

"Some people are made that way, Cal, you know they are. Harry's like that, so is Maria. You don't see it because you're not."

"Am I not?"

Elizabeth laughed and stroked the back of his hand. It was getting to be a habit he could get used to.

"You don't see it in them because it's not part of you."

"Is it of you?" he asked.

"I suspect so. But I can have fun as well when I want." She looked into his eyes. "As you already know."

Calum wanted to say something about that night in her room, but the words remained stubbornly inside, trapped somewhere between chest and lips. Before he could force them into the open, Elizabeth turned and looked at the imposing edifice set back from the roadway. Most of the work would be done in a series of units behind, but from here, it might have been the house of a rich merchant. Perhaps at some time, it had been. Calum knew nothing at all about the Royal Arsenal.

Elizabeth started across the road, and after a moment he followed and entered into an outer lobby.

"Are you the girl who rang?" The man who asked was into his sixties, hair slicked down, so it lay tight across his skull as it fought a losing battle to hide a bald patch. A cigarette burned in an ashtray already piled with butts.

Calum saw Elizabeth bridle at being called a girl, but her voice was sweet when she answered, a flirtatious edge to it he hadn't heard her use before, not even on him.

"Indeed, I am, sir. Did you ask someone to find information on Mr Harrison for me?"

"Sent a message. Got a message back. He's not here, girlie."

It was a step too far, and Calum suppressed a smile as Elizabeth took a pace closer to the desk. She rested her fists on the top and stared into the man's eyes.

"I didn't ask about where he was. I asked what information you had on him. And do you allow all your employees to swan off at any time they please? I assume you are aware we are fighting a war?"

The man didn't appear intimidated. "Winning it more like, with our help. It'll all be over by Christmas."

"I think they said that in 1914. They were wrong then, and they're wrong now. I want to see any paperwork you have on him."

"You know where you are, don't you, girlie? This is the Woolwich Arsenal. Not just any old Tom, Dick, or Harriet can come waltzing in here making demands." It seemed the man had so far failed to learn his lesson.

Elizabeth rummaged inside her thick jacket and pulled out a folded card with a dark blue cover. She opened it out and held it in front of the man's face.

"This should tell you I'm not just anybody, matey. If you think this is fake, then there's a telephone number here." She jabbed her finger at the document. "Call it now and ask about Elizabeth Grierson. *Doctor* Elizabeth Grierson. And then prepare to pack up whatever personal items you have and fuck off home like a good little boy."

Calum watched the man flinch, flinch again at the curse word. Even so, he picked up a pencil and wrote the telephone number on a slip of paper. He got to his feet.

"Wait here, I'm going to have to check."

After he had gone, Elizabeth smiled. "I like him. Most men would have rolled over, but he's doing the job he's supposed to."

"There won't be anything here," Calum said.

"I know. But despite him being right, nobody calls me girlie. And certainly not twice."

It was five minutes before the man returned in the

company of another, this one dressed in a pin-striped suit. He was around the same age as the first but had worn significantly better.

"I am sorry to have delayed you, Dr Grierson. If you would follow me, I will show you everything we have on Mr Harrison."

As Elizabeth and Calum wound their way through tight spaces between an array of desks, the man asked, as casually as he could, "I hope there is nothing amiss. No, ah, information gone astray?"

"You have nothing to be concerned about," said Elizabeth. "Mr Harrison contacted my department some time ago offering his services."

Calum could see the man wanted to ask what department that would be before deciding it was inappropriate under the circumstances. They came to a small office where a single desk sat squarely in the middle. Two chairs were set on the far side. A single buff folder lay on the desk.

"I will leave you to read what we have, but you cannot take anything with you." He glanced at the overnight bag Calum still carried. "Perhaps I can take that from you, Mr..."

Calum handed the bag over without giving his name. He was enjoying the secrecy, and how even powerful men treated Elizabeth. He wondered who had been on the other end of the telephone number she gave the receptionist.

He took the chair next to Elizabeth, their shoulders touching. He leaned forward as she opened the folder. Inside was a single sheet of typed paper.

"It's a fresh copy," said Elizabeth, running her thumb across the ink to smear it. "I wonder what they left out?"

"Are you going to get him back in?"

She gave a shake of her head. "Let's see what we've got first."

"What are we looking for?"

Elizabeth's eyes scanned what little information lay on the sheet then placed her fingertip on one line. "This. What's your memory like, Cal?"

"Pretty good."

"Then remember this. Forty-seven Gill Street, Limehouse. Got it?"

Calum repeated it once out loud, three times in his head. He'd had a brief fling with a girl called Gill once, and he made the association, together with the lime tree in his mother's garden at home.

When he nodded, Elizabeth said, "I've got it, too. Now, do we put on a pretence at looking for anything else, or do we get out of here?"

"Are we going there now?"

Elizabeth shook her head. "In the morning. I'm exhausted, and I'd like to…" She gave a brief laugh. "I don't even know what time it is."

Calum consulted his repaired watch, surprised when he saw the hour.

"Ten minutes after eight," he said.

"Where did the day go? Let's find somewhere to stay. We can go to this address in the morning."

Outside on the street, waiting at a bus stop with a crowd of workers from the Royal Arsenal, Calum asked, "Is that where you think Bill Harrison might be?"

"According to his employer he's been missing for two days, and it's the only lead we have. It's the address he gave for his mother when he started work. With luck, the street hasn't been destroyed by a bomb. It lies close to the docks, so it may have been. With even more luck, his mother still lives there. And with the best kind of luck, Bill Harrison is holed up at her house."

"That's a lot of ifs," Calum said. A bus approached, but it was not the one Elizabeth had in mind. "Where are we going, by the way?"

"I have a little treat for you. Pulled a few strings when we were in the War Room this morning. A suite in the Fitzroy, Great Russell Street. It's reserved for Cabinet Ministers and such when they need to stay over, but it's free tonight. We can get dinner, fall into bed and dream the sleep of the innocent."

Calum said nothing, wondering if she was trying to tell him they would fall into bed together or, as she had mentioned a suite, there would be more than one bed. As for sleeping the dreams of the innocent... he hoped not.

It was starting to grow dark as they arrived at the Fitzroy in Great Russel Street. It pleased Calum to discover their suite consisted of only one bedroom and only one bed. Even if it was so enormous, they might never find each other. He thought the only thing he had ever seen wider was a battleship. There was a small lounge where they ate a sparse dinner, and a bathroom that was significantly larger. Elizabeth had signed in as Mr and Mrs Grierson, making sure the desk clerk saw the wedding ring on her left hand. Not that the man was likely to say anything. When Calum asked her how much the room was costing, she told him it was better he didn't know.

Now he sat in one of the plush armchairs in the bedroom while Elizabeth was in the bathroom. It might be another week before she found her way out again.

A glass of single malt sat on the round table next to his chair and Calum had his stockinged feet resting on the deep windowsill. Only one lamp burned beside the bed, and he had opened the curtains only a crack so he could see out. Across the street, well-appointed terraced houses stood shoulder to shoulder, none of them showing any lights. Beyond them lay an equally dark London. The blitz was over, the air battle long won, but the lights remained dimmed. Calum's eyes were heavy, and he kept finding himself startling awake. He reached for the whisky and swallowed it in one. A waste, he knew, but he needed something to keep him awake. He poured another two fingers from the bottle Elizabeth had ordered. Calum thought this was a luxury he could get used to but knew he'd better not. This was for one night only, he suspected.

He turned when the bathroom door opened. Elizabeth stood silhouetted, wearing not a stitch of clothing.

"I've run a bath," she said.

Calum nodded. Light silhouetted her body from behind, but he could see enough to trigger memories of the last time he had seen her in this state of nature.

"I wondered if you'd like to come and scrub my back."

"Only your back?"

"We could always check one or two other places, I suppose. Come on, Cal, we might all be dead tomorrow."

He needed no encouragement. When Elizabeth turned away, rewarding him with a brief side view, he undressed and followed her through.

Some time later, washed and clean and then made sweaty again, he woke with a start from a dreamless sleep. Despite the size of the bed, he was aware he lay in it alone. When he had finally drifted off, Elizabeth was curled beside him, her arm across his waist. They were both sated from their love-making. At least Calum was. He gained an impression Elizabeth might have been content to carry on all night.

He sat up to see her standing at the window, the curtains drawn so she could look out. Calum walked across and wrapped his arms around her.

"You'll catch your death standing here. Let me keep you warm."

Elizabeth gave a low laugh and put her arms over his, hugging them tighter as she leaned back into his embrace.

"Plus, you'll give some Tommy the treat of his life if he looks up and sees you."

"They all deserve a treat, don't they?" she said. "What time is it, Cal?"

He glanced at his watch, which by some miracle had remained on his wrist throughout their fevered love-making. The faint green glow of the dial showed him it was a quarter before four. He held the watch so she could see for herself.

"Are you coming back to bed? It'll be getting light before long."

"I'm not sleepy."

Calum kissed her shoulder and felt her react. He wanted to ask her a question. At least one. He was afraid of the answer she might give but not as afraid of not knowing.

"About tonight," he said.

"Mm-hm?" Elizabeth stroked the back of his arm with two fingers.

"Is this going to be like the last time?"

"Why do you ask that?"

"You know what I mean. Will tomorrow be business as usual?"

Elizabeth drew a breath, let it go.

"You know the others can never know about us. It would cause problems."

"Is there an us, then? Or is it just, I don't know… am I an itch you have to scratch now and again, or am I something more to you?"

"I do like you, Cal. I like you an awful lot. Can't you tell after what we did?"

It was no answer.

"That was sex. I need to know if there's more than just sex. Great as it was."

Elizabeth giggled, the first time he had ever heard her make the sound. "It was rather good, wasn't it? I believe I might even have worn you out a little."

"More than a little. Is this what we're going to be from now on? Bedmates every few weeks?"

"More, if we can find a way. I told you, I like you."

"Yes, I heard. A lot."

"Don't go all soppy on me, Cal. Don't go mentioning the L word."

"It was you who said like." Calum was relieved when Elizabeth laughed, her belly moving beneath his touch. "But no, I won't. What's with the wedding ring? In some other life away from this one, are you married?"

Elizabeth shook her head, her hair brushing his shoulder where she stood three inches shorter. "No."

"Were you married?"

"Once," she said. "A long time ago."

"How long ago can it have been? You're not even thirty."

"You don't know that, Cal."

"You're certainly not forty. How long is long ago? Ten years? It can't be twenty."

"Let's not talk about it."

"What happened?"

"War happened. He died."

"Did you love him?"

Elizabeth made no reply. She twisted out of his arms and walked past him. Calum thought she might lock herself in the bathroom. Instead, she went on her knees and opened her bag. She searched inside until she found what she was looking for, then came back and stood facing him. The temptation to reach out for her was almost overwhelming, but Calum knew he could do nothing. Not yet.

Elizabeth's face was shaded as she looked up at him. She handed him a photograph.

Calum angled it to catch what little moonlight remained. It showed a man in uniform. Slim, good looking, with a neat moustache and dark hair. The rank of captain showed on his epaulettes, but the uniform was dated, as if it belonged to an earlier war than this one. Which was impossible.

He handed the photograph back. "What was his name?"

"Peter. Captain Peter Watson."

"Did he die in the war?"

She nodded, resting her forehead against his shoulder.

"I'm sorry." Calum wrapped his arms around her.

"I know you are, but it's not your fault. It's not my fault. It wasn't Peter's fault. It was the *fucking war's* fault." She looked up at him. "Come back to bed and make me forget the memories, Cal. I do like you, I really do, and maybe one day there can be more, but tonight I don't want love. I want lust."

He kissed her mouth, intending to lead her back to bed. Instead, he threw her to the carpet and covered her with his body.

"No – in the bed!" Elizabeth complained.

The explosion Calum had seen ten seconds in the future arrived, rattling the window panes. It was a tremendous roar of thunder as if someone had fired a cannon, followed a moment later by a massive fireball that lit up the night sky.

They both rose to their feet and stared out at a plume of roiling smoke rising in the distance. Already the clatter of bells sounded as fire-engines sped from their depots. One flashed by on the street below, followed by an ambulance.

"What the hell was that?" said Elizabeth.

"A bomb. It has to be a bomb."

"Not one I've ever heard about before. No bombers. No doodlebug. I know people are working on–" Elizabeth stopped herself when she realised she might be about to reveal too much. She turned away, going to her knees again. "Come on, Cal, get dressed. We're going to find out what it was."

He walked past her and started searching for his clothes. "It's nothing to do with us."

"You're right, it's not, but I know a man who's

obsessed with explosions and armament. Bill Harrison won't be able to help himself. If he was close enough to hear it, he'll be there somewhere."

Calum almost told her they wouldn't be allowed through before remembering Elizabeth appeared to be able to go anywhere she wanted.

He found his underwear, socks and trousers in the bathroom. His underwear was still damp from where he had rinsed it through, but it was the only pair he had.

Out on the street, they ran to Euston Road. Instead of turning east to where the roil of smoke continued to climb into the air, Elizabeth crossed to where the doors of a Fire Station stood open. She went inside and spoke with someone. When she came out, she said, "I've got us a lift, but hang on tight, Cal. These fellows don't mess around."

The fire-engine stopped barely long enough for them to climb aboard. Calum clung to a metal hook on the side. Elizabeth perched herself on the knee of a man inside. From his expression, it looked as if she had made his night.

They careened through the dark, weaving from side to side, skidding around corners until ahead of them a cordon caused them to slow, but only long enough for the barriers to be raised to allow them through. While the fire-engine was stationary, Elizabeth climbed out, and Calum dropped to the ground. They followed the fire-engine as it entered the danger zone. Nobody challenged them.

A row of terraced houses stood with a vast gap in the middle. Flame and smoke continued to rise, and Calum was sure there must be scores of dead.

"Neither of us heard a doodlebug, so what the hell did this? A gas main?"

Elizabeth looked at him. "No doubt that's what the authorities are going to say."

"But you don't think so, do you?"

"I think I know what it was, but it's classified. The government doesn't want word of it getting out because they're convinced it will cause panic. Our boffins have nothing like it, but the Nazis do."

"Some kind of new bomb? I heard no plane, the same as you."

"Not a bomb." Elizabeth stared at him, and Calum knew she was wondering how much to tell him. As she decided, he saw a change in her eyes and knew her following words would be the truth. "The Germans have a new weapon that makes the doodlebug look like a toy. It's a rocket. A great big bloody rocket. I heard yesterday they'd tried it in France but missed their target. Seems they got this one almost spot on, though I suspect it was Winnie they were after."

"I heard nothing before the explosion, so what is it, supersonic?" Calum had talked of the possibilities with the others. He knew Germany had jet fighters, the same as Britain did, but even they couldn't approach the 760 miles per hour needed. Most of the men on Calum's base believed the speed of sound was a solid barrier. To hit it would be like hitting a concrete wall.

"That's the gen they gave me," said Elizabeth. "The powers-that-be hoped the war might be over before the Nazis got them into service. Our planes have already bombed a couple of their bases and made them draw back from the coast. From what I've been told, they've been trying to increase the range. Seems they did it." Elizabeth looked around. "Go that way and see if you can find Bill Harrison. If he's still in London, he'll have heard the explosion, just like we did."

"I don't even know what he looks like."

"He'll be the man standing as close as he can with an expression on his face like he's won the pools. He's taller than you, around forty, and dresses like he works in a factory rather than an office." Elizabeth pressed something into his hand. A silver police whistle. "If you see him blow on this." She held a similar one up to show him. "I'll do the same."

"What if someone stops and asks what I'm doing?"

"Tell them you're with me."

Calum shook his head and turned away. He was beginning to think his life had been more straightforward when he flew over Germany every night.

All around him, men worked trying to douse the flames, attempting to get close enough to check for survivors. Uniformed nurses and doctors hovered, darting forward at any sign someone might need their help – just as likely to be firefighters and police as civilians. The darkness and flames made their faces demonic. The heat reached Calum, bringing an instant sweat to his skin.

He circled the site of the damage until he came out on the far side. There were fewer people here, otherwise he might have missed the man he sought. Bill Harrison, if it was him, stood closer to the flames than seemed sensible. As Calum came up behind him, he had a moment of doubt. What if this wasn't the man he sought? He was tall enough, dressed in corduroy trousers and a tweed jacket, but so were other men. But there was nothing for it. He could always apologise afterwards.

Calum was twenty paces away when some instinct caused the man to turn. He caught sight of Calum and ran.

Calum blew his whistle and shouted out, "Stop, Police!" He felt like an idiot, but it didn't stop him from sprinting after the man. He was almost twenty years younger and significantly fitter. He caught Bill Harrison before he could disappear into the maze of alleys on the far side of the road, where most of the houses' windows were blown in. He leapt and tackled the man to the ground, rolled him over and sat astride him.

"God, but I hope your name's Bill Harrison." He blew on the whistle again, the sharp sound making the man beneath him wince.

"Who wants to know?"

"Secret Service," said Calum, hoping he wouldn't need to prove it. No doubt Elizabeth would have documents for that as well.

"You took your sweet time finding me, chum," said Bill Harrison. "I'm glad to hear you're a spook because I thought you might be a Nazi assassin."

CHAPTER TWENTY-FOUR

Bill Harrison sat in the back of a Vauxhall 12, Calum in the middle of the rear bench seat with Elizabeth to his left. As the uniformed driver sped through the narrow country roads north of London, they slid from side to side on the polished leather. Dawn had arrived an hour earlier. The driver switched off the headlights, not that they had been much good for anything.

The man Elizabeth had been searching for appeared to accept his fate. So much so that when she asked him to prove he was who she sought, he asked Calum if he had something personal on him.

Calum slipped his watch off and handed it across. "Will this do?"

Bill Harrison took the watch and held it cupped between his palms, exactly as Harry had done at their first dinner together. He closed his eyes, his body swaying as the car took a series of tight corners with a squeal of protest from the tyres.

Elizabeth leaned forward and tapped the shoulder of the driver. "How much further?"

"Half an hour, ma'am. Give or take. Not much on the roads, fortunately."

"You were a fly-boy." Bill opened his eyes and looked at Calum, who nodded.

"What position was I?"

"Cramped. Not too loud. Gunner? No, bomb-aimer." He met Calum's eyes. "Lancs?"

Calum nodded again.

"What are you doing in Hereford?" asked Bill.

"God damn it," said Elizabeth, "you can't go saying things like that!"

Bill looked at her and smiled. "Would you rather I talked about what the two of you got up to last night? It wasn't the first time either, was it?" He handed the watch back to Calum. "There's something funny about that watch, but I can't work out what it is." He glanced across at Elizabeth before looking back at Calum to offer a wink she couldn't see. "Can't say I blame you."

Calum slipped the watch back on his wrist, aware of an unusual warmth.

"Why did you make yourself scarce after asking to talk to me?" said Elizabeth.

"There have been people watching my house," said Bill. "A couple of times I saw someone on the bus home, too. I thought it would make sense to get out of town for a while, so I called you."

"And then you weren't there. How on earth did you expect me to find you?"

"You did, didn't you? I heard you were resourceful, so it must be true."

"Heard from who?"

"I'll keep that to myself for now."

"I saw a man in the street outside your house," Calum said.

"Ordinary looking cove in a suit?" said Bill, and Calum nodded. "There is a couple of them, but they all look the same."

"Who are they? When I caught up with you, you said you were glad I wasn't a Nazi assassin. Is that who you think they are? And if you do, why do they want to kill you?"

"Were you good at your job?" asked Bill.

"I was the best bomb-aimer in the world."

"Calum has a talent which made that possible," said Elizabeth.

"Then you'll believe me when I say I understand weapons better than almost anyone else."

"Is that what all those schematics and pictures on your wall are for? Where did you get them?"

"Can't say," said Bill.

"Stole them, I expect."

"Still can't say. But yes, most are weapons. Ours, those of the Third Reich, some American. Seems the Nazis heard something about me. I think they either want to kidnap me or kill me. Not sure which of those two would be the best option."

"Why would they do that?" Calum asked.

"Because I can look at a blueprint and tell you in a

couple of minutes what the weapon is. I can also tell you what's wrong with it and how to make it better."

"We've got a man back in our team you're going to get on well with," said Elizabeth. "Was that bomb last night one you already knew about?"

"It was. I'd like to get hold of a piece if you can arrange such a thing, my dear. Doesn't need to be big. Something six inches by six should do. I'll make it worth your while. I might even be able to tell you where it came from and who made it."

"I'll see what I can do," said Elizabeth.

The three of them were thrown forward as the driver braked hard to avoid a tractor that had pulled out from a field. He cursed and started the stalled engine. Ahead, the tractor proceeded at walking pace, and the driver cursed again without repeating anything he had already muttered. It seemed he had a rich vocabulary of such words.

"Are you going to help us?" Elizabeth asked Bill.

"I told you, the Nazis want me dead. I'm hoping I'll be safer with others around me, in a nice little out-of-the-way location in the countryside. It will make strangers easier to spot." Bill looked at Calum. "What's Hereford like, chum?"

"Nice," Calum said. "They have dances every month. Lots of women who work in munitions there. I think you'd like them."

"Ah, the scent of ammonium nitrate. It works for me, mate. How many of you are there?"

Calum said nothing.

"Six, if we include you," said Elizabeth.

"Do you have anyone else like me?" asked Bill.

"If there was I wouldn't have had to chase you through half of London."

"I wasn't hiding. If you'd telephoned to let me know you were coming, I'd have arranged a meeting somewhere safe."

"What about your job? I thought you enjoyed it."

"I did when I worked with ordnance. Now all the Arsenal want me to do is fill in forms and oversee other people's work. The war will be over soon. Not by Christmas, that's only a pipe-dream, but next year, I reckon. You and your little outfit might be the future. What's the pay like?"

"Lousy," Calum said with a laugh.

"Government, so I wouldn't I expect anything else. Ah well. Are the vittles any good?"

"Best you'll get anywhere." Calum rested his head against the back of the rear bench seat, suddenly tired. Too little sleep and too much excitement. He smiled to himself as he recalled the nature of some of that excitement. The car's rocking movement was a comfort, even when it accelerated hard to overtake the tractor.

He opened his eyes when Elizabeth nudged him.

"Sorry, was I snoring again?"

"How would I know whether you snore?" Her face was expressionless.

Calum sat up to look through the window. A substantial stone building stood at the end of a curved driveway, its elegance spoiled by a bedraggled gathering of huts of various shapes and sizes scattered across what might once have been an impressive lawn. A few people moved from one building to another, most of them female.

The driver pulled up but stayed behind the wheel. Elizabeth climbed out on one side, Bill Harrison the other. Calum slid across the seat to stand beside him. After his flight through the streets of London, the man appeared to have accepted his fate. The real reason puzzled Calum, and he knew he'd have to discuss it with Elizabeth when they found a chance.

A uniformed man came down the stone steps of the main house and crossed to them. He ignored Calum and Harry and went straight to Elizabeth.

"Thirteen?" he asked, and when she nodded, "The rest of your people are inside. Breakfast's finished, but I'll try to rustle up a cup of tea. There are people ready for you." Without waiting for any acknowledgement, he turned and strode back to the house, making them walk fast to keep up.

When Calum glanced back, the car was pulling away. His head spun from all the different forms of transport he had taken in the last twenty-four hours.

The man handed them over to a uniformed woman who took them into a conference room. Maria, Harry and Richard sat on one side of a long table. On the other were three men and a woman. At the head of the table sat a man in a crumpled suit, his face marked by the blandness of someone senior and used to keeping the country's secrets close. He gave a nod to acknowledge their presence and indicated they should join their companions.

Elizabeth took the seat closest to him. Calum sat next to Maria, and Bill slumped into the chair next to his.

"I hope they don't forget that tea," he whispered.

"If we can start," said the man at the table's head.

"I apologise for the delay," said Elizabeth. "Did you hear what happened in London?"

What might have passed for a smile in the Secret Service briefly touched the man's lips. "Gas explosion is what I heard. The people sitting opposite you work for me, and none of us have names as far as you are concerned. You can call them one to four if you like."

The three men and the single woman showed no expression.

The man steepled his fingers and leaned forward.

"To be perfectly frank with you, your presence here is against my better judgement. However, I have been issued an order, and I can't ignore it. So, here we all are. I have been briefed on the, ah, unusual nature of Unit-13, Dr Grierson, and appraised my companions of the same. They share my opinion, but..." He trailed off, as if unwilling to state exactly what their opinion might be.

Calum realised the man was afraid of them.

Perhaps Elizabeth saw it as well because she offered her best smile. The one she had used on Calum when she invited him into the bathroom the night before.

"My understanding is that you are aware of a problem but could not effect any solution. I assume because we are here, you are desperate enough to seek more unusual methods."

"Something along those lines." He sat back. "If you would start, um, one."

The man closest to him opened a manilla folder but shielded the contents with his arm, like a schoolboy trying to stop his homework from being copied. He stared at the contents for some time. Calum pushed into the future to see what his intention was.

Twenty seconds passed before the man pushed four pages across the table, followed by half a dozen black and white images.

"This is what we have so far. We know secrets are being divulged to enemies of this country. The evidence is in front of you. What we cannot find out is who is divulging it, or who has received the information – though I think we can be pretty sure who wants it the most."

Elizabeth scanned the first sheet then pushed it along the table to Harry, who only passed it on to Richard, who gave it to Maria. She read it then looked up.

"Some of this is in German, some in Russian," she said.

"I understood you could read both," said the man who had passed it across.

Calum leaned over to look at the words he understood. Several sections had been blacked out.

"These pages show nothing about what has been taken."

"I am not at liberty to pass that information on."

"Let me get this straight. You expect us to track down one or more spies who have taken information about something you will not allow us to know anything about?"

"Knocked the nail on the head, old son."

"I assume your own people are fully appraised of its contents?"

"They are."

"But we are not to be."

The man glanced at Elizabeth. "I was told that divulging the nature of the information is not required."

"You are correct in that assumption," said Elizabeth.

Calum waited for her to say more, but she sat with her hands folded in front of her. He glanced at each of the pictures as they reached him then passed them on to Bill. For a moment, it felt strange to do so. The man had run from him only hours before, and Calum was still making his mind up about him. Yet here the man was, already drawn into their strange, secret world.

Bill leaned over to study the photographs. He arranged them in front of him, moving each until they sat in a formation that satisfied him. He touched each with the tip of a finger, moving from one to the other, then started again. He repeated the process seven times.

He said nothing, but his eyes locked on Calum's and he offered a nod, as if he knew what had been taken.

Calum glanced at the pictures, leaving them where they lay. They showed men in white coats, a long stretch of coastline, some industrial machinery, what looked like the inside of a laboratory, some gears and shaped pieces of metal. None of it offered any meaning for him, but it surprised him to discover he trusted Bill. He knew what the man's obsession was, which was enough to hazard a guess about what the stolen information might contain.

"Why give us these if you're not telling us what they represent?" Calum asked.

"I am trying to play fair with you." The man ignored Calum and spoke to Elizabeth. "The full nature of what has been taken cannot be divulged, but I was told to offer you something, at least. That is what I am doing."

"Thanks for nothing," Calum said.

The man ignored him.

"Can you divulge what investigations you have carried out so far?" asked Elizabeth. "And perhaps more pertinently, why you believe anything has gone missing?"

The man appeared to think for a moment before nodding. "I believe I can. My people are highly skilled, as you must know. They have broken many undercover rings that had been working in this country since the thirties. They are experts in this manner of work, but they have reached a dead-end in this case. What they have discovered is that it has all the hallmarks of an inside job. Every employee with access to these records has been questioned, then questioned again. In two instances, men found their employment terminated, together with their freedom. But they were accidental victims, and we are no closer to who might have taken the information."

"How can you be sure something has been taken?" asked Elizabeth.

"As you know, the Services work closely together, even more so during wartime. Our people over there have picked up small scraps of intelligence to indicate there is great excitement among high-ranking Nazis. It goes all the way to the top, I understand. They are expecting receipt of secret information relating to the matter we cannot discuss. Still, I understand that information has already been stolen and is on its way across the Channel, unless we can find out who took it."

"I assume this theft occurred fairly recently?" asked Elizabeth.

"It did."

"How can you be sure they are still in this country and not already in Nazi hands?"

"As I said, we have our resources. Resources that come at a high price but which provides invaluable intelligence. That intelligence indicates nothing has reached Germany yet."

"How can someone have stolen these documents? From what you are telling us, they are highly classified."

"Very highly classified. Top secret has nothing on these boys. And you may already have noted that I have been careful not to mention documents. We have done an audit, and as far as anyone can tell, nothing is missing. Nothing at all. Except the Nazis are expecting something that could even yet change the course of the war." The man ran a hand across his face, and for the first time, Calum saw the fear in him. Was it fear of the theft, or because of who he had been forced to call in to assist?

"I think we can probably help," said Elizabeth. "Despite your childish insistence on secrecy. We are all on the same side. All of us fighting to end this war." She looked along the line at each of them, but it was clear she was not seeking their approval. This was a side to her Calum had never seen before. How someone so young, so pretty, could exude such authority was a mystery. As she was becoming ever more of a mystery to him.

The man looked at his staff.

Calum wondered why he had brought all four when only one had revealed anything to them. Perhaps they were witnesses.

"Give them the rest of the information," he said. "The A file should suffice." The man rose and walked from the room without acknowledging either Elizabeth or the others. One by one, his staff also rose and followed.

"Bastards," said Bill.

Elizabeth said nothing. She put a finger to her lips and pointed at the ceiling, letting them know someone might be listening.

Calum looked at Harry and cocked his head in a silent question. Harry nodded, then rose and walked along each wall. He raised a hand high, moving slowly as if in a trance. When he returned to his place he nodded again, slow and deliberate. Yes, someone was listening.

So they sat patiently until the woman who had sat opposite entered with a cardboard box. She set it on the table and left without a word.

"If you would be a gentleman, Harry," said Elizabeth. "I believe the day is improving, and seeing as that promised tea has not arrived perhaps we should sit outside in the fresh air for a while."

Harry rose and picked up the box, which despite its size, appeared to be remarkably light.

CHAPTER TWENTY-FIVE

Outside, a concrete yard held two canvas-sided army trucks. To the right stood a tall, barn-like structure within which a group of boiler suited men worked under a jacked up car. Set at right angles was a long wooden building with a set of double doors thrown wide. The shade within hid whatever was being worked on there. Beyond the yard, a small lawn dipped away to a metal fence, and Elizabeth led them in that direction. There was nowhere else to sit but on the grass, and as soon as they were partially out of sight from the main building Elizabeth tucked her skirts between her legs and sat cross-legged. She indicated for Harry to pass her the cardboard box, which she opened and took some papers from.

"You knew what those papers they showed us were about, didn't you?" Calum asked Bill.

"I had a pretty good idea, but I want to see if there's anything in this box to confirm it."

Elizabeth glanced up from where she was studying a

sheet of paper. "Take a look at all of these and see if they corroborate what you think. Then I'm going to see if I can get you into the room where all the secrets are held."

"What good will that do?" Harry wasn't content to give up his role as the sceptic among them.

"It's what Bill does," said Elizabeth. "He doesn't need to see the documents directly. He only needs to be where they are stored. Tell Harry who those people are, Bill"

The Government Code and Cipher School are based here," said Bill. "GCCS was set up a century ago to decode secret messages, but it's a damn sight more than that these days. That'll be who those people work for. They're turning into the best intelligence unit in the world, even if they do come across as arseholes. One day they're going to fly the nest and want their own lodgings away from this place. Somewhere more private."

"And your point is?" Calum asked.

"They'll be the ones who were listening in on the meeting we had. On whose behalf they are working, I don't know, but someone will have written it all up by now."

Maria looked around. "Do you think they can overhear us out here?"

"Not unless they've planted devices under the grass and in the trees," said Harry. "I sense nothing. Unlike in that room."

"Is that what you can do?" Bill Harrison looked at Harry. "You feel hidden things?"

Harry glanced at Elizabeth, who offered a nod to let him know Bill Harrison had passed from outside to inside. He was one of them now.

"Wasn't aware I could," said Harry. "Now I am, thanks to Elizabeth and the rest of the team. We've come a long way together in a short time. I've got this affinity for machinery, but I always believed I was nothing more than a skilled mechanic." He shook his head as if at his own stupidity.

"I've always known what I can do is odd," said Bill.

"Tell us what is it you do." It was Maria who asked this time.

Before he could reply, Elizabeth said, "Bill can hear conversations in rooms after they've taken place." She didn't hide the impatience in her voice. "You can share what each of your talents are once we get back to base. Right now, we need to discuss the matter at hand."

"Which is?" Calum asked. "Were they telling the truth in there?"

"What would be the point of bringing us all the way here only to lie to us?" said Elizabeth.

"Lying is what they do, isn't it?"

Elizabeth waved the papers she was holding. "Here, I'll pass these around. Each of you take what you can from them, and then we'll decide what to do next. I believe I already know, but I want your input."

"Blimey," said Harry, "I'm not sure I can get used to being consulted. Are you sure we're part of the Service?"

"Just read the papers," said Elizabeth, her voice curt. "There's more here than they showed us in that room, so perhaps they're trying to offer us something."

Calum wondered if she was as exhausted as he was.

He took each sheet as it came to him, scanned it then passed it on to Richard, who sat to his left, though he kept forgetting the fact. Calum understood the words but gleaned nothing from them. He hoped one of the others might.

"All right," said Bill Harrison, when he had read each page, scanning the contents quickly. "Are there any photographs in your magic box?"

Elizabeth tilted the box to show it was empty.

"No problem, but they would have been useful as confirmation. They're trying to build a bomb. A bomb of enormous power. And they're scared the Nazis have stolen their research."

"They?" asked Elizabeth.

"There's an organisation called Tube Alloys, set up before the war to investigate just such a weapon. As some of you know, I have an interest in such developments. I suppose it's a hobby of mine."

"Tube Alloys?" said Harry. "Funny old name for a bomb factory, if you ask me."

"Deliberately named to disguise the nature of their work."

Elizabeth leaned forward. "How do you know about it, Bill? It's not mentioned in any of these documents. You already knew, didn't you?"

"Like I said, it's a hobby of mine."

"A hobby that seems to have revealed national secrets to you."

"My other abilities might have something to do with that. There have been certain visitors to the Royal Arsenal, though none for a few years now. I picked up quite a lot after the meetings took place. Never said a word to anyone, of course. They've moved all the work to

America now. We gave them our work, and they put the resources into making the damn thing work. Apparently, they promised to share the results with us once the war is over. The papers here show nothing to dispute that fact, do they?"

"It's not whether the work is going on here or over there. The knowledge that it's going on at all is dangerous." Elizabeth reached out and picked up the stack of papers deposited in front of her. She riffled through them quickly. "Here, I knew I saw it somewhere. It says, 'Despite the effort now being concentrated in Nevada, our scientists have communicated developments to their seniors, which will interest those parties in Great Britain'. I assume it's that information that's gone missing."

"When did they first know about this?" asked Bill. "If it was months ago, I won't be much help. After a few weeks, the things I hear melt into the background and I can't pick them out anymore. They're still there but not clear enough for me to make any sense of."

"I can help with that," said Elizabeth. "Just like I helped the others, though it will take more time than we have at the moment. I was told our presence is urgent, so I'm assuming the information went missing recently. That man who called us here is inside, waiting for my response. He's going to want to know if we can help or not. What do I tell him?"

"Are we talking about secrets or bombs?" asked Harry.

"Secrets in the main," Elizabeth said. "Secrets about bombs. And a rogue Nazi unit placed over here, no doubt years ago. A sleeper cell waiting for exactly something like this to fall into their hands."

"Between us, we can do things that would make the average bloke's hair stand on end," said Harry, "but we don't know what we're up against. I'm handy with my fists, and I can use a gun. I suspect Cal's the same, but what if it comes to a fight? We could do with some backup."

"Which I'll try to get us if we agree to go ahead. I can call John Simpson in for extra muscle if we need him."

"I can fight, too," said Bill. "Count me in."

"What this information contains isn't the point, is it?" said Maria. "It's the fact someone has stolen it and the fact that it's no doubt out of the country by now or planning to leave soon."

Elizabeth gave a nod of agreement. "Which is why we need to move fast."

"If we find out who took it are they going to send in the reserves?" Calum asked. "They can't expect us to handle it ourselves, can they?"

"All good questions, to which I don't have any answers. But I intend to go back inside and demand some. All I need to know right now is if you are all willing." She looked at each of them, waiting until they gave some sign of assent.

"When you go in," said Bill, "see if you can get me access to wherever they store their documents. Tell them I don't want to see any – I assume they'll all be locked away, in any case – but say it might offer us a clue as to who took them."

"Except they claim nothing is missing," said Elizabeth.

"No documents are missing," said Bill. "That doesn't mean the information hasn't been taken."

Elizabeth rose and brushed down her dress to remove a few strands of grass sticking to it. "Very well. I'll try not to be too long, but I believe you can probably get yourselves some lunch if I'm away more than a few minutes. I'll meet up with you here or in the canteen, so don't stray too far."

With that, she strode away. Calum watched her go, aware they had been together for the last two days, aware of what they had shared. He felt the loss of her leaving more than he ought.

When Elizabeth didn't return within ten minutes, Harry suggested they try to get something to eat.

"What time did you get here this morning?" Calum asked as they walked towards where men and women were streaming into a long, low building which had to be the canteen. At least half the crowd were female, almost everyone dressed in civilian clothes.

"Six-thirty," said Harry with a snort. "They put us on the mail train to London, then shunted us across the country. And then we had to wait around for you two to arrive."

"Us three," Calum said.

"Of course. I like Bill; he's my kind of fellow. Can he really do what Lizzie says?"

"I haven't seen it myself, but I know he's obsessed with explosions and weaponry. Elizabeth's not been wrong so far, has she? Even you've accepted you're not like most people."

"I did nothing to fix your watch," said Harry. "I held it, that's all." He glanced at Calum. "That's pretty much all I ever need to do. How was your flight, by the way?"

"Smooth as butter," Calum said. "Thanks."

"You'd likely have made it without my help, but I've decided I like you both. Better safe than sorry, eh?" He gave a wink. "Are you and Lizzie an item now? Can't say I blame you if you are. A man needs some distraction to take his mind off his troubles."

"What gives you that idea?"

"Let's just say intuition." Harry tapped the side of his nose, then looked ahead to where Maria was walking beside Richard, a sensible space between them.

"What about you and Dottie?" Calum asked. "I've seen you hanging around the kitchens more than necessary."

Harry laughed. "She was playing hard to get, but after the dance she finally weakened."

"Because of your charm?"

"That too," said Harry. "If she hadn't, there are plenty of girls in Hereford. Some of them are even quite pretty. None are like Dottie, mind."

Calum recalled the ease of finding romantic distraction off base. WAAFs, Land Girls, local girls. He had tried not to take advantage but, as Harry said, sometimes a man needed something to take his mind off his troubles.

They were fifty paces from the canteen when Calum came to an abrupt halt. When Harry turned back, he said, "Go ahead, I'll catch you up. I've just seen someone I know."

Harry snapped off a sloppy salute and ran to catch up with Maria, Richard and Bill.

Calum stayed where he was as two figures followed a concrete path roughly lain through the grass. His sister Jeannie hadn't seen him, and he was unsure whether to call out. No wonder she had been elusive when he asked what she did. Her skill with numbers and codes, a natural ability rather than the kind Calum possessed, should have given him a clue she might work somewhere like this. Until Elizabeth had briefed him on the code centre, Calum wasn't even aware it existed. The same as almost everyone else in the country.

Jeannie was deep in conversation with her companion, a man close to Calum's height but a little stockier, wearing a tweed jacket and white shirt without a tie. His hands moved as he tried to make some point to her.

Calum continued to watch, having decided to remain where he was. He was pleased to see Jeannie had found a place here to suit her abilities. She was never the best at dealing with people. Symbols were her friends, but not the human kind of symbol, which she had always failed to understand. Calum smiled as he recalled all the times she had come to him with a question about what someone had said or how they had acted. He tried to explain emotion, anger and love to her, but she only shook her head in bemusement. She had tried, he knew, but it came hard to her. He wondered – no, hoped – the man might mean something to her.

He was still standing there watching as they entered the canteen. Calum decided to give them a few minutes before going to join the others. He was still standing in the same spot when an arm snaked around his waist and Elizabeth kissed his cheek.

She gave a laugh and glanced around. "I hope the others didn't see that, but you looked so forlorn and handsome standing there I couldn't help myself. What are you doing out here on your own?"

"I saw someone I knew."

"So why are you still here?"

"I don't want to impose myself on her."

"Her? Do I have a rival, Cal?"

"If you consider my sister a rival."

Elizabeth looked away for a moment, and Calum knew she was scanning her prodigious memory.

"Jean," she said when she met his eyes again. "I'm not surprised she's working here."

"Do you know everything about her as well as you do me?"

"Pretty much. It's my job to know everything about those who work for me, together with their families. But I've also taken an extra interest in you, in case you haven't noticed."

"Now that you mention it."

Elizabeth slapped her hand against his side. "Come on, let's eat. I'm starving. And then I've got us a half-hour in the room they store the documents in. We can't touch anything, but let's see if Bill's as good as he claims."

CHAPTER TWENTY-SIX

Calum left Elizabeth to scan the sea of heads for the others while he went to fetch them both a sandwich. When he joined her, she pointed to a table in the far corner. His eyes were on the group as he followed her, so when a hand circled his wrist he gave a start. He looked down into the expressionless face of his sister.

"Hello, Cal," she said. "What on earth are you doing here? Or shouldn't I ask?"

He nodded towards Elizabeth, who had reached the others but remained on her feet as she told them what she had achieved.

"Working," he said, looking back at his sister.

"Here?"

"Passing through, that's all. I saw you before but didn't want to butt in."

Jeannie gave a frown. "Why not? If you're already here, you must have clearance. Nobody comes to Bletchley without clearance."

Calum was aware of Jeannie's companion staring at him and offered his hand.

"Jeannie's never going to introduce us," he said with a smile. "I'm her brother, Calum."

The man reached across the table, his handshake soft. "Alan," he said. "Alan Turing. You're sister's a genius."

"I know." It pleased Calum when the man smiled.

"Are you staying around later?" Turing asked. "We're going to decamp to the pub tonight and get a little drunk in celebration. At least we hope it's going to be worth celebrating. You're welcome to join us."

"Is it somebody's birthday?"

"Even better than a birthday. We've managed to–"

"No, Alan," said Jeannie, and the man's face lost a little of the brightness that had come to it.

"Sorry," he said.

"Me too. But I suspect we'll be long gone before tea-time."

"Are you in cyphers as well, Calum?"

"Something like that." He shook the man's hand again, then bent to kiss Jeannie's cheek because he knew it would annoy her.

"Another time," said Turing.

"When the war's over, perhaps," said Calum and set off to join the others.

They were standing as he approached, and he looked down at his sandwich, wrapped in greaseproof paper, and knew it would have to wait.

As they made their way back through the tables, Elizabeth said, "I saw you talking with Alan. How do you know him?"

"I don't. Jeannie introduced us."

"He's a little eccentric," said Elizabeth. "I heard he chains his coffee mug to a radiator so nobody else can use it. An absolute genius, mind."

"If he's working with my sister, that's probably a good thing. He said the same about her. I think she was pleased, though it's not always easy to tell with Jeannie."

Outside, Elizabeth slowed a little, allowing the others to get ahead. "Have you ever suspected some of your sister's ability might be like your own, Cal?"

"Spooky, do you mean?"

"Different."

"Jeannie's certainly different, but no, I don't think in the way you mean. She's just brilliant."

"What about your mother or father?"

"Dad? No, never. Mum…? Sometimes I wonder."

"Have you ever spoken to her? Does she know about you, by the way?"

"I thought you knew everything about my family and me."

"Not everything. Some things aren't written down, are they? So, does she?"

"I tried to talk to her a few times when this thing first started. After George died. She listened, then told me some people are just different and not to draw attention to myself."

"Except you drew my attention," said Elizabeth. "Your name came up when I put the request out."

Calum slowed. "What request?"

"For people with abilities that couldn't be explained.

Yours was the second name that came up after Bill Harrison, but it took me longer to get to you."

"You were looking for people like us?"

"You saw what the Russians are doing, Cal, same as the Germans and Americans. I've even had reports from our troops in India that something is going on over there, though it's different, less organised. Britain needs to play catch up, but we're good at doing that. Good at taking the lead."

"How long have you known about talents?"

"Longer than you might think."

"How did you even start looking?"

"I told you about the professor in Oxford. He introduced me to the esoteric."

"Did you go to Oxford, then?"

Elizabeth laughed. "What, a mere girl like me? No, but I lived in the city for a while. It was a stroke of luck, really. I lodged in this man's house, and we talked. I think he liked talking to someone who didn't dismiss his ideas out of hand."

"So what are they? Harry calls them spooky. Is he right, or are they something else? Something my sister might understand?"

"I'm still working that through. My tame professor is old-fashioned. He thinks talent is connected to the mystic, the other world that lies alongside this one."

"Which might go some way to explaining what I can do," Calum said. "Perhaps I tap into that other world, one that is slightly ahead of ours."

"Perhaps."

"But you don't believe that, do you?"

Elizabeth's feet slowed, and she turned to Calum. "I believe talent has a more scientific explanation. I just haven't worked out what it is yet. If I ever do, it could make a huge difference. There will be rules, theorems, perhaps even a way to make our talents stronger using machinery of some kind." She stared at Calum for a moment, and he felt a strong connection between them. Then she shook her head and turned away. "Come on, let's concentrate on the matter at hand. We can talk again when we find some time, and I'll try to explain to you what I do believe."

The others were waiting for them at the main entrance. Two armed soldiers stood guard in the corridor to the inner rooms. They were staring hard at the group until Elizabeth and Calum arrived, though Calum knew their change in attitude owed nothing to his presence. Elizabeth crossed the vestibule and spoke softly with them. When they parted, she called the rest of their group to follow her.

They entered a reception room staffed by three women, each sitting behind a desk, together with the tall man from their meeting. He gave a nod to Elizabeth and turned away, taking a bunch of keys from his jacket pocket and unlocking the far door.

He led the way into a room fifty feet by forty. It was lined with steel cabinets that rose ten feet to the ceiling. Every inch of the walls, other than the door, was given over to the cabinets. A small rectangular table sat in the room's centre, a narrow library ladder pushed into one corner. There were no chairs. The man watched as they all filed inside then cocked his head at Elizabeth.

"Do you need all these people?"

"They are here as observers. My thanks."

The man made no move to leave.

"I take it the cabinets are locked?" asked Elizabeth.

"Of course, and I have no intention of changing that state of affairs. I have offered you access only because of the name you provided me, but I don't have to like doing it."

"Your secrets are safe with us. We're all on the same side, aren't we? But we'll work more effectively left to our own devices."

The man remained where he was. He shuffled the chain of keys through his fingers in a sign of possible nervousness.

"Do you want me to make another telephone call?" Elizabeth reached into her bag. "I have the name and number here." She held a slip of paper out. The man glanced at it, looked away.

"Very well. One hour, no more."

"We should be done well before then."

When they were alone, Harry put his back against the door. It remained unlocked, but he would form some kind of barrier should anyone seek entry. Elizabeth came to stand beside Calum, Maria and Richard.

Bill Harrison walked around the room. He trailed his fingers across the smooth surface of the table, then went to one wall of cabinets and laid his hands flat across them, arms spread. He closed his eyes.

Nobody moved. Calum tried to still his breathing, as if the whisper of it might disturb the man in front of him. He grew aware of a static charge in the air and felt his hair stand on end. When he glanced at Elizabeth, he saw the same thing happening to her. Her longer blonde tresses stood out from her head. Calum turned to Maria to see the same. He looked at Harry, the sceptic among them, but saw all trace of it gone. Whatever was happening in the room made Bill Harrison one of them. More than one of them. He made Calum feel like an imposter.

The charged air crackled even more. Without warning, the door of one of the locked cabinets sprang open and clattered back against the one beside it.

Bill Harrison pointed. "There is a red file in there." His voice was soft, calm. "If you would be so kind as to place it on the table, I might be able to find out a little more."

Elizabeth crossed and pulled out a folder. She laid it on the table and flicked through the papers before stepping back. Bill took her place, but instead of reading what was there, he picked up the folder and closed his eyes. For several minutes nothing happened. Bill swayed slightly, but the sense of electric charge had subsided.

Finally, Bill spoke, his eyes still closed. "It's what I thought. An atomic weapon. These documents contain the original British research, together with what the Americans have done since. It's all locked up here in a place where it has always been considered safe. But that's only the what. I'm still searching for the who."

Bill opened his eyes, set the folder down and took out several sheets of paper, his choice seeming random to everyone but him. He laid them out side by side, then leaned close. Calum saw him breathe in deeply, like a dog examining a scent. He ran his fingers over the papers several times, then set his hands flat on two.

"She typed all of these, but these are the most recent."

"Who is she?" asked Elizabeth.

"I'm trying to find that out. I can almost… no… yes, I can describe her, but there's no name. She works in London, but all the top-secret stuff is held here. It's safer than in the city." Bill remained where he was for another few minutes, then turned away. "You can put them back now, my dear. I've got everything I can from them."

Elizabeth gathered the papers and returned the folder from where she took it. When she pushed the broken door it locked back into place with a soft click.

"There's more," said Bill, "but that's the meat of it. An atomic weapon. Unfortunately, not ours. Not any more." He looked into Elizabeth's eyes. "How much do you know about it?"

"Less than you, I suspect."

"But you are not obsessed about such things, whereas I am." He looked around the room, meeting the eyes of each of them before returning to Elizabeth. "How much am I allowed to tell the others?"

"Everything. I decided that a long time ago when I first pitched my plans for Unit-13," said Elizabeth. "We are all equals. There can be no secrets between us. None. What one knows, we must all know." She gave a brief smile. "We already know so much about each other there can be few secrets."

"Then I'll explain what I can while we travel because we are going to have to go back to London. I can describe the woman who stole the information, and have a vague sense of a street of terraced houses close to the docks, but no name. Did you notice the numbers on each of the pages?"

"Of course. We can use them to track where they were produced. We might even be able to find out who typed them up. I'll get onto it as soon as we're out of here. How did she do it? Some miniature camera smuggled in beneath her underwear?"

"I believe they check everywhere," said Bill. "So no, she didn't take anything either in or out. She memorised the information."

Elizabeth stared at him. "How could she do that? There were pages and pages of it."

"She didn't type them all the same day, did she? She didn't even work on all of them. When we catch up with her, I think you'll discover she has an eidetic memory. She can reproduce whatever she reads or types."

Calum went with the others while Elizabeth disappeared to make some phone calls. He watched Bill, who walked at a small distance. His face was grey, and every few steps, his feet scuffed against the ground. There was a cost to his talent that he was paying for now.

It was a shock when he saw his sister walk from the canteen. It felt as if hours had passed since they were inside the canteen, but when he glanced at his watch, it showed him they had left it only twenty minutes before.

Turing remained at Jeannie's side, and once more Calum wondered if he and his sister were a romantic item, though something told him they were likely not.

Jeannie glanced up, saw him and gave a wave. She came across, and after a moment Turing followed.

Calum nodded. "Alan."

The man nodded back before looking at the rest of them, his eyes resting for a moment on Richard, who had drawn himself fully into the present as an act of politeness.

"Did you find what you were looking for?" asked Jeannie. "You came looking for something, I assume."

"We did," Calum said.

"I wish we could stay and chat," said Turing, "but we need to get back to work, Jean. There must be a reason for the glitch, and it won't fix itself." His eyes came back to meet Calum's. "Good to meet you again. All of you." He hesitated, then gave a shy smile. "I assume you have the highest clearance?"

"The very highest," said Harry before Calum could reply.

"In that case, come and take a look at what we're doing."

Jeannie looked at him. "Are you sure, Alan? We're not meant to show our work to anyone."

"Half this damn place knows what we're doing, and I'm fully aware most consider it a joke. Can I not show it off a little, for once? And didn't you tell me your brother could be trusted? He is one of the good people, is what you said." He turned away before Jeannie could object.

"I'm sorry, Cal, but he's under a lot of strain. People are starting to ask questions. They think he's failed. That what he's trying to do can't be achieved."

"We all understand that feeling," Calum said.

"Come if you want," she said, "I don't suppose it will do any harm. There's not much point keeping a secret about something that only works when it feels like it." She led the way to the tall barn-like structure Calum had noted before. Inside, a small group of men were manipulating wires plugged into some kind of switchboard that stood twice as high as them.

Calum had no idea what the device was meant to do. Harry walked up to the tangle of wires and leaned closer to examine them. Turing said something to him, pointing to various elements. After a moment, Harry turned to him and asked a question. Calum smiled, sure he knew what it was.

Turing appeared reluctant, then shrugged.

"He's getting desperate," Jeannie whispered to Calum.

"Are you all right, sis?"

She gave a brief nod. "I'm fine, Cal."

He hesitated, then asked, "Are you and Alan an item, by any chance?"

Jeannie gave one of her rare laughs. "Alan? I think not. I'm pretty sure he likes you a lot better than he does me. Sometimes I think I'm little more than camouflage for him."

"I don't understand."

"No, I don't suppose you do. I'll explain when you grow up."

Calum frowned, as much in the dark as he was before. He watched as Harry reached out to the device. He touched the wires, wiggled the connections as if it might make a difference. Then he closed his eyes and laid both palms on the surface in a near-copy of what Bill had done in the storage room. The men working on the machine stood aside, glancing at one another in confusion.

A static spark ran across the mechanism, touched Harry and made him jerk. He stepped back and looked across the jumble of wires, then gave a nod, turned and walked back to join them. Turing accompanied him while his men fussed about looking for any damage.

"You have a marvellous machine there, Mr Turing," said Harry.

"Thank you. I'm afraid not everyone shares your opinion. It needs to work more reliably before my bosses believe in what I have created." He shook Harry's hand, then did the same with each of them. He spent longer grasping Richard's, staring at him as if trying to work something out. Richard was on his best behaviour, not fading at all.

Finally, Turing came to Calum and shook his hand. "It has been a pleasure to meet you, Calum. Maybe we can get that drink some other time."

"It would be my pleasure. Look after Jeannie for me."

"Of course I will."

Calum kissed Jeannie's cheek, and this time she didn't flinch. She even squeezed his hand.

"Nice couple," said Harry.

"Yes," Calum said. "Maybe they are."

"I think his contraption will work fine now," said Harry with a grin.

They were playing a make-do game of cricket with a plank from some pallets and a ball formed from rolled-up paper when Elizabeth emerged half-an-hour later.

"Any luck?" asked Harry.

"Lilian Hamer," said Elizabeth. "She lives the other side of the river. Works nights but didn't turn up yesterday. I don't see how she might have got wind of us, but according to the clerk I managed to track down, it's the first time she's ever missed work. So we go there now. All of us."

"Do we need support?" asked Calum.

"She's a middle-aged woman. Do you think you won't be able to manage her, Cal?" She patted his cheek. "If it makes you feel safer, I made a phone call while we were inside."

CHAPTER TWENTY-SEVEN

John Simpson was standing next to the long Rover when they emerged into the car park. They all managed to squeeze in, this time Calum and Elizabeth in front. Maria sat on Richard's knee in the back seat between Harry and Bill. By the time they reached London, the streets were dark, their own headlights scarcely brighter than a candle in the dusk. The car crossed the river using Westminster Bridge, then turned east. There were rumours the blackout might end soon, but it hadn't yet. There was little traffic until they approached their destination, then Calum saw a fire-engine and a police car blocking the road ahead.

"Bugger," said John Simpson. "Looks like another house has come down."

Elizabeth leaned forward, trying to see through the gloom. "Can you tell which one?"

"Would it make a difference if I could?" He slowed the car, stopped three yards from a policeman who was waving them down. He climbed out and approached the man. Elizabeth slid from beside Calum and followed.

Calum stayed where he was, watching as Elizabeth performed her own kind of magic. Once again, she didn't need to reach into her bag for Churchill's letter. The man nodded and stepped aside, but another brief conversation ensued. When she finished, Elizabeth strolled back to the car while John Simpson walked towards the destroyed building.

Calum suspected he knew who the house belonged to – at least when it had been a house rather than a pile of bricks. Elizabeth confirmed this when she opened the door and leaned in.

"Everyone out, though this might be a waste of time. The demolished building is the address our suspect lives at. I have been informed there are no survivors, but I'd rather we confirm the fact for ourselves." She leaned over the front seat. "Do you think you might get anything from the ruins, Bill?"

He smiled. "A bomb site and whispers trapped in bricks? I think so, my dear. Let me at it."

The policeman snapped off a salute as Calum passed, some instinct telling him he was a fellow uniformed man despite the way he was dressed. The house was a middle terrace. Those on either side remained standing, but only just.

"Bloody lucky kind of bomb-strike, if you ask me," said Bill. "Any idea what it was?"

"The policeman claimed a doodlebug," said Elizabeth.

John Simpson overheard the comment as he returned from talking with a clutch of firefighters who had finished damping down the last of the flames. A small group of neighbours stood around, watching the entertainment.

"Not a doodlebug, according to others in the street and the firefighters. Their theory is a gas explosion. They say a bomb would have taken more than the one house out."

"It would," said Bill. "But gas would have done less damage than this." He glanced at Elizabeth. "Do you think I can get closer?"

"I'll ask." She looked across at the others. "You come as well, Cal. The rest of you go back to the car. John, ask around and see if there's anywhere we can summon up some grub from. Sandwiches will do; soup would be better."

They approached the group of firemen who, it appeared, already had sandwiches. One neighbour, a pinafore over her dress, was handing out mugs of tea from a tray.

"My man would like a closer look," said Elizabeth to the officer who appeared to be in charge. "Is it safe enough?"

"The neighbours' walls won't fall down, but there's a lot of rubble underfoot. He can go in if he wants, but it's on his head if he falls through into the cellar. Some of the floor's missing."

Elizabeth looked at the man. "Is the cellar intact?"

"Might be, but we haven't been down there."

"Could there be anyone trapped?"

"The dogs have been over the site and found nothing, so I'd say no, but we'll check it out in a while." The man glanced to where Bill was already picking his way into the remains of the building.

Calum watched him, recognising the signs now. Bill was listening to whispers, stitching together the last week of conversations held in the fabric of the house that now lay broken around him. Calum wondered how it felt. Was it like his own talent, always there in the background, ready to be used when needed? Or was it silent until required? He realised he had met Bill only earlier that day. There was so much he didn't know about him. So much the rest of them didn't know about each other. Who their families were. Where they were raised. He didn't even know where any of them worked when they were picked to join Unit-13. He felt it was an omission, one he intended to correct as soon as he found the time. When that might be, he had no idea.

"What does he think he's doing?"

Calum returned to the present as the lead fireman spoke. He directed two of his men to go check on Bill, but Elizabeth stopped them.

"It's what he does," she said, offering no further explanation.

The fireman stared at her. After a moment, he moved away as if wanting nothing to do with the strange group that had descended on their work.

Bill was sitting on a pile of bricks, his hands spread to either side, with his fingers buried into shattered plaster. His eyes were closed, his chin almost touching his chest. As Calum stared at him, he was sure he could make out a faint halo of light surrounding the man.

Calum started when something touched his hand, but

it was only a neighbour handing out tea. She had made more sandwiches, perhaps a contribution from the entire street, and was pressing one into Calum's hand. He took it, expressing his thanks, then took the mug of hot tea in his other hand.

"Can you see it?" asked Maria, who came to stand at his side.

"If you mean the light, then yes, I can."

"It's coming from his body." She glanced around. "Do you think the firemen see it, too? Is that why they've moved away?"

"Can you read them?" Calum asked.

"I need to be closer than this."

Calum glanced down at her. "Has Elizabeth been trying to help you with that?"

"A little. Has she been doing the same for you?"

Calum gave a nod and bit into his sandwich. It was paste, but whether fish or meat he couldn't decide.

"That's not all she's been doing with you though, is it?"

He tried to hear some judgement in her voice, some hurt he had not chosen her. In other circumstances, he knew she would make a pleasant companion. Perhaps on another day, in another place. Who knew what tomorrow might bring?

He swallowed the plug of bread and whatever it was. "You tell me, Maria. Read what's in my head."

She looked down. "It feels like spying when I do it to someone I know. Someone I like."

"Do it anyway. I want you to."

"Are you sure?"

Calum offered a nod, unsure exactly why he was

making the offer. Perhaps he wanted only to find out how skilled she was. His own talent had improved tenfold since he started taking Elizabeth's advice. Perhaps Maria's was the same. Or better.

"Can I hold your hand?" she asked, her voice tiny. "It helps."

Calum set his mug of tea on the ground and held his hand out. Maria slipped hers inside it.

She closed her eyes.

Calum looked past her to where Bill continued to sit like a statue. The rest of the world faded away as if it no longer existed. Somewhere people spoke, but it was all distant, wrapped in cotton wool. Something coiled through his mind, not physical, but a presence all the same, and he knew it was Maria. What was she seeing? What was she hearing, reading, knowing? Calum was suddenly unsure this was such a good idea, but he felt trapped now, unable to break free. As his awareness of himself shrank, so his awareness of those around him grew. Except it was not their physical selves but the spark of their essence, the things that made them unique. Maria was sharing her talent with him.

Harry was the calm at the centre of a storm, his thoughts simple and straightforward. His mind worked like the machines he had an affinity for.

Richard was sharper, like a finely honed knife. For him, existence was a constant danger of being discovered. It was part of the reason he had learned to be what he was, to hide his real self. The thought sparked another, something Maria must have seen when they were at

Bletchley. Jeannie and Turing were the same as she and Richard.

Calum closed his eyes because sight was a distraction as he drifted like mist across the ground.

John Simpson was stone and iron, all unquestioning duty. A spark of emotion shone dimly in one corner, and Calum saw who was the recipient of his love and felt a smile touch his own lips.

And then there was Elizabeth. He had avoided her, unsure if this was not even more intimate than the physical closeness they had shared the night before. He sensed Maria could read every thought that slid through his mind. Confirmed when he sensed a sadness in hers. Calum was aware of Elizabeth's shape in this ether, a shape different to the one she showed the world. She was stillness and surety. Confident, with an awareness far in excess of her years.

Then he felt her close herself down as she felt their psychic attention on her. His eyes snapped open to see her staring at him with a look of almost horror. Her entire body was tense, and he saw she was trying to hold herself in check. He had invaded her without permission, and she was angry.

Maria released his hand and stepped away.

"I'm sorry, Cal, I didn't know."

"Of course you did."

"Not about the two of you. Nobody has to be a mind reader to see that. I didn't know about your brother. I'm sorry."

"It was a long time ago."

"Was it? You know..." She let whatever thought she

was going to express trail away as Bill rose to his feet. Instead of returning, he went deeper into the chaos of the rubble, knelt and picked something up. It was a small, well-loved teddy bear, almost white with plaster dust. Bill held it by the paw, then turned and walked back to the firemen.

"There's a little girl in the cellar. She's alive, and she's scared. All the others are dead or gone."

The lead fireman stared at Bill. "How the hell do you know all that?"

"Don't worry about how I know it, just get her out. She's six years old and in fear for her life. There are rats down there. She's soaked from a broken water pipe, and thinks she's about to drown. Go fetch her, for God's sake." Bill turned away, his face once more white as snow.

Elizabeth reached out and touched his arm, and Bill looked up.

"Go sit in the car. You've done good work tonight. We'll talk to the girl when she comes out."

Bill shook his head, wiped his face with his free hand, the teddy bear still hanging in the other. "I've got more work to do yet. The girl doesn't know what she saw, what she heard. Yes, I'll go in the car, but I want you and Cal with me. I need witnesses. Sometimes when I go deep I don't always remember everything."

"What do you know so far?" Elizabeth took his elbow and steered him in the car's direction. As she passed John Simpson, she said, "As soon as the girl's out, come and fetch me."

Calum followed. He slid into the front seat as Elizabeth pushed Bill into the back and got in beside him.

"It was no doodlebug," said Bill, settling himself. He lifted the teddy bear and stared at it, then clutched it against his chest as if he needed the comfort it might offer. "It wasn't a bomb that brought the house down. There were explosives planted. Cleverly planted to make it look like a bomb." He lifted the bear and stared into its face, gave a smile. "Snoozle knows everything."

"Snoozle?" said Elizabeth.

Bill lifted the teddy to show her, wiggled it from side to side and said, "Hello, Elizabeth," in a high voice. He laughed. "The girl – her name is Sally, by the way – calls her bear Snoozle. She was sitting at the top of the cellar steps and heard everything. Fortunately, she only heard, not saw, because her parents had their throats cut before the killers left with the papers." Bill set the teddy bear in his lap, his hands supporting it. "Cal, go fetch Maria; we're going to need her. The girl didn't understand what they said because the entire conversation was in German."

CHAPTER TWENTY-EIGHT

Maria came back with Elizabeth and got in behind the steering wheel before leaning over the seat back. She waited as Bill raised a hand. He lifted the teddy bear again, hesitant, then his gaze turned away from the outside world as he clutched it against his chest. Watching him, Calum knew this is how the girl had sat, taking what comfort she could from her best friend in the world.

Minutes passed. Bill rocked backwards and forwards. Elizabeth shifted to the corner of the rear seat to give him space.

The air inside the car changed, carrying a now-familiar electrical charge. It felt like standing close to a big generator. Then Bill spoke, slow and deep in a voice that didn't sound like his own, unless that was because the words were German.

Maria translated, then stopped and listened. When Elizabeth started to ask her something, she held up a hand. "He's reciting every word, and it will only confuse you. Wait, and I'll tell you the important parts as I work them out."

Calum watched Bill, the static in the air making the hairs on his head itch.

"Three men," Maria said. "Plus the woman and her husband."

"Only the one child?" Elizabeth asked.

"Only the one."

Bill stopped speaking German and said in his normal voice. "They didn't want any more kids until the war was over. Thought it wouldn't be fair on them. They weren't sure they would survive. Didn't want to leave them orphaned." He took a deep breath, like a man about to dive into deep water, then closed his eyes again. A moment later, the German returned to his tongue.

"Both of them were in on the plan," said Maria. "Husband and wife. They… no, it's not there, but I don't think they were sleepers, not German but British." She waited, listening, then said, "Yes, one man mentioned money. Had they not been paid enough already? They wanted the documents she had transcribed. She had given them a single page as a teaser, and they wanted the rest."

"I don't understand," said Elizabeth. "A single page?"

"It was enough if she put the right information in it. I can sense Bill can work all this out. The Nazis are already working on their own atomic weapon. They're behind the Americans and us, but close enough that getting their hands on the right information would let them catch up, maybe even overtake us. Lilian Hamer transcribed at least forty pages, as close as I can determine from what Bill discovered, but her husband persuaded her the material was worth more money. Now don't interrupt again until I finish. This is hard enough as it is without having to explain myself all the time."

Elizabeth closed her mouth and sat primly, chastised.

Maria reached out for Calum's hand, seeking some comfort from the story she had to tell. To him, it felt like a small betrayal, the contact hidden from Elizabeth behind the seat.

"They're arguing," said Maria. "The Nazis are refusing to pay more... more than a thousand pounds." She interjected her own opinion. "A thousand pounds? Can any pieces of paper be worth that much?"

"If what Bill says they contain is right they'll be worth millions in saved effort and research," said Elizabeth.

"There's noise. A fight, I think," said Bill. "Chairs knocked over, china smashed, and then... then everything goes quiet for a while. The couple are dead now. Then more sounds. Drawers being opened, tossed to the ground. One of them has sent the other two out to the car for explosives while he continues the search. He's talking to himself, muttering, discarding useless papers, newspapers, books. Then he makes a sound. He's kneeling. His voice is strained. Perhaps he's on his front, reaching deep behind something. Then he laughs and swears, says he's found them. He claims the English must be stupid if that was the best hiding place they could think of."

Bill started to speak German again, and Maria translated. "The others have returned. They're laying charges. One of them comes towards the cellar and puts his hand on the latch. He says they need to check the rest of the house, but he's told it doesn't matter if there's anyone else because they'll be dead in five minutes. The girl runs down the stairs when she hears his hand on the latch. She presses herself into the old fireplace. It's the only reason she's alive because the rest of the cellar will fill with rubble. She hears the men leave and wants to go upstairs to Mummy and Daddy, but she's scared the men might try to trick her. So she stays where she is with Snoozle and tries to cry as quietly as she can. Then there's an enormous bang and the house falls in on itself, and when she searches Snoozle is gone."

Maria sat back, breathing hard, tears in her eyes. Her fingers squeezed Calum's hard.

Bill slumped against the back of the seat, and from the colour of his face, Calum was afraid he might be having a heart attack.

Harry tapped on the window beside Calum, and he opened the door.

"The girl's out. She's alive and in pretty good shape, considering, but she's crying because she lost her teddy bear."

Bill smiled without opening his eyes and held it out. "Here, take it to her. It's told me everything it knows."

Calum took the bear and passed it to Harry.

Elizabeth cursed, a single word that made Maria giggle and cover her mouth as if the same word might have been on the tip of her own tongue.

"We know what happened, but we're no further forward," said Elizabeth.

"There's something else," said Maria. "It wasn't part of the story, so I set it aside until now, but it's the most important part. One man said, 'This is what Carlton has been searching for the last three years. We have to take it to the house in Elmsted at once. He will reward us. Herr Hitler will reward us. This might yet save the Fatherland.'"

"Indeed it might," muttered Elizabeth. She frowned. "Are you sure that's what they said? They used the name Carlton?"

"They did."

"I heard it, too," said Bill, "but there must be a thousand men in Britain called Carlton."

"Bill's right," Calum said. "It's far more likely to be a different Carlton."

"Perhaps," said Elizabeth, "but do you really think so?" She swore again. Twice.

Bill sat up and opened his eyes. He would have no idea who they were talking about.

"So you know him? Who is he?"

"If it is him, his name is Sir Edward Carlton," said Elizabeth. "If you had joined us at the same time as the others, you would have met him. He's supposedly in charge of Unit-13, except he appears to take no notice of us at all. No wonder if he's been running a spy ring for the Nazis." She shook her head. "It makes sense, with his links to Mosley and visits to Germany in the thirties."

"Where's Elmsted?" Calum asked. "If it is Carlton, that's where we'll find him. I wouldn't mind giving him a black eye."

"Get in line, chum," said a returned Harry. "The bastard. He's been selling our country out to the Third Reich. I'll give him more than a bloody black eye."

"Elmsted is in Kent," said Elizabeth. "And we don't

know for sure it's our Carlton, but if it is, he'll be hanged for what he's done and good riddance." She looked at each of them. "Elmsted is a small hamlet eight or nine miles north of Folkestone. An excellent location for a spy ring to set themselves up."

"Wouldn't that make them stand out even more?" Calum asked.

"Not if they're a sleeper cell. They could have been there for decades. They might even have been born there. The Service has uncovered scores of similar cells throughout the war, but news of them never gets out." Elizabeth smiled. "Elmsted is small enough. We can probably work out where they are." She glanced across at Bill, who was recovering. "Can you travel?"

"Of course I can. I'm exhausted, not sick."

Elizabeth opened the door and stepped out. "Stay here while I fetch the others. If we leave now, we might catch them before they can take the documents across the channel."

John Simpson drove faster than Calum had ever seen him do. The car, enhanced by Harry's talent, sped through a countryside bathed by the light of a full moon. It illuminated the road ahead far better than their headlights. Elizabeth had taken the middle front seat, with Harry on her left. Maria had decided Calum's lap was more comfortable than Richard's, who sat on Bill's other side. Calum grasped the strap above the door to stop himself from tipping over as the car screeched around every turn, his right arm around Maria's waist to stop her from doing the same. If they survived the journey, they might stand a chance.

John Simpson followed the A2020 as far as he could before cutting across country on smaller roads once they passed through Ashford. They followed the scarp slope of the Downs until a milestone flashed past. The cement used to obscure it at the start of the war had crumbled and the etching could just be read. It said Elmsted 2 miles. Calum glanced at his watch, which told him it was a little after four in the morning.

Finally, John Simpson slowed. The roads they had traversed should have made him do so before, but he had ignored the danger of meeting whatever might come the other way, and they had been fortunate.

"How do you want to do this?" he asked Elizabeth.

"If we see a pub stop, we can knock the landlord up. They're bound to know everybody in a place this small."

"And if the landlord turns out to be who we're after?"

"Then it will save us having to look any further, won't it," said Elizabeth.

John Simpson shook his head, and Calum shared his judgement. As it turned out, there was no pub. In fact, they drove right through the scatter of houses before they realised that was all the hamlet consisted of. John Simpson braked hard and reversed into an open gate, drove back more slowly. The moon outlined six houses set back from the road.

"Nothing much here." John Simpson glanced over his shoulder at Bill. "Are you sure you heard them right?"

"I am."

"John, go and knock on some doors," said Elizabeth. She twisted around so she could see the rear seat better. "Have you still got that pistol you stole, Harry?"

He reached under his jacket and pulled out the Webley.

"I've also got a couple of machine rifles in the boot," said John Simpson, "and another pistol in the glove box."

"Go with John as backup," she said to Harry. "If anyone answers and they're not who we're after, ask if they know of someone nearby."

"They won't be acting like spies," said John Simpson. "They'll be regarded as just another neighbour."

"Do you think I don't know that? But maybe someone has a germ of suspicion. And if it is Sir Edward Carlton, they'll remember him. Besides, what else have we got?"

John Simpson killed the engine and climbed out. Harry followed, the pistol held down at his side. Calum watched as they went to the nearest house and knocked on the door.

"You should have gone with him," he said to Elizabeth. "You could have flashed that letter of yours and they'd tell you everything they know."

She said nothing. Moonlight reflected in her eyes, which were on the two men.

John Simpson continued to knock. Eventually, the light of a candle showed behind the front door and it opened. A brief conversation ensued, then the door slammed shut. The pair continued to the next house.

Ten minutes passed before they returned.

"Nobody much enjoyed being woken up in the middle

of the night," said Harry as he slid into the back seat beside Bill.

"Was it a total waste of time?" asked Elizabeth.

"The last house belonged to a farmer," said John Simpson. "He was already up getting ready to milk his cows, so he was in a better mood than the rest. He told us there's a house set on its own a mile further along this road."

"And?" said Elizabeth.

"He said they're funny buggers, and funny goings-on. Told me he's reported them twice to the local bobby but nothing came of it. He rubbed his fingers together as if to say money might have changed hands. I asked him if whoever lived there might be well off. Stinking rich, the farmer said. Tall bugger. Posh accent." John Simpson smiled. "Does that sound like someone we know?"

"It does. Did the farmer say who else was there?"

"People come and go, but he thinks there are four at the moment. He's got land not so far from there and sees their comings and goings. I omitted to mention why we are looking for them, of course, but he didn't appear surprised somebody was."

Elizabeth looked ahead along the road, which climbed the shoulder of a low hill. Dawn was only an hour away, and already the sky to the east showed a faint glow.

"That direction's south," she said. "They'll want to be as close to the coast as they can be without drawing suspicion. They'll also want to have some height if they have a radio for communication. Go slow, John. Everyone else, keep your eyes peeled on either side. We're looking for… I don't know what we're looking for, but with luck something will jump out at us."

Calum didn't consider it much of a plan, but he had nothing better to offer, so he turned as far as he could with Maria on his knee and stared out at the moonlit countryside. High hedges obscured the land from the road most of the time, and any houses would show no lights, particularly this close to the channel. He had heard bombers passing overhead as they returned home from their night raids. He recognised the sound of their own planes flying east and south. Once, he heard the crack of a rocket as it passed overhead, presumably on its way to London. No doubt it had landed only seconds after the sound reached them.

They moved slowly along a road barely wider than the car until, without warning, the engine missed a beat. It caught again, then died entirely.

John Simpson tapped the dials. "Plenty of fuel." He looked back at Harry. "Can you take a look, old chap?"

Harry climbed out and opened the bonnet.

"Turn her over," he called out.

John Simpson pulled the starter but nothing happened, not even the click of a dead solenoid. Calum slid Maria from his knee and got out, went to stand beside Harry, who had his hands as close to the engine block as the heat would allow.

"Nothing there," he said. "Dead as a dodo."

Calum looked around. He saw a wooden field-gate twenty yards along the road and went to it, lifted himself up so he stood on the middle bars and stared around. In one direction, he could just make out the small cluster of houses that marked Elmsted. In the other, a single house stood alone two hundred yards away. It sat at the end of a grassed driveway, trees rising behind, the moon hanging above. He looked around as the others joined him.

"That place has got to be worth a try," he said.

Elizabeth climbed up beside him, clinging to his arm, and he knew she would come to the same conclusion he had but would have to do it for herself. Eventually, she nodded and jumped down.

"What did you say you had in the boot?" she asked John Simpson.

"Got my service pistol here," he patted a bulge beneath his jacket. "There's another in the glove box and a brace of Sten submachine guns in there." He looked at Bill, who nodded and walked back to the car to fetch the SMGs.

"Some poor farmer's in for one hell of a shock if he's an innocent party in all this," said Harry.

"We'll worry about that if it happens," said Elizabeth. "Calum, take the other pistol. Harry, give yours to Bill and take one of the machine guns. Richard, take the other. Four of us go to the house. Bill, you stay here with Maria in case someone tries to get past us."

"You might need me," said Bill. "If they've fled the nest, I can tell you what they said. And you'll need Maria to translate."

He appeared to have accepted the strangeness of their group as if it was normal. Perhaps to him, it was. Calum knew he had grown used to his own talent and rarely gave it much thought anymore. Except now, as the idea came to him, he grew aware of its lack.

He pressed out, using some invisible muscle in search of the future, and failed to find it.

"Elizabeth, something's wrong," he said.

"I know something's wrong, but standing here won't get those bloody secrets back."

"Not that. I can't see the future." He looked around at the others. "Harry, when you had your hands over the engine, you said you couldn't find anything wrong."

"There wasn't anything wrong, or I would have known."

"Or your talent has stopped working, like mine." He looked at Bill, who had returned with the machine guns and the other pistol from the car's front. Calum held his hand out and took the pistol, checked it over. He watched as Harry took one of the SMGs, Richard the other.

Harry gripped the dark metal sheened with oil and frowned. "I should be able to feel this gun," he said, "and I can't. There's nothing there. Nothing at all."

"Maria, try to read my thoughts," Calum said. He waited as she came closer, the distance unnecessary, and saw a realisation come to her.

She shook her head. "I can't, Cal."

"Looks like we'll have to do this the old-fashioned way," said John Simpson. "Just how I like it." He drew his own pistol and spun the chamber.

"Try firing it," said Harry.

John Simpson shook his head. "And warn whoever's in that house? Are you nuts?"

Harry didn't bother with a reply. He turned and pointed his SMG out into the field, snicked the safety off, and pulled the trigger.

Nothing happened.

He worked the slide again, checked the mechanism and tried a second time – still nothing.

John Simpson stared at his own pistol. He raised it, cocked the hammer and drew on the trigger. It fell with a dull click on the cartridge.

"What the hell?"

Elizabeth looked back at the car. It sat with all four doors open, the bonnet and boot both raised, completely open to the night air.

She turned to Richard. "Disappear," she said.

Richard remained where he was, no need to do anything on the surface. They all watched, waiting for him to fade as he always did. Except this time, nothing happened.

"Shit," said Elizabeth. "Looks like we really are going to have to do this the old-fashioned way. All right, change of plan. Richard, stay here with Maria. John, give him your pistol and take the SMG. Who knows, if we can work out what's going on, we might actually get to shoot someone. If they haven't seen us and done a runner. Come on." She turned away and walked towards the metal gates marking the driveway to the house.

After a while, Calum started after her, wondering just what was going on.

CHAPTER TWENTY-NINE

Calum glanced across at Elizabeth as he fell into step beside her. The moonlight was harsh on her features and seemed to add twenty years to her age. She even walked differently, with a slight limp on her left side. He had never seen her look so exhausted, and he was aware neither of them had slept in over 24 hours.

He was about to reach out to offer some support when she said, "Never try that trick on me again, Cal."

He stopped dead in his tracks. "What trick?" He had no idea what she was talking about.

"Don't pretend you don't know. You and Maria looking into all our heads. Looking into *my* head." She turned her back on the house and stared at him with cold eyes. "What were you thinking of? Didn't our time in the hotel mean anything to you at all?"

"It meant everything to me. You know it did. And I'm sorry, but..." Calum's voice trailed off as he became aware that any excuse he might make was only that – an excuse.

"Well, I hope you found what you were looking for."

"I've already told you, I'm sorry. And for what it's worth, neither of us could read anything. Nothing at all."

Elizabeth made a huffing sound and turned away. Calum wondered if she was actually studying the house or only putting on a show for him.

"What are we going to do?" she said. "Walk up and knock on the door?"

"You tell me." Calum was still angry with her. "That's what you do, isn't it? Direct the rest of us."

Elizabeth shook her head. "My head is filled with cotton wool. No wonder you couldn't see anything in there." She looked at Calum, anguish on her face. "I don't know what to do, Cal."

He caught her elbow, and this time she didn't shake him off. "Then go back to the car and stay with the others. You're no good to any of us like this." He saw his words hurt, but not as much as her failure of leadership would hurt them all.

John Simpson and Harry reached them and halted, waiting for instructions.

"I can't go back," said Elizabeth. "I have to be here. I know I have to be here. But…" She looked at each of them, fear in her eyes. "John, I'm putting Cal in charge. I'm not feeling too good, so I want you to follow his orders."

Calum didn't know if the man would. He was a major, a man of rank, and Calum had been a lowly flight sergeant when he had a rank. But John Simpson nodded.

"Sure thing, old girl."

For the first time, Elizabeth looked like an old girl. A very old girl.

"Stay back," Calum said to her. "Is there anything you know about Carlton that might be useful?"

Elizabeth shook her head. "I always considered him one of those inept aristocrats that get pushed into positions where they can do the least harm. If he's involved in this, then I got him all wrong. Very wrong."

"Do you think he has talent?" Calum asked. "Is the lack of our own anything to do with him?"

"I don't know!" Elizabeth's response was a wail of anguish. "If it is, it's nothing like I've ever come across before. And it means he knows we're here. Do what you can, Cal. I think I might go back to the car after all. I'm not doing any good here."

Calum watched her walk away, shoulders hunched, feet stumbling. If pressed, he'd put her age at eighty if he didn't know better. He turned away from watching, aware they were wasting time. He took a breath and considered their options.

"John, go around back in case anyone tries to sneak out that way. Harry, with me." Calum turned away and started towards the front door. When he looked up he saw a shadow cross an upstairs window and walked faster.

"Straight in and see what happens?" asked Harry.

"Can't think of any other option," Calum said. "How many in there, I wonder?"

Harry brandished the SMG. "This might not fire anything, but it makes a damned good club. Use your pistol the same way. Go in fast and go in hard. Hit the first one, then the next."

Calum was trying to remember the last time he had

been involved in a fight and couldn't. Probably when he was a teenager in school. There had been a few run-ins as word spread about his strangeness. He recalled he had acquitted himself pretty well in those skirmishes. But he had his talent to use then and could see the blows coming, avoiding them with ease. Now he was locked in the present, but if the people in the house had the stolen information now was the time to stop them, before they left the country.

He slowed as they approached the front door. Reached out and tried the handle. It turned, but the door remained obstinately closed when Calum put his shoulder against it.

"Here," Harry hissed. He stood below a window, which stood open a crack. Harry reached in and eased the catch up. The window swung out and Harry wriggled through, his legs waving for a moment before he fell inside with a curse.

Calum followed, lifting himself up on the window-frame so his feet entered first. He landed on his toes and looked around the dark room. A single chair stood in one corner, but there was nothing else. This wasn't a place to live in, merely a stopping off point on the way to somewhere else. A faint light came from the hallway beyond and he crept towards it, expecting resistance but encountering none.

The hallway stretched away into a lighted kitchen revealed through a half-open door. As Calum stood there, he heard faint voices talking in English, their accents perfect. From the little he overheard, they were waiting for someone else, and he wondered if that was Carlton.

He tried to work out how many voices there were but couldn't decide between three and five, all male. He glanced upwards to where a light marked the head of a staircase which descended to the left of the front door. Calum went there first and turned the key so they had an escape route. Then he took the steps one at a time, testing each tread before continuing. The light increased as he climbed, and he grew aware of a strange tension in the air. The same static charge he had felt when Bill recalled the information the girl had overheard. It was another ability. Another talent. At the head of the stairs it charged the air with its power and Calum hesitated, confused. Their weapons and their own abilities had been neutralised by what was unmistakably a product of talent. Which meant not all of it was disabled.

Harry nudged him forward, not taking the risk of speaking even in a whisper. Calum took a step, another. On the third, a figure appeared in the doorway of the lighted room. The man cried out in German and raised a pistol. Calum didn't need to see the future to know what was coming. He leapt to one side. As he did so, he heard a click as the gun failed to fire, just like theirs had. Whatever power was causing mechanical objects to fail was working on their enemies weapons as well as on their own, even if not on the talent of at least one person.

Calum bounced off the wall and ran at the man, who took a pace back. Calum lashed out with the butt of his pistol, but the attacker was too fast and ducked aside. Fortunately, Harry was right behind him. The barrel of the SMG crashed into the man's face, opening his cheek. He stayed on his feet, ignoring the blood that ran from his chin, and struck out with his own weapon. He caught Harry on the arm, and the SMG fell to the floor. Calum grabbed the man in his arms and pushed hard, toppling them both to the ground. Before he hit the floor, he glimpsed a second man sitting in a straight-backed chair, some kind of machine next to him, his hand resting on the upper curve of a gleaming apparatus. It was a glimpse, nothing more, and then Calum was fighting for his life.

His adversary twisted enough to free a hand and reached down to his waist. He withdrew a long-bladed knife and slashed at Calum's neck, but he threw himself aside just in time. Then Harry picked up his SMG and brought it down against the attacker's face so hard they both heard a sharp crack as his skull broke.

Calum got to his knees, reached out and took the knife from the dead man's limp fingers. Only then did he get to his feet.

"Check him for any other weapons," he said to Harry, then turned to look at the seated man, only now taking him in.

Sir Edward Carlton's tall, cadaverously thin body sat in the chair as if at ease. His dark hair was slicked back from his forehead, his chin freshly shaved. His eyes were closed. One hand rested in his lap, the other lay on top of the machine. When Calum tried to approach, it felt as if he was swimming through treacle. The closer he got, the further away Carlton seemed to be.

Calum looked at the machine. It was fashioned of brass, the outer casing open in places as though offering a skeleton on which the inner workings could be attached. There were cogs and wheels, small bottles of liquid, one of which shone with a silver sheen. Two others contained something more viscous, one green, the other dark blue. An acrid stink of ozone hung in the air. Calum shuffled to one side, because it was easier than going forwards. He was four feet to the right of the machine now and began to move towards it again, finding progress a little easier. He didn't know whether Carton or the machine were the source of the repulsive force, but it seemed they must combine to create it, one useless without the other.

He heard raised voices from downstairs.

"I think we're about to get company," said Harry

"See if you can lock the door, or put your shoulder against it at least. I'm going to try getting that contraption away from him."

"What the hell is it?" Harry asked as he slammed the door shut and pressed his back to it.

"Maybe Elizabeth will tell us when she has time to examine it."

"I want a closer look, too," said Harry. "I like machines, but I've never seen anything like that. Clever buggers, these Nazis. It's a damned nuisance." He shuddered as someone barged against the far side of the door. "Don't want to rush you, chum, but now might be a good time to try something." Harry's feet skidded on the floor as what sounded like two people crashed into the other side.

Calum turned back to Carlton, who had remained unmoving the entire time. He took a step sideways, the resistance almost impossible to move against, but he forced a few more inches of progress. He was three feet away now but knew he could get no closer. Calum raised a hand to wipe his face. That movement was allowed. He had forgotten he still held the now useless pistol in his hand, and it cracked against his forehead. Calum winced and jerked his hand away. Again, it was easy.

He looked at the gun. Looked at the machine. He judged the openings in the side, then tossed the gun at one of them. It caught on the edge of the casing and teetered, then fell back to land on the floor.

Calum cursed, before remembering the knife he had taken from his attacker. It was longer, slimmer. He took aim and threw it underhand. The blade slid between the casing and lodged on top of an inner metal strut.

Nothing happened. The machine continued to do its work. Calum tried to move forward again but couldn't. He tried to retreat, only to discover he couldn't do that either. He was locked in place. When he looked up, Carlton's eyes were on him, and he started to rise.

The whine of the gears in the machine increased in pitch as if it needed to provide more power now Carlton was no longer in contact with it. And then, one of the gears, turning faster, must have caught on the lodged knife because all at once there came a loud grinding sound, and the tension left the air with an almost audible crack.

Calum threw himself at Carlton, but his foot caught on the gleaming machine and he fell onto his side. Carlton backed away, turned and threw himself at the closed window, the shattering of glass accompanying him as he fell through.

Calum got to his feet in time to see Harry move away from the door and wondered what he was doing. Then, as the first man ran through, Harry lifted the SMG. It rattled and spat fire as a line of bullets sprayed the intruder, almost cutting him in half. Whoever was beyond the door heard the gunfire and their feet crashed down the stairs.

A single shot sounded from below. Calum hoped it was John Simpson doing the shooting. He leaned over and retrieved his pistol, then reached for the knife. As he did so, the cogs began to turn again, and he pushed it back in to stop them.

"Harry," Calum said, "come over here and see if you can work out how to turn this bloody thing off. I think we're safe enough now he's gone, but just in case."

Harry knelt and set the SMG down. Calum walked from the room. He stopped at the head of the stairs, listening. Nothing, but he was aware of the return of his talent. The future shimmered its promise of what was to come.

He descended the stairs slowly and turned towards the kitchen, which remained lit. As he approached, he saw Simpson with his back to him. His arms were raised ahead of him, both hands gripping his pistol as he pointed it at someone. Calum pushed the door fully open to discover Carlton with an arm around Elizabeth. The other held a wicked-looking blade to her throat.

"Drop the knife," said John Simpson.

"Shoot me," said Carlton, his voice urbane, "but you'll need to be damned quick if you want to save her."

Calum walked into the room and raised his own pistol.

Elizabeth's face was waxy, but the lines that were etched into it earlier had disappeared. She looked more like herself again.

"Shoot him," she said, her eyes on Calum.

He fired.

In the future, the bullet missed Carlton by six inches. Calum adjusted his stance and fired again in the present. By which time, Carlton had also moved. Calum had never experienced the response before. Was Carlton someone who shared his own ability, who could see what was going to happen and adjust for it?

"Both of us," said John Simpson, and Calum nodded.

He watched the future unspool. Saw them both fire. Saw the tall man flung back onto the floor.

And then everything changed, and Calum hadn't seen it coming. Carlton raised the knife and thrust it down. Once, twice, three times. The blade made a soft whisper each time it entered Elizabeth's body. Carlton flung her to one side like a rag doll as Simpson fired, but the man had already gone, running through the door.

Calum crossed the room and went to his knees. He clutched Elizabeth against him, her head lolling. He pressed his hands against her wounds, even as he knew there was nothing he could do. She was already dead.

CHAPTER THIRTY

Calum watched the Rover Light Six power away, its engine restored to life now the intricate machine in the house had stopped, and Sir Edward Carlton fled the scene. Elizabeth's body lay across the back seat. John Simpson said he would return her to her family home. It was, he said, the right thing to do. Calum was numb. He knew the sensation was self-imposed because to allow his emotions full rein now would bring the world crashing down.

"We should check the rest of the house in case the documents are still in there," said Harry. "And I'd like another look at that device."

Calum heard the words, but they washed past him without imparting any meaning.

"Elizabeth told us you were in charge if anything happened to her," said Harry. "So do your job, Cal. We're all upset, but there's work to do. The longer we put it off, the more chance those bastards have of getting clean away." He shook Calum's shoulder hard.

Calum jerked his arm away, but the shaking broke through where words had failed. He looked around at the others, looked beyond them as the countryside sparked into solidity with a rising sun that remained hidden behind high clouds. He glanced at his watch. Six-thirty. A darker band of cloud to the south offered a chance of rain before midday. They would have to travel in that direction if they wanted to pursue the survivors from the house.

"Tell us what to do, Cal," said Maria.

She stood close to him, and he saw she wanted to reach out but was unsure of his response. He looked at the expectation on the faces of the rest of their group.

"It's a long drive to Shrewsbury," Calum said. "I hope he gets there in one piece." He raised his shoulders, a tightness in them he couldn't release, his head fuzzy from lack of sleep. "All right. First thing, we search the house like Harry says. There's also a shed at the bottom of the garden, with what looks like an aerial winding up a pine tree. I expect we'll find a radio hidden away somewhere." He turned to Harry. "Go on, take a look at the contraption. See if you can start it up. I want to know what happens if you do."

"Do you think if it worked on him it might work on us?" asked Harry.

"It's a possibility. Though if it's a Nazi machine, we might have to try it out on Maria."

"You're not wiring me up to any machine," she said.

"No wires, but let's see. I expect it takes years of training, but at least we can make a start. Come on, while we stand here they're escaping justice."

As Maria turned away, Calum gripped her wrist.

"I told you, I'm not–"

"I want you to go down the road to the last house we passed. With luck, they'll have a telephone." He reached into his jacket and pulled out a sheet of paper. One edge was stained with dried blood. He had taken it from inside Elizabeth's dress, where he had seen her hide it after using it in London. "Can you remember a number if I tell it to you?" he asked.

"Of course."

He recalled the one Elizabeth had dialled. "If you get through, tell them where we are and what happened. Mention Elizabeth's name. That should do the trick."

"Do I tell them she's dead?"

The starkness of Maria's words brought a fresh wave of anguish. "No, just tell them we've found the spy group's lair, and where it is."

"Do I go alone?"

"I need the men with me."

"You're sending me away, aren't you? Sending me off on some make-work errand so I don't see what's inside the house."

"The Service needs to know what happened here, and I trust you to do the job."

Maria shook her head, making it clear she didn't believe his explanation. She walked away fast along the road as if she wanted to get away from him. Calum tried to remember how far it was to the last house they had passed. Over a mile, and there was no guarantee there would be a telephone. If not, they might have transport, even if only a bicycle. He trusted Maria's powers of persuasion would be sufficient to make use of whatever there was.

He caught up with Harry, Richard and Bill as they were about to enter the house. Work is what he needed. It would stop him dwelling on the conviction he should have saved Elizabeth.

"Harry, see if you can bring that contraption downstairs. If Maria rustles up some help, I want to take it away with us. I suspect there are people in Bletchley Park who'd like to get their hands on it."

"Not the same sort of machine they're used to, I don't suppose."

"Not even that one you fixed for Turing?"

"Maybe that one, now you mention it." Harry went inside and climbed the stairs.

"What about us?" asked Bill. Richard stood beside him, fully present.

"Can you hear anything in the walls of the house, Bill?" Calum asked. "It would tell us how many and what they were planning."

"Already tried it and got nothing. Which is strange. I've never failed to pick up on at least a little conversation. Which means either the house has been empty for months and nobody who was here said a word, or…" He glanced at Calum, "…that device wiped whatever was held in the walls. Just like it killed our talents, it killed the words. It's like the whole place has been put through the washer and hung on a line to dry. It's all gone, Cal. Everything."

"Bugger, though it makes some kind of sense. At least as much as anything else about this mission. All right, then I need you to search the shed. Check if there's anything in the walls there. It's further from the house, so it's possible, yes?"

"I'll try it, but don't get your hopes up."

Richard, you're with me," Calum said after Bill had left. "We go through everything in the house. Agreed?"

Richard nodded. "I'll take the upstairs."

As they separated, Calum knew the information Lilian Hamer had stolen was unlikely to remain in the house. Carlton, and whichever of his compatriots remained alive, would have made sure to take them. Unless they had been forced to leave before they could salvage anything.

There were three rooms downstairs, the kitchen where Elizabeth had died, a small bathroom, and a sparsely furnished sitting room which looked as if it had never been used. Calum opened the sideboard doors, but it contained nothing other than a pack of cards and a chessboard with no pieces. He pulled the drawers out and reached back into the spaces behind, finding nothing. Then he tipped the sideboard away from the wall and checked the back, with the same result. He cursed and looked around the room. The only other furniture consisted of a single, dilapidated easy chair. He went to the kitchen for a carving knife, then cut into each surface, but found nothing. He used the knife to tap at every wall, every floorboard. The floor sounded hollow, but wooden floors always did. He made a note to ask Bill if there were any tools in the shed they could use. If there was a crowbar or axe, he might lift the boards to check beneath.

Calum went back into the kitchen. There were more places here, so it took longer, but the result was the same.

He went to the foot of the stairs and called out. "Anything up there?"

"Nothing so far," Richard replied. "Harry needs a hand to bring the machine down. It's a lot heavier than it looks."

"Do you want me?"

"I think we can manage."

Calum went into the bathroom. The high-level cistern was the first place to check according to all the detective films he had ever seen. He stood on the cracked toilet bowl and reached into cold water, making sure he examined every part of the cistern. Once again, he found nothing. He climbed down and looked around. A single towel rail stood next to the bath, but no towel. There was no enclosure around the sink. Nowhere to hide anything.

A grunting noise brought him to the door to see Harry and Richard struggling with the brass contraption. It did indeed look to be a lot heavier than its delicate nature suggested.

"Put it on the kitchen table if it will hold it," Calum said.

"Do you want me to see if I can get it working?" asked Harry.

"I need one of you to see how Bill's doing first; he's been a long time in that shed. There can't be that much stuff down there."

"What about the bodies upstairs?"

"Leave them," Calum said. "If Maria can get someone down here, they'll know what to do with them."

"Stick them in the belly of one of those Lancs you used

to fly," said Harry. "Drop 'em off back over Munich. With a bit of luck, they might land on Hitler's noggin."

Calum shook his head at the barbarism of the idea, but wasn't sure he blamed Harry, not after what Carlton had done to Elizabeth. The thought was still too painful, so he pushed it away and returned to the bathroom, even as he knew he was finished there. He turned back, then stopped and went to one knee. A badly painted wooden panel was screwed to the side of the bath to hide the plumbing. Calum leaned closer to examine the brass screws. Everything else in the room was old, corroded, but the four screws were bright. He leaned closer still to discover marks on the head of one where a screwdriver had slipped.

Only Harry remained in the kitchen. The brass device sat on the table, which looked as if it could only just support it.

"I don't suppose you've seen a screwdriver anywhere?" Calum asked, rewarded only by a shake of the head. Harry bent close to the mechanism, studying it.

Calum went to the kitchen drawer he had already searched and pulled out a flat-bladed knife. He returned to the bathroom and tried it on the first screw, but it slipped and nearly cut his hand. He cursed and punched the bath panel, which was harder than it looked.

"Need a hand, mate?" Harry stood in the doorway.

"What I need is a screwdriver."

"No, you don't. Not when you've got Harry Parker. Shift over." Harry knelt and took the knife from Calum. He placed the rounded end against the screw. When he turned, the screw moved easily and dropped into his palm. Harry removed the other three screws. They tilted the panel off and set it against the wall. Both knelt again to look beneath the bath.

It was remarkably clean. There were no spider-webs, no dust to speak of. What there was instead was a brown cardboard box wedged under the end opposite the taps. Calum dragged it out and opened the top. It was half-filled with manilla folders, almost all with a government mark and the words Top Secret stamped in red.

"Well, bugger me," said Harry. "You clever sod."

"Nearly missed them. Here, look through some of these with me."

Calum took the folder from the top, which by logic should be the most recent. When he opened it, he discovered notes relating to an Allied landing at Calais and Dunkirk and knew they had been meant as a subterfuge. He wondered if someone had deliberately put them in a place they could be stolen from. If so, the plan had worked. Calum had heard enough to know the Nazis had heavily fortified the Calais area back in June, the Normandy coastline relatively less so. He discarded the folder and reached for another. Harry had skimmed the contents of a dozen, but none were what they sought.

"That tall bugger's taken it with him," said Harry. "The Service will want to see these, though. I doubt Lilian Hamer was their only source. They might be able to expose the entire spy ring from what's in this box." Harry smiled. "There'll be a few doors getting knocked on in the middle of the night over the next month, mark my words."

Calum reached down to the bottom of the box and

retrieved the last file. He wondered if it might not have been placed there to hide it, but when he opened it, he saw a date from 1935. The only thing it told him was the spy ring had been working from this house for almost ten years. And Harry was right – this information could help shorten the war.

Calum put the files back into the box and carried them through to the kitchen. He set it on the floor as there was no room on the table.

"I'm going to see what Bill and Richard are up to."

"I'll stay here if that's all right with you. I want to get a closer look at this contraption. It's a nightmare. Nothing seems like it's going to work. The gears and cogs are crazy, but we've both seen what it can do."

Calum went through the back door and walked down a clear track through the uncut grass of what passed for a lawn. Richard stood outside the shed, smoking a cigarette. Calum offered a nod and went inside, confused when he found the room empty.

"Down here." Bill's voice came from beneath his feet. "There's a hatch in the far corner. Wooden ladder. Careful, it's a tight squeeze."

Calum walked over and peered into the narrow space. A yellow light showed there was illumination down there, so he eased himself through the opening, his feet searching for the rungs of the ladder.

The space below was at least four times larger than the shed above. There was power, which ran to a single unshaded bulb. A second wire snaked down to the back of a radio set.

"There's some stuff here, but I can't make head nor tail

of it," said Bill. "We need Maria. I think it's German, but if it is, it's probably coded as well. But there is this…" He smiled and turned a dial on the radio set, and voices sounded. "Another reason we need Maria," said Bill. "I think there might be someone at the other end trying to communicate."

Calum listened. The voice sounded stressed even through the static.

"Do you think they know you've turned it on?"

"It was on when I came down here. I suspect someone was in the middle of sending a message when we interrupted them. Whoever's on the other end has lost his temper once or twice because nobody's answering anymore. Oh, and there's another one of those machines over there." Bill gave a nod. "Not my field of expertise, but it looks like a spare to me, or a prototype. It's tarnished and covered in dust. I tried to get it through the hatch, but it's a lot heavier than it looks."

"We've already found that out. Turn the radio off. We don't want to give them any clue we've discovered their hideout."

"Too late for that, I suspect. Better to leave it on. At least then, they might not know we've rumbled them. Whoever was down here left in a hurry. They left the hatch open, or it wouldn't have occurred to me all this was down here. I suspect they might have already passed the information on about what happened. They'll have arranged for some means of crossing the channel and running for home by now."

"Not as easy as it would have been six months ago," Calum said.

"No doubt, but it's chaotic over there. For all we know, they might have a U-boat coming to take them out. It could carry them all the way into friendlier waters. Or a small plane. How many escaped?

"That's a good question, but one I don't have an answer for. Only one I can be sure of, but I suspect there are others. Whoever was down here for a start. Only two men are dead, so the rest are gone. No doubt better people than us will turn up soon enough to find all that out. They'll question everyone in the area, check the records."

"So we do nothing?" said Bill.

"We go after Carlton. He's the man behind all this. With luck, we'll catch him before he can escape."

"And if we don't?"

"Then we follow him. The information he has cannot fall into Nazi hands."

CHAPTER THIRTY-ONE

When Calum emerged from the hidden cellar, he found Maria had returned. She stood next to Richard, both of them sharing a cigarette between them. Maria's lipstick had stained the filter.

"Did anyone have a phone?" Calum asked.

"They didn't. But a farmer drove me to the nearest village with a police station – manned by a single constable – who let me call through once I woke him up. They're sending a team down from London, but they're also getting some local people here sooner. We are to stay here until they arrive to take over."

"Did you tell them Carlton is running?"

"I did, and they said it was their job to stop him. They're sending people to the coast to watch for any suspicious activity. I got the impression they think we've exceeded our remit in acting as we did." She handed the cigarette back to Richard and came to stand in front of Calum. "I'm supposed to tell you to stay here. They're sending transport to get us back to Hereford."

Calum shook his head. "That's a waste of time. We're on the ground, and we know what's going on. We also know how powerful Carlton is." Calum wondered how they had missed any clues to what the man could do.

As if reading his thoughts, which she might well have done, Maria said, "He fooled us all, Cal, even Elizabeth, and there's not much gets past her."

"Except she's dead." Calum spoke more harshly than he intended, a reaction to his grief. "When we catch up with him, I'm going to kill him with my own hands. We should be chasing him down right now. He can't be far ahead of us."

"The man at the other end didn't sound like he made idle threats. We are to stay here. Under no circumstances are we to attempt pursuit. Is there anything we can do until they arrive, Cal?"

"First thing is to get that other machine out from under the shed. The next is to take it and the other one somewhere they won't be found. I don't want them falling into the hands of anyone in government. They won't understand them, and they'll disappear forever."

"What about that man in Bletchley Park?" asked Maria.

"He's a scientist, like my sister. I doubt either of them would get anything from it. However it works doesn't owe much to science. Not any science we know at the moment. But we have the right man to find out what it can do, don't we?" Calum turned away and walked to the house.

In the kitchen, Harry was still tinkering with the machine. Calum told him to stop, and between the four of them, they rigged up a pulley system, hauled the second machine up into the shed, and then carried it out on two planks held between them. Calum set it in the corner of the garden where it was half-hidden beneath an overgrown juniper, then they went back for the one in the kitchen. They had only just finished when a police car pulled up in the driveway, and Calum went to talk with the two men who got out.

He returned to the group five minutes later.

"They're local bobbies. We're to stay outside and do nothing. Someone's bringing transport for us, and we're expected to leave. They warned me none of us is to mention a word about what happened here."

"We're being sidelined," said Harry. "After all we've done, they're going to take over and get all the credit for themselves. Sod's law, ain't it?"

"They'd never have done this if Elizabeth was still in charge," said Richard.

"No, they wouldn't. But she's not in charge anymore, is she?" Calum didn't try to soften the sharpness in his voice, his grief still too raw. Every mention of her brought a fresh wave that threatened to engulf him.

"So who is? You?"

"I don't want to be. John Simpson, I expect."

"Only he's not one of us, and he's not here," said Maria. "It has to be one of us." She met Calum's eyes. "Elizabeth put you in charge. She did that for a reason. She believes you capable. I'm not; I know I'm not." She looked around at each of them. "What about you, Richard?"

He gave a shake of the head and offered a soft laugh. "You know me, anything not to draw attention to myself."

"Harry?" asked Maria.

"I'm not the sort of bloke people take orders from, or the kind to give them."

"Bill?" Maria turned to face him.

Calum watched the man. He saw he wanted to make a claim on the position. He probably believed himself qualified, but he was too new to their group. His eyes rose to meet Calum's and must have seen something there that gave him pause.

He shrugged. "Cal should be our leader until we can work things out. Who knows, your cushy little number might be about to come to an end now Elizabeth's gone. I ought to walk away from you and disappear back into my safe obscurity, but…" He shrugged. "I'll give it a try, at least for a while."

It wasn't much of a recommendation, but Calum suspected it was all he was going to get. He could live with it. Like Bill said… for now, anyway.

An army truck arrived and pulled up behind the police cars. Two more vehicles drew into the drive, and men in dark suits climbed out and looked around. All but one went into the house. The other approached their group.

"My name's not important, as I'm sure you understand, but I'm taking over. Your work is complete, but know that your government is grateful for what you have done here. Take a well-earned break. Mourn the death of your leader." The man took a notebook from his inside pocket. "Which one of you is Calum Auger?"

"I am."

"I have authority to appoint you as director of Unit-13." He handed a small folded card over. When Calum opened it, he found an official-looking stamp inside, together with his photograph. It had been taken in his RAF uniform.

"I believe this will give you all the authority you need, Mr Auger. The rest of you are to remain in your positions for now. It seems you have friends in high places. Friends in very high places. There is a car out on the road at your disposal, but no driver, I'm afraid. The tank is full, and there are two petrol cans in the boot. I would like you to leave at once. I assume you brought nothing with you?"

"A couple of guns," Calum said.

"They stay here. There are bodies inside, I understand?"

"Two of them."

"We'll take care of those."

"And there's a chamber under the shed at the bottom of the garden," Calum said. "There's a radio in there with a frustrated German on the other end."

"I have someone who speaks the language. Thank you, that will save us time searching for it."

"What about Carlton?" Calum asked. "He's known to us, of course, but how long has he been working for the Nazis?"

The man was silent a long time, so long Calum decided he wasn't going to answer. Instead, the man offered a shrug as if the information didn't matter. Perhaps he felt they deserved to know something.

"He's not been in our sights of late, but he did do a few silly things in the thirties, except we have never been able to prove anything. Sir Edward Carlton has connections in almost as elevated positions as your ex-leader appears to have, but there's always been something fishy about him.

He was part of Mosley's group before the war but escaped without a stain on his character. I believe someone assigned him to oversee Unit-13, but whoever that was isn't owning up to anything yet."

"Another mistake, I expect," Calum said.

"Oh, I think not. They most likely thought it was someplace he could be shunted off to where he would cause the least harm. He was always considered too inept to be a problem, but now this." The man looked past them at the house. "There will be questions asked about how he managed to avoid our attention. This place must be where they hole up because he has a substantial property in Surrey. Old family manor-house going back a couple of hundred years. And money. Pots of money."

"So why risk everything to do what he did?"

"His family has roots in Germany, and some of the aristocracy became rather enamoured of Herr Hitler at one time. I believe Carlton was one of those. He visited Berlin and Munich several times in the thirties, but I'm afraid that's all you're going to get from me. It's probably a little more than I should have revealed, to be honest, but too late now, what? Have a safe journey back to Hereford."

When he was gone, Harry said, "He made it clear he knows where to find us."

"I suspect he knows everything about us," Calum said. "Down to our shoe size and inside leg measurement." He looked around. "Harry, go check out this car he mentioned while we see what we can do with those machines. I think I saw a wicket gate into the next field. We'll carry the old one through first, then come back for the other."

Harry gave a nod and loped off across the grass. Calum checked nobody was watching, but it seemed they no longer existed. Suited men and soldiers streamed in and out of the house, a constant chatter between them. Calum and Bill lifted the older device onto the planks while Maria offered some kind of cover for them. By the time they emerged into the field on the far side Harry had pulled a black Sunbeam into the gate and opened the rear door. Calum recalled it was the spot they had parked in earlier to observe the house from. That moment seemed like days ago rather than hours. And Elizabeth had still been alive.

They put the machine in the middle of the back seat because, as promised, two petrol cans filled most of the boot. When Calum returned with Bill for the second machine he stopped short. Two uniformed men were pulling back the juniper to examine the object. Calum waited, hoping they might leave, but one stood guard while the other ran back to the house. A few moments later, the man who had spoken with them emerged, and Calum drew Bill away.

"Looks like we're going to have to make do with the old one," he said.

CHAPTER THIRTY-TWO

Each of the men took a turn behind the wheel of the aged Sunbeam. Harry drove the first leg, heading east while Calum sat beside him and tried to remember the towns they would need to drive through to reach Hereford. There was no map in the car, no doubt in case they were captured by German paratroopers, or some such nonsense dreamed up in the higher echelons of power. Maria and Richard sat in the back, pressed together on one side of the machine, Bill on the other.

Tunbridge, Guildford and Basingstoke would give them a good start, Calum thought, then a climb over the North Wessex downs into Swindon. From there, it was a simple run through to Gloucester, and then they were almost home.

Home, he thought, his mind spinning without gaining traction. Hereford wasn't home, but was anywhere now? Shrewsbury is where he had been raised, but that was no longer home. It was something the war had done to a lot more people than him. Shaken up the old ways, and nobody yet knew what the new ones would be like.

They stopped a little after noon and found a hotel that offered them a sparse meal once they showed their ration cards, then carried on. Calum climbed in the back beside the machine while Bill drove. Their progress was less than half what John Simpson would have made, but it would get them there in the end. Darkness came as they descended the twisting road down the steep northern scarp slope of the Cotswolds. The shadow of Gloucester and its docks was arrayed below, the tall warehouses rising above everything in the city apart from the cathedral. The sight reminded Calum of the last time he had seen them as he and Elizabeth flew over the city on their way to London. He dismissed the thought as too raw and looked north to the Malvern Hills. In the west, the mountains of Wales showed, faintly visible against the last of the light. The same peaks he could see from the house at the foot of Credenhill. Almost home.

It was almost midnight before they drew up in front of the house and staggered out of the Sunbeam. Harry said he would see if there was any whiskey, but Calum plodded up the stairs to his room. He hesitated a moment outside Elizabeth's room, where some faint remnant of her perfume still hung in the air. He gave a shake of his head to dispel his demons but knew he would fail. Somehow, he got out of his clothes but made no effort to wash. Sleep engulfed him almost before his head touched the pillow.

When he woke, a faint light came through the window

from where he had neglected to draw the curtains. It outlined the figure of a woman.

Calum sat up fast, his heart threatening to beat out of his chest. Elizabeth stood in the same dress she wore when she died. A bloodstain marked the material above her breast, part of the seam torn.

"No," he said, his voice catching. "You're not there. I don't believe in ghosts."

The figure he knew was a figment of his imagination offered a sad smile.

"Oh, Cal," it said, walking towards the side of the bed.

"No. Go away."

"I can't. I can never go away." She reached the side of the bed and stopped. Cal could smell her perfume again, but nothing else. No underlying odour of death. But Elizabeth's presence was impossible.

"What do you want?"

"You know what I want, Cal. I want you. I wanted you from the first moment I met you, even more so now. You're special. So am I."

Her words brought a deep chill to him. It brought a memory of Alice Clare and her ghostly companions.

"You're dead is what you are. Go back to wherever you came from and leave me alone."

"I am back where I came from. I'm back where I belong. At your side." She reached out her hand. "Here, feel this and tell me I'm dead."

He stared at her fingers, afraid to touch them.

"Do it, Cal. I need you to take my hand." There was a tension in her voice, a reality that was not part of any dream, and he reached out.

Her hand was warm.

She raised his hand and laid it between her breasts. The same breasts he had caressed and kissed in their hotel room in London… how long ago? Two nights? Three? He didn't know anymore.

Beneath his fingers, Elizabeth's heart beat.

"I saw you die," Calum said. "I put my hand where it is now and there was no heartbeat. You were dead."

"And now I'm not dead. Let me lie beside you, and I'll tell you the truth about myself."

Calum felt another shiver run through him. Was she dead or alive? Was he still dreaming?

Elizabeth removed her clothes. When she was naked, he recognised the curves, dips and crevices he had grown familiar with. A mark showed above her left breast where the knife had entered, but it was no more than a faint scar. Which was impossible.

"How?" Calum shifted across the bed as Elizabeth came to lie on it. He made no move to reach for her, still trying to process what was happening.

"Do you remember when we went to your house and I confused your father?"

"He thought he knew you, and you said it must have been your mother."

"I did, but it was a lie because I couldn't reveal the truth. It was me he knew. I was there during the Great War."

"That's not possible. Dad is fifty-eight. You're nowhere near fifty-eight. You can't be."

"You're right, Cal. I can't be the same age as your father. Of course I can't." She reached out and stroked his chest, ran a finger along the sharp stubble on his cheek. "I met your father in 1917 when he was twenty-nine years old and serving in a field hospital outside Abbeville. At that time I was eighty-four years of age."

Calum stared into her eyes. The gathering light beyond the window illuminated every inch of her body, but none of it looked more than twenty years old. He had estimated her age in the late twenties only because of her apparent seniority.

He laughed. "Good joke. Now tell me how old you really are. And why you're not dead."

"I was born in 1833, which makes me one hundred and eleven years old."

"No."

"Yes."

"How?"

"If I knew that, I'd bottle it and sell it. I could live the rest of my days in luxury. Though I might need a very great deal of money because I suspect the rest of my days are going to extend far into the future."

"I don't understand."

"Neither do I. All I know is it just is. I never grow older than I look now. I did as a young girl, then when I reached puberty, ageing slowed for me. Slowed so much my parents grew afraid of me, and I left home. It's what I've done ever since. As soon as someone notices I never age, I move on."

"Carlton stabbed you." Calum reached out and touched the faint marks, sure they were less than when she had lain beside him. He ran his finger along one of the faded scars, then inward to her breast. He watched her nipple respond to his touch. It was this simple response that convinced him. He wondered what he was doing but knew himself incapable of resisting her.

"Yes. And I died. Except I can't die, Cal. Not that way. Perhaps if one of those rockets landed on me and blew me into a million pieces I would. But I've been stabbed before and shot. I was poisoned once."

"It all sounds a little careless to me."

"I suppose it does, but knowing you can't die makes you a little careless. Will you do what you're doing on the other side now, please?"

Calum obliged. And then, before his courage left him, before he woke from this dream, he did a lot more – a great deal more.

When he woke, much later in the day, Elizabeth remained at his side. He watched her sleep for a time, accepting what she had told him. Because was it any stranger than what the rest of them could do? He wondered if her immortality was a talent, or something else.

She made a sound and rolled her head. Her eyes opened to look into his, and he kissed her. Before she could pull him down, he said, "What the hell are we going to tell the others? I assume John Simpson already knows about you. He doesn't have any talent, does he?"

"Yes, John knows. He's known me for a long time and carried out the same service for me as he did last night. But no, he has no special talent, unless you count driving fast."

"How long have you known him?"

"Ten years."

Calum wanted to ask the obvious question about her and John but didn't want to hear the obvious reply, so he kept it locked inside.

"What are you going to tell the rest of the team?"

She laughed. "That you made a mistake. That I didn't die. I was just hurt."

"Some hurt."

"I can make them believe it."

And Calum knew she could.

CHAPTER THIRTY-THREE

When Calum dropped into the games room three days later he found Harry still working on the stolen device. The outer casing had been cleaned and shone with a dull glow, as if the metal was lit from within. The construction was different from the one Edward Carlton had used, but Calum only knew this because Harry told him so. He had taken the mechanism apart, breaking it down into individual components, stopping only briefly to eat and sleep. Now he was starting to reassemble it.

"Any news?" asked Harry, no need to explain regarding what. They all had only one thing on their minds.

"Elizabeth's on the phone to London now."

"I expect she'll let us know as soon as she hears anything. Those bastards had better not try to cut us out from events now."

Calum drew up a chair and sat on the other side of the machine from Harry. He leaned forward to watch as he screwed a cog into place, then tested it with his fingers to ensure it met with another, and that turned yet another, and another. Harry had the remaining parts spread out on the nearby card table, with a warning nobody was to touch them. Nobody had. Nobody dared.

"Will you finish it today?" Calum asked.

"Should do. Whether it works is another matter."

"Is this a prototype that didn't work, do you think, or simply a spare? Is that why they abandoned it in the cellar?"

"It's different to the other, but until I put it back together we won't know what it can do. When I examined the one Carlton used it had a phial of mercury at its centre. This one has the container but no mercury. I went into Hereford yesterday and got my hands on some. Whether it's important or not I've no idea until I start it up."

"How is it powered? Electricity?"

"Clockwork."

Calum raised his eyes to meet Harry's. "Clockwork?"

"You know, like a–"

"I know what clockwork is. It just seems so old-fashioned."

"Maybe so, but it means it doesn't need any other power source so you can use it anywhere."

"If it works."

"There is that."

Calum got to his feet. "I'm going to get some breakfast. Do you want me to bring you something?"

"Bacon and egg sandwich if there's any bacon, sausage otherwise."

"And if there are no sausages?"

Harry didn't look up from what he was doing, his

hand deep inside the mechanism. For a man with such rough hands, his fingers moved delicately. "Since when has there never been any sausage? Wherever the grub comes from here, it's plentiful, and nobody's ever asked to see our ration cards." He waved his free hand to dismiss Calum.

Maria, Richard and Bill were already in the dining room. Maria had been cool towards Calum since Elizabeth's miraculous recovery. It had been a twenty-four-hour wonder, but now it was simply a part of life. Whether any of them believed Elizabeth's explanation that her wounds looked worse than they were, Calum didn't know. Nobody talked about it. They didn't talk of much at all. Maria and Richard went on long walks across the wooded slopes of Credenhill, climbing to the old fortification wall that circled the summit. Bill spent a lot of his time with Harry, the pair of them talking, trying to decide if the mechanism was a weapon or something else. Whether it needed a person to make it into a weapon. Calum spent hours with Elizabeth, but she had not come to his bed again, as if she needed to ration out her favours to keep him strung along. If she feared he would tire of her, then she was wrong, but Calum hadn't told her that. Not yet. They would need to talk about their relationship at some time, but he was content to let her choose that time and place. It surprised him, the ease with which he had accepted her strange claim that she could never die. That didn't mean he had no questions.

He put together Harry's sandwich, but Bill said he'd take it through. He'd finished eating and wanted to watch Harry work. Calum sat opposite Maria and Richard, wondering once more at their relationship. It was clear one existed. Maria had hinted it was only camouflage, but Calum wasn't so sure. Whatever form it took was strange, for they were not what anyone might regard as a match. He was still searching for some safe topic of conversation when Elizabeth's arrival saved him.

"Goodness, but I'm starving." She went to the array of food and loaded her plate high. Bacon, sausage, two fried eggs, plus a pile of scrambled egg as well. She brought it back and sat down.

"Any news?" asked Maria.

"A little, but it's both good and bad."

Maria smiled. "Give us the good first, then."

"I can give you both at the same time." Elizabeth put bacon and dripping egg into her mouth, a delicate manoeuvre she managed without spilling a single drop on her dress. "Two nights ago, a coastal cutter caught sight of a U-boat periscope. It was approaching an isolated beach west of Eastbourne. A motor torpedo boat was despatched from Portsmouth and reached the area just before dark. It encountered the U-boat an hour later and sent it to the bottom. It wasn't all that deep, so they sent divers down to make sure they had destroyed it."

"Which part of that is the bad news?" asked Maria.

"I'm getting to it," said Elizabeth around a mouthful of food she had just started on. She chewed and swallowed. "The divers brought up half the crew, who were in an air pocket. But no sign of Edward Carlton. No sign of anyone other than the crew, but they're still being interrogated. A couple of them caved almost at once, unless that was also a plot. They were sent to pick him up from the beach, together with two companions, but were sent to the bottom before they had the chance."

"Are they trying to throw us off the scent?" Calum asked.

"Could be, but there was no sign of Carlton among either the living or the dead."

"Do you think he escaped?"

"That's the other bit of good and bad news I received." Elizabeth wiped her mouth with a napkin and sipped her tea. "I think he's been sighted in France. One of the advance guard sent a message back that they'd encountered a Panzer tank in the Allied sector. It was taken on but escaped."

"Doesn't mean much, does it?" said Richard. The last few days, he had been visible most of the time, either his own doing or because they were growing more used to him.

"They saw three men running after the tank as it fled. It stopped and allowed them to board. One man was unnaturally tall and thin, the report said."

"Do you think it was him?" asked Maria.

"Sounds as if it could be, but we've no proof unless we go out there."

"To the front?" said Maria.

"Beyond the front. If that tank picked him up and kept going, it will be in Nazi territory by now. Though the word is the Allies are advancing fast, even if some of my contacts tell me the advance is chaotic. Men can find themselves behind enemy lines without even realising it. We've lost people that way but killed a lot of Wehrmacht as well. Not so many captives, which would be useful if we could get them to talk."

"Are you saying we're going over there after Carlton?" Calum asked.

"He's got the documents that woman copied," said Elizabeth. "We can't let them to end up in Nazi hands. Special Services have been sent across to hunt them down, but they don't know what they're up against. We do."

"Are you sure about that?" Calum said. "He fooled us all, didn't he? Us and everyone else."

"Except we're all there is, Cal. The six of us. If we can confirm where Carlton is, I've been told there are six Mosquitos loaded and waiting for our word. They'll strafe and bomb the area into oblivion, but only if they're sure."

"So we're going to the front lines?" Calum thought the idea completely crazy.

"Today. I've arranged for transport to fly into Credenhill base so we can cross to France."

"What is it?" asked Calum.

"An Avro Anson. It won't be comfortable, but it's fast enough and has the range and room for all of us. If everyone wants to go, that is. I think you and I might be enough, Cal."

"You're not leaving me behind," said Harry, who had come into the room to make himself a second sandwich, the first clearly not enough. "And Bill will be handy, too. I've never known anyone understand armament the way he does."

"So four passengers," said Elizabeth. She looked towards Maria and Richard. "I'd like it to be all six of us if the others are coming. We may need your language skills, Maria, and your ability to pass unnoticed would be useful, Richard. But I won't order any of you. It will be dangerous, and there's no guarantee any of us will come back."

"Except for you," said Maria, a sharpness in her voice that told Calum she didn't believe Elizabeth's story about her wounds.

"You can take your time making your decision," said Elizabeth, nothing showing in her voice. "I need to know by eleven, so I have time to make arrangements."

"I want to bring the device," said Harry.

"It weighs a bloody ton," said Richard.

"Not anymore. I've made improvements, and I think the unnatural weight is a by-product of it being used. I wish we'd managed to keep hold of the other one."

"The Anson is big enough that weight isn't a problem," said Elizabeth. "But there's no point taking the device if it doesn't work, however much you can't bear to part with it, Harry."

"Oh, it works all right," said Harry. "I've finished putting it back together. Apart from coming in here for this," he held up his sandwich, "I came to see if anyone wants to watch me start it up."

Nobody spoke for a while, then Calum said, "We need to discuss how we want that to work. You saw what Carlton did when he was with it. We need to decide which of is going to be the guinea-pig." He looked around at each of them.

"There are only two here who are suitable," said Elizabeth. "If it does what I suspect, the subject needs to be someone who can easily demonstrate an improvement in their talent. Which means it has to be Cal or Richard." She gave a smile. "Assuming it works at all."

"Don't worry about that," said Harry. "It might even work better than the one we saw. They didn't have Harry Parker on the case."

"Then let's do it sooner rather than later," said Elizabeth. "Volunteers?" She looked at Richard, then Calum before rising to her feet. "I'll let you talk it out between yourselves while Harry shows me his handiwork."

"Any time, old girl," said Harry, with an exaggerated wink, and Elizabeth laughed.

She's good, Calum thought. He also knew there was only one person who could prove if the device worked or not. As soon as Elizabeth and Harry left the room, he leaned over the table to the others. "I'll do it," he said.

Richard faded, returned. "I don't mind if you'd rather it was me."

"I'm more used to taking risks than you. Apart from which, how can you disappear more than you already do? Besides, Maria will kill me if I say no and something happens to you." Calum saw Maria's face flush. He thought her reaction rather sweet.

"Thanks, old man," said Richard.

Calum got up and went through to the games room. Bill stood off to one side while Harry and Elizabeth argued over whether to leave the device where it was or carry it outside. Elizabeth's argument seemed to be that it might affect the surrounding structure if it was as powerful as they thought. Harry's argument was that

Edward Carlton had operated his within a small upstairs room. They stopped when they caught sight of Calum.

"What do I have to do?" Calum asked.

"I'm not too sure," said Harry, "but Carlton had his hand on it when we saw him, so let's try that to start with."

"Do you think it's going to work?"

Harry grinned. "I started it up before coming through. I couldn't let everyone come in here and it turns out to be a dud, could I?"

Elizabeth stared at him. "That was foolhardy and stupid."

"I showed Bill how to turn it off if my head started to smoke."

Elizabeth's anger seemed a little mollified. "And what happened?"

"I now know dozens of ways to make the device better. It gave me that. Or improved my talent, so I understand it better. I also think I can knock together something a lot smaller. Something any one of us could carry in their hand or pocket. Bill said he felt something too, so we think it's not limited to just one person. We suspect Carlton was the only one in that house with a strong enough talent to use the apparatus. The others were nothing more than foot soldiers."

"I've been giving that some thought," said Bill. "His talent, that is. It's not like mine, nor any of yours."

"What we felt was a negative talent," said Calum, who had also considered the matter. "He sucks the ability out of those around him. He makes machinery stop. Even when we thought he was on our side, there was always something odd about him, wasn't there? Do you remember when my watch stopped working that first day? I think it must have happened when he shook my hand. I suspect if we track him down your bombing raid will fail, Elizabeth. The bombs will simply not go off."

"Maybe one will hit him on the head," said Maria, who had come into the room with Richard.

"I wouldn't bet on it," said Harry. He looked around at them all before his gaze settled on Elizabeth. "Well, old girl?"

She took a breath. "Do it, but everyone except Harry and Cal stand back, just in case."

CHAPTER THIRTY-FOUR

Harry took Calum's elbow and sat him in a hard-backed chair within touching distance of the device. He waited until the others had taken up their positions, then reached into the mechanism and did something Calum couldn't see. Later, he discovered there was no switch. At least, not one any ordinary person could operate. The device responded only to talent. As soon as the cogs began to turn, a soft thrum filled the air. The sound came not only from the device but seemed to fill the entire room. Harry drew a second chair up and stared into the spinning wheels. He reached in and made a minute adjustment.

Calum looked away, trying to work out if he felt different or not. On balance, he thought not.

"Close your eyes," said Harry. "Carlton had his eyes closed when we first saw him."

Calum gave a nod and tried it. The device's soft hum washed through him, together with a faint vibration that entered where his hand rested and warmed his skin. Then he felt the vibration sink beneath the surface and lodge inside his body. He heard another sound, the rattle of twin air-cooled engines that identified an Avro Anson. It flew over the house as it came in to land at the base.

"Our ride's here early," he said, but there was no response.

He opened his eyes to see if anyone had heard him. At first, nothing appeared to be different, then he saw that nobody was breathing. When he looked at the device the wheels had stopped turning, but the effect remained. He felt it crawling inside him like some kind of parasite.

Calum stood, his body heavy. Movement was difficult, exactly as it had been in Carlton's presence in Kent. He waited a moment to see if taking his hand from the device would break the connection, but nothing changed. The power continued to flow through him. He studied the others, but he appeared to be the only one affected. Was that because he had been the only one touching it, or because it could affect only one person at a time? Calum knew they would have to discuss all these questions later, but only once he could prove the device worked.

When he tried to move again, he found progress easier, and wondered if he was learning to control the power of the device. If so, he had no idea how he was doing it. He went to stand in front of Maria and stared into her open eyes. There was no blink response, and when he touched her shoulder, there was no rise or fall. He moved across to Elizabeth and put a finger against the throat he had kissed, searching for a pulse. He found none. It came to him slowly as knowledge rose from some inner depth he had never acknowledged before. It had always lain there, just out of reach, but the device had released it. These people were in the past. He was in the future. He had broken the thread. Now he travelled ahead of them by... how far? He had no way of knowing. Or did he?

Calum walked to the window and looked out. Nothing moved. The trees were static. A training plane taxiing across the base was stationary. A second plane hung motionless a hundred feet in the air. All locked in the past.

Calum cursed. What was the point of this talent? What advantage would it bring? This was different to what he could do. He had been thrown too far ahead and could see nothing, affect nothing. He existed in an alternate dimension, totally disconnected from the present.

He suspected when Harry turned the machine off everything would return to normal. Which meant he could prove nothing.

Or could he?

Calum looked around and went to Maria because she was the lightest of them. He put his hands beneath her arms and tugged. At first, he thought she wouldn't move, then she tipped away from the wall and Calum dragged her across the floor like a length of wood. There was no give in her body. Even her clothes were stiff. She felt like a marble carving beneath his touch, and almost as heavy. He dragged her to the games table, then heaved her up to lie on her back on top of it. Her hands remained suspended in front of her. Calum went back and moved every person other than Harry until they all faced the table where Maria lay. Sweat stood out on his face by the time he finished. He wiped a hand across it, which came away damp. He became aware movement was easier.

Everything that happened to him was normal. Only the rest of the world had fallen into a fugue state. Calum saw now how this state might be useful to him. Once he learned to control it.

He returned to the chair, but instead of sitting he put his foot on the seat, intending to stand, then stopped. How much longer would he exist like this? When would Harry turn off the machine? Calum looked at it, at Harry. What if this was all he had now? No past. No future. No life. No death. Nothing but this stasis?

He reached out and laid his hand on top of the device. Despite everything else being locked in a moment, a vibration passed through him. Somewhere, cogs still turned as the mechanism wound down. That thought gave him some hope. Eventually, the spring would wind down and the device stop. But he didn't want to wait. He wanted it to stop. To stop now!

"For God's sake, Cal, don't touch it." Harry reached out and grasped his wrist, then his mouth fell open. He looked at the others, at Maria struggling to sit up, at Richard helping her down from the table. Elizabeth turned and stared at Calum. Then they were all staring at him.

"What…?" Elizabeth shook her head.

"I need to do it again," Calum said. "I have to learn how to control it."

"Tell me what happened." Elizabeth crossed the room and took his arm. "Come to my office. The rest of you stay here. Or not. Do whatever you want."

When Calum looked back, he saw Harry and Bill leaning close to the device, discussing how to improve it.

"You need to ask the others if they experienced

anything," Calum said as he took the seat in front of Elizabeth's desk.

"How could they in such a short time?"

"Short? I was under at least twenty minutes."

"Twenty seconds, Cal, no more. How did you make us move in that time? More to the point, how did you do it?"

He stared across the desk at the woman he had shared a bed with on three occasions and wondered how they could be so close and yet so far apart.

"I dragged you," he said. "It was like dragging rocks, even you and Maria, but I did it to show I could. I needed some way to prove what was happening to me, and I couldn't think of anything else."

"What about the future?" asked Elizabeth. "How far could you see?"

Cal watched her write something in her journal, the same red-backed one she had made notes in all those days ago when he first arrived at Carden House.

"I couldn't see anything, not as far as I could tell. Except now..." Calum trailed off, aware of a change in himself. The double vision he had grown used to was different, the future image stronger. It was the present he struggled to hold on to, and for a moment dizziness swept through him as he wondered which conversation he was having with Elizabeth, and how he could tell. He closed his eyes.

"Are you all right, Cal?"

He heard her voice. Heard the echo of her voice – past, present and future combined.

"I can see further," he said, his eyes still closed. It made the sensations that washed through him easier to manage, or perhaps easier to ignore.

"How much further?"

"I don't know. Two minutes, three, I don't know."

"How about four and a half minutes?" said Elizabeth.

Cal opened his eyes and stared at her. "Why that exact amount?"

"I'm sure you can tell me if you think about it."

He could. Calum recalled the moment when he and George had first found their birth certificates and compared them. George was born at 11:34 in the morning. Calum at 11:38½. He remembered how they'd laughed at the fact some nurse had taken the trouble to record the half minute. Then George had said he had to give the orders because he was older.

"What you're suggesting is even stranger than seeing into the future. If that is what you're suggesting." He stared at her. "Is it?"

"I don't know. It's a theory, that's all. What do you believe, Cal? Do you ever hear George's voice?"

Calum held up a hand. He wanted this to stop. The idea of what Elizabeth was suggesting scared him, made even worse because of his own guilt at his brother's death.

"It's impossible," he said.

"Most people would say what you can do is impossible. But if I'm correct, it raises even more questions because your talent is different from others. The others were all born with them. Yours came only when your brother died."

"Even if what you claim is true, I was further in the future than four minutes just now."

"I told you, twenty seconds is all it was."

"You're wrong. I know you're wrong."

"Tell me, Cal… do you ever hear your dead brother's voice?"

He shook his head and stood.

"If you've got nothing positive to say, I think we're finished here." He turned away before she could speak, only to hear a sound for the second time that day. A plane came in low over Credenhill. The note of the twin engines changed as it banked to line up with the grass runway. Calum turned back. "You sent for two Ansons?"

Elizabeth rose. "Two what?"

"Avro Ansons. That's the second one landing now. And I hope you're not expecting me to fly it. I managed that Magister as far as London, but the Anson has twin engines, and it's a damn sight bigger."

Elizabeth glanced through the window, but the plane was already down, hidden behind a bank of trees obscuring most of the base from the house.

"I only sent for the one, Cal, and had to pull all kinds of strings to get my hands on that. I needed something we could all fit in, though I've been told it won't be comfortable. We leave later today. You know we do. And I've arranged for a pilot, so you won't have to fly it." She gave a smile as she glanced through the window again. "You heard the plane landing before?"

"As I went into whatever it was. Nothing else sounds like an Anson. Those air-cooled engines are noisy buggers."

Elizabeth looked at her watch. "That was twelve minutes ago, Cal. You experienced an event twelve minutes in the future. And you affected events in the present when you moved us." She stared at him, an expression that might have been fear on her face. "How far *can* you go, Cal? What has that machine given you?"

Calum's anger faded as the realisation of what Elizabeth was saying sank through him.

"You're scaring me now."

"What about the others?" said Elizabeth. "Will it be the same for them if they use the device?"

"You're the expert, you tell me."

"Not me. Harry's the expert. We've got a little time yet. We should ask if anyone else wants to try it." She came towards Calum, stopped in front of him. She stared up into his face, then put her hands on his cheeks and kissed him hard on the mouth. "Oh, the wonder of it."

Then she was gone, leaving Calum even more confused than ever.

When Calum entered the Games room, Harry sat beside the device. He had taken apart the tall grandfather clock, as well as a smaller one which had hung on the dining room wall. Their constituent parts lay across the table. Bill sat beside him while Maria had one hand on Harry's shoulder as she leaned close to observe what he was doing. Elizabeth wasn't present, neither was Richard.

"What are you up to?" Calum asked as he approached.

"I need a frame of some sort. I'm sure I can knock something up if I can get my hands on some metal. Brass would be best, like the device." He patted it with his hand as if for good luck. "And I'll need some jewellers' tools."

"Tell me why," Calum said. "I'm sure Elizabeth can get anything you want. Where is she, by the way?"

"She took Richard to the dining room," said Maria. "She wants to talk to each of us separately. I'm next. Harry thinks he can create a smaller version of the device. He claims this one is inefficient, the one in that house only a little better. He thinks a lot of the mechanism is for show. He's sure he can whittle it down to the essentials. Something you can hold in your pocket, or a rucksack at least."

Calum watched as Harry moved the cogs from the clocks, separating them, his eyes going from his hands to the device sitting next to him and back.

"I might have to take this one apart," he said. "I can salvage the bits I need from it. Maybe even make two from what's there, even three."

"You're not touching that device." Elizabeth had entered the room without anyone hearing. "Maria, I'm ready for you now."

Richard came and took her place once the two women had left.

"What did she want to know?" Calum asked.

"She talked to you first, so I'm sure you already know. She asked me if I felt anything unusual."

"And did you?"

Richard shrugged. "Might have, old man, but it's hard to say. Harry claims he did, so does Bill, but they were both closer to the device than the rest of us. And everyone knows what you did." He laughed. "That was some trick, Cal."

"I'm trying to use what the device gave me," said Harry, his eyes not moving from his work. "It's fading, but there's something still there. Bill says the same. He's been a great help. I think working with weapons is not too different to what I do."

"Except he hears words trapped in walls," Calum said.

"I also have a connection to armament," said Bill. "I believe none of us has a single talent. I want to talk to Elizabeth about it when my turn comes. What if we can all extend ourselves? Just knowing what we do is real, can be improved on, might be enough to let us go further even without the device. What do you think, Cal?"

"You're asking the wrong man."

"I don't think I am."

"Fuck!" Harry pushed away from the table. "If she won't let me cannibalise the device I don't think I can do what I want. Maybe if I get access to a workshop with all the right equipment, but not here, and not now."

Maria and Elizabeth returned.

"Harry and Bill, I'll talk to you both together. The rest of you get ready to leave. You've got twenty minutes. We take the device with us. I overheard what you said, Harry, and as soon as we get back I'll make arrangements. Give me a list of what you need, and I'll get it for you." She clapped her hands. "Now, everybody move."

CHAPTER THIRTY-FIVE

The weather took a turn for the worse as the Avro Anson flew south. Squally rain streaked the screen. Wind crabbed at the wings, making the plane shudder and lurch. Calum had no worries sitting in the co-pilot's seat because he knew the pilot could manage anything the weather threw at them and more. Seeing Guy Jordan again had been a shock, but a pleasant one. They had shaken hands, and Calum had to force himself not to embrace the other man, even if he was no longer his skipper. There had been no chance to catch up as a tanker refuelled the plane, and the others settled into the unpadded seats arranged in the space behind the cockpit. Harry and Bill manhandled the device onboard and strapped it down. Calum's right arm still ached from having to wind up the undercarriage by hand once they were airborne. One hundred and forty turns of the metal handle it had taken, and he had counted every single one. He wasn't looking forward to lowering it again when they came in to land. Wherever that might be.

Beneath their wings, the south coast drifted past, almost completely obscured by rain. The plane rocked again in the turbulence that almost always accompanied passing from land to sea. Calum and Guy were both familiar with it and barely noticed. When Calum turned in his seat to check on the others he saw Maria clutching Richard's hand. Even Harry looked nervous.

Elizabeth was sleeping, a blanket draped over her to keep out the cold.

Calum toggled his headset. "What's the plan, skip?" He saw Guy smile at his use of the word.

"Straight south to Normandy, then hang a turn to port. Less chance of meeting any stray fighters that way. I've been told there aren't many this far west. They've been pulled back to the fighting in the east." He tapped at a map strapped to his left leg. "They gave me a location of an airfield near Ghent. It's about as close to the front lines as they're going to let us get." Guy studied his instruments before turning to look at Calum. "What have you got yourself involved in, Cal? And what's that bloody great contraption strapped in the back – some kind of bomb?"

"Something like that, but you know I can't tell you any more. Not even you, Guy. Maybe when the war's over we can sit down together in some London club over a good single malt, and I can give you something, but not now."

Guy nodded to show he understood. They were all used to secrets. Calum was only glad Elizabeth had assigned Guy as their pilot. He trusted the man to get them to their destination. Trusted him more than anyone he could think of.

"What happened to the crew?" Calum asked, talking as

much to pass the time as anything else, though he was curious. A promise had been made to him, and he wanted to know how it had worked out.

"Recycled," said Guy. The mask hid any expression he might have shown, but the disgust in his voice came through even over the static in Calum's headset.

"I was told they would give everyone easy duties. They promised me."

"Promises mean nothing in war, Cal, you know they don't."

Calum stared ahead through the window. The weather was clearing, and a band of blue showed beyond the edge of the squall. There was an obvious question to ask, but he didn't raise it, unsure he wanted to know the answer. He didn't have to because Guy was aware of it as well, and less circumspect.

"They were all assigned to separate crews to make up the numbers. Last I heard, Bob was in a prisoner-of-war camp after bailing out from a crippled bird. Pete Marshall didn't make it. A Messerschmitt got the better of him and his crew over Hamburg."

"And the others?"

"Heard nothing about them, so I assume they're still flying."

"And you?"

"Another crew, another Lanc. You know that's what I wanted. I assumed that would be it for the duration until I got a call from the Wingco and given this posting. Came as a bolt from the blue, I can tell you."

"I'll have a word with Elizabeth and see if she can't get

you assigned to us permanently. It'd be handy to have a good pilot on the books. Or even you."

Guy reached across and punched Calum on the arm. It felt good – a brief taste of the old camaraderie he missed.

"Look over there, Spits," said Guy, pointing. A half-dozen of the unmistakable fighters flew two hundred feet above them and half a mile ahead. No doubt they were returning to their base in the south of England after a sortie over the front lines.

Calum watched the fighters disappear, then leaned over to look down at the ground, which had become visible with the weather's improvement. The buffeting of the airframe smoothed out, which would come as a relief to the passengers. Two thousand feet below trucks, jeeps and columns of uniformed men snaked along a roadway. Tanks ignored the road and ploughed across fields and through woods. A stain of smoke drifted over the land. Everything moved in the same direction as the aeroplane above. East, to where the defending Nazi army continued to offer stubborn resistance. Within twenty minutes, that resistance became clearer.

Guy brought the Anson down to a thousand feet. Twenty miles ahead, more smoke rose to mark where the front line lay, and beneath them, the troop movements were heavier. Fighter planes streaked across the skies, but fortunately, so far they were all either British or American. Guy brought the plane lower still.

"Time to get winding, Cal. It'll be a good exercise for that right wrist of yours." Guy laughed. "Unless one of the girls back there is taking care of that for you now."

An American Mustang curled from the sky and fell in

alongside them, the face of the pilot clearly visible. Calum suspected he was checking them out, and after a while he must have satisfied himself because he turned away with a friendly wave. The Anson settled into its final approach. Guy caressed the stick, his feet active on the pedals as a line of trees flashed by below. Calum had finally lowered the undercarriage, but his arm ached again. Guy reduced power and eased back on the stick, waiting until their wheels kissed the runway. Calum smiled. Guy always managed to show off his prowess during a landing, and he was sure there was no better pilot anywhere. Their last flight together had proven that. Nobody else could have saved their Lancaster that day. It seemed a long time ago rather than a few months.

They braked, turned and headed to a hangar where a man stood waving his arms. As they came closer, Calum saw it was John Simpson. He must have come over ahead of them. Calum unbuckled and ducked through to check on the others. Elizabeth was just waking, or pretending to wake from a pretend sleep. He wouldn't put it past her. The others were leaning over to stare out at the airfield. To look at Belgium. Not that it differed much from any other base Calum had ever been on, other than there were more fighters. More than he had ever seen gathered in one place before.

Calum opened the side door, lowered the flimsy ladder and stepped down. He waited for Bill to join him, then they reached up and took the supporting arms of the device and drew it out. By the time they were all out, John Simpson had walked across to join them.

"Any news?" Elizabeth asked him.

He shook his head. "Nothing, but I only sent word out last night. Most people have got more on their minds than looking out for a tall man. Apart from which, there are so many Yanks on the ground now there's a surfeit of tall men. Though I admit, few are as skinny as Carlton. I arranged transport so we can move as soon as we hear anything. There's a place arranged for us off base. I thought you might like to grab something to eat and clean up." He glanced across as Guy came out from the plane. He raised an eyebrow. "New recruit?"

"Our pilot, a friend of Cal's."

Simpson held his hand out. "John Simpson. Good to meet you. Nice landing, by the way."

"Guy Jordan," said Guy, shaking the offered hand. He glanced at Elizabeth, waiting for some decision from her.

"You can come along with us to this place, wherever it is," she said. "Unless you have to get back?"

"I was told to bring you out here then hang around to transport you home. Possibly with a prisoner."

"Then join us for dinner. Not that I expect it's going to be very salubrious." Elizabeth glanced at Calum, something in her eyes he couldn't interpret, and he wondered if the obvious friendship between himself and Guy made her feel an outsider. If so, she had nothing to worry about.

Simpson led the way to the hangar he had been standing outside. Inside was a small lorry with two rows of wooden seats in the open back. He climbed into the cab, and Elizabeth joined him in the front. It looked like she intended to drive, which came as a surprise. Calum went with the others, sitting between Guy and Maria, the rest opposite them. The lorry drove around the base and out through a guarded gate. They had travelled a mile before Calum realised they were driving on what he considered the wrong side of the road, and John Simpson was behind the wheel.

The bustle around the base faded as they passed through a flat landscape where trees lined the road. They passed an occasional farmhouse, then slowed for a village where only half the houses remained intact. Even those that were showed evidence of a fierce firefight. Windows shattered, walls pock-marked from the strike of bullets. A few people stopped what they were doing to watch them pass, their faces impassive.

Beyond the village, Simpson turned into a long driveway before pulling up at a large mansion. Though Calum expected that over here they called it a chateau. There were people in white coats, doctors and nurses manning a field hospital. Trucks and jeeps sat around, having brought wounded from the front.

"They have let us use a barn around back," said Simpson. "Sorry there's nowhere to sleep, but it has a well and hand pump if anyone wants to wash, and I believe they've left us some food. With luck, we won't be here long."

Except they were. Each of them ate some food then sat around on bales of straw as the afternoon faded into dusk. Trucks brought more wounded, each arrival accompanied by a sudden burst of activity from the white-coated men and women. Elizabeth and Maria had disappeared somewhere. Calum was unsure if Richard had stayed or not. Harry and Bill fussed over the device, both men obsessed with it.

"What is that thing?" asked Guy, for the second time. He had manhandled some bales into a semblance of a couch and lay back, his long legs stretched out.

"As soon as I find out, I'll let you know."

Guy gave a soft laugh. "Whatever it is, those two can't leave it alone."

Calum watched the pair working. "I want to ask you something, skip."

"That sounds ominous."

"Maybe it is." Calum rolled his head to look at Guy. A languor filled him, softening his bones, eroding his will. "You know why the men wanted to fly with me, don't you?"

"All except Phil."

"Phil didn't like me, but he'd rather I was with you in that plane than any other bomb-aimer. So tell me, Guy, you do know, don't you?"

"I know you're not altogether normal, Cal. You know things before they happen, but to be honest I never gave it much thought. Too grateful you were with us to jinx it, I suppose." He looked around the barn. "Is that why we're here?"

Calum gave a nod. He decided Guy deserved answers to his questions and knew he would reveal nothing told to him.

"And the others?" asked Guy.

"The same. We all have a talent. Just like you have a talent for flying. Just like George Formby has a talent for making people laugh and Vera Lynn for cheering up the troops."

"Except what I do is nothing but skill. You have something else, don't you?"

"We can stop talking about it if you prefer," Calum said.

"No, I'm fine with it. In fact, it's a bit of a relief not to have to tiptoe around the subject. So tell me, how far into the future can you see? Based on experience, I'd say about ten or twenty seconds."

"It used to be that, maybe a little more, but now it's longer." Calum glanced at the device. "Elizabeth changed me. She brought out more of my ability, stopped me from being afraid I was different. She changed us all. That thing changed me, too."

"So what the hell does it do?"

"It enhances whatever talent I possess. Same as it does for the others."

"What can they do? Walk through walls? Levitate?"

"We don't know what any of us are fully capable of yet. This is only the start. It's scary, and it's exciting."

"Are these talents, as you call them, the reason we're here?"

"Have you ever heard of a man called Edward Carlton?"

"Sir Edward Carlton? I heard he'd scuttled off to Germany when the war broke out. Good riddance, too."

"He came back with his tail between his legs when he saw which way the wind was blowing. The man has connections in high places, and he used them. They assigned him to oversee our unit, amongst other things. I'm pretty sure he made sure they gave him the job because he's like me. Like Bill and Harry, like Maria and Richard. There are others, too, all over the world. Some of them…" Calum shook his head. "Well, let's just say they scare the pants off me."

"So what's this Carlton done?"

"Stolen something. And we're here to get it back. If we can."

Guy gave a laugh. "God, Cal, there's a bloody army out there. Tens of thousands of men. Wouldn't it be a better idea to give the job to them? You're six people. What can you do an army can't?"

"Defeat Carlton," Calum said. "At least I hope we can. The army won't be able to find him. Only we can do that because in our own small way, we're the same as he is." Calum wondered if he was revealing too much but knew he couldn't take any of it back now.

Guy was silent for a long time, watching Bill and Harry as they arranged pulleys and ropes from a beam. When he spoke, it was as if he had forgotten their conversation. Or accepted everything Calum told him.

"What are they doing?"

Calum raised his gaze. "No idea. Let's go find out." He stood and walked across to them. "What's this all about, chaps?"

"We're tired of hanging around," said Bill. "Carlton is getting closer to the Nazi lines with every passing minute. He might even have crossed them by now. We need to know where he is."

"And this is going to tell us?"

"Harry thinks so, and I'm willing to give it a try."

"How is it going to tell us anything?"

Harry finished what he was doing and turned to Calum. "When you went under its influence, I saw something. Felt something might be a better way of putting it. The device moved. Only very slightly, but it was drawn towards you." Harry looked at what he and Bill had accomplished. "I believe it has an affinity with whoever uses it, and I'm hoping I can make use of that to find out where Carlton is. It's a long shot for sure, but better than sitting on our backsides doing sweet Fanny Adams."

"If you turn it on it's going to affect us all, isn't it? Why would it find Carlton? He has to be miles away, maybe even further. And if it does locate him, isn't he going to feel it too? He'll know we're after him."

"I've changed it so I can control the power. I'll use only as much as we need. With luck, it won't be enough to alert him. If it was drawn to you, even though it was your first time, I'm convinced it will draw even more to Carlton, who must have used it hundreds of times. I don't think it's a general-purpose machine. Only one person possessing talent can use it at any one time."

"Who manufactured it?" Calum asked. "The Nazis?"

"It's German engineering, right enough. You can't see it now, but there are tiny etchings on some of the parts that say Bayerische Motoren Werke AG. I wouldn't be surprised if Carlton wasn't involved in its manufacture, which is all the more reason it would be drawn to him."

Calum looked at Guy, who listened to the conversation without offering any sign of surprise or that he failed to understand what they were talking about.

"All right, do it," Calum said. "Before Elizabeth and Simpson get back. They'll stop us. Do it now."

"Stand back," said Harry. "You too, Bill. Everyone stand as far back as you can, or go outside. If I'm right, it will draw towards talent it knows."

Calum shook his head. "Wherever Carlton is, he's not in this barn, Harry. And it knows me as well, now."

"Which is why I need you to concentrate, Cal. Picture Carlton. Draw him in your mind. I'm hoping the device will recognise you and use what's in your mind. I made a couple of adjustments to it that might help."

Calum frowned. "When this fails, or not, you're going to have to explain to me how you did all this."

"You know how I did it," said Harry. "The device gave me the ability."

Calum went to the barn door, turned and looked back. He tried to conjure a picture of Carlton sitting in the house in Kent. He drew on the fear he had felt at the time, his grief at what occurred after. Harry ran across to join them.

Nothing happened.

CHAPTER THIRTY-SIX

The silence in the barn lay so deep Calum could hear the faint ticking of his wristwatch. When he raised it to read the time, it surprised him to discover it was almost 1800 hours. He glanced over his shoulder, concerned Elizabeth might return and call a halt to Harry's experiment, but there was no sign of either her or John Simpson. From a distance came the sound of mortar fire, the faint rattle of small-arms, the deeper cough of a Bren gun, the fighting made safe by distance.

Harry tapped Guy on the shoulder. "Help me close the doors. And Cal, keep thinking of Carlton."

Between the two of them, the heavy wooden doors were drawn shut, then everyone stood with their backs to them facing the device.

"Good, that's what I was hoping for," said Harry.

At first, Calum didn't know what he was talking about, but as his eyes grew accustomed to the gloom, he made out a faint glow coming from the device. It was the same as he had seen in the house when they first encountered

Edward Carlton, but now more focussed, no doubt thanks to Harry's tinkering.

Sparks of faint light floated within the device, then narrow beams lanced out to dance against the walls. Not on any specific wall, but on any surface, including the roof beams.

"What the f–"

Harry cut Calum off. "Shh, it's searching. Keep the bastard in your mind."

"How can it know what it's looking for?"

Harry put a finger to his lips, the meaning clear. Calum set his questions aside for later. He watched the pattern of lights dance. Then they coalesced. One beam merged with another. That with yet another, until only six remained. Four on each quadrant. One on the roof. A sixth speared down to the ground. That was the first to wink out, followed by the one rising to the roof. Slowly, the other beams drew towards each other.

"Picture him," said Harry. "Think about Carlton."

Calum drew on all the memories he had of the man. Carlton at Carden House when he seemed no more than an inept buffoon. Then he pictured the unbeatable power that had come from the man, like the heat of a roaring fire. He forced the image into focus. The colour of the man's eyes: a pale grey, almost no colour at all. The smoothness of his face. His hair. Eyebrows. The slope of his shoulders.

Four beams became one. They tracked the far wall, slowed, settled.

"He's there." Harry's voice was barely a sound at all.

With a jerk, he moved fast across the barn floor, his

eyes never leaving the dot of light. He reached out and set his finger on it just as the beam died.

"Someone come here and put their finger where mine is. Bill, do it while I find a nail."

The men changed positions. Anyone else would have taken an age to find a nail, but Harry wasn't just anyone. He had a magical affinity for machines, for metal… nails too, it seemed. He found one almost at once, came back to Bill and pushed it into the soft wood. Only then did he allow himself to relax. He turned back to where Calum and Guy remained at the door.

Calum staggered forwards as someone pushed on the door from the other side.

"What on earth is going on in here?" Elizabeth stood outlined in the fading light from outside. "What are you all doing?"

"I need a compass," said Harry. "I think this wall faces north-east, but we need a better reading than that."

"There's one in the lorry," said John Simpson, who had also arrived. He turned and loped off across the grass.

Calum crossed to Harry. "Are you sure that's what all this means?"

"Nobody else is telling us where the bugger is, so this is the best chance we've got, isn't it?"

Elizabeth joined them. "What are you talking about?"

"Harry did something to the device. He thinks it's showing us where Carlton is."

Elizabeth made a sound to express her scepticism.

John Simpson returned with a metal encased army issue compass and handed it to Harry, who stepped back and took a reading.

"Forty-three degrees," he said. "Someone try to remember that." As if it was likely he wouldn't. He closed the top on the compass and slipped it into an inside jacket pocket.

"This is ridiculous," said Elizabeth. "And get the device down from those ropes. While you boys have been playing games, I've had a conversation with an American captain. Some of his advance troops encountered a man who sounds as if it could be Carlton. He was dressed as a British Colonel, but the uniform was too small for him, making them suspicious. The captain offered to provide us with some men and take us to where this sighting occurred."

"Which was where?" asked Harry.

Elizabeth reached into her shoulder bag and pulled out a map. It was one of the British ones, more accurate than the American versions because of the Pathfinder Mosquitos that had crossed and re-crossed this ground throughout the war. She unfolded it, her finger hovering until it stabbed down.

Calum leaned over, his shoulder pressing against her. "Hulst?"

"That's what the colonel told me. It's a few miles west of Antwerp, so almost at the front line."

"When was this?"

"Around 1500 hours, while we were still in the air."

Harry pushed his way in. He flipped open the compass and turned the map until it was aligned correctly. He set the compass over their current location and read off the dial. "Forty-nine degrees," he said. "Carlton's moved on since the sighting."

"God, but I hope you're right about this," said Elizabeth. She rose to her feet, brushing off her skirt.

"What have we got to lose?" Calum said. "This captain says Carlton's in that direction in any case. Harry's right, we can't lose him now, not with what he has in his possession."

Elizabeth gave a shake of her head, but not in disagreement. Calum sensed it was more to express her frustration that they were challenging her position.

"Let me talk to Ray," she said.

"Who?"

"Captain Raymond James, of the United States Army Corps."

"Ray," Calum said, his voice flat.

"I'll get him to show us where they saw Carlton, then perhaps we can track him from there." She turned and strode from the barn.

"Well, that's your love-life put on the back burner, old chap," said Harry. "Bloody Yanks come over here and try to steal all the best-looking girls."

Calum shook his head. "Does everyone know about Elizabeth and me?"

"You can't keep something like that a secret." Harry gave a laugh. "Besides, Bill said he could hear you in the walls of your room, and you know Maria can read what's in everyone's heads. She also said both your auras change when you're around each other."

Calum stared at him. He shook his head. "It's lucky Bill can only hear and not see, isn't it?" He glanced at Bill, who was studying his nails as if the conversation had nothing to do with him.

"Elizabeth and you?" asked Guy, and when Calum nodded, "Well, all I can say is you're one lucky bugger, Cal. Bit out of your league, but well done all the same. I expect any plans I had in that direction are well and truly scuppered now."

Darkness had fallen before they could arrange everything and strap the device down in the back of a lorry. A dozen American soldiers led the way in their own transport. While they waited, the team tried to catch up on whatever sleep they could, wherever they could. Elizabeth took them all into the chateau before leaving and made them change into British Army uniforms in case they fell into enemy hands. All except Guy, who stayed in his RAF flight suit. Better to be captured as a defeated soldier than shot as a spy, she said. Calum thought the khaki uniforms fitted her and Maria, even with their dresses still underneath, a lot better than they did the rest of them. He sat beside Elizabeth in the cab as John Simpson followed the American truck ahead – big, brash and loud; just like the soldiers. Calum believed that was exactly what the situation required. They passed through villages where barely any houses remained standing, others that appeared almost untouched. Ahead, flashes of light punctured the darkness as tanks and heavy armament fired into the night. Progress was slow because of the amount of traffic, all moving in the same direction – towards the front line.

"What are we going to do if Carlton's already crossed over into Nazi territory?" Calum asked.

"He won't have yet," said Elizabeth. "Let's hope we catch up with him before he does."

"Do you have a plan? After what happened last time, we're going to need more than rifles and handguns."

"He doesn't have his device anymore. We do."

"Except it was his device, wasn't it? How do we know he won't draw all the power to himself? We should have left it behind. It's a bugger to transport, and he'll know how to tap into it far better than we do."

Elizabeth glanced at him, her face lit red in the pale illumination from the truck's rear lights ahead. "I considered that option. I assume Carlton knows his talent far better than we do ours, but the device might be the only edge we have on him. And Harry's pretty much rebuilt it. That must be worth something." She gave a shake of her head. "All the times he visited us, and nobody knew what he could do. How is that possible, Cal? Can't you sense each other?"

"You know it doesn't work that way. From the outside, we all look ordinary. I suspect Carlton must have more talents than we saw in that house. If not, stripping us of our abilities and stopping weapons and engines from working will only get him so far."

"Yes, I suspect he will have other talents," said Elizabeth.

Calum waited, but when she said nothing else, he said, "What talents? How long have you known about him?"

Elizabeth shook her head. "I didn't know it was him. Don't you think I'd have had him arrested if I did? If I'd known it was him he'd never have come within a hundred miles of Unit-13. There have been rumours for years about an adept far in advance of anything I have ever heard of before, but nobody had any idea who it was. Carlton fooled us all. I'm afraid the rest is above your pay-grade for now, Cal." She reached out and squeezed his hand as if to offer an apology.

"The talent, or how long you knew about him?"

Elizabeth gave a long sigh. She stared ahead, unwilling to get into this conversation.

"Tell him," said John Simpson. "Tell Cal what you know. He deserves that much. They all do."

Before Elizabeth could say anything, the American truck ahead of them came to a halt, and half the soldiers climbed out and walked to the side of the road to relieve themselves. The captain walked back and stepped up onto the running board.

"One of our tanks took a hit. We have to clear it from the road before we can get past. Could be here a while yet."

John Simpson turned off the engine and got out. He took the offered Camel cigarette, and the two men walked away to the side. Calum turned to face Elizabeth.

"So, are you going to tell me what you know or not?" It felt to him like some kind of test, some confirmation of the relationship between them.

"There will be better places and better times, Cal."

Beyond her, he saw Guy and Maria walk along the road to the group of American soldiers. The Americans always seemed to have cigarettes, even if they did taste different.

"Except now is when I need to know," he said. "Not next week, not next month or next year. I need – no, we *all* need – to know what we're going up against."

Elizabeth avoided his gaze. "If I tell you, you might not want to continue."

"That's our choice, isn't it? Right now, you're making it for us." He leaned closer and took her hand. For a moment, there was resistance, then she stopped and met his eyes.

"We've known about someone for close to ten years." She gave a lopsided smile. "As you are aware, I would have looked exactly the same then as I do now. That information you keep to yourself, though. The others don't need to know anything about it. Carlton first came to my attention through his dubious friendships, as you know, but I never suspected he possessed talent."

"Was he a Blackshirt?"

"Not as far as anyone knew. Carlton remained strictly on the periphery. He's always been clever that way. Nothing ever sticks to him. Not even when he was in the orbit of Aleister Crowley – I assume you know who he is?"

"He used to be in the papers often enough, though pretty quiet since the outbreak of hostilities. I heard he also spent some time in Nazi Germany in the '30s."

"The same as Carlton. Both of them met Hitler, another man who has an interest in the occult. I wouldn't be surprised if that machine wasn't built under his orders. But all that is beside the point. What isn't is that it's clear to me now that Carlton is the adept I heard about. Rumours, whispers, nothing more. He hid the fact he could do what he does from me and everybody else. He has abilities both Crowley and Hitler lack, as much as Crowley always wished he had them himself."

"You said 'we' before. Who are 'we'?"

"The Service, of course. I worked with them from 1928 until a year before I recruited you."

"Were you looking for people like me all that time?"

"Of course not, though I've always had an interest in the paranormal. It makes sense, doesn't it? Considering my own ability."

"Do you consider that a talent?"

"Can you explain it in any rational way?"

Calum shook his head. "Of course not."

"That's what talent is, Cal. Abilities that defy rational explanation. We're only just scratching the surface of what everyone is capable of. Once the war is over, we can buckle down to finding out exactly how they work, and why only some people have them."

"But we're always going to be a secret, aren't we? All hell would break loose if the general population discovered there were people like us."

"Which is why we're buried deep inside the Service," said Elizabeth. "Where better to keep secrets hidden."

"How come Carlton ended up supervising Unit-13 if he's been under suspicion in the past?"

"When war was declared, Carlton was all at once squeaky clean. Knowing what we do now, I suspect he made sure he was involved with us. I always considered him a bit of a fool. You know the type, all the money and property but none of the brains to go with it. The

Commons and Lords are full of them. We're going to need a better quality of politician when the war ends."

"Good luck with that."

Elizabeth smiled and touched Calum's arm. For a moment, the closeness between them was renewed. He tried to dismiss it, knowing it would prove temporary.

"Sometimes you're too cynical for your own good, Cal."

"Better that than too naïve, wouldn't you say? You of all people should have more than enough experience to come to the same conclusion."

"Perhaps."

"So you had no idea what Carlton could do before this week?"

Elizabeth stared into space, and Calum saw her disappear into herself. When she returned, she said, "No, and I should have. I blame myself for everything that happened. I should have seen him for what he is. I did think this mysterious adept might be Alice Clare, but I know now she's just a damaged girl and not who the rumours were about."

"Don't go thinking it's your fault," Calum said. "If Carlton's as skilled as he appears to be, he'll have used his talents on you all along so you didn't see what he's capable of. Even Maria missed it, and she can see everything about people." He looked around, noting where the others were, wondering how much longer before they would get moving again. He was tense with the awareness of Carlton escaping them, even as he didn't know how they might defeat him.

"The information he has in his possession has the

potential to save Nazi Germany, even at this late stage," said Elizabeth. "The weapon they detail would allow them to take over the entire world."

"Except they're playing catch-up," Calum said.

"Don't underestimate their industry, Cal. Bill told me the Nazis are already advanced with their own atomic weapon. Not as advanced as the Americans and us with our shared research, but this information could close that gap. A madman might lead them, but German engineering is the best, as is their manufacturing capacity. The Tiger tank is the most fearsome weapon on the battlefield. Their fighters are a match for ours. And they are totally ruthless." Elizabeth's head dropped. "I don't know how we stop him. Only that we have to."

"You've already told us how we do it. Find the man and call in the bombers. Obliterate wherever he is. Raze it to the ground. Finish it. If he's as powerful as you say, nobody else can find him. Only those of us who share some small part of what he has. We can do that, at least, can't we?"

Elizabeth raised her eyes. "Can we?"

Which is when Harry opened the door on the driver's side and slid onto the seat. "Carlton's moving. I've rigged the device up in the back, and he's going south and east. I've got a strong reading, which means we're close."

"And how can we go after him with the road closed?" asked Elizabeth.

"Cross-country, of course. We'll have to leave the device, but I'm sure we can track him ourselves. I've rigged up a little something to help us. He leaves a particular trail, doesn't he? Bill claims he can feel it, and

I've no reason to doubt him." Harry leaned closer and showed them the compass, but he had heavily modified it. Now it sat on a square metal box, and Calum felt the same thrum of power from it as he did the device. "Tonight, Lizzie," said Harry. "We finish the bastard tonight."

CHAPTER THIRTY-SEVEN

They drifted away in ones and twos to disappear into the cloak of darkness. John Simpson remained with the lorry as some small measure of cover. He said if they cleared the blockage, he'd bring it through and try to find them.

They needed no light to come together, some inner talent drawing each to the other. Harry carried the compass but had no need of it. He led the way, and Calum hoped Harry's talent for machinery matched its promise, or none of them would see the sunrise. Elizabeth walked beside him, the ground underfoot rough, so they stumbled and sometimes fell. Now and then, they passed groups of soldiers moving back from the front line to get some sleep. They sat around small fires, and those who couldn't sleep talked or sang. Somewhere a man played a harmonica, the plaintive sound drifting across to them. They avoided such groups, passing at a distance, sheltered by the night.

Ahead, the sound of shelling and small-arms fire grew louder.

They came to a hedge and followed it for several minutes until they found a gate where they stopped to decide how to proceed.

"What does your compass tell you, Harry?" asked Elizabeth, all trace of her previous scepticism gone.

"We're closer, not that I need the compass to tell me that. Can't you feel it?"

"It's like I've got spiders crawling around inside my skull," said Maria. She looked at them, her face pale in the light of a moon that had risen as they crossed the fields.

Bill nodded, as did Richard. Guy showed nothing, which was understandable. At least he had been keen enough to come along with them, which demonstrated a great deal of trust.

Calum considered what he could feel within himself but couldn't decide if there was anything or not. He had put his tension down to their situation. No spiders. At least not yet.

"How close are we?" asked Elizabeth.

Harry opened the compass. He had fiddled with it the entire journey in the back of the truck. The original compass sat on top of a new metal frame. The open sides revealed its inner workings – cogs and mechanisms only Harry understood. He turned a key on the side, winding the spring, then flicked a brass toggle and the cogs moved.

Now Calum felt the spiders. He scratched at his head even as he knew they didn't exist. Not that the knowledge helped, because they felt real enough. He glanced at Guy, aware he would experience none of this. Aware his friend had accepted their strange abilities without question. In the same way he and the crew had accepted what Calum could do.

"Less than a mile in that direction." Harry pointed beyond the gate. "And there are others with him."

"Others with power?" asked Elizabeth, a catch in her voice.

"Come on, old girl, this is all new to me. You don't expect me to know that, do you?"

"Give the compass to Bill," said Maria.

Harry looked at her, and for a moment, Calum was sure he would refuse. The device was his baby. No doubt he believed it only responded when held in his hands. Then he shrugged, as if he didn't care, and passed it across.

Bill stared at the device. "What the hell am I supposed to do with this?"

"Listen," said Harry. "It talked to me. It told me how to make it. I believe it can talk to each of us in our own way. It understands our talents and enhances them. I made this device myself, so it's ours, not his. Listen to what it says."

Bill closed his eyes, then Maria stepped close and placed her hand on top of his, her fingers slipping between his to grip the device.

"If we hear anything, it's going to be in German," she said, then closed her eyes.

Calum watched Elizabeth wrap her arms around herself as if she felt the cold. He went to her and enclosed her slim body inside his own arms, drew her back against his warmth. He recalled the last time he had done the same thing in their hotel room. Except then, she had been naked.

She tilted her head so only he could hear and whispered, "I don't know if any of us are up to this, Cal."

"Of course we are." He hoped none of his own doubt showed in his voice. The fear he had felt when he was in the air was nothing to the fear he felt now, but Calum knew he had to fight back before it defeated him. "We've made it this far, thanks to Harry. He's a whiz with that thing he knocked together. I bet when we get home he can refine it and make more, one for each of us."

"This is all moving faster than I thought possible. Too fast. We need another six months to learn what we can do. To understand everything."

"War doesn't wait until you're ready. We have to stop Carlton tonight, before he can cross the front lines into Nazi territory." He offered her a hug, and Elizabeth gripped his hand and pulled it beneath her jacket so it lay against her breast. Calum smiled. "I think we'd better wait until we get home for that."

"I'm trying to take my mind off things."

"Well, you're certainly taking mine off them."

"Sixteen men, plus Carlton." Maria released the device and stepped away from Bill, who shook his head as he handed it back to Harry. His eyes followed Maria as she came to join Elizabeth and Calum, a new respect in them. "He's lost the others he crossed the Channel with but joined up with a band of Wehrmacht soldiers," said Maria. "Notionally, they're part of the defence line, but it's patchy, and there are sizeable gaps. Ahead of us is one of them."

"You heard all this?" asked Elizabeth.

"I just listened in to what Bill heard. He didn't understand any of it, but I did."

Calum didn't understand how she could do that, only grateful she could. He realised there was still a great deal they didn't know about each other.

"They're planning to pull back as soon as it gets light," said Maria. "There's a car waiting for Carlton, and a plane nearby to whisk him away. It's now or never. The soldiers don't know what he can do or what he's carrying, only that he's important enough to sacrifice themselves for if that's what it comes to." She stared at Elizabeth. "This is going to be hard. They're all armed with submachine guns, and they're all battle-hardened."

"Perhaps we should have brought some of those Yanks with us," Calum said.

"Couldn't," said Elizabeth. "They're not allowed to know anything about this. Orders from the very top."

"Then why let them bring us this far?"

"Because if that damn lorry hadn't got stuck they'd have taken us all the way to the front by now. They were our escort, Cal. But I admit, a couple of rifles would come in handy right now."

"We can get rifles," Calum said. "In fact, we can get submachine guns." He finally released her and turned away. "Richard, when we get close, I want you to do your trick and get among them. See if there are any spare weapons and bring them back. Can you do that?"

Richard gave a nod of confirmation, but even as Calum saw it the man faded. He didn't disappear; he was simply not worth the bother of noticing.

They climbed over the gate and started across an open

field. The rising moon washed the grass with silver, and if anyone on the far side was keeping watch, it would be impossible to miss their approach. All except for Richard.

A water-filled ditch blocked their path. They tracked sideways until they came to a narrow bridge made from an old railway sleeper. Beyond the next field lay a roadway and a clutch of houses. The sound of gunfire and artillery was louder now, the stink of cordite drifting through the air.

"Carlton's on the other side of those houses," said Harry, consulting his modified compass once more.

"What about his bodyguards?"

"They're normal, so they could be anywhere, but if what Maria said is right, they'll be with–"

"Everyone down, now!" Calum shouted. Ever since climbing the gate, he had pushed his talent to call the future into vision. That vision showed a bullet entering Harry's chest and exploding out through his back.

Now, the bullet flew on through the clear night air to bury itself a mile or more behind them.

A rattle of submachine gunfire came, then fell silent.

They had found Carlton's bodyguards, and if they had found them, they had found Carlton as well.

Calum rolled onto his back and looked around. "You're up, Richard," he said, keeping his voice low, and the man rose to his feet. He hesitated, waiting to see if the soldiers directed any fire his way, trusting in Calum to warn him in time if they did.

There was nothing.

Richard started across the field, fading as he walked away.

Elizabeth rolled across the damp grass to Calum. "He's only one man, and there may be no weapons he can steal. We should try to crawl closer."

"We can stand and walk; it'll be quicker."

"A quicker way to die, Cal. I think not. The rest of you aren't like me. You won't come back."

"Trust me." He rose to his feet, knowing what the next thirty seconds would bring. He looked around for Harry, found him sitting up. "All right if I take your device for a bit, old chum?"

Harry grinned and tossed it across. Calum caught it one-handed, the weight of it a surprise, the warmth not. The metal sent a current along his arm that sparked into his mind, and the future became crystal clear.

An echo of gunfire sounded. Calum stepped a foot to one side to avoid the bullets. The whistle of them through the air passed harmlessly to his right. He looked around as the others rose, then started to walk.

"Elizabeth, left." A brief hiatus, then "Bill, down... Harry, right a yard... Guy, kneel..." They all continued to walk, each of them doing exactly as Calum ordered. The German bullets whined away through the night. Carlton would be watching as his men were shooting and know what was happening. Others with talent were coming for him.

The spark of gunfire showed where men crouched behind a low stone wall. Calum tried to count how many rifles but couldn't do both that and keep everyone safe, so he concentrated solely on the latter task. He saw the bodies of his friends ripped apart in a future that would never come to pass. His own body moved without conscious thought to avoid the bullets aimed at him, but it was getting harder the closer they came. And there was something else. The spiders were growing more insistent inside his head.

Calum saw Richard drift among the German soldiers, passing like a phantom. Then, as they came close enough, Guy drew a revolver from inside his jacket and returned fire, aiming at the flashes of light. He hit one man, who gave a sharp cry before slumping to one side. Richard moved and retrieved his rifle, turned and raised it.

"No," Calum said. "Guy, give me the pistol. The rest of you down, now."

There was no hesitation as Guy tossed it to him. All those hours listening to Calum's voice telling him what to do had burned a trust into him.

Calum plucked the pistol from the air with his left hand and ran forward as fast as he could. They were too close to the Germans for him to protect everyone, but he knew he could protect himself, and by attacking he would draw their fire.

He put another man down, weaving from side to side, ducking to avoid his future death. Then Richard fired the submachine gun and took three of the men. Calum was fifty feet from the wall when the rest turned and fled. As the remaining soldiers reached the house behind, Carlton's tall figure appeared and joined them, issuing instructions. When Calum reached the wall, he knelt and took a submachine rifle from a dead man. The weapon was hot in his hands from the firefight. When he looked up again there was nothing to see. Carlton and the soldiers had disappeared into thin air, and an electric tension ran through the air.

Calum was sure Carlton must be using his own talent to spirit them away, but exactly what that talent was, he didn't know. He raised the gun and sprayed a rain of bullets into the last place he had seen them, but the move was made out of frustration rather than any hope he would hit anything. Carlton and his remaining men were gone.

CHAPTER THIRTY-EIGHT

Bill went to one knee and reached out to place a hand on a dead soldier's forehead.

"Which side of the lines are we on now?" asked Guy.

"No idea," said Elizabeth. "What about you, Harry?"

He shook his head. "The device only tells me where Carlton is, nothing else. If I'd had more time I might have managed to get it to do more, like the bigger device." He looked at Guy. "Why? It doesn't make any difference, does it? We go after him wherever he is."

"I was wondering about our uniforms," said Guy. "There are three dead Germans here, and it looks like their uniforms might fit some of us."

"And if we meet Allied troops?" asked Elizabeth. "What then?"

"In that case, we're prisoners until you explain what happened. If we encounter the enemy, then we play it the other way."

Calum nodded. "It's a good plan." He was looking at Elizabeth as he spoke.

"Any sign on your device where Carlton is now, Harry?" asked Elizabeth.

Harry shook his head, but Bill opened his eyes and rose to his feet.

"He's east of us, but distance is harder to judge because of all the buildings. They're heading for a pick-up point in some ruined building in Antwerp, which is on the other side of the river."

"What river?"

Bill pointed. "It's a quarter mile that way. The Allies crossed it closer to the docks, but this side is still enemy-held territory."

"And you know all that how?"

"The dead soldier told me. It's the way they came to pick up Carlton. He's recent enough deceased I can access almost all his memories. Only the visual stuff, of course, but that's enough. I suspect they'll retreat the same way they came, which is across the Bercham bridge, if it's still intact. It was being shelled when they crossed it."

Elizabeth shook her head. If it was meant to show disbelief, it was far too late for that. She looked down at the three dead soldiers.

"Cal, Guy, and..." she considered, "...Harry. Strip out of your British uniforms and put theirs on." She glanced at Maria. "Did you keep your dress on under your uniform, like I did?" And when she received a nod in return, "Then we're just two unlucky *fräuleins* who got caught up in the fighting. We can both play innocent if we want to. You explain the situation if we need to talk. Bill and Richard will play the captives."

"And if they question any of us?" Calum asked.

"I've got a little German, but let's hope they don't. Even better, let's hope we don't meet anybody. All right, get changed so we can be on our way. Carlton's getting further away from us the longer we stand here." She led Maria a short distance away, and both turned their backs as the three men stripped and pulled on the German uniforms. Calum's was a little snug, but he was the slimmest of them, so he had to make do with what was left. They discarded their British uniforms on the ground, and Bill led them past the farmhouse.

They encountered the river where Bill said they would, but the bridge no longer existed. On the opposite bank, Allied soldiers fought with their German counterparts, both of them using whatever cover they could. None were close, but the sound of competing gunfire was almost deafening.

To the south, the ground was clearer, and they headed that way, hoping Carlton had been unable to cross. The sound of the fighting faded as they followed a narrow track above the slowly moving water of the river, dotted here and there with floating bodies. On both banks, barely a single house remained intact.

Calum searched out the future, worried that snipers on the far bank might take aim at them, but nothing showed. What did was a quarter mile ahead at a bend in the river he foresaw a boat being rowed from the far shore to this, two Wehrmacht soldiers using makeshift oars.

Calum fell back to walk beside Maria.

"We're going to need you." He glanced at Elizabeth, who was on Maria's other side. "You're going to see a boat soon. Use the story about Richard and Bill being prisoners and ask them to take us across." He allowed Maria to go ahead.

"I've got a bad feeling about this," said Elizabeth.

"We've made it this far, haven't we?"

She gave a shake of her head. "God knows how. This is chaos, Cal. Men fighting on all sides of us. Carlton is going to get away. I know he is."

Calum thought she looked on the verge of tears. He reached for her hand, surprised at her reaction. He had always believed Elizabeth would be the last of them to buckle under the strain. His own fear nestled within his chest like a coiled spring, prevented from overwhelming him only through sheer willpower. Perhaps all those hours fighting his fear in the nose of a Lancaster had given him a better training. All the same, however scared she might be, Elizabeth had to be strong. Now more than ever. Calum only wished he could lend her some of his courage but knew it didn't work that way. All he could do was act strong, and hope.

Ahead of them, Maria slid down to the riverbank. She waved to the two men, who both waved back. Calum heard her voice reach him as she spoke in fluent German. She turned and pointed at their group, chatting away as if the three of them were the best of friends. The boat reached the shingle bank and slid a little way up it. Maria made her way back up the slope to meet the others.

"They're happy to take us across." She kept her voice low so the boatmen wouldn't hear her speaking English. "I explained about the prisoners, and they told me they must come over one at a time with a guard. They won't take responsibility for watching them. They say Elizabeth and me have to cross first, then they'll come back for one prisoner and one guard, then the rest."

"What about Carlton?"

"They took him and what was left of his men over ten minutes ago."

"Were they suspicious?"

Maria smiled. "Of me? Of course not. One of them is convinced I'm from his region because he recognises my accent. I'm afraid I flirted a little."

"I don't like you and Elizabeth going across without us," Calum said. "What if they don't come back for us?"

"Guy, give me your pistol," said Elizabeth, her voice firm, and Calum knew she had recovered her courage from somewhere. "If they threaten to do that, I'll shoot them both and come back for you myself. No need to bother with any of this silliness then." She glanced at where the men were waiting, each smoking a cigarette. "In fact, it might be easier to just shoot them now and go over without them."

"The boat's not big enough for all of us," Calum said. "And if anyone hears gunshots, they might come to investigate, and we don't know which side they'll belong to. I say we do what they want. It might be necessary to kill them after, if they get suspicious, but we go along with them for now." Calum wondered when he had grown so cynical, so uncaring for the lives of others. Then he recalled the nights he had hung in the skies above Germany to release a rain of death on those below and knew the war had changed him. As it had changed them all.

One man called out to them, and Maria called back in German.

"They're getting impatient. I think they're going to want paying, which might get awkward."

"I have pounds, dollars and reichsmarks," said Elizabeth. "Come on, this isn't getting Carlton caught." She stepped out, then slowed to allow Maria to join her. They clung to each other for balance as they slid down the steep bank, and Maria had a brief conversation with the men. Each offered a hand to help the women into the boat.

Calum had a bad feeling. He reached ahead, pushing hard, but could see only as far as the boat in the middle of the river. The rest would be revealed, he knew.

"Let's get down there," he said to Guy. "I don't trust either of those men."

"So why did you let the women go with them?"

"Because Maria's right, we can't afford to draw attention to ourselves. Come on. And Harry, Bill and Richard, try to look more like prisoners, or I might have to threaten you."

"Do it anyway," said Bill. "One of them is watching us standing here talking."

Calum lifted the sub machine gun he had taken and pretended to smash it into the side of Bill's face, looking forward far enough to judge when he would pull away. Bill played his part by crying out and going to his knees. Out on the water, both soldiers laughed.

Calum stood to one side of their three prisoners, Guy on the other. They covered them with their guns, but

Calum's sight was on what was happening thirty seconds in the future.

The boat made slow progress, the languid current causing it to drift downstream, so it headed for a point twenty yards north on the far bank. Calum watched the boat jerk as it hit the grassed bank, and Maria lost her balance. One soldier jumped out and offered her a hand.

"Guy," Calum said, nodding to the boat. "Get ready. We're going to have to shoot them."

The other man took Elizabeth's hand and guided her to shore. Then he put his boot on the boat and pushed it back into the river, where it spun slowly as it drifted downstream. He turned back and ripped the front of Elizabeth's dress away. The other man pushed Maria onto her back and stood over her as he started to unbutton his trousers.

"The bastard on the right is yours," said Guy. "I'll take the other one."

Calum nodded and raised his rifle. He scanned ahead, watching where their rounds went, and then he saw ten seconds away Elizabeth pull her own gun from beneath her skirts, raise it and fire at point-blank range into the face of her attacker. The man standing over Maria spun around. As he did so, Guy shot him square in the chest. He flew backwards to land with his arms splayed out.

Maria rose to her feet. Elizabeth tried to repair the damage to her dress with little success.

"Shit." Calum handed his rifle to Harry, slipped out of his jacket and dived into the water. It filled his nose and mouth, tasting of petrol and worse. He stroked for the boat, then dragged it back to where Elizabeth and Maria waited on the far bank.

"Are you both all right?"

"We're fine," said Elizabeth. "Go get the others."

Calum retrieved the makeshift oars and rowed the ungainly craft back to the far shore. When he got there, everyone piled in, making the return journey precarious as water slopped in over the sides. As they started up the far bank into what was undoubtedly enemy territory, Maria aimed a hard kick at the head of the dead man who had tried to rape her. She cursed in German, but Calum was pretty sure he knew what the words meant. As they reached the top of the bank, the eastern flank of the city lay ahead. Buildings stood in ruins, fires burned, and smoke rose into a sky that was showing the first faint glimmer of the coming dawn Calum feared he might never see arrive.

"There," said Harry, pointing. "They think they're safe."

Carlton and the remnant of his escort stood in front of a house lacking a roof and half its walls, the bricks of which blocked most of the road in front of it.

"Why aren't they running?" asked Maria.

"They're waiting for the transport promised to Carlton," said Elizabeth. She glanced around, but there was nobody else in sight. "Does anyone have a better plan than the last one?"

"It worked, didn't it?" Calum said.

"And he got away. This time that isn't an option."

"Same as before," said Richard. "I go across and do what I can. Cal keeps everyone else safe. We storm them before anyone arrives to take him away." He looked around at each of them. "Unless anyone can come up with a better idea?"

"They'll be expecting us to do the same as last time," Calum said. "They'll be ready for us."

"That doesn't mean it won't work," said Elizabeth.

"No, only that it'll be a damn sight riskier."

Calum looked both ways along the street. Still nobody in sight. Whatever Carlton was waiting for wouldn't arrive in the next thirty seconds. Calum pushed further. One minute. Two. Four. A headache started up so suddenly it scared him, but he knew they had time for what he planned. He relaxed whatever mental muscle he used and let the future recede from him until all that remained was the shadow of ten seconds ahead.

"Yes, Richard, go across," he said. "The rest of us split up. Half go left, the others right. Look for some way to get in behind that house. From the looks of it, there's not going to be much to stop us coming at them from behind."

"What do I do when I reach them?" asked Richard.

"Wait for us. Don't make any move until we arrive." Calum looked at each of them. "Maria, go with Harry and Bill. Elizabeth, you're with Guy and me. As soon as we get the chance, we shoot them all."

"Not Carlton," said Elizabeth. "He has to stay alive."

"He's the most dangerous of them all. Better he gets a bullet in the back of the head."

"This is non-negotiable, Cal."

"Are you pulling rank?"

"If that's what you want to call it. Carlton stays alive."

Calum was aware of time passing. He reached out, but

only two minutes into the future. He still saw no transport arrive.

"All right, he stays alive. But the rest of them die. They're our enemies, and we already know they'll kill us in an instant if the boot's on the other foot." Calum looked around, wondering when Elizabeth had passed control of the group over to him.

"Give me the device." Richard held his hand out to Harry, who looked down at it.

"Why? It's not like the big one, all it can do is find Carlton, and we can see where he is now."

"Nobody else is going to need it, are they?" A sharpness entered Richard's voice he had never shown before. "It can do more than you think, Harry. We all felt those spiders back there, so I'm not going anywhere near Carlton without it. Can't you feel his power, even from here?"

Harry looked at the device again, then wound the mechanism before handing it across. "Just make sure he doesn't get his hands on it, or we're all buggered."

CHAPTER THIRTY-NINE

Calum pushed his talent hard, scanning the future for danger and finding none. He took the lead, Elizabeth behind him, Guy at the rear. None of them had any idea what was happening with Carlton and his protectors, nor with Richard or the others. All they had was hope, and what little talent they possessed. But was it enough to defeat Carlton? At the house in Kent, his power had been phenomenal. How strong would it be without his device? Still formidable, Calum believed. If they had the time, he would have discussed it with Elizabeth. But there was no time. They had to do this now.

They made their way along an alley barely wider than their shoulders. The cobbled ground was covered in scattered mounds of bricks where the surrounding walls had come down. They were further from Carlton than Calum liked, but any closer and they might be seen crossing the roadway. He hoped the others had also gone unobserved.

When they came out on a street that ran parallel to the

one they had left, Calum held up a hand to halt them. He peered out, checking both ways, both in the now and the future. He saw nothing. This area of the city was abandoned. Perhaps Carlton knew that, and it was why he was here. Neither side laid claim to the ruins. Calum stepped out, waving Elizabeth and Guy to follow. They could walk side by side in the wider roadway as they made their way back towards the rear of the building Carlton was using. Calum had counted their progress on the way out. They had taken three-hundred paces to reach the alley, and now he counted them again until he reached fifty then stopped. On their left, the neighbouring house had almost completely collapsed to block the entire street. They could climb over it, but there was no need because the side of the house they wanted had come down as well. All they needed to do was pick their way through the rubble. Calum held a finger to his lips to tell them to keep silent, then climbed across the scattered stone and beams, taking care not to dislodge anything.

The interior of the building was precarious, the upper floors half gone, broken pipes cascading water. As they went deeper, Calum heard voices speaking German. He called them to a halt, pointed at Guy, then off to the right. Guy gave a nod to show he understood and crept off. Elizabeth cocked her head, and Calum patted his chest to show he wanted her with him. She raised the rifle stolen from the dead soldiers at the river, her expression harsh with fear. Calum wondered if his own matched hers.

As they came within twenty feet, he saw Carlton. Calum had half-expected the man would be able to sense them, but whether their own talent was stronger, or he believed his pursuers were normal men, he appeared to have dropped his guard. He sat in a salvaged armchair, his long legs stretched out as if he was in some gentlemans' club in London. To his right stood Richard. To Calum, he appeared to be in full view, and he wondered how that was possible because neither Carlton nor his minders could fail to see him. Richard gripped the small device in his left hand, a revolver in his right. His head turned to look back into the ruined buildings for the others. Calum raised a hand, hoping he would see the gesture.

Elizabeth came close and put her lips against his ear.

"I can see Harry and Bill over there. Your friend Guy is between them and us. We're all here now, Cal."

He gave a brief nod, disappointed when she moved away. However brief the contact had been, it raised memories of what they had shared. He raised his rifle to his shoulder and took aim. Glancing across, he saw Guy do the same, then beyond him Bill and Harry followed their example. Over a dozen uniformed men stood in front of Carlton, all in plain sight. Two each, Calum thought, maybe three, depending on the others' accuracy, but he was sure of his own.

As he pressed his finger against the trigger and fired, the man he was aiming at moved to the side suddenly and his round ricocheted off a wall into the darkness. Calum adjusted without even thinking and fired again, this time hitting his target, who fell forward, dead before he hit the ground. He swung the barrel of the rifle around, seeking a new target. The sound of shooting surrounded him. He saw four other men fall, then the rest reacted even though only seconds had passed. They went to the ground, raising their own rifles and returning fire. Elizabeth took one of the men in the forehead, Guy another in the chest. Bill and Harry made their own contribution.

Calum knelt to make himself less of a target, but he knew his role in events had changed. He pushed ahead, but only by fifteen seconds, and looked around at his friends. He shouted warnings, each of them reacting without hesitation. When Calum looked ahead again Richard stood directly behind Carlton. The gun was gone, and the hand that had held it lay on top of Carlton's head. It made a strange picture, and Calum couldn't work out why Carlton was putting up with the contact, why he hadn't taken cover like his men. In Richard's left hand, the small device glowed as if lit from within. Calum felt a bullet tug at his sleeve and brought his attention back to the remaining German soldiers. Only six now. Then four.

Calum stepped forwards, deliberately making himself a target. As he did so, a German staff car pulled up on the roadway beyond and four more men piled out, their own rifles already raised. Carlton's transport had arrived, but the man stayed where he was. Richard remained fully visible, his hand still on Carlton's head.

Calum thought back to a teasing conversation with Maria several weeks before. She had told him how Richard could draw the very essence from her. Told him how it made sex with him – for her, at least – more pleasurable. She had theorised that as well as making himself disappear, Richard could draw the life force from those he chose. Was that was what he was doing now? The question was, could he control Carlton, who should be the strongest of them all? Except he no longer had his own device, and Calum wondered if the man had grown too reliant on it, so his innate talent was weaker. Richard, gripping the miniature device fashioned by Harry, appeared to have the upper hand. They were a team, and in this instance the team was stronger than any individual.

As he turned his attention back to the staff car, Calum saw one of the soldiers struggle with something as he attempted to lift it from the rear seat. When he turned, Calum saw the man held a second shining device, identical to the one Carlton had used against them in Kent.

Calum raised his rifle and fired a hail of bullets at the man. None of them found their target. When he narrowed his eyes, he saw the cogs within the device were already turning, a point of light shining from the mercury capsule at its heart.

Calum pushed hard into the future, ignoring the sudden pain in his temples, forcing his way past it to see how events were going to play out. What he saw wasn't good. The device deflected their bullets, protecting itself and whoever held it even if they lacked any talent. The soldier staggered across the rubble-strewn ground, almost falling twice, but each step took him closer to Carlton.

Calum started forwards, leaving the others to take care of the remaining resistance. He saw a grimace on Richard's face and knew he was using whatever ultimate resources he could call on to fight the new device. Carlton moved for the first time since Richard had laid his hand on him. Richard's fingers turned white with the strain of trying to keep his grip, but it was all too late, too weak compared to the power of the man who rose from the chair. Carlton reached out a hand, the glowing device only feet from his fingertips.

Which is when Calum ran towards him. He fired blindly, uncaring who he hit, uncaring if his bullets hit Carlton or not. Elizabeth was wrong. The man had to die. Had to be defeated. Even as the conviction rose through him, Calum's vision of the future told him he would be too late. Except he had learned that the future wasn't fixed. He could change it. Not the past, but the future could be manipulated. Calum threw himself forwards, knowing he was about to die, but knowing it was their only chance.

Calum landed on his belly and rolled over. He lifted the muzzle of his rifle, seeing only the glowing orb, Carlton's fingers inches from it. Calum raised his own hand and placed it against the shining device. The shock of its roiling power made his head feel as if it was about to explode, but he managed to press against the trigger of his rifle, with no clue how many rounds remained in the magazine. The bullets tore into the man holding the device, and it fell from his hands. The unnatural weight of it crashed down on Calum's leg with an explosion of pain, and he knew the bone was broken. Still he continued to fire, this time into the guts of the device. His bullets ricocheted, sparking a flame that had nothing to do with their contact. He ignored the searing pain in his leg and kept on firing. He saw the capsule of mercury hit and split apart, the silver liquid falling to the ground. Then the magazine emptied and a sudden silence rang in his ears.

He looked up.

Carlton loomed over him, a rictus grin on his face. His hand came down and clasped the side of the device.

Nothing happened.

Calum had damaged it. Not beyond repair, but beyond anything Carlton could do.

Richard closed the distance and placed his hand back on top of Carlton's skull and the man went still, his eyes focusing on something no one else could see.

"Get this fucking thing off me!" Calum screamed.

He yelled again when Bill and Harry lifted it, once more when Elizabeth went to her knees and pulled away what remained of his trousers. He raised his head to look at the damage. White bone showed, and there was blood. A great deal of blood. He tried to see his own future, but it was clouded, hidden from him.

"Lie still," said Elizabeth, and only then did Calum realise he was writhing about.

Other hands reached out and held him down. Only Richard stayed where he was, controlling Carlton. Guy tossed his uniform jacket aside, then removed his shirt. He tore it into strips, handing each to Elizabeth, who first tied a tourniquet. Which brought more agony.

She waved a hand. "Someone go find me some wood. There has to be something in the building." She sat back on her heels, her fingers tracing the damage to Calum's leg.

Maria knelt and took Calum's hand, clutching it between her breasts. *Another time, another place*, he thought, and laughed at the incongruity of it. He saw her frown, no idea of the thoughts tumbling through his mind. Or did she?

Bill returned with four lengths of wood that looked as if they might once have made up the side of a dressing table. He placed them on the ground and used his heel to snap them into shorter lengths. Elizabeth reached out and took two.

She glanced up at Calum. "This is going to hurt like blazes. Nothing I can do about it, I'm afraid."

"It already hurts."

Calum heard a noise, not recognising it at first and then, as the others looked up, he did. It was the engine of a vehicle, approaching fast.

"Oh, for fuck's sake," said Harry.

"Maria, put your hands over Cal's eyes." Elizabeth ignored the approaching reinforcements. "Guy, Bill, Harry, hold him down. Hold him hard."

Calum felt hands grip him as Maria placed her palm across his face. Why didn't they abandon him and save themselves? He shook his head from side to side in an attempt to see, but Maria only pressed harder. And then Elizabeth used her hands to push the jagged bone back into place. The final small tatters of sanity he had held onto fled and Calum descended into a chaos of darkness.

CHAPTER FORTY

Calum woke to a gentle rocking motion. His body felt detached, but at least there was no pain. He wondered if this was what death felt like. He tried to open his eyes but couldn't. It seemed too much effort for too little reward. He welcomed the darkness because it meant he might see George again. If he made it to heaven, that is. Calum tried to think what sins he had committed, and if they amounted to enough in the debit column to send him to the other place. Then he heard familiar voices, one of them American. He was sure he had heard it before but couldn't place where. All the Americans sounded the same to him, as no doubt the British did to their ears.

"Watcher, old cocker," Calum said, making himself laugh.

"He's awake." Maria's voice, then hands on him, female hands.

When Calum opened his eyes, he discovered Elizabeth leaning over him. He wanted to kiss her, but even that seemed too much trouble.

"What happened?"

"Not now," she said. "Maria, go ask the nurse if we can give him another shot of morphine."

The soft female hands left his arm, and he experienced a sense of deep loss.

"Tell me what happened." He managed to half sit up, the searing pain in his leg dulled only by the drug in his bloodstream. He liked the feeling. He wanted it to never end.

"Ray found us," said Elizabeth. "Lie down again."

"Now you tell me?" Calum said. He shook his head. "No."

Elizabeth's lips thinned. "Then sit up properly, but don't blame me if it hurts." She helped him to sit until he could lean against the side of the moving vehicle.

He looked around. They were in the back of an American truck, metal-sided rather than canvas, wider, the engine louder and more powerful than the British equivalent. Of course it was, and Calum was glad of it.

"The nurse says nothing more for two hours," said Maria when she returned. She knelt beside Calum and took his hand again, and he smiled, pleased when he saw Elizabeth frown. He tried to move his hand so it lay between Maria's breasts, where it had been earlier, but she deflected his attempt without effort.

"Where's Carlton?" Calum asked.

"He's got shackles around just about every part of his body. Richard's with him in case he needs to control him again. Harry's with them too, because the device needs recharging now and again, and only Harry can manage that without it stopping."

"What about the other device?"

"Harry says he might be able to work with it, but if not it'll be useful for spare parts. You did a pretty good job on it. He says without you, Carlton would have destroyed all of us."

"Where are we going?"

"To the airfield. The Anson is still there, and the Americans have told me they've assigned a B-17 to take Carlton. We can't risk him coming with us in case anything goes wrong. Richard and Harry will have to go with him in the other plane, of course. As well as the shackles, they have him heavily drugged, but God knows what he might do if Richard isn't there. We're going to fly into Northolt so the authorities can deal with Carlton."

"It's only our team who can deal with what he's capable of."

"Which is what I'll tell them once we're safely back in Blighty," said Elizabeth. "I'm going to ask them to take Carlton to Porton Down and keep him drugged. We need to work out how to control him so Richard can get back to us. I'm sure we can find something. Harry already has an idea about redesigning the device so it can dampen talent instead of enhancing it." She smiled. "We'll keep Carlton safe until Harry works it all out, which I'm sure he'll do."

"So it's over?" Calum said with a smile.

"Yes, it's over. Try to rest, Cal. It's going to take us an hour to reach the airfield, then another before we land in London. I want you in hospital as soon as I can get you there."

"The others?"

"All safe, thanks to you." She leaned close and pressed her lips against his. When she straightened up, it surprised Calum to see unshed tears glittering in her eyes. "We might have won this battle, but the war isn't over yet, and we need to find out if there are others like Carlton out there."

"What about the documents?"

Elizabeth smiled and patted a canvas bag slung over her shoulder. "Carlton had them under his jacket. I've checked them, and so far as I can tell, nothing is missing. Bill took a look and confirmed they are what he thought. He said if Carlton had succeeded in handing them over the Nazis could have leap-frogged us. It hardly bears thinking about what would happen then."

"Burn them," Calum said.

"I was planning to return them to their rightful place."

"No. Burn them. Do it as soon as you can. Whatever is in there is too dangerous to risk being stolen a second time."

"It's too late for that," said Elizabeth. "The Americans already know all about the bomb. We gave them the information on how to build it before the war, and they put their boffins to work on how to make it all work. We couldn't have done it ourselves. The Nazis have been doing similar work, but Bill says they won't get anything finished now without these plans. Not before the Allies reach Munich, in any case."

"So what was the point of it all?"

"The point is, we were asked. And we do as we are asked. We got the documents back for them." Elizabeth leaned over and kissed him again. "Now sleep. With luck, you'll wake in a hospital bed and can forget about everything for a few months while your leg heals."

"I want to go home to recover," Calum said. "I have things I need to ask my parents."

Elizabeth looked into his eyes. "You know you can't say anything about me."

"This isn't about you. It's about George and me. And my mother and father. This thing I can do didn't start with me. It can't have done. I want to know where it came from."

"Have you ever mentioned it to them before?" Elizabeth sat back, a visible tiredness seeping through her. They were all tired, every single one of them.

"Tried once and got shot down."

"What makes you think they'll talk if you ask again?"

"They may not, but I have to try. I've been thinking about Jeannie, too. She's clever, but there might be more than clever involved. Perhaps that's what genius is. Some part of whatever it is we possess turned in a different direction."

"Possibly," said Elizabeth. "Once you're safe in a hospital, I'm going to see Winnie again. I want him to provide funds for more research. If I'm lucky, he'll be in a good mood when I tell him we got his precious secrets back."

"Good luck with that. I'm sure Winston's got other things on his mind."

Elizabeth shook her head. "You've seen what it's like over here, Cal. We've got the Nazis on the run. The Russians are pushing them even harder in the east. More men and women are going to die on all sides, but we're winning the war. All we have to do now is win the peace and not make the same mistakes we did after the last one." She stared at him for a long time, her face showing no expression. Then she gave a deep sigh and reached into her shoulder bag. She pulled out a slim manilla folder. It looked as if it held only half a dozen sheets of paper.

"What have you got there, old girl?" Calum asked, pleased when she smiled.

"I was going to save it for later, but just in case you don't make it…"

"Oh, thanks a lot. What is it, then?"

"Carlton had it on him." She waved the folder as if he could see through it to what lay within. "It's a list of the German paranormals. A few captured Russians as well. As soon as you're healed, I'm going to ask Winnie if we can come back over here and track them down. Let's see if we can't recruit them to work on the right side of the fence."

I set an Imperfect Future in an imaginary version of the Second World War, but the book sticks closely to actual events and timelines. As far as I am aware, no special organisation such as Unit-13 ever existed. However, I discovered a brief mention of MI13, an arm of the secret service disbanded after the war that supposedly investigated paranormal phenomena.

Most events and dates are accurate, but I have inserted fictional characters into the real world. Sometimes I have stretched the realms of what could have happened, partly for my amusement and, I hope, for the reader. You will no doubt recognise these deceits when you come across them.

Credenhill base in Herefordshire is the Special Air Service's current home, but it did not move there until 1994, though the SAS were stationed in Hereford since 1960, having moved there from Malvern. During the Second World War, Credenhill was a training base for RAF pilots. The wooded hill of Credenhill, topped with an ancient fort, is described as accurately as my memory serves.

GCCS was based at Bletchley Park and was the precursor to GCHQ, which moved to Cheltenham when they wanted to distance themselves into a separate organisation.

Bletchley Park requires no explanation. Neither does Alan Turing. A genius who was taken from the world far too soon.

David Penny 6th April 2021

THE THOMAS BERRINGTON HISTORICAL MYSTERIES

The Red Hill

Moorish Spain, 1482. English surgeon Thomas Berrington is asked to investigate a series of brutal murders in the palace of al-Hamra in Granada.

Breaker of Bones

Summoned to Cordoba to heal a Spanish prince, Thomas Berrington and his companion, the eunuch Jorge, pursue a killer who re-makes his victims with his own crazed logic.

The Sin Eater

In Granada Helena, the concubine who once shared Thomas Berrington's bed, is carrying his child, while Thomas tracks a killer exacting revenge on evil men.

The Incubus

A mysterious killer stalks the alleys of Ronda. Thomas Berrington, Jorge and Lubna race to identify the culprit before more victims have their breath stolen.

The Inquisitor

In a Sevilla on the edge of chaos death stalks the streets. Thomas Berrington and his companions tread a dangerous path between the Inquisition, the royal palace, and a killer.

The Fortunate Dead

As a Spanish army gathers outside the walls of Malaga, Thomas Berrington hunts down a killer who threatens more than just strangers.

The Promise of Pain

When revenge is not enough. Thomas Berrington flees to the high mountains, only to be drawn back by those he left behind.

The Message of Blood

When Thomas Berrington is sent to Cordoba on the orders of a man he hates he welcomes the distraction of a murder, but is shocked when the evidence points to the killer being his companion.

A Tear for the Dead

As the reign of Moorish Granada draws to a close, dark forces gather to carve a new Spain. Can Thomas Berrington overcome the plot to destroy not just one civilisation, but two?

THE THOMAS BERRINGTON PREQUELS

A Death of Innocence

When 13 years old Thomas Berrington is accused of murder he must enlist the help of pretty Bel Brickenden to prove his innocence. And then another kind of death comes to Lemster.

THE THOMAS BERRINGTON BUNDLES

Purchase 3 full-length novels for less than the price of two.

Thomas Berrington Books 1-3

The Red Hill

Breaker of Bones

The Incubus

Thomas Berrington Books 4-6

The Incubus

The Inquisitor

The Fortunate Dead

Thomas Berrington Books 7-9

The Promise of Pain

The Message of Blood

A Tear for the Dead

ABOUT THE AUTHOR

David Penny is the author of the Thomas Berrington Historical Mysteries set in Moorish Spain at the end of the 15th Century.

He is also writing in the Unit-13 series of Paranormal spy thrillers.

He is currently working on his book.

Find out more about David Penny
www.davidpenny.com

9 781912 592616